BLUE EYES

Hema Macherla

For the three wonderful people in my life
Radhamanohar, Littoo and Smitha.
Without you my existence has no meaning.

ACKNOWLEDGMENTS

Firstly, my heartfelt gratitude goes to my publisher and editor, Lynn Michell, for believing in my writing and also for her patience, guidance and tireless mentoring.

My immense thanks to John Farley, creative writing tutor at Fairkytes, for his invaluable comments, suggestions and honest criticism.

Thank you Russ and Alice for nitpicking my grammar.

I would like to thank my writer friends, Frances, Connie, Mary, Maureen, Alice, Val, Bill, Peter and Russ for listening to my readings every week and giving me helpful comments.

I feel very fortunate to have my wonderful family – Radhamanohar, Vamshi (Littoo) & Sandy, and Smitha & Mathew, for their unconditional love, support and encouragement. Thank you for putting up with me.

To my beautiful little Leo, Sophia and Eliana for filling my writer's block spaces with fun and laughter.

I thank my large loving families in India and in the USA for their eagerness to see my books in print.

Special thanks to Rama Naidu garu and the members of TAL, and Smita Singh (Founder of Vaani) for their interest and support.

RESOURCES FOR BLUE EYES

India 100 Years Ago by Reverend W. Urwick.
Originally published in 1885. Published by Bracken Books. 1985.

The Life of Mahatma Gandhi by Louis Fischer.
HarperCollins. 1997.

With all our love
Mary D[...]

[signature]

© 2011 Hema Macherla

Published by Linen Press, Edinburgh 2011
1 Newton Farm Cottages
Miller Hill
Dalkeith
Midlothian
EH22 1SA

Email: lynnmichell0@googlemail.com
Website: www.linenpressbooks.co.uk
Blog: linenpressbooks.wordpress.com

Events that take place in India in the 1920s, while in chronological order, do not always coincide exactly with actual dates. Historical events are loosely interpreted as a backcloth against which fictional characters play out their own narrative.

ISBN: 978-0-955 961 861
Cover photographs: Brígida Brito
Cover design: Submarine, Edinburgh

BLUE EYES

Hema Macherla

Chapter 1

Anjali was sitting on the floor of her room. Earlier she had not realised what was going to happen to her, but once she had understood, she had wailed and screamed and fought like a tiger with all the women who held her down and forced the ceremonial clothing on her. She lashed out. She shouted.

'Be quiet!' a stout female relative said and hit her across the face.

Anjali rubbed her stinging cheek and stared wide-eyed at the woman. The shock of the blow stopped her from protesting, but not for long.

Again she fought.

'You'll be beaten if you don't behave. Better just let us dress you.'

Afterwards, Anjali had leaned against the wall, but her legs would not support her and she had slid down, landing with a thud. A crumpled rag doll in the *sari* and jewels she had worn once before, long ago, as a child bride. She tried to suppress her terror but it was impossible. Another surge of panic erupted like a volcano, making her giddy and sick.

Someone washed her face with cold water and her step-mother, Parvati, forced her to drink some bitter green liquid from a cup, saying it would calm her. In minutes her head felt light and her vision was blurred. The liquid brought tranquillity, making her oblivious to what was going on around her. Other women took over and finished dressing and decorating her limp body.

She didn't know how long she remained in a state of stupor but some time much later the sound of a bullock cart crunching across the gravel woke her and brought her to her senses. Confused by the silence where before there had been shouting and noise, she looked around and saw that all the women in the room were now asleep. An eerie silence filled the house, broken only by the occasional *mantra* chanted sleepily by the priests.

The numbness wore off and once again the horror of her reality gripped her. Her teeth chattered, and icy shivers ran up and down her spine. Trying to make as little noise as possible, she struggled to suppress the sobbing that rose to her throat. What could she do now? She tried desperately to think. To make a plan. How could she escape? She looked at the only exit from the room. It was blocked by two servants, who slept one on each side of it. Above her head was a tiny window, too high to climb out of and secured with iron bars. There was no way she could run away while the house was full of people. Despite their outward signs of distress, she knew that her mother-in-law and her step-mother were guarding her like hawks. The harsh truth was that there could be no escape.

Would it be painful? She shook her head, trying to dislodge the horrible images that burned in her imagination. Would it take long? She shivered again. How would it feel? As if to answer the question, she stretched out her index finger and placed it in the orange flame of an oil lamp that was placed nearby. *Ow!* She put her stinging finger in her mouth. Just a sharp pain from the heat of the lamp. It was nothing. She trembled as she imagined the huge flames of the pyre, fanned to a fierce heat, licking and hurting and burning her whole body.

She thought of her husband's lifeless form, newly clothed and garlanded, lying on the front veranda, ready to be taken to the cremation grounds at the crack of dawn. They had made her a bride once again, but this time to accompany him on his final journey when they laid him on the funeral pyre.

'Why me?' Anjali had asked a hundred times, willing someone to give her a different answer. 'Ratna is also his wife. Why does it have to be me?' She had asked anyone who would listen. Each time she was told the same thing.

'His first wife, Ratna, has his children to look after. You are a barren woman. You have borne him no children. The least you can do for him is to accompany him on his last journey.'

Remembering, Anjali flinched. At the age of eighteeen, branded a barren woman, her life was about to end. Leaning back against the wall, she tried to brace herself for the inevitable. Resting her head on to her knees, she closed her eyes and tried to block out all feelings and pain.

Where would her spirit go once her body was burned? To heaven or hell, should either exist? Would she see her mother there? For the first time in years she tried to remember a young, slender woman with a beautiful smile. She had been only five years old when her mother had passed away, but she still remembered how her devastated father would sit her on his knee, hug her, and tell her how much her mother had loved her.

'Your mother was a beautiful woman, Anjali. You are the spitting image of her,' he would say, and there would be tears in his eyes.

'I will try to grow up to be like her,' Anjali would reply, saddened by her father's grief.

But Parvati, her father's second wife, had changed all that. Three years later, he had married again and his loving conversations with his daughter had ceased because they displeased his new wife. He never took her in his arms in front of Parvati. Then never at all. It seemed he no longer had time for her. Anjali wondered why he had married Parvati when he always looked so wretched. Soon father and daughter were separated further, each in their own quarter of the house as Parvati's power increased and she enforced new rules. Her final act to sever Anjali's connections with the outside world was to dismiss her teacher. Lilly Garland, an Anglo-Indian lady, who had been coming to the house for years to teach the young Anjali to read and write. Anjali was left with no one.

Anjali was only ten years old when Parvati started nagging her father to marry the child off to her own cousin's son. Initially her father had protested.

'For god's sake, Parvati, Anajli is only a child.'

'Are you blind?' she shouted back. 'Open your eyes and look at her properly.'

But he could not look, nor meet his daughter's gaze.

'Anyway, at the age of ten she is not a child.' Parvati waved her hands dramatically in front of his eyes. 'Do you hear me? She will start her periods any time now, and if that happens before you have arranged her marriage, you will have to hide your face in shame.'

'All right, all right, I will search for a boy.' Her father's voice was meek.

'There is no need to search elsewhere. The right boy is under your nose. Ranjit will make a fine husband for Anjali.'

'You mean your cousin's son Ranjit?' Her father sounded shocked. 'Are you mad? For god's sake, he is already married.'

'Of course he is married, but so what? The point is that his wife can't give him any children.'

'So?'

She grimaced. 'Can't you see, if our Anjali could give him a child, all that property would fall into her hands!'

'Money is not everything, Parvati.'

Her father's voice did not convince.

'You're talking rubbish. Just imagine how you would feel if your daughter could live like a queen.'

A rueful smile came to Anjali's lips as she remembered that

conversation, which she had heard one evening whilst sitting on the back veranda, picking out little stones and husks from a measure of rice – one of the tasks that Parvati had set for her after she had married her father and put an end to her studies. It wasn't difficult to imagine how Parvati had finally persuaded him.

At the age of ten Anjali became Ranjit's second wife and took her place in his house. 'Palace' would be a more appropriate word.

Only then, as she was leaving her own home, did her father finally stretch out his arms and hug her. He clung to her crying like a baby. He was pitiful and his tears provoked tears of her own, tears which she had suppressed for so many years. Together they wept and silently acknowledged how much they had missed each other and how hard this parting was for both of them.

It was midnight by the time they arrived at her husband's grand house. She was tired and sleepy-eyed but remembered travelling in a palanquin, sitting opposite a big strange man, garlanded, dressed in silks and gold jewellery. She wanted to sleep but it was impossible as she had to sit upright, holding a tassel that was dangling from the middle of the roof. The loud rhythmic sounds of the band and the singing of the four men who carried the palanquin kept her awake throughout the journey.

She was glad when all the formalities that accompanied the arrival of a new bride were over and they sent her to bed. She slept like a log next to her step-mother, Parvati, on a feather-soft bed in a huge room. It was only when the next morning dawned that she began to take in and marvel at the grandeur of it all.

Parvati stayed with her for three days before leaving her in her mother-in-law's care.

Chapter 2

Anjali soon learned that her husband, Ranjit, was an only son. His younger sister was already married and had her own family. Anjali's new father-in-law was a powerful man, not just the head of the village but also the landlord of hundreds of acres of paddy fields. Her mother-in-law saw her role in life as keeping the servants in order and making sure they did what they were supposed to do. She ruled the magnificent house. Ratna, Anjali's husband's first wife, was delegated to do all the cooking. During Anjali's first few days, her mother-in-law, Kousalya, repeatedly explained the house rules, and told Anjali that her task would be to help Ratna in the kitchen.

If Anjali's mother-in-law was the queen of the house, Ratna was queen of the kitchen. She guarded it so possessively that she wouldn't let Anjali do anything except perform the specific tasks that she had set aside for her. These were to boil the milk, cut the vegetables, clean the rice and carry in the drinking water from the well in the back garden. Ratna wouldn't talk to her except when it was absolutely necessary, and then she was curt and almost rude. Anjali smiled wryly at the memory. She may have been only ten years old but she recognised the loathing in Ratna's eyes.

Ratna made it clear that Anjali had to avoid being seen by the men in the house: 'If you have to serve them meals, Anjali, make sure you pull your *sari pallu* over your face.'

Actually, she didn't mind that. She felt safer hiding her face from the men, and anyway, it only happened once a month, when Ratna had her period, because it was the custom for menstruating women to be banned from the main rooms of the house. They had to sit in a separate room at the back for four days.

Anjali only saw her husband properly when she was serving meals. The rest of the time she hid from him, glad that she was never summoned.

A year passed and on her eleventh birthday Anjali had terrible stomach cramps. Blood trickled between her legs and soiled her clothes. Kousalya, her mother-in-law, made her sit in a corner of that separate room for ten days. Ratna brought her meals but left the plates just inside the door, on the floor. Then on the tenth day, after a wash with turmeric water, she was allowed back inside the house. Her step-mother and numerous other women relatives were invited to celebrate her new maturity.

The next day they called an astrologer to the house to discuss and decide on a good day for the physical union of Ranjit and Anjali.

'Please look for a favourable *Muhurtam* for their names, *pundit-ji*,' her mother-in-law pleaded. 'If this girl can give us just one grandson to save our family, I will be thankful to you.'

'Don't worry, Kousalya, the sun and moon are in very good positions this coming Wednesday, and I can guarantee your new daughter-in-law will give you a beautiful grandson.' He chuckled and looked knowingly at Anjali.

Two days before the appointed date, Anjali had a surprise visitor: the mistress of a zamindar who ruled the county. Anjali had heard her name mentioned as a celebrated beauty and a renowned dancer. According to the villagers, the young zamindar had fallen in love with Chandini when he had visited her at a brothel and had taken her away to live with him. He built a huge mansion for her in his own town and settled her there in luxury. During his youth, his mind was constantly unsettled by her seductive beauty and he could think of nothing but love and poetry. He was known as The Love-Mad Zamindar and Chandini was called *Prem-Devi* – Goddess of Love. In their early months together, respectable housewives despised her, but her obvious devotion to the zamindar changed their minds and they began to respect her. Before long, mothers and mothers-in-law were inviting Chandini to their reputable homes to advise their young, innocent, newly married daughters and daughters-in-law on the taboo subject of love-making.

Now Chandini had been invited by Kousalya to advise Anjali.

After they had exchanged polite greetings and small talk, and after Kousalya had served her visitor with light refreshments, she called for Anjali: 'Come, Anjali. Come and sit next to Aunty.' She gestured at a place beside Chandini on a blue and red Persian rug.

The visitor, cross legged and leaning on a blue velvet cushion, smiled warmly at Anjali. Anjali stared back, unable to hide her admiration for this woman's extraordinary beauty, even though she must have been fifty.

'Pay attention to what Aunty is going to say to you,' her mother-in-law said.

'Yes *ma-ji*.' Anjali nodded obediently.

'I must go now. I have lots of things to organise,' Kousalya said, getting up to take her leave.

Anjali followed her departure with puzzled eyes, leaving her alone with the visitor.

'Anjali is a beautiful name and it suits you,' Chandini smiled.

'Thank you,' Anjali said in a small voice.

'Come on, relax, there is nothing to be scared of.' Chandini patted Anjali's slim shoulder. 'Do you know there are nine *rasas* in us?'

'No.' Anjali shook her head.

'The word "*rasa*" has many meanings,' Chandini began. Then, counting on her fingers, she said, '*rasa* means juice, flavour, delicious

17

taste, art and emotion. We are going to talk about the last one – emotion. It contains nine *rasas*. The first one is *karuna*. This means kindness and compassion, but at the same time it can mean grief, despair and utter hopelessness. The second is happiness, joy or mirth. The third is disgust. The fourth, anger in all its forms.'

She glanced at Anjali to see if she was paying attention, but the girl was totally absorbed, fascinated by what she was being taught. Chandini continued. 'The fifth is fear, a subtle nameless anxiety. The sixth is wonder or curiosity, the seventh is bravery or self-confidence. The eighth *rasa* is serenity, calm and peace. The ninth is love, beauty and passion.'

Chandini paused and gave Anjali a knowing look. 'Do you understand so far what I have taught you?'

Anjali nodded.

Chandini cleared her throat. 'Now we are going to talk about the last and most important *rasa, shringara* – love, beauty and passion – the sweet anticipation between a man and a woman as they wait for each other for the ultimate, the actual act of love…'

Chandini revealed the secrets and the mysteries of the physical act of love, explaining it all carefully, while Anjali listened, awestruck but horribly embarrassed.

Chandini's teachings did not have the effect her mother-in-law had anticipated and desired: while Anjali understood the details perfectly, she felt only horror at the thought of what would happen, and was filled with fear. As the time approached for her physical union with Ranjit, the thought of sleeping with a man whom she hardly knew, and who frightened her, became a daily terror.

The day arrived sooner than expected. A delicious meal was cooked and consumed by the family and their guests. In the evening, the women sat Anjali on a low chair, ready for the preparations. While a local band played and all the women sang, her mother-in-law put vermilion on her forehead, smeared fragrant sandalwood paste under her chin, and smoothed turmeric paste on her feet. Then she presented her with a shimmering red silk *sari* with a gold border. Anjali held it in her hands and touched its silky softness, but still she felt nothing but anxiety and trepidation for what was ahead. Later, towards night, they applied *attar* and arranged jasmine flowers in her hair. Giving her the traditional glass of milk to carry with her, the women took her into a room she had never seen before. Inside, a grand four-poster bed, sprinkled with rose petals and decorated with garlands of flowers, took centre stage.

Knowing what was coming after the door had been closed behind her, Anjali trembled like a leaf. Then her name was called and she lifted her eyes. Ranjit was already sitting on the bed, leisurely chewing an aromatic betel-leaf. He looked straight at her. In that split second when their eyes met, Anjali noticed that he was tall and well built, but then she quickly averted her eyes, staring down at the carpet beneath her feet. She didn't know how long she stood there, holding her breath and fixing her gaze on the floor.

Again his voice reached her, making her jump. 'Come here,' he beckoned.

Her body shook as she took a few steps forward.

'Don't just stand there wide-eyed like a frightened deer,' he smiled. 'Come nearer.'

Her muscles tightened and she clenched her fists. Trying to control her fear, she slowly took another few steps closer to the bed.

Not saying anything, he stretched out his hand and took the milk from her. He gulped it down and set the empty glass to one side. Then he stared at her, taking in every detail. In his eyes was an unmistakable and joyful admiration for her lovely face and slender body.

Chapter 3

'Anjali!'

It was only a whisper. Someone was calling her very softly. Then her name was called again, slightly louder, startling her back to the present – to the room full of relatives and her fate on the funeral pyre.

She lifted her head and stifled an urge to scream as she saw a figure moving outside the window in the darkness. With her heart pounding, she looked again to make sure that she wasn't imagining it. Yes, she could definitely make out a figure wearing white clothes, who once more called her name. She froze but the figure outside beckoned to her to come closer.

Something about the gesture seemed familiar. When she got up to take a second look, she recognised the person waiting outside. Moving as softly as possible towards the window, her eyes now accustomed to the darkness of the night, she saw that it was indeed her father standing below.

'Come out!' His lips mouthed the words with barely a sound.

'How?' she whispered.

'If anyone wakes up, tell them you need to go to the bathroom.'

She nodded and looked around her. She moved as silently as she could but the jingle of her anklets, toe-rings and bangles woke her mother-in-law. The older woman stirred, half opened her eyes and called, 'Who is it?… Anjali?' She was shading her eyes against the faint light of the lamp and squinting to see what was going on. 'What are you doing?'

'I… I am just going to the bathroom.'

'Take the lamp with you. It's dark outside.' Kousalya yawned and turned over. Once again she was fast asleep.

Anjali crossed the threshold. There, in the corridor, were the servants, stretched out on the floor, dead to the world. They had stayed the night in case they were needed. Snaking along the corridor, Anjali finally reached the back door and unbolted it.

In the back garden, her father was waiting for her.

'Anjali…' he whispered. His face, crumpled with worry, looked ashen even in the glow of the lamp. He blew out the flame before taking her in his arms. Darkness enveloped them as the moon slid behind the clouds.

'Listen to me,' he whispered. 'Go in to the bathroom and remove your bangles and anklets. He pressed a bundle into her hands. 'This is a *burqa*. Put it on.'

'A *burqa*?'

'Yes, yes, a *burqa*, go on… quickly… wear it over your head and no one will recognise you.'

Going into a room at the far corner of the garden, she removed all her jewellery and placed it in an alcove. She opened the bundle and slipped the garment over her head, wondering where on earth her father had found it. Emerging fully covered in black material, she followed him silently out of the back gate and into a narrow street.

'This way! Quickly!' Her father took her arm and rushed her to the corner of the road, where there was a sharp turn. Under a *tamarind* tree was a bullock cart with a domed roof, hitched and ready to depart.

'*Pita-ji!*' Anjali looked up at her father.

'Go… *Beti!* Just go! *Jiti raho, jiti raho*; be alive and live longer.' He blessed her, wiping away her tears. 'Saleem will take you far away from here.'

'Saleem?' It was a name she hadn't heard for a long time.

'Yes, Saleem… you remember him…' His voice trailed away as he pressed a bundle of money into her hand. 'Look after yourself.'

'*Pita-ji*,' she called, clinging to him.

'God will protect you, my child.' He kissed her forehead and held her waist to help her climb into the cart. After securing the screen at the back so that she could not be seen, he tapped on the roof. It was the sign that it was time to go.

Saleem, in the driver's seat, made clucking noises with his tongue and slapped the bullocks. As soon as he loosened the reins the animals began to move. The wheels made a crunching noise on the gravel and the cart jerked forwards on the uneven dust road. Pushing the fabric of the screen slightly aside, Anjali watched her father through the net of her *burqa* until he was nothing but a blur. The cart carried her away into the darkness.

Saleem drove in silence. Even in the faint light of the early hours of the morning it was dark behind the curtains of the cart. The waves of panic that had rocked her earlier were slowly ebbing away, and her nerves stopped jangling until she felt a calmness like a sea settling after a cyclone. Anjali leaned against the walls of the latticed bamboo sides and closed her eyes. Once again her thoughts went back to the past, to her dead husband, and that first encounter with him in his room after the women had dressed her and sent her in to him.

*

That night, Ranjit's eyes had swept over her body and Anjali had cringed as she remembered everything that Chandini had told her. She stepped back, desperate to run away. She wanted nothing to do with this ritual. This violation of her body.

'How old are you?' His deep voice made her freeze.

'Eleven…'

'Of course!' He was smiling at her. Laughing gently. Not understanding why her age amused him, she summoned the courage to look up.

He pointed at a roll of straw mat that stood in a corner. 'Go and roll that out,' he said.

She obeyed his instructions and laid the mat on the floor on the far side of the room.

'You sleep there, Anjali.' He threw her a pillow and some bed clothes.

She could not believe her luck. Had he read her thoughts? Did he know she was terrified of him? Still keeping an eye on him, she lay down and covered herself with the bed clothes.

It was very late, way past her bed time and, despite being exhausted from the day's extraordinary events, she could not sleep. Very aware of lying in the same room as a strange man, the slightest sound made her jump. She listened to him tossing and turning for a long time but eventually she must have dozed off.

In the early hours the squeaking of the door woke her from her sleep. She heard the jingle of glass bangles and silver anklets and the pad of soft footsteps crossing the room to Ranjit's bed.

Then she heard Ranjit whisper, 'Please don't cry.'

In the dark silence of the night she couldn't make out the woman's reply, but she knew it was Ratna.

After a while, she heard the door of the adjoining room open and close again and even though she hadn't once opened her eyes, she knew that she was alone.

Chapter 4

The darkness faded and the early sun struggled to rise from the horizon. The birds on the *neem* and *tamarind* trees alongside the track broke the silence with their wake-up calls.

Saleem, driving the cart on the dusty road, realised that this was the exact moment when Anjali should have been accompanying Ranjit on his last journey to the funeral pyre. A strong desire to check whether Anjali was really there, in the cart, made him turn round and stretch out his hand to lift the curtain, but then he paused, not wanting to disturb her in case she was asleep. He withdrew his hand and twisted the tails of the bullocks to encourage them to run faster. If the animals maintained their speed, they could reach Adhira in half an hour and he could deliver Anjali safely to Chandini, who had promised to look after the girl for two days while he visited his sister in Amritsar. Then she would help Anjali to board a train to Kalipet Junction, where he would meet her at the station.

It was a fortunate coincidence that his mother had asked him to take this opportunity to visit his sister before continuing on his way to his work in Harikonda, South India. He thus already had a perfect reason for leaving the village, and could agree to help Anjali as soon as he heard the dreadful news from her distraught father. Everyone in the village knew that he had set off to see his sister last night and no one would suspect that Anjali had escaped with him. There was no reason to connect the two events.

It had been so long since he had seen her, but he had thought about her often and had wondered what had happened to her. She might have married and left the village. Such thoughts were painful and he tried very hard to supress them. Any feelings he might have for her were irrelevant and pointless. Sometimes when his mind wandered off course, he had to rein it back in and remind himself that not only was Anjali from a higher caste and of a different religion, she was now a married woman. Their lives ran along parallel tracks, destined never to meet.

A smile played on his lips as he remembered them playing together as children. His father, Abdul Khan, used to work for Anjali's father, Narayan, as a mattress maker in his factory. His mother was the personal tailor for Narayan's family and he was her little helper, handing her bits and pieces that she needed for her work – scissors and thread and buttons.

He had been seven when he had first met five-year-old Anjali. His mother, Tahera, took him to her house. On the way she told him about this little girl who had lost her mother in a tragic accident. At that tender age, it was hard for him to digest this information. He tried to imagine life without his own mother and a lump came to his throat. He pulled his ma's *sari pallu* hard and she stopped to look at him.

'Please ma, promise me you won't die like Anjali's mother.'

Tahera smiled, scooping him up in an embrace. 'God forbid, my little one. I am not going to leave you so soon.' She kissed him on both cheeks and he felt secure. He snuggled closer and wrapped his arms around her neck.

As soon as they entered the house, Anjali, small, like a doll, with big innocent eyes, captured and melted his heart. From then on it became a routine for him to accompany his mother, who went every day to look after Anjali. He found he didn't mind sharing his mother's attention with her. Soon they became firm friends, playing together, running around the garden, making fabric dolls with his mother's discarded bits of cotton and silk and linen. When Anjali's teacher, Miss Garland, came to the house to give the girl lessons, Anjali persuaded her father to allow Saleem to sit in with her so that he too could learn reading and writing.

Three years later, when Narayan married Parvati, everything changed abruptly. Parvati stopped Miss Garland coming to the house. Tahera was immediately dismissed. Saleem was prohibited from seeing Anjali. It saddened him. Whenever he found an opportunity or an excuse, he went to the house on an errand in the hope of seeing Anjali. Even then, he rarely caught more than a glimpse of her. Sometimes they would manage a few words in conversation, but even then she had to remain hidden from him, standing behind a door or a curtain.

Soon, even those brief meetings ceased. At the tender age of twelve, he understood full well that marrying ten-year-old Anjali to forty-year-old Ranjit was a sin and something that should never happen to any young girl. The thought of not having her in the village was beyond his imagination. It hurt him. He wanted to do something, anything, to stop the wedding, but he was only a child, and also a Muslim. Of course he couldn't get involved in their affairs. He could only express his frustrations to his mother.

In the end, she told him to stop talking about Anjali. Who did he think he was to even think he could change anything or interfere? 'This is nonsense, Saleem. You must always remember that you are only their servant boy. You must never, never try to act above your station.'

And so he waited helplessly as the wedding day approached, and when it arrived, he watched, sitting amongst the servants, while Anjali was married to a man old enough to be her father.

No one had noticed as a young boy, frowning and furious, had followed the procession in which his childhood friend was carried high by the palanquin bearers to her husband's house. Without Anjali, life in the village would be so much less than it had been before.

Chapter 5

By the time the cart carrying Anjali entered Adhira, the morning sun was shining brilliantly.

The town was wide awake with people hustling and bustling, doing their everyday chores.

'Hi, hi, *rockho*, *rockho*!' Saleem was talking to his bullocks. He twisted their tails to manoeuvre the cart and bring it to a halt under the shade of a huge *banyan* tree.

'Anjali-ji,' he called, without touching the curtain. The word 'ji' sounded strange because it was a term of respect. When they were children, he always called her by her first name. But now she was not only a married woman but the daughter-in-law of an upper-class, wealthy family. At the age of twenty, he knew his boundaries and it was only appropriate to address her properly.

The curtains parted and he could tell that she was looking at him through her veil.

'I am taking you to Chandini's house…'

'Chandini's house?'

'You remember Chandini, don't you?'

'Of course…'

Picking up her embarrassment, he rubbed his brow, upset that he had to mention something that was painful for her.

When Parvati had ordered his father to collect Chandini from Adhira in a horse-drawn buggy, and to drive her back to the house, Saleem had accompanied him. At the time, he hadn't understood the purpose of her visit to Anjali, but when he was older he remembered that day and the truth dawned on him. The thought of Ranjit even touching Anjali was painful to him. Unbearable. Sometimes, when the world slumbered soundly in a cloak of darkness, images of Anjali and Ranjit together came unbidden, making him sick to his heart and appalled at his own hopeless jealousy and desire.

'Saleem...' Anjali's voice broke into his thoughts and he quickly composed himself.

'Anjali-ji,' he called back gently. 'I am sorry but I have to travel on now to Amritsar to visit my sister. Your father has arranged for you to stay with Chandini just for a couple of days. I hope you don't mind. She is a kind woman. She will look after you and make sure that you are safe. On Monday she will take you to the station and there you will board a train and get off at the Kalipet Junction. I will be there on the platform.'

'Kalipet Junction? Where is that?' Anjali asked, not really taking in all this information. She still felt numb with the shock of escaping.

'It is in the south,' Saleem replied. 'It will be a long journey, I'm afraid. At least twenty-four hours.'

'That far... but why?'

'Because I work in that area, in a city called Harikonda. Besides, the further we go, the safer you will be.'

Anjali just stared at him, unable to make any decisions for herself.

'But please don't worry,' he said, hiding his own concern. 'I know you've never travelled on a train before but you will be fine in the ladies' compartment. It will be full of other travellers like you. I am going to take an earlier train from Amritsar to reach Kalipet before you, and I will be there waiting for you.'

She nodded silently.

He knew there were tears in her eyes, but he controlled the urge to lift her veil and wipe them away. Instead he gave her a bright and brittle smile of reassurance.

Anjali peered through the gap in the curtains as Saleem drove the cart through some huge gates and was bemused at the grand, whitewashed mansion. The gatekeeper greeted Saleem as if he were expecting him and guided him through the front courtyard to the left side of the house, into a vast outdoor area. As soon as the cart stopped, a woman servant came out of the house carrying a stool, which she placed on the ground so that Anjali could climb down.

Chandini was waiting on the doorstep. She opened her arms wide to embrace Anjali.

'Oh, my child, my child!' There was pity and motherly affection in her voice.

It was as if Anjali had been frozen by fear ever since she had escaped and had suppressed all thoughts of what had almost happened to her. Now, in the embrace of this kind and caring woman, she broke down and wept on Chandini's shoulders.

'It's all right, Anjali. There is no need to be afraid anymore. Sometimes we become the victims of ill fate.' She held the young woman to her and let her cry until there were no more tears left.

As Anjali was being led into the house, her fears calmed for now, she turned and saw Saleem standing on the steps, his head bowed, waiting to take his leave. He bid her a silent goodbye before climbing back on to the cart, where he pulled the reins to turn the bullocks around and drove away without looking back.

Chapter 6

Mentally and physically exhausted, Anjali hardly noticed her surroundings as she walked from room to room, following Chandini like a silent ghost. She was so tired she could barely put one foot in front of the other. She politely refused lunch because she had no appetite, but she accepted a glass of water.

Chandini took Anjali to her room in the inner quarters of the house, and told her to rest until she felt better. Finally alone, she slept for hours as morning turned into late afternoon. No one disturbed her.

But during the night, feelings of panic returned and kept her wide awake as she contemplated the uncertainty of her future and thought about never seeing her father again. She lay awake troubled by the stuffiness of the airless night, then got up and pulled aside the bolt of the window to breathe some fresh air. The wooden shutters parted, revealing the adjoining hall.

There, on one wall, a life-size portrait caught her eye. The dark shadows from the oil lamps cast a strange light, making it look macabre, but when she looked more closely, she saw that it was just a painting of a man wearing a turban. As her eyes adjusted, she could see his lavishly embroidered silk outfit, studded with pearls. He was wearing gold jewellery on his chest, wrists and fingers. She felt sure that the handle of his walking stick, carved in the shape of a swan, was also made of gold, with emerald stones for eyes. Ah, she thought. So this is the love of Chandini's life. Even though he had died long ago, this evidence of her devotion and love remained here in the dancing flames of the little silver lamps, in the garlands of fresh jasmine draped across the portrait, and in the fragrance of camphor sticks and sandalwood powders. His stature and up-turned moustache reminded her of her own husband.

And with that thought, Anjali saw once more Ranjit's dead body lying on the veranda. With the image came pain and guilt, because she had grown fond of him, in spite of everything. She had accepted him, not as a husband, but as a father figure. In that entire household of in-laws and servants, he was the only one who had been kind to her.

It was at the *Diwali* festival that she had finally come face to face with him. She was collecting almond fruits in the back yard when she heard her name being called. Recognising his voice, she hid behind the wall of the well. He came searching for her and called her from her hiding place. Feeling foolish and frightened, she walked round to face him. He observed her in silence for a few seconds, then told her to come to him.

The kindness in his eyes gave her the courage to walk towards him.

'Here, these are for you. A *Diwali* gift.' He handed her a large parcel.

That was all. He smiled at her, then nodded as if to dismiss her, and, having taken the gift from him, she ran to her room. There, in haste, she untied the string and to her joy and excitement, out from the brown paper tumbled a pile of story books. How did he know that there was nothing she wanted more?

After that, her fear of him ebbed away and gradually affection took its place. If ever she happened to see him during the day she would offer him a smile, and he would give her a friendly word in return.

After the night of the nuptials, her mother-in-law and step-mother would check on her every month. As time passed, their waiting turned to frustration and they began scolding her for not getting pregnant. Despite having her husband to herself, his first wife, Ratna, didn't show any mercy either.

Anjali lived in an atmosphere in which she constantly felt the hostility of women who waited intrusively. Only Ranjit treated her with dignity and kindness.

Chapter 7

Saleem reached Delhi by midday. Catching the 1.30 pm train, he travelled all night – three hundred and sixteen miles north-west – to arrive at Amritsar in the early hours of 13 April 1919.

After taking part in the naming ceremony of his sister Ruksana's new baby, he wanted to leave immediately in time for the earliest possible train back to Kalipet, but his sister and brother-in-law insisted that he should stay on and see the celebrations of *Baishakhi*, the harvest festival at the Golden Temple.

'I have to go. I have something important to see to and I really have to leave now,' he said. He knew that his behaviour appeared rude, but he was worried about Anjali.

'Please, *bhayya*,' his sister pleaded. 'Since I live so far away and you rarely visit me and it's been so long, can't you take the evening train instead? Please stay a while longer. I don't often have the pleasure of your company.'

Saleem did a quick calculation. If he took the early evening train, he would still reach Kalipet at least three hours before Anjali.

'Of course,' Saleem finally agreed, moved by his sister's affection.

On the way to the Golden Temple, Saleem asked, 'But Ruksana, are we allowed into a Sikh temple?

'No, *bhayya*, we can't go into the temple, but we can watch the celebrations all along the way.'

Saleem saw little stalls on the pavements selling beautifully carved ivory and woven Kashmiri shawls.

'Look, *bhayya*!' Ruksana called to him, stopping at one. 'Isn't it beautiful?' She pointed at an elegantly carved figurine.

'Yes, it is.' He took the figurine in his hands. The delicacy of the face and the sophistication of the curves reminded him of Anjali. He wondered whether her skin was as smooth and as flawless as the polished ivory. At another stall he saw a crimson shawl, draped on a hanger, and imagined it around her shoulders. A smile came to his lips. Maybe he should buy it for her.

'Come on, Saleem, that's enough admiring that figurine,' laughed Ahmad, his brother-in-law. 'Lucky you are not married. By marrying your sister I lost my licence to look at anything beautiful.' He winked at his wife.

As they walked on, Saleem saw the streets filled with men, women and children in brightly coloured outfits, dancing *Bhangra* and *Gidda* to the beat of the drums and the melody of the music. On the side of the road, some people were cooking *nans* and curries, snacks and sweets to offer to those who passed by as a gesture of goodwill.

His first sight of the temple took his breath away. It was built from pure white marble and rose from the centre of a large lake. The doors were solid silver, the windows golden, the upper half and the roof a mass of gold. The imposing dome on top represented an inverted lotus shape.

'It is so beautiful' whispered Saleem.

'Isn't it, *bhayya*! They say that the interior of the temple is decorated with precious stones, frescos and glass work.'

Saleem looked at the rippling blue waves washing against the polished marbled courtyard. Hundreds of pilgrims were walking towards it along a bridge that stretched across the water. In the glare of the sunlight, the building's structure was dazzling, its surface reflected in the sparkling waters. The floating lamps in the blue lake looked like a thousand moons that had fallen out of the sky to bathe in the sacred waters.

'The name "Amritsar" means "pool of nectar". They say that this water has powers,' Ahmad said.

'Really?'

'Oh, Saleem, ask your sister! She is fond of telling stories,' Ahmad teased. 'You don't believe anything I say.'

'I believe you. Tell me the story.'

'A very long time ago, even before the temple was built, a king used to rule this area. He had three daughters and during one Bisakhi festival, he brought gifts for them. His eldest two took them happily, but the youngest, Rajni, said, "This is a gift from the God but you are only a mediator". The king was angry and in his fury he married her to a poor leper and sent her away to live with him. Thinking that this was the God's wish, Rajni happily went with her husband. One day, she sat her husband near the Amritsar lake and went to work. He sat staring at the water and found that it made him feel at peace. Then he saw a crow fly down to drink. As soon as the bird touched the water, its darkness vanished and it became pure white. After watching, mesmerised, the leper crawled to the water and immersed himself in it. When Rajni came back from work, she was astonished to see her husband in full health and looking strong and handsome. So people still believe that the water has healing powers.'

'Um… very nice story.' Saleem smiled absentmindedly at his brother-in-law. Despite all the festivity and the hustle and bustle, he could not think of anything but Anjali. He knew it had been a wise decision to leave her at Chandini's for two days but he was concerned at making her travel such a long way on her own. Had he made a terrible mistake? What if she became confused and got off the train at the wrong place? He felt restless with worry. It was only on the way back from the temple that Ahmad's question, 'Have you heard about that horrible Rowlatt Act?' jolted Saleem back to the present.

'Yes, I have. Last month.'

'What exactly is it, bhayya?'

'The British judge, Sidney Rowlatt, has authorised the government to imprison, without trial, any person living in India suspected of aggression towards those in power. But Gandhi, among other Indian leaders, is extremely critical of the Act and has argued for leniency, saying that people should not be punished for expressing their political views nor for isolated acts of rebellion.'

'That's why last week on the sixth, a *hartal* was organised and Indians suspended all trading and fasted in protest against the legislation…' But before Ahmad had finished speaking, the two men were interrupted by an uproar and into the street poured an angry mob of men, women and children, shouting and holding placards inscribed: '*Jaihind*! Hail India! We want freedom!'

'British Raj, down, down! We want home rule! Long live Gandhi-ji!'

As the protest passed, everyone in the street stopped to watch.

'Hey, *bhai*,' one of the men greeted those who stood around. 'Why don't you join us at the meeting at Jallianwala-Bagh?'

'What is the meeting about?' someone asked.

'Haven't you heard? The Brigadier-General Dyer has given orders to prohibit all protests and stop the meetings of the freedom fighters who are speaking out against the Rowlatt Act. So this meeting is to protest against Rowlatt's orders.'

'Is it under Mahatma Gandhi's instructions?'

'On his principles.'

'We must go,' Ahmad said.

Saleem looked down. Lately he had started to admire Gandhi-ji and his principles. He admired what he had achieved in South Africa and now what he was doing in India, especially with his chosen weapon of non-violence. At any other time, he would have joined the protesting crowd without question, but now, with Anjali on his mind and a train to catch, it was impossible.

'Take the baby and go home,' Ahmad said to Ruksana. 'Come, Saleem.' He grabbed Saleem's hand.

'But Ahmad, I must catch the five o'clock train.'

'Don't worry. You'll have plenty of time for that.' Ahmad looked serious. 'It is important that we should join the march, Saleem. This is the only way we can teach the British that they can't stop us doing what we want to do in our own country.'

Before Saleem had time to utter a word, another mob appeared shouting the same slogans and joined the first crowd. Suddenly Saleem found himself pushed into the midst of a human river, which swept him away, leaving him little choice but to be carried along.

The Jallianwala-Bagh didn't look anything like the garden its name would suggest. It was a rectangle of unused ground. Some parts were covered with building material and debris. High walls completely enclosed it and in the middle was an empty well. The place was jam-packed with men, women and children. Looking at the massive crowd, Saleem estimated it to be about fifteen- to twenty-thousand strong. He knew that most of the protestors would have come from the neighbouring villages to celebrate *Baishakhi*.

The meeting got under way, and Saleem became totally engrossed, especially in the passionate speech of one of the leaders of the freedom fighters, who shouted from a raised platform. But then he sensed a disturbance in the audience and turned to see what looked like figures of authority standing on the raised ground that surrounded the meeting place. Some were already squeezing in through the only gate. Next he heard a voice filled with hatred and anger: 'Fire! Fire! Fire where the crowd is thickest! Block the exit.'

Before Saleem had time to react, an army of soldiers rushed into the grounds and aimed their rifles at the crowd.

'Using violence is a weakness! We must have the courage to face their anger!' The voice of the leader on the platform rang out even as a rain of bullets hit the crowd from all directions. Someone shouted, 'Dyer is the devil! He has come to kill us.'

Panic erupted as people screamed and shouted and cried for help. They were running in all directions, trampling on each other's feet, trying, in desperation, to climb the high walls around them. Some even jumped into the empty well in an attempt to escape the bullets. The only exit was blocked by Dyer and his soldiers.

Stunned, Saleem stood motionless, a witness to the massacre.

'Stop! Stop! Stop firing! Practise non-violence!' his inner voice screamed, but not a word came out of his mouth. *We don't want to punish and we have no desire for revenge. Our weapons are only the Truth and Non-violence. With that we want to change the system that produces brutality.'* Mahatma Gandhi's words echoed in his mind.

Close by, a woman clutching a child fell to the ground. Saleem caught hold of the child, and as he did so he remembered his sister's baby and his brother-in-law. Where was Ahmad? He couldn't see him. He shouted his name several times over the deafening noise but there was no answer.

'Please protect him, Allah!' Saleem prayed.

Holding the child close to his chest and shielding her with his arms, he ran to a five-foot wall. As he tried to climb it, he felt a sharp pain in his thigh and warm liquid trickled down his leg. He fell backwards. His head hit the ground hard and his eyes saw darkness. Then he lost consciousness. The child ran from his arms. Did she escape, or was she too shot and killed like so many thousands of others on that terrible day?

Chapter 8

For the first couple of days, Chandini left Anjali alone to recover and to regain her strength. The decision was well intentioned but it was counter-productive. The long periods on her own made Anjali worried and restless and she spent most of the time pacing her room like a prisoner. She would have loved to walk outside to release some of the pent-up energy, but she was unable to leave the house for fear of someone recognising her. Although it was reassuring to know that Chandini was there somewhere in the house, at night she had nightmares about her in-laws coming to claim her and take her back to the funeral pyre. She slept badly, jumping at the slightest sound and the faintest shadow.

To make matters worse, one morning Chandini came up to Anjali's room with distressing news.

'Anjali… I have just heard that all the trains to and from Punjab have been cancelled for the next few days, so Saleem can't travel and you can't leave here until the trains from Amritsar run again.'

'Why have the trains been cancelled?'

'No one knows. Perhaps some mechanical problem. Saleem will be worrying about you, Anjali,' Chandini said, immediately regretting her words. Anjali looked shocked. 'But knowing him, he'll jump on the very first train from Amritsar to Kalipet,' she added quickly.

It did not reassure Anjali. The waiting felt like a great weight as again she paced up and down her room, unable to find any outlet for her growing anxiety. What would happen to her now? When would Saleem be able to get there? The days passed.

*

Anjali had just dozed off, after hearing the distant chimes of a grandfather clock in Chandini's living room, when she was disturbed by someone calling her name. She stirred but her eyes were heavy and her body resisted being dragged from sleep. She moaned, burying her face in her pillow, wanting to be allowed back into the darkness of deep sleep.

'Anjali! Open your eyes. It's me…'

There was an urgency in the voice that forced Anjali fully awake. She saw Chandini looking down at her.

'I'm so sorry, Anjali, for startling you like this, but we have to go to the station very soon. The trains are running again. Saleem might have been travelling for several hours already.'

It was still dark outside and the stars were bright in the sky. From the depth of the blackness, she knew that dawn was a long way off. A dim glow from the hurricane lamp that hung on a post on the veranda lit a small part of the front yard. It felt much cooler than inside the house, and Anjali didn't know whether she shivered because of her rising panic or because of the cool breeze that came from the trees. Pulling the *burqa* over her head, she followed Chandini towards what would be her second journey in a *tonga*, this time towards the station, and this time with horses, not bullocks, hitched to the buggy.

'Don't ever lift the veil from your face,' Chandini advised her, checking the long garment that covered Anjali from head to toe.

Even at four in the morning the station heaved with people carrying trunks and bags, grain sacks and milk pitchers. Some, with fruit and vegetable baskets on their heads, rushed around shouting at each other at the tops of their voices. The vendors were singing, 'Tea, Coffee, Buttermilk, Biscuits!' The paper boys, weaving through the crowds, ran along the platforms, shouting out the latest headlines. All this activity overwhelmed Anjali and she looked at Chandini for reassurance.

'Don't worry, Anjali, you will be fine. Just remember what I said to you. Whatever happens, you must never reveal your identity to anyone.'

Anjali nodded, only half hearing, as a high-pitched whistle momentarily deafened her. She stared open-mouthed at the brick-coloured express train, puffing great clouds of dirty smoke, that thundered into the station and, wheels squealing and steam hissing, finally ground to a halt just inches away from where the two women were standing at the edge of the platform.

As another piercing whistle announced that the train was about to depart, Chandini hugged Anjali and bid her farewell. Anjali climbed the steps and stood at one of the windows to wave goodbye. She was thrown sideways as the engine lurched forwards, making its first gigantic effort to drag the carriages behind it. Then they were on their way, the great, noisy machine taking Anjali alone to some unknown destination.

Chapter 9

It felt incredibly strange and frightening to be sitting in a train that rocked at such great speed along the tracks. The rhythmic thudding of the wheels matched her heartbeat. She had never been on any sort of motorised vehicle before, let alone a long gigantic train that puffed out steam and rocked her from side to side with its lumbering motion.

Anjali kept her face turned to the window and observed the passing scenery. As the town was left behind, she saw makeshift huts built with pieces of fallen tree branch and cardboard. This was where the poor lived: she wondered how they could bear the stench that came from the sewage nearby. Then the shanty town gave way to luscious green rice fields, followed by a thick jungle that reminded her of the forests she had read about in the books Ranjit had given her. She saw all these places but they made no impression on her as her emotions were blunted by fear.

At times, despite the speed of the train, it felt stationary, with everything else travelling backwards. It picked up speed when it entered the Vindhya Forest and Anjali found it difficult to keep her veil over her face in the strong wind. She closed the window, and for a while stared at the flying sparks of burning coal, which looked like fire flies. Only when the train was moving through a tunnel did she dare turn her head and take note of the people in the carriage.

It was full of young and old, rich and poor. Some, well dressed, sat on the wooden seats, reading books or knitting woollen garments. They made polite conversation, keeping their voices low. The poor labourers and working classes sat on the floor, surrounded by their baskets, sacks and work tools. They yelled at each other at the tops of their voices, while all the time chewing betel or tobacco leaf.

'Where are you going, *beti*?' It was a middle-aged woman sitting opposite Anjali who spoke.

'Ka... Kalipet,'

'Are you travelling alone?'

'Yes.'

'Where is your husband?' she leaned forward. 'Is he sitting in the gentlemen's compartment?'

Of course the woman assumed that Anjali was married. At her age any girl would be married and have children. A lump came to her throat and she didn't know how to answer the question.

The woman smiled at her and said, 'I understand. You are shy. I was like you when I was your age. Even the mention of my husband would send my heart fluttering and make me cast my eyes down. Do you live in Adhira?'

'No,' Anjali answered quickly.

'So, I assume it is your mother's place then?'

'No.'

'No? Then who lives there?'

Anjali didn't know what to say. She wished the woman would leave her alone.

'Oh, the poor girl might not understand what you are saying,' another woman piped up.

'Perhaps.' the first woman nodded. 'Some Muslims don't understand any local languages, and can only speak Urdu.'

Of course. Anjali realised that she must look like a Muslim because she was wearing a *burqa*. She was glad of it and hoped the questioning would stop.

The train stopped at another station and the usual hullabaloo started up again. The sellers of tea, coffee, snacks and newspapers surrounded the train. Anjali had to shoo the vendors away from her. She watched a girl, hardly ten years old, in tattered clothes, climbing all over the train, and a boy, perhaps her younger brother, following her. Only when the girl began playing the mouth organ while the boy collected money from the passengers did Anjali realise that the girl was blind. It was obvious that this was their only way of making a living.

Her thoughts turned to her future. What was she going to do? How on earth was she going to earn money? She knew Saleem would look after her but she could not impose on him the burden of feeding her as well as his own large family. She had heard that since his father had had an accident at the factory, Saleem was the sole bread winner. That was why he took a better paid job far away from home, in Harikonda. Anjali wondered if she could ask him to find her a job, but what sort of job could she do? She could cook. That was the only skill that she had managed to acquire over the years, thanks to Ratna taking her under her wing in the kitchen.

Another shrill whistle from the train interrupted her thoughts and she watched as the talkative women in the opposite seat were replaced with a mother and two little children. Anjali was reminded of the cherubic faces of Virinchi and Lakshmi, her husband's children. A longing for the little ones seized her and she closed her eyes.

Darkness was falling when a delicious, pungent aroma reached her nostrils. She immediately recognised it as spicy mango pickle. Her tastebuds tingled and her stomach grumbled as she remembered the *roties* that Chandini had packed for her. She saw that the mother on the opposite seat was feeding her children and the sight reminded her of Ratna, the woman who at first had hated her and then became her friend.

Soon after her first encounter with Ranjit, the miracle that no one had expected had happened: the announcement that Ratna was expecting a child echoed around the house. Not only the family but the whole village celebrated the news. Except Parvati. She turned on Anjali and scolded her with a fury that took the young woman by surprise.

'It has been three months, Anjali!' she screamed. 'What have you been doing? Why are you not pregnant?'

Turning away her gaze, Anjali did not answer.

'Are you not sleeping with him?'

Anjali lowered her head.

'Why? What's wrong with you?' Parvati gripped her shoulders and shook her. 'Answer me, girl! Didn't Chandini teach you anything?'

Anjali bit her lip but remained silent.

'You are a stupid girl, you know, Anjali. You are young and pretty and if you tried, it would have been so easy for you to hold Ranjit in your fist. What bad luck! It's your karma that has taken away an opportunity to be mistress of a gold mine.'

The months progressed and Ratna ordered Anjali to become her personal maid, at her beck and call at all times. Anjali cooked according to her taste, rubbed aromatic oils into her aching back and feet, and fanned her with peacock feathers to help her sleep during the airless summer nights. When the first child Virinchi was born, Anjali was promoted to be his Ayah and later she looked after his sister Lakshmi as well. She didn't mind her new role. The children filled her life with fun. They always slept in her room at night. She loved playing with them, enjoyed telling age-old stories to them. When they were little, she used to sing them to sleep with lullabies. She felt like a second mother and in return they gave her pleasure. Anjali longed for them now.

Putting her feet up on the seat, she leaned on the window, and Ratna came to her mind. She had guarded her husband possessively and had spent every minute of the day doing things for him. It must have been unbearably painful to lose him suddenly like that. When Ratna had realised that neither Ranjit nor Anjali was interested in forming a loving relationship, she had become softer and more friendly. She would, after all, have Ranjit to herself.

On that fateful night, Anjali had been the first to hear Ratna's screams and had alerted the household. People had panicked. Someone had fetched the doctor but within minutes of his arrival, he emerged from Ranjit's room and announced that he was dead. He had died of a heart attack. Nothing could have saved him. Like others, she had been numb with shock for a long time, and as the dreadful truth sank in, she too cried her heart out – for him, for Ratna, and for their children.

Anjali moved restlessly in her seat, the memories disturbing her. For the first time since she was married, she realised that she had loved that strange, big man almost as much as her own father. Once more tears welled up, but this time for him.

Chapter 10

Another piercing whistle jolted Anjali from her fitful dozing. Another station. How many had they been through already? Was this one her final destination? She looked round the carriage and saw that everyone was asleep except one woman on the upper berth opposite who was reading. As the train gradually slowed down, Anjali asked in Hindi, 'Is this Kalipet Junction?'

The woman yawned, closed her book and said, 'Yes it is.'

Anjali thanked the woman. She felt uneasy. For the last twenty-four hours the train had sheltered and protected her and now she had to leave it. 'Don't panic,' she told herself. 'Saleem will be waiting at the station!' Once she had found him, she could stop worrying. He would look after her. With this reassurance, she looked out of the window. It was still pitch black, except for the tiny sparks that flew around the train from the burning coal which stoked the engine. They looked so beautiful. Like ruby dust.

The train ground to a halt and the vendors quickly surrounded it. They held their baskets on their heads, tiny oil lamps flickering in them so that the passengers could see their contents.

'Hot hot *pakoras*…!' 'Batthanies and peanuts…!' 'Biscuits and bread…!' 'Tea and coffee…!' the vendors sang loudly. 'Papers, newspapers, *Young India*, *The Hindu* and *Swaraj*…!' 'Please buy one. There was and still is trouble in Punjab.' 'Dyer the devil! Last week he massacred hundreds of people at Jallianwala-Bagh.' 'And the cowards, fearing for their lives, banned all transport to and from the Punjab, making it impossible for people to travel and contact each other.' 'Heartless British and the brutality of them! Read it!' The paper boys ran along the train holding up pictures and shouting out the headlines to tempt passengers to buy a newspaper.

As Anajli gathered herself to follow her fellow passengers descending from the train, she heard slogans called out, faintly at first and then louder and louder.

'General Dyer – Down! Down!' 'Long live Mahatma Gandhi!' 'We want home rule!' 'We want freedom not detention!' *'Jai-Hind!* Give us our country back!'

At the doorway, Anjali craned her neck and saw a crowd of people, shouting and surrounding the train. In minutes they were everywhere, holding batons, knives and other weapons. Everyone in the carriage became alarmed. 'What's happening?' puzzled passengers asked each other sleepily.

'Look, look...' someone pointed through the door. 'There is trouble brewing in the first-class compartment.'

What had begun as individual cries and slogans was now a furious mob chant.

'Murderers! Leave India! Get out of our country!'

'Expel them! Beat the blood suckers!'

Anjali couldn't get out of the train because the crowd blocked her way. Some of the passengers joined it, swelling its numbers. The voices rose higher as people expressed their anger, frustration and anguish. Soon there was only a ferocious roar and she could not make out a single word. The station had turned into a battle field.

'Come on, girl, get out of the train, fast.' Someone grabbed her hand.

'They may de-rail the train or set it alight.'

Anjali struggled to step down on to the platform, but there was not an inch, not even when she stood on tip-toe.

Where was Saleem? How could she find him in this sea of people churning in a storm? She tried to scan the faces but the human wall blocked her vision. She had to get out of the station – Saleem must be waiting outside.

As she struggled to inch her way forward, she saw some English passengers being dragged out of their first-class carriages. Shocked, she watched as they were beaten by the mob until they collapsed on the platform, unconscious, in a pool of blood.

Nothing seemed real; it was like a horror scene out of a story book.

And then suddenly the armed police were everywhere, beating the crowd with batons and gun barrels, trying to gain control of the uncontrollable.

'Fire!

'Something is on fire!'

'Something's burning…'

People were shouting and trampling on each other as they tried to run from the flames that rose from one of the snack stalls. Anjali could smell burning oil. The whole station filled with smoke as the blaze spread rapidly from stall to stall.

Sweat poured down Anjali's face. She struggled to breathe.

Chapter 11

Saleem heard his name being called. Someone was trying to wake him. At first it was like a distant whisper and he couldn't understand what the voice was saying, then slowly it became clearer and nearer. He wanted to see who it was. Why was he being woken? He felt exhausted after the previous night's violence and it was an effort to open his eyes. Everything was blurred and out of focus but he could make out a woman in white clothes. She smiled at him. Who was she and why was she here? He raised his head slowly and looked around. He was in a hospital. He realised that the woman in white was a nurse.

'You are all right now,' she said to him.

Then the green curtain across the door twitched open and in ran his sister Ruksana, followed by her husband Ahmad.

'*Bhayya*, oh, *bhayya*!' Ruksana cried. 'Thank god, you are all right. Thank god, you are awake.' She put her arms around him, while Ahmad squeezed his hand affectionately.

Saleem saw concern and worry etched on their faces and asked, 'What happened?' His throat hurt and his voice was groggy from the after-effects of anaesthesia.

'Don't worry about it now,' Ahmad said.

'Just tell me why I am here?' Saleem felt too weak to whisper more than a few words.

Then yesterday's events came back to him. He re-lived the visit to Amritsar, the massacre at Jallianwala-Bagh, the baby crying, the mother lying dead on the ground, his thigh being hit by a bullet.

He was drifting back to sleep, longing for rest and oblivion, when another thought jolted him back to consciousness. Anjali! Oh, my god, Anjali! He didn't catch the train. What had happened to Anjali? What could he do now? He moved in a futile effort to get up.

'Don't move your leg, Saleem,' Ahmad said.

'Do you want anything? Water?'

No, nothing… but I must go. I must get out of here. Can you take me to the station?'

Ahmad put a hand on Saleem's shoulder and gently pushed him back down. 'Now? In the state you are in? You can't even walk.'

'But it's very important… please…'

' You are in no state to travel,' said his sister.

'You got hurt at Jallianwala-Bagh. They had to operate,' Ahmad said. 'And you have been in a coma for a week now.'

'A week? My god! Anjali! I have to go. You don't understand how important it is,' Saleem moaned. Only when he tried again to sit up did he realise that it was impossible.

'Saleem, the trains have been cancelled ever since the shooting. Even if you were not injured you wouldn't be able to travel. They only started running again last night.'

'This can't be happening!' he cried weakly. 'Please, someone help me. I am sure there is a train now! I have to go…'

Hearing his cries, the nurse came running. 'Are you in pain?'

'No… no… but I need to leave here. Now..'

'You can't. Not yet. You have been very lucky. The bullet only penetrated the soft tissue of your leg. You know it could have been much worse if it had penetrated the major blood vessels.' She loaded a syringe with a drug from a tiny bottle.

'How long will it be before he can walk again?' Ruksana asked.

'It depends, sometimes it can take more than two weeks. Perhaps three.' The nurse looked at her watch. 'The doctor will be here on his rounds in an hour and he will let you know.' She pricked the needle into Saleem's arm. 'This will ease the pain and help you relax and sleep.'

As the drug poured through his veins, Saleem leaned back on his pillows and closed his eyes. It was hard to think clearly but images of Anjali floated before him. She must have reached Kalipet by now. How would she cope without him? What a dreadful mistake. He should never have gone to the meeting. He shouldn't have let her travel on her own. Chandini would have looked after her for another few days until he could have collected her.

These thoughts came and went until the drug finally kicked in, rescuing him from his torment. He closed his eyes. He had no choice but to drift back to sleep.

Chapter 12

Anjali didn't know how she got out of the smoke-filled station but somehow she managed to detach herself from the tangled web of people and make her way to the exit. The sudden brilliance of the sunshine hurt her eyes. It felt much cooler outside than inside where the fire still burned. She took a deep breath and lifted her hand to her brow to shade her eyes. She saw people, panic-stricken and confused, crying, shouting and running, haphazardly and without any direction, as if a mad bull was chasing them.

Feeling tired and very thirsty from the smoke, she searched for a source of water and, after wandering about, found a well under a huge *neem* tree. With trembling hands, she drew up the fresh water and splashed it over her face, feet and hands before allowing herself a long, cool drink. Refreshed, she sat down on a big root as wide as the wooden train seat on which she had sat for so many hours only a short time ago.

Where was Saleem? She looked around, searching for him. Why was he late? Perhaps the train was early. Had Saleem forgotten that she was coming today? No. She shook her head. He would never do that. He was always reliable. He would come soon. With these thoughts she tried to reassure herself and settled to wait under the comfortable shade of the *neem* tree.

From here she could see each and every person who emerged from or entered the station. She guessed that the stretchers being carried in and out were for casualties. People were helping those with minor injuries and dragging them into the waiting *tongas* and rickshaws and bullock carts. Police came out with those they had arrested, handcuffed, and threw them into waiting vans. She knew the fire was under control but it would take hours to clear the chaos and get the trains running again.

As the minutes turned into long hours, and as the midday sun crossed the sky from east to west, the noise gradually died down and the crowd subsided. Seeing the place deserted, except for a few men in uniform, she began to doubt if Saleem would ever come for her. What had been anxiety turned to panic, and she stood up over and over again, staring desperately in every direction. And then a new thought struck her. What if Saleem had arrived early and had been injured himself in the mob or the fire? It was a horrific idea, and after all those hours of waiting, had only just occurred to her. Horrified at her lack of clear thinking, she got up again and ran to the closed gates of the station.

'Stop! Stop! The station is closed. You can't go in,' shouted an elderly gentleman in a blue porter's uniform, holding out his arm to block her.

'Please let me go in. I am looking for a man called Saleem,' she begged.

The man stared at her disbelievingly. 'There is no one inside the station. He must have come out.'

'No, I didn't see him come out of the station. I have been waiting since four in the morning.'

'Was he supposed to arrive on that early morning train?'

'No, I was on the train, and he was supposed to meet me here.'

'Don't worry. Go and sit over there.' He led her to the shade of the *neem* tree again.

'I just hope he hasn't been injured...'

'No, he couldn't have been,' replied the porter. 'No one has been allowed into the station since the incident. Only the authorities. Don't worry, you wait here. In a few hours the station will be reopened and if the man comes asking about you, I will let him know that you are waiting here.'

Comforted by his words, Anjali sat down again on the root of the tree and waited and waited until she lost count of the time.

*

She stayed there without moving for a very long time and as the light faded, so did her hope. Except the porter had said that the station would be reopened for the nine o'clock train, and perhaps Saleem had assumed that she was arriving on that and would be at the station then, in time to meet it.

She didn't know what time it was but she stood up when she heard the sound of a train's arrival in the station. Minutes passed. No one went in or came out. Then she heard the piercing screech of the whistle – the train was about to depart..

Where was he? She ran like a madwoman, in and out of the station, looking everywhere, unable to believe that Saleem had not come.

The porter came across to her with a couple of bananas. 'You haven't eaten anything since this morning…'

Her stomach was full with worry but she didn't have the heart to refuse his kindness.

'Where does this Saleem live?'

'I have his address with me but I don't know how to get there.'

'What does he do?' the porter asked, taking the piece of paper with Saleem's address from Anjali.

'He is a jeep driver.'

'Ah!' he said. 'Motorcars are completely unreliable. They're always causing trouble for their drivers.' He smiled, gesturing at a *tonga*. 'Give me a horse any day and I would swap ten motorcars for it. Now you know why he hasn't come.'

She didn't say anything but looked down, hiding the tears in her eyes. In her heart of hearts she knew that this man's explanation was wrong and that something awful had happened to Saleem. She kept seeing an image of him injured and lying in a hospital bed.

The porter had moved to stand under the light of a street lamp where he could read the address on the paper. 'This is in Harikonda. A long way away, and at this time of night you will find it almost impossible to travel there. See – there are no rickshaws or *tongas*.'

Anjali stared at him.

'Look, there are no trains until six in the morning and it's certainly not safe for a girl to stay here alone at night. I will accompany you to a lodge near the temple, which is not far, and you can sleep there tonight.'

'A lodge…'

'Don't worry, the owner is a nice lady. She will look after you. You can come back here in the morning… and you might meet Saleem… who knows…'

As she had not the slightest idea what else to do, Anjali did as she was told and followed him to the lodge near the temple.

Chapter 13

Anjali sat motionless under a *tamarind* tree in the compound of the lodge, staring at the star-lit sky. She had been staying there for more than a week now. The porter said it was the only cheap accommodation in town. For a modest amount of money, she was getting two meals a day, and a straw mat to sleep on in a room which was allocated for women only. The men slept on the front veranda.

It had become a daily ritual for her then to hire a rickshaw and go to the address that Saleem had given her. The door of the tiny house was always locked. Eventually, when she plucked up the courage to ask, the neighbours said that they hadn't seen Saleem for weeks now. She returned to the station and sat and scanned every face. She even visited all the hospitals – a Mission hospital, a homeopathic clinic and an Ayurvedic dispensary, but to no avail. No one knew anything about Saleem.

With each day that passed, Anjali's hope faded. She sighed, leaning against the trunk of the tree. What could she do now? Over and over again, she asked herself the same impossible question. What had happened to him? Was he badly injured, or worse…? She looked up to the sky through the thick foliage of the tree. She could not stay here forever. The fifty rupees her father had given her would not last much longer. The eeriness of the night made her heart lurch.

When the temple bells rang out, Anjali got to her feet. and She found herself walking towards the temple on the lower slopes of the Harikonda hill, with its high, exquisitely carved *gopuram*. She had heard that it was the largest Shiva temple in Harikonda district with its high, exquisitely carved *gopuram*, the pyramidal roof. It was built by King Krishnadeva of the Surya dynasty in 1163. From the outside she could see that it was a star- shaped structure with five angles, following an ancient architectural rule.

Its polished black granite gleamed in the red glow of the blazing torches set high on posts all around it. Beside the temple was a small lake with a flight of steps descending into the water. After climbing the stone steps leading up to the *mantapam*, Anjali entered the inner quarters of the temple, where she noticed a slightly raised circular dance platform in front of the shrine, where Lord Shiva presided. There were many intricately carved pillars, with divine figures, dancing girls and musical instruments, supporting the flat stone roof, domed at its centre. The sculpture of *Nandi*, the holy bull of the Lord, was carved out of a monolithic black stone. With its glossy finish, it was a splendid piece of art. The soft light of the oil lamps soothed Anjali's nerves. She inhaled the fragrance of fresh flowers and incense sticks. At that time of the night, only a few devotees lingered about this hushed worshipping place. Anjali had prayed to *Nandi* before walking up to the shrine. The low-pitched rhythm of the priest's chanting and the sacred sight of the deity calmed her troubled spirit. After praying for Saleem, she sat with her back against a pillar.

*

'Here, have some *prasadam*.'

Anjali looked up to see a middle aged woman with a plate of offerings standing over her.

'Thank you.' She stretched her hand to take a sweet pastry.

'I am Mohini. I have come from a neighbouring village to attend the Ugadi festival at the temple. What is your name, *beti*?' The woman sat down beside her.

'Anjali…'

'Oh, nice name.' She smiled as she settled next to her.

Feeling under some obligation, Anjali said, 'This is a very beautiful temple, with its star shape and surrounded by the gardens and the lake…'

'Yes, it is.'

Mohini nodded.

'I saw you coming out of the lodge. I don't think you have been here before, have you?'

For some reason the woman's friendliness comforted Anjali and she answered all her questions, revealing the purpose of her visit to Harikonda, telling her about the fire in the station and about not finding Saleem anywhere. Apart from the kind porter at the station, Mohini was the only person who seemed to understand her anguish.

'What are you going to do now?'

'I don't know. I am thinking of finding some work.'

Mohini looked her up and down for a few seconds before asking, 'What sort of work are you looking for?'

'I can cook and do housework. I have been doing it for years.'

'Of course, but don't forget it is very different working for other people compared with looking after your own house. They might treat you like a slave.' Her eyes became softer as she added, 'You look too delicate to do any kind of hard work. With your beauty and grace, you should become a dancer.'

'A dancer?' Anjali was astonished at Mohini's suggestion.

'Yes, why not? I can teach you.'

'You are a dancer?'

'I used to be when I was young, but now I only teach.'

Anjali became silent, not knowing what to say. Many thoughts buzzed in her mind. She had heard that dancers did not command respect, but Chandini was also a dancer and her in-laws held her in high regard.

'I know what you are thinking,' Mohini interrupted her thoughts. 'There are many people who respect the art and grace of a dancer. The zamindar in our village adores all the fine arts. In our village, there are no festivals or *pujas* without music and dance.'

'I don't know what to say... can I think about it?'

'Of course, take your time. I will be here until tomorrow afternoon.'

Anjali stayed wide awake the whole night deliberating, calculating the pros and cons of a decision one way or the other. When she finally made up her mind, birdsong was already heralding the dawn.

Chapter 14

Saleem had no choice but to spend several miserable weeks in the hospital, worrying all the time about Anjali. During the first few days, he had desperately wanted to get a message to her to tell her not to set out on her journey and not to get on the train, but the distance between Amritsar and Adhira and the lack of communication facilities made it impossible. Then it was too late. Feeling utterly helpless, he decided to send two letters to Harikonda: a short note to his employer, Mr Robert Harrison, asking his pardon for the delay in returning to his duties, and a more detailed one to his roommate Prakash, explaining the whole situation and begging him to look for Anjali at the Kalipet station. He knew it might take several days for the letters to reach them but he prayed for a miracle and hoped that Prakash at least would receive his soon. The anticipation that his friend would find Anjali was the only thing that kept him from going insane over the following two weeks.

His anxiety seemed to double his will to get stronger. As soon as he could take a few steps with the aid of a walking stick, he persuaded the doctors to discharge him. Ignoring his sister's plea that he should stay with her until he was fully recovered, he immediately ventured forth on the long journey to find Anjali.

Once aboard the train, he fretted about its speed and looked at his watch every few minutes. Time was passing so slowly. And of course he was worried. What if his letter hadn't reached Prakash in time? What would Anjali do once she realised he was not going to meet her? Where would she go? He shifted uncomfortably in his seat. With the fingers of his right hand he rubbed his aching brow while his left hand fidgeted with his shirt buttons.

After two long, agonising days, the train finally reached its destination. Saleem wanted to rush out and begin his search for Anjali, but his leg was still painful and he had to be careful. Holding on to his walking stick he tried to stand up but as he leaned on his injured foot, he felt dizzy and his legs trembled. He sat down again on the seat, waited for a few seconds, took some deep breaths and had a sip of water. He collected himself, and, wincing with pain, managed to get off the train and on to the platform. Moving slowly, he scanned every female face in and around the station, just in case Anjali was still there. Then he hired one of the waiting rickshaws, hoping that he would find Anjali waiting for him at his home. Perhaps Prakash or a neighbour had let her in.

As he was climbing down from the rickshaw outside his home, there was Prakash turning the key in the padlock.

'Prakash!' His voice was urgent.

'Saleem! Welcome back. I'm glad to see you.' But then Prakash saw the bandages on his friend's leg and the pallor in his face and the painful thinness of his body. His eyes widened with shock. 'What has happened? Your leg…'

'Have you seen Anjali?' Saleem asked, ignoring his friend's concern.

'Anjali… who is Anjali?'

'Didn't she come here?'

'No. No one came here…'

'Didn't you get my letter?'

'What letter?'

'What do you mean "what letter"?' Saleem felt the ground swaying beneath his feet.

'Come inside and we can talk.' Prakash offered Saleem his arm for support. 'Do you know there have been riots everywhere? I went home two weeks ago and was stuck there for a week.'

'So you weren't here when Anjali came… and you haven't received my letter…'

'The mail bags must have caught in the fire at the station.'

'You mean in Kalipet station?'

'Yes.'

'Oh my god! Anjali!' He looked at Prakash. 'Please can you take me back to the station?'

'Look, Saleem, you have just travelled a very long way. Look at you, you are so pale, and your leg… you can't even walk properly. Get some rest, Saleem, and I will go with you later to enquire about the girl… I mean Anjali.'

'No, Prakash, it is already too late. She came here several weeks ago and I was supposed to meet her then!'

'Relax, Saleem. You have waited two weeks. Nothing is going to happen in the next two hours. At least freshen up and have some tea before we go and search for her.'

Defeated by his friend's common sense, and his own exhaustion, Saleem agreed. He lay down for a couple of hours, and then had something to eat. Only then did the two friends set off together back to the station.

Kalipet station was as busy as ever. Police were everywhere, closely guarding it on all sides. Sitting on a bench in the waiting area – Prakash had insisted – Saleem waited anxiously while his friend went round all the officials and passengers asking about a young woman of Anjali's description. An hour later, disappointed and forlorn, Saleem followed his friend out of the station.

Once at home he called out to her, 'Anjali-ji!' He covered his face with his hands and wept hot tears. 'Your father rescued you from a fire, and now look what I have done! I've sent you straight into another.'

'Saleem, I am sure nothing terrible has happened to her.' Prakash squeezed Saleem's shoulder, trying to reassure him. 'We will find her soon.'

For the next three days Saleem walked every inch of the town searching for Anjali. He asked everywhere. He looked everywhere. When Prakash offered him food, Saleem refused, and at nights he tossed and turned in bed. He hardly spoke, even with his friend. Only on the third evening, when once again he had returned to the station, did he finally bump into the porter whom Anjali had met when she had first waited for him at the station.

'You will remember that fire at the station two weeks ago. By any chance, did you notice a girl of eighteen? She had travelled on her own,' Saleem asked him.

'A girl, on her own… on the day of the fire at the station?'

'Yes, did you see her? She didn't have much luggage.'

'She is very pretty,' added Prakash.

'What did you say her name was?'

'Anjali,' they both said at the same time.

'Yes, I met her,' nodded the porter. 'She was on her own, scared and worried…' He looked at the two friends again, and recognising Saleem's Muslim style of clothing, he smiled at him and asked, 'Are you Saleem?'

'Yes, I am.' He was surprised that the porter knew his name.

'She worried about you so much. She even went to your house, and was so disappointed when she didn't find you.'

'Please… tell me where she is now.'

'I know she stayed in that lodge near the temple for a week, but I haven't seen her lately. I am not sure if she is still staying there. The owner might be able to help you.'

Saleem thanked the man and touched his feet with both hands in the traditional gesture of gratitude.

'See, I told you that she would be safe. Now that you know where she went, will you have something to eat before we set off for the lodge?'

Saleem smiled at his friend.

'And don't you dare say that you can't eat because your belly is full with relief,' Prakash teased, leading Saleem to a snack stall beside the station.

Chapter 15

Anjali's legs trembled as she climbed on to the tonga and sat next to Mohini. She pulled her *sari pallu* over her head and put her hand in her bag, feeling for the fabric of the *burqa*. In this area of the south, where she was a complete stranger, far away from her in-laws, she didn't feel any need for the garment, but she didn't want to discard it either. With so much uncertainty in her life, she never knew when she might need it again.

The *tonga* passed through the busy streets of Harikonda before turning on to a quieter country track. As it reached its maximum speed, a cool breeze brushed Anjali's cheeks, and she looked at the lush green rice fields on either side and listened to the music of the jingling bells that hung round the horse's neck. She wondered whether her decision was wise, but Mohini's words, 'A pretty young girl like you can't survive in a town like Harikonda,' echoed in her mind, and she decided that perhaps she was right. She had waited for Saleem for more than a week until her hope had dwindled. Now there was no choice but to follow the older woman's advice. Reassured, she closed her eyes for a moment. But anxiety about Saleem's fate soon put an end to her peace. She stared blankly at her surroundings, winding and unwinding her cloth bag's thin straps around her fingers.

'Are you all right, Anjali?' Mohini asked, looking at her sullen face.

Anjali nodded, but turned away.

'Have a drop of water.' Mohini unscrewed the lid of a brass decanter and poured some into a small glass.

Anjali took a sip. 'What if Saleem comes looking for me…?'

Mohini looked at her kindly. 'If he is looking for you, I am sure he will find you wherever you go. Relax now. Stop worrying so much.'

*

Anjali hardly noticed the time passing. They had been travelling for three hours across thirty miles, passing rice and maize fields, palm and mango groves, and orange and lemon gardens, when she saw a milestone bearing the engraved letters 'Roypuram'.

On Mohini's orders, the driver had stopped the *tonga* for a moment to pull the curtains down at the back and the front, but Anjali moved the material to one side with her finger and saw that the sun was sinking, painting the sky with red and yellow streaks. She heard a flock of birds prattling, flying low to reach their nests for the night. At the same time, groups of field workers and herds of cattle appeared on the track, walking home after a hard day under the scorching sun. The men held their tools on their shoulders, while the women balanced their baskets on their heads and carried their babies on their backs in cloth cradles.

As they entered the village, the *tonga* made its final journey through the narrow uneven gullies separating small mud huts crowned with palm-leaf roofs. Smoke was rising everywhere and Anjali could smell the food; women were crouching, standing and squatting over clay pots, cooking their only meal of the day on a stone or mud stove over a log fire. While stirring, they kept up a tirade of abuse, scolding their men, who sat around rolling tobacco for a smoke or drinking *kallu* from pots; it was the familiar evening ritual. Half-clothed children ran around and played in the dust with broken tiles, pebbles and sticks, while naked babies gurgled on straw mats or in cloth swings dangling from *tamarind* or mango or *neem* trees.

Then Anjali saw the huts give way to small houses with terracotta roofs. She knew that they at least had separate kitchens, if not bathrooms.

A small stream divided the village, just as it divided and defined the two separate classes. Having crossed to the other side, Anjali noticed that the streets were much wider, with large houses, some two-storied, with tiled or flat roofs. Their stone-floored verandas gleamed, housing magnificent furniture. It was dusk still, lighting-up-the-lamps time, and no Hindu would welcome the misfortune that might be visited on them if they closed the doors of their houses to Lakshmi, the goddess of wealth, so the painted metal or polished wooden gates remained wide open.

Here, only men were visible, returning from their walks or talks, holding, prodding or swaying their gold- or silver-headed walking sticks. Some sat in groups on their verandas, discussing village affairs or playing chess. Children played in their different territories.

Anjali recognised the high-caste society and she knew the women would be in the inner quarters of the house, ordering their servants about and telling them to do the evening chores. Her heart ached as she thought of her husband's home.

Finally the tonga made a sharp turn, before a long driveway, and jolted to a halt. Anjali stared at the fabulously carved wooden gates of a grand mansion hidden by tall *ashoka* trees, which had grown higher than the compound wall. She stretched her neck and leaned backwards to see magnificent arches and pillars. Awestruck, she looked at Mohini. Mohini returned the girl's astonishment with a knowing smile and told her to close the curtain properly. Anjali quickly took her finger away and stretched the silky material to cover the gap.

A few seconds later, she heard the gates opening smoothly on their well-oiled hinges.

Chapter 16

Once inside the gates, Anjali could see, through the curtain, a huge courtyard, where torches burned in tall ornamental posts. In their illumination, the grand mansion was fully visible, glowing in burnished pink. It stood well back from the gates, surrounded by emerald lawns with fountains at their centres and gleaming white marble steps leading to its magnificent entrance. Its countless arched windows, balconies and verandas sat behind a dense barrier of flowering bushes, so that it was completely cut off from the hustle and bustle of the outside world.

'This is the famous Gadi palace, where Zamindar Jeevan Roy lives. He rules not only Roypuram but several other villages in this neighbourhood.'

'And you are…?' enquired Anjali.

But before she could finish her question, the cart began moving forward once more, this time turning towards the back of the building. Mohini remained silent, so Anjali sat and observed; they passed a cattle shed on the left, a stable on the right, and a sanctuary for elephants. Last came a row of small huts which she guessed were servants' quarters.

The cart stopped at a whitewashed bungalow with a stone-floored veranda. The pillars on either side, entwined with jasmine creepers, were smothered in pink and white flowers. Anjali inhaled the sweet fragrance. Everything looked so enchanting in the moonlight.

'Welcome home,' Mohini smiled.

Anjali nodded her thanks.

A servant boy rushed from the house, holding a lantern for them, while a woman servant carried water so that they could wash their feet.

Anjali climbed the stone steps behind Mohini. Inside, the room looked cosy in the dim light of oil lamps. The scent of camphor and sandalwood hung in the air. It was cool and refreshing after the heaviness of the humid air in the streets outside.

Mohini pointed to a divan covered in velvet cushions and asked a female servant, 'Where is Kalyani?'

'She is in her room, *dorsani*.'

'Go and tell her that I am calling her.'

'Yes, *dorsani*.'

Hearing the servant address Mohini with a title of respect, one reserved for a high-caste woman, Anjali wondered whether she was related to the Zamindar Jeevan Roy – but if so, why was she living in an inferior residence like this? What was she supposed to call Mohini in future? Perhaps '*dorsani*' as well!

'*Amma!*' A voice interrupted her thoughts, and Anjali saw a girl of her own age coming from the inner quarters of the house. Aware of the stranger, the girl stopped in the doorway.

'Come and sit here, Kalyani,' said Mohini. 'This is Anjali.'

Anjali smiled at Kalyani.

'She has come here to learn dance.'

'Dance?' Kalyani muttered and her face fell.

'Yes.' Mohini looked at both girls seriously and her voice was firm. 'From today onwards, you will be sharing your room with Anjali. Anjali, please go with Kalyani, who will see to your needs.' And with this final statement, Mohini rose from the couch and left the two girls to their own thoughts.

After watching Kalyani biting her nails for several minutes, Anjali stood up, gathered her small bag, and asked, 'Can you show me where the bathroom is, please?'

'Yes, of course, come with me.' Kalyani led the way.

*

Next morning Anjali woke to the cooing of a cockerel. Confused for a second, she sat upright and blinked her sleepy eyes. The room was dark still, but she could see the traces of misty morning light struggling through window doors that had been left ajar. Outside, she could hear the swishing sounds of people sweeping the yard and sprinkling it with water. She saw Kalyani stir in the next bed and wondered how the girl would receive her today.

Having slept deeply and well for the first time in weeks, Anjali felt relaxed, in mind and body; but her relief was short-lived, for her nagging worry about Saleem again flooded her mind. She leaned back on her pillows and closed her eyes, reminiscing over past events. Finally, after so many weeks of uncertainty and deliberation and worry, she made a decision. She would continue to pray for Saleem's safety but apart from that she would put aside her constant thoughts of him and get on with her new life. What other choice did she have?

New life? The thought itself surprised her. Yes, she had already stepped into it, not knowing what it would bring her. The only thing she knew for certain was that Mohini was going to teach her dance, whether she liked it or not, and whether or not she had the slightest talent for it. Apart from a swirl or two at some celebration, she had never danced in her life – but then a girl like her, from a respectable family, would never have been allowed to. Would she be able to learn it? Mohini seemed to have more confidence in her than she had in herself. And what was Mohini going to gain by teaching her? She sat bolt upright as another question occurred to her. Would she have to pay for her lessons? Did Mohini expect remuneration? Or was she just acting out of kindness? But why, when there were plenty of girls out there on the streets, begging for food and much poorer than she was? Niggling doubts that she had pushed aside during her journey started to surface until she was sure that there must be some other motive behind Mohini's interest in her. And when her training was finished, where would she perform? Perhaps in the temples, or…?

A knock at the door woke the other girl. She stared at Anjali, startled that she had company.

'Good morning,' smiled Anjali.

The girl's expression changed and she smiled back. She rose from her bed and went to open the door.

*

For breakfast there were wonderful savoury pancakes which Kalyani devoured, but Anjali was too unsettled to manage more than a glass of sweet, hot milk that the cook had brought her. She sipped it absentmindedly.

Not long afterwards, a woman servant called Rangi arrived, bringing orders from Mohini that she would like to see Anjali now. Anjali followed the woman to the front room. Mohini was already seated on a divan. She greeted Anjali with a smile and said, 'I want to take you to the astrologer so that he can set an auspicious time for your first dance lesson.' And so they set off, Anjali walking behind Mohini towards the astrologer's house on the next street.

'Over there,' said Mohini, pointing at a house with a tiled roof, as small as Mohini's own.

Anjali saw an elderly man in a chair on his front veranda, immersed in a great volume of the Bhagavad-Gita that lay on his lap. His head was clean-shaven, with a few strands of grey hair twisted into a small coil on top. He was wearing a fine white cotton *dhoti* and a shoulder cloth that covered his chest. A long chain of *rudraksha* beads hung loosely around his neck.

'*Namstay Ayyagaru*,' Mohini said in greeting, and bent over to touch his feet. Anjali knew she must do the same as a mark of respect for an older and more learned person.

He looked up at the two women over his reading glasses. 'May you live a long, healthy and prosperous life,' he said in blessing, placing a hand on Anjali's head before looking at Mohini questioningly.

'This is Anjali, sir.' said Mohini. 'She has come to me to learn dance.'

'Good, good,' he nodded, and his small eyes twinkled kindly at Anjali. 'My child, I wish you all the best.'

'Could you please tell me when is the auspicious time for her to start the lesson, sir?'

'Of course!' He gave her a wide, toothless grin before counting something on his fingers. 'According to the positions of the planets linked to her name, this Friday at eight fifteen in the morning will be an auspicious time for her to have her first lesson,' the astrologer said.

On the way back, Mohini started to explain the history of dance; its rules and regulations. It was complex and detailed, and Anjali was worried that she would not remember much as they walked along the dusty path. Her mind was not yet clear enough to take in so much new information.

*

It was very early on Friday morning and Rangi was applying coconut oil mixed with the extract of hibiscus flowers along the whole length of Anjali's hair. While massaging in the sweet-smelling oil, she commented, 'You are so beautiful. You will make the zamindar very happy.'

'What do you mean, Rangi? Why would I make the zamindar happy?'

The woman gave Anjali an enigmatic smile and said, 'I mean with your dance.' Then she quickly changed the subject. 'I have put the warm water in the bathroom for you, and *sunnipindi*, instead of soap.

'What is *sunnipindi*?' Anjali asked. She had never heard the word before.

'It is a mixture of chickpea, sandalwood and saffron powders. *Dorsani* believes that it is better for your skin than harsh soap.

Later, while washing her hair with warm water mixed with perfumed oils, Anjali wondered at Rangi's words about her making the zamindar happy, and sensed a hidden meaning behind them. She wanted to ask Rangi but knew that a loyal servant like her wouldn't reveal anything that might jeopardise the plans of her mistress. Anjali had noticed that since Mohini had returned to Roypuram, she smiled less and was much more serious. There was an air of authority about her that intimidated Anjali a little, deterring her from freely expressing her thoughts and doubts. Instead she waited for an opportunity to talk to Kalyani.

Her busy schedule started precisely at the time prescribed. Wearing a yellow dance *sari*, she walked into the dance room, where she was met with a wall full of mirrors. In a corner stood a huge statue of the Lord Natraj, the God of dance, adorned with garlands of flowers, and in front were lighted lamps and incense sticks in silver holders, reminders of a prayer that Mohini had performed earlier. In a corner, sitting down on a Persian rug, was Kalyani, tuning the *tanpura* strings with her fingers. Anjali folded her hands and closed her eyes to pray to Natraj, before touching Mohini's feet in blessing.

'The first lesson is always unpredictable,' said Mohini, presenting Anjali with ankle bells. 'You might like it or you might hate it, but believe me, Anjali, if you prepare your mind positively and focus on what I teach you, I am sure you will learn to love dancing, and I have a feeling that you will be a talented pupil.'

And so, with Anjali looking on and marvelling, Mohini began to bend and move her agile body, demonstrating the first elegant steps and graceful movements. Anjali tried her best to follow and copy her. At the beginning her legs felt like a ton of lead but gradually she relaxed and her anklets jingled rhythmically to the beat of the *tabla* in Mohini's hands, while Kalyani sang the haunting dance tunes.

From that day on, Anjali woke regularly at four in the morning to perform her warming-up sessions in preparation for her lesson, which always took place as the first rays of the sun shone over the horizon. Anjali danced until noon, acquiring skills and confidence. This was now her life.

Chapter 17

Hearing Prakash enter their rented room, Saleem quickly turned towards the wall and averted his face. He was thankful for the curtain that divided the room into two separate sections. Whenever he wanted to, he could hide behind it, pretending to be asleep. Pulling the thin bed cover up to his shoulders, he listened to the sounds that came from his friend's part of the room. Over Prakash's loud and cheerful whistling, he heard a match being struck to light the coal stove. Then came the familiar thudding as Prakash fanned the flame with the cover of a discarded notebook, which he banged hard on the floor.

'I know you are not sleeping, Saleem,' he called. 'How long are you going to mourn like this? It's been a month now.' He walked across to Saleem's portion of the room and tugged back the curtain. He was holding two glasses of hot milk but Saleem had lost his appetite. His mouth felt bitter and his stomach heaved at the smell of any kind of food.

'For god's sake, get up,' Prakash said, placing the glasses on a small bedside table and tugging viciously at the bed cover. Not having the heart to keep up the pretence, Saleem pulled himself up to a sitting position.

'At least be glad that she is not dead.' Prakash handed him a glass. 'You know she is somewhere safe and there is hope that you will meet her some day.'

'I know,' Saleem mumbled, doubtful that a young girl like Anjali with such amazing looks would be safe anywhere.

'Oh Saleem!' Prakash grimaced, guessing what Saleem was thinking. 'You heard what the lodge owner said, didn't you? Anjali left with a woman, not with a man.'

'Yes,' Saleem looked down.

Placing a hand on his friend's shoulder, Prakash continued, 'You can't blame yourself, Saleem. It wasn't your fault that you were injured and were stuck in the hospital. You did your best. You searched not only Harikonda but also every neighbouring village as well. What more could you do?'

Saleem looked up helplessly.

'This won't do, Saleem. It's time to move on. In many ways you have been fortunate. If it wasn't for the kindness of the engineer sahib you would have lost your job by now. You are lucky that he has been so generous with you…'

'Stop it!' shouted Saleem. 'After all that has happened… I can't believe you are praising him.'

'What crime has he committed? You can't blame him just because he is English?'

'Yes, I can. Don't you remember how many innocent men, women and children were killed in that massacre? I lost Anjali because of those brutal monsters.' Saleem glared at his friend. His eyes were bloodshot and his breath was rapid. Saleem stood up, still unsteady on his feet, and pointed towards the outside of the house. 'You actually still want me to work for them?'

'What else can you do? Don't you know the old saying: the worst enemy of a poor man is his own anger?'

Saleem stared at his friend, unable to utter a word in case he lost control and lashed out in fury. He stomped out of the room and set off for *chowrasta*, the town centre, where he could buy the crude palm wine that he used to drown his sorrows.

While he sat drinking and brooding, Saleem found himself hearing again his friend's sensible words. Remembering his constant kindness and caring, something finally shifted. With the change of mood came a flood of self-criticism and disgust. Prakash was right. Saleem had been selfish and self-pitying. It was time to move on.

The next morning Saleem forced himself to get up early. If he were to lose his job, not only would he starve, but so would his whole family back home. Standing in the back yard, he poured buckets of cold water from the well over his head. He pulled his uniform from a tin trunk and for the first time in weeks got dressed.

Hitching up his trousers so that they would not get soiled, Saleem stepped carefully along the muddy path, which was filled with little puddles of murky water. Scattered cow pats and pig droppings were everywhere. Wrinkling his nose at the stink of the over-flowing gutter, he crossed the narrow gully, where under-nourished children were playing, fighting and crying in front of straw-roofed huts. Skeletal dogs and starving pigs wandered lethargically, searching for food.

After walking for two miles, Saleem reached the British settlement area. He breathed in deeply. The air felt cooler and fresher here. Gulmohar trees, with their flame-coloured flowers, stood on either side of the much wider roads, providing shade from the hot sun. The neat rows of big houses, with their open verandas, balconies, lush green lawns and flower gardens, had a distinctive colonial style. The iron gates of the compound walls were guarded by Ghurkas or gatekeepers. No native would dare enter that area; only the very rich or one of the servants. How proud he used to feel just to be able to step into the British settlement! But now he felt nothing but hatred towards the race that was ruling his country. He loathed the fact that he was helpless and had no choice but to walk back to his old job.

*

'Good morning, sir.' Saleem saluted Mr Robert, who was climbing down his white marble steps.

'Ah, Saleem! There you are!' Mr Robert exclaimed, receiving his salute with a smile. 'I am sorry to hear that you were injured.' His eyes were concerned as he asked, 'How is your leg now?'

'Its fine, sir,' Saleem answered with cool politeness.

'You look pale still, and there is no hurry. You can have a few more days off, if you want to.'

'Thank you, sir, but I am fully recovered now,'

'Are you sure you want to come back to work?'

'Yes, sir.' Saleem opened the jeep door for his employer.

In the eyes of many an Indian, the English officials were mysterious, inaccessible, selfish and arrogant, but Saleem had to admit that he had always found Mr Robert kind and considerate towards his employees. After passing tennis courts and a golf course, and the clubhouse with its swimming pool, where the English sahibs and memsahibs went during the day for a cool dip and in the evenings for a drink, Saleem drove on for several miles out of town, taking the engineer sahib to the construction site of a big main road.

Saleen swallowed his bile and drove on. He would give nothing away. His thoughts, at least, were his own.

Chapter 18

After dropping Mr Robert off at his office, Saleem went to a small roadside stall for a cup of tea. Seated on a wooden bench that wobbled on the uneven mud floor, he ordered his milky chai and puffed his cigarette unhurriedly. A small tunnel of light filtered through one of many holes in the roof and fell on his watch, and the metal glinted, catching his attention. It was Mr Robert's old watch. When he had received a new, gold-strapped watch from London, instead of discarding the old one, he had presented it to Saleem, mainly to encourage him to keep up with Memsahib's precise time-keeping. He made a face, remembering Miss Edwina, who, unlike her husband, was always restless, short-tempered and intolerant of her servants' making mistakes or being late. He glanced at his watch again and remembered Mr Robert's instructions to take his wife to the clubhouse. He was already half an hour late. Normally he would have panicked and rushed off to fulfil his duties, but today his heart didn't race and his legs didn't rush to drive at top speed to pick up the memsahib. To his surprise, he just didn't care.

Taking his time, he drove slowly. As he pulled in through the gates of the beige, two-storied colonial house, he could see the memsahib angrily pacing up and down on the veranda. She reminded him of a frustrated lioness in a cage. Her floral dress, tightly fitted around her slender waist, was blowing in the breeze, as were her ginger ringlets around her shoulders.

Hearing the sound of the jeep, she turned, fussed with her hat and stomped down the steps. She gave him a furious look. 'Where were you? Do you know how late it is?'

'Sorry, memsahib. The jeep broke down on the way,' he lied, opening the door for her.

'Excuses, excuses, excuses!' she shouted, looking pointedly at her watch. 'Bloody servants and bloody drivers. I was supposed to be there an hour ago.' Ignoring her complaints, and without a word, Saleem opened the back door for her.

He drove for fifteen minutes, while Miss Edwina fretted out loud about being late for the club, and about Mr Robert being too lenient with the servants. By the time they reached the whitewashed club house building, he had more than enough. Once, he would have been able to block out the incessant complaints, but not now.

Saying nothing, Saleem drove the jeep slowly up the gravelled drive, bordered with ornamental palm trees, and came to a halt, tyres crunching, in front of the steps that led to the main entrance. He got out and went to open the door for Miss Edwina. With a polite bow, he said, 'I will wait for you, madam.'

'Of course you will!'

He stood and watched while a doorman in a fancy crimson uniform came running to escort Miss Edwina inside. Saleem started up the jeep again, ready to park it in its designated place.

There, in the car park, in the sweltering heat, Saleem decided to stretch his legs and went to seek the shade of the *banyan* tree, where all the other drivers were sitting chatting. As soon as they saw him, they greeted him kindly, and, gathering round, asked him to tell them in detail all about the shooting at Jallianwala-Bagh. At first, moved by their concern, he answered their questions, but soon he found that he was becoming upset talking about the event, and the sympathy they showered on him was too much to bear. It was like reliving the whole thing again. Feeling mentally exhausted, he leaned against the tree trunk with his handkerchief draped loosely over his face against the glare of the sun. The other men took the hint and left him alone.

Saleem closed his eyes, stretched out his legs, and tried to empty his mind of the unpleasant thoughts, but his ears pricked up again when he heard what the others were discussing.

'Have you heard what happened last week in Madras?'

'No, what?'

'A Hindu, who was just minding his own business, walking along a road, was punished, just because he did not salute an English officer who was walking on the other side.'

'Really! Why didn't he salute?'

'His argument was, why should he?'

'What was the punishment?' someone asked.

'Apparently the officer seized him by the neck, threw him on to the ground, pushed his face into the dust and ordered fifty lashes.'

'Good god! That's brutal for such a trivial crime.'

'Crime!' exclaimed another driver, imitating the way the English spoke, 'What nonsense! My foot!'

Then there was silence and Saleem knew that every man there was thinking the same thing. He, too, felt sorry for the victim, and as he imagined the humiliation that this innocent man had suffered at the hands of the arrogant British, his thoughts turned swiftly to revenge.

*

It was past midnight by the time he reached home. Prakash was fast asleep and snoring. Making as little noise as possible, he went into the back yard and, drawing a bucket of water from the well, washed his face, hands and feet. His stomach grumbled as he sat on his bed. He opened a banana-leaf parcel that he had picked up from a food stall on his way back. The aroma of spicy potatoes and a well-roasted chapatti made his mouth water. Quickly tearing off a piece of soft *nan* bread to scoop up the curry, he realised to his surprise that he had not thought of Anjali so much today. He winced, feeling guilty. 'Oh, Allah, where is she?' he whispered.

Chapter 19

The relaxed atmosphere around the Gadi palace had changed. The servants were running around doing their chores with an increased urgency and care.

After finishing her usual warm-up, Anjali climbed the steps and went out on to the rooftop. Outside, leaning on the parapet wall, she could see part of the palace and the courtyard through the gaps between the branches of a tree. The arches of the gateways, doors and window frames were decorated with flower garlands. Hundreds of clay lamps, filled with oil and cotton wicks, were placed in the numerous alcoves of the compound wall, ready to be lit. From the scent that drifted upwards, Anjali was surprised to realise that even Mohini's house was filled with the fragrance of musk and sandalwood.

'There is no dance lesson today.' Kalyani had climbed the steps too and came out to tell her.

'Why? What's happening?' Anjali asked, without turning from the spectacle.

'We've had news that the zamindar is arriving from his hunting trip tomorrow.'

'Tomorrow!' Anjali exclaimed. 'But you said he wouldn't be back until full moon's day.'

'Yes, but he is only two days early. Apparently he succeeded in shooting a tiger this time,' Kalyani said with enthusiasm.

'Oh. He must be very brave.'

'Yes,' Kalyani shrugged her shoulders. 'But you know, once he is here, it's a different story.'

'What do you mean?'

'No one will be able to relax. The whole atmosphere will become very tense and not even an ant will dare to move without seeking his permission.' She sighed. 'You know what? If he hadn't gone on that hunting trip, Mohini wouldn't have gone to that temple in Harikonda, and you wouldn't be here today.'

Ignoring the remark, Anjali asked, 'Is that the reason my lessons have been cancelled?'

'No, no. I don't think Mohini will even mention you to the zamindar. Not yet.' Kalyani laughed. 'You see, she is saving you as her secret, for when the time comes.'

'The time for what?'

Kalyani didn't answer. 'Look at those lamps. Once they are lit, the whole place will look beautiful. Like... as if we are celebrating *Diwali*.'

But Anjali wanted an answer. 'What has his arrival got to do with my dance class?'

'Mohini is preparing herself for his arrival.' She nudged Anjali's elbow and giggled.

'I don't understand.'

'Go and see her room.'

'You know I've never been there before. What is there to see? It's only her bedroom, isn't it?'

'No, I mean it,' Kalyani said seriously. But she laughed as she saw Anjali's puzzled expression. 'Don't worry, she's not there at the moment. She's in her dressing room with the hairdresser.' Kalyani rolled her eyes. 'It takes ages because she has to dye her hair jet-black with the extraction of *jeedi* seeds, then she massages it with perfumed oils, and combs it until it shines like silk.'

Anjali followed Kalyani, the two of them tiptoeing down the stairs, then along the corridor to Mohini's room.

'See,' Kalyani whispered as she pushed the door slightly ajar.

Anjali peered through the gap and gasped. She had never seen a room like it. All the walls and the ceiling were fitted with gleaming mirrors. Reflections of the four-poster bed multiplied over and over. It brought back memories of her husband's bed, all those years ago, on that first night, but this was on a much grander scale. The mattress was covered with lavishly embroidered gold and white silk sheets, strewn with flower petals. The canopy was draped with a flimsy gold material, fringed with long white and gold beads, which hung down and shimmered. A silver bowl of fresh fruit was placed on a small carved table beside the bed. Fragrant flowers were everywhere – in the vases, and on the windowsills.

'Why all this?'

'Because the zamindar might come to her tomorrow night.'

'Why?'

'What do you mean, why? Anjali, you are not a child that you need to ask why,' she mocked. 'Stop pretending to be such an innocent.'

Anjali's eyes widened. 'But Mohini is a dancer.'

'Yes, but also… you know… a courtesan.'

'No!' Anjali was shocked.

'Yes!' Kalyani threw back her head and laughed.

*

By late afternoon most of the preparations were finished and the exhausted servants took a break sitting or lying down under the trees or wherever there was some shade. The heat of the afternoon was so severe that even the birds in the trees seemed to be sleeping. Anjali hadn't seen her teacher all day, but she knew Mohini too would be having a nap after lunch.

A lulled silence enveloped the place. As she rested in her room, Anjali's mind drifted back to the past and inevitably to Saleem. Her heart refused to believe that he was dead. How could she find out what had happened to him? Who else could she ask? Suddenly an idea flashed through her mind and she sat upright in excitement. Yes, the astrologer. He might know the answers. All at once, Anjali could not keep still. She got up and paced the room. She wanted to find out about Saleem. She wanted to find out now.

She wasn't allowed to go out without Mohini's permission, but if she waited for that, she might wait forever. Now was the only possible time. Everyone was asleep and she must seize this rare opportunity. She had to go and ask him now, because from tomorrow, from what Kalyani has said, everything might change. Anjali had no idea what would happen once the zamindar arrived home.

Not wanting to wait in case she became afraid and changed her mind, Anjali quickly pulled her *sari pallu* over her head, and stepped out of the back door and into the street.

Chapter 20

It felt very strange and very daring to be walking alone along the empty streets. Never in her life, not even as a child, had Anjali been allowed to go anywhere on her own. Fortunately she remembered the way from their previous visit. She turned right at the end of the street into Brahmin *Bazar* and walked on towards the astrologer's house.

Once inside the gate, Anjali was disappointed to see that the astrologer's chair on the veranda was empty, but at the top of the stone steps the front door was ajar, so she knocked gently and waited. Then came soft footsteps from behind the door and a female voice asked, 'Who is it?'

'It's… me, Anjali,' she answered nervously.

'Anjali? Who?'

The door opened fully and a young woman stood on the doorstep, looking out. She could not have been any older than Anjali herself. She was wearing a coarse white *sari*, her head was bare and she was without a dot of vermilion on her forehead. Her body was painfully thin, the result of an enforced diet. It was obvious to Anjali that she was a widow. How very sad, Anjali thought. This woman is much too young to be the victim of such a cruel fate. Only a man could have invented such harsh rules for women whose husbands are dead. They are unfair. How come a man is allowed to re-marry within three months of his wife's death while a girl and or woman has only two options, either the funeral pyre alongside her dead husband, or to live like an ugly corpse with a shaved head on a meagre diet meant to suppress her own desires? Rules to keep them hidden and to make sure they do not attract the opposite sex, let alone re-marry.

'What do you want?' the girl asked, pulling her *sari pallu* over her shaved head.

Realising that she had been lost in thought and hadn't answered, Anjali cleared her throat and asked, 'Is the astrologer at home, please?'

'No, he went into the city this morning. He won't be back until tomorrow. Is it anything urgent?'

'No, nothing urgent. I will come back later.' Bitterly disappointed, Anjali turned and left.

*

'Where did you go?' Rangi hissed at Anjali as she sneaked back in through the back door. 'Good thing *dorsani* didn't send for you. Go, go inside quickly. Kalyani is fuming.'

Anjali hurried to her room, where Kalyani was restlessly pacing up and down.

'Where did you go?' Kalyani glared at her.

Surprised by her tone, Anjali answered, 'I went to the astrologer's house.'

'Why?'

'Just to ask him about Saleem.'

'Do you really believe that he will know the answer?'

'He might, because Mohini said he could predict the future.'

'So, what did he say?'

'I didn't see him. He wasn't at home. I saw his daughter.'

'Oh, that widow.'

Anjali was surprised at the lack of sympathy in Kalyani's voice but had the sense to realise that this was not the right moment to discuss their differing feelings.

'You went on a secret mission and it was a total waste of time. Surely you know by now that you are not allowed to go anywhere without seeking Mohini's permission?'

'Yes, but…'

'Do you know what will happen if she finds out about your little secret trips into the village…? We will both get into trouble. You are being selfish, Anjali. If you do wrong then I will get blamed too.' Kalyani paused to take a deep breath to try to control her temper. 'It is my job to watch over you.'

'I'm sorry. I won't go anywhere in future without asking you. I'm sorry I alarmed you.'

Kalyani said nothing. Without a backward glance, she walked out of the room.

Alone, Anjali thought about her situation and realised that her freedoms were very limited. But her fate was nothing compared to the young girl at the astrologer's house, who, simply because her husband had died, was imprisoned forever, hidden from the world, as if she had done something terribly wrong. And only then did Anjali make the connection. Of course. She and this girl had so much in common. She felt a deeper sympathy, and a clearer understanding of the unfairness of the way all women who were widowed were treated.

Chapter 21

A commotion outside woke Anjali from heavy sleep but she felt too lethargic to open her eyes. A band was playing cheerful tunes and she could sense excitement and exhilaration.

'Anjali, wake up.' The voice was as brisk as the hand that shook her shoulder. 'The zamindar is arriving in the village. Don't you want to see the procession?'

Kalyani's excitement was so infectious that Anjali got up at once. They climbed the stone steps and went out on to the flat rooftop to see the crowds that had already gathered around the Gadi palace. Leaning over the parapet wall next to Kalyani, Anjali watched as the sleeping village came to life. People rushed around talking at the tops of their voices over the pounding of drums. Children ran towards the procession, wild with excitement.

'By the sound of the drums, I think he must be visiting the temple now,' said Kalyani.

'Is that where the astrologer works as a priest?'

'Yes.' Kalyani turned her head to look at her. 'So you saw his daughter yesterday?'

'Yes,' Anjali sighed. 'I feel sorry for her. She is so young... and already a widow.'

'Why do you feel sorry for her,' Kalyani interrupted, 'when you yourself are in exactly the same situation? Both of you are widows.'

Yes, thought Anjali, but I have been mourning the loss of a father figure who had cared for me. She had hardly thought of Ranjit as a husband. Lost again in memories of her past, she stared into space for a long time before answering Kalyani. 'Are you not surprised that I don't practice widowhood?'

'No,' answered Kalyani. 'Nothing in this world will ever surprise me.'

Anjali gazed at her in puzzlement. What bitterness was this in someone so young?

Kalyani laughed. 'Don't look at me like that. You are going to be a dancer – a *devadasi* – a servant to Shiva!' She laughed again. 'No, no, a servant to the zamindar. And as long as he is alive, you won't be treated as a widow.'

The reality of her situation slowly dawned on Anjali. How stupid I have been, she thought. How foolish and innocent.

'Kalyani… what are you saying?'

'Oh, don't take any notice of me. I just talk too much.'

By the time the procession reached the palace, the sun was blazing in the sky. From where they were standing, they could see the courtyard and up as far as the grand gates, which were never opened to anyone except the zamindar. Through them now marched the band, playing with great gusto. Next came a gorgeously dressed elephant, whose trunk, forehead, large ears and massive legs all shimmered with designs painted in brilliant white, red and yellow. The fringes of its red velvet covers reached almost to the ground on either side. The elephant rocked gently as it paced forward, one foot at a time, as did the man who sat tall on its embossed gold and silver seat, dressed in a hunting uniform that was Euopean in style. Anjali guessed that this was the great Zamindar Jeevan Roy.

'Why is he dressed like that?' she asked Kalyani.

'He likes English fashions. He even hired an Anglo-Indian lady to teach his children English.'

'That's strange!' said Anjali, remembering her own teacher, Miss Garland.

'Did you know he sent his son to Oxford to study law?'

'That's what my father told me, that nowadays it's fashionable for the maharajas and the richest of the rich to send their children to study in England.'

As the procession reached the main entrance, the band stopped playing and came to an abrupt halt, and Anjali heard the *mahout* shout a single word of command, loud and clear. The elephant halted and stood still, while a couple of turbaned servants rushed forward with a ladder and held it against its massive side so that the zamindar could dismount.

As soon as he climbed down, a servant rushed to take his shoes off and another washed his feet with water from a silver container. Female servants sprinkled flower petals at his feet as he climbed the marble steps to sit on a throne that was set for him on the veranda. A few very important looking people greeted him with respect and stood to one side with their arms folded.

'Look, look!,' Kalyani exclaimed, pointing at an open-topped cart that was now emerging through the wide-open gates. Anjali gasped when she saw what it contained: a dead tiger, its limbs sprawled across the cart, once a magnificent creature of the forest. And then behind the cart bearing the tiger came the villagers in their hundreds, shouting, shoving, hoping to get a glimpse of an animal that they had no chance of seeing when it was alive and in the wild. The whole Gadi palace and its surroundings throbbed with people who called their congratulations to Jeevan Roy for his bravery.

The crowd kept up the celebrations until the evening – dancing, singing and feasting – until the butchers took away the lifeless beast.

For hours, the two young women stood transfixed on the rooftop, hiding behind the branches of an almond tree. As they watched through the gaps of the leaves, Anjali felt sorry for the animal. She knew that from tomorrow its skin would be a doormat in front of the main entrance and its head would be a trophy on a wall in the main hall. With the other animal heads already there, it would serve to remind everyone of the zamindar's valour.

Chapter 22

The letter that Saleem was dreading had arrived that morning.

Anjali's father wrote asking about his daughter's welfare. Saleem quickly scanned the letter and paused when he came to the name 'Ananth'. He remembered how they had mutually decided to give her a code name, so that it would give people the impression that they were writing to each other about one of Saleem's male friends. As he read the last few lines of a personal note for Anjali at the bottom of the page, and the words 'Eagerly waiting for your reply,' his hands shook. How could he reply to Narayan? What would he say? Would he write 'Sorry, the daughter you had rescued from the funeral pyre has been lost in the station fire?' Rubbing his brow he got up to place the letter in a tin trunk. He wondered if there were any other places where he hadn't searched for Anjali. He listed the names of all the villages on his fingers and realised that there were still some where he had not looked.

Ideally he would have taken more time off to look for Anjali, but already Mr Robert had granted him so much leave and he didn't want to take advantage of his employer's generosity and compassion. There were plenty of drivers who would jump at the chance of working for a man like his engineer sahib. He didn't want to risk losing his job. So many responsibilities weighed on his shoulders. On top of providing for his family, he had to pay off a large loan that he had taken out to pay for Ruksana's wedding. So far he was only paying the interest every month. God only knew how he was going to pay back the capital.

That evening as he waited in the car park to collect the engineer sahib and his wife Miss Edwina from a social meeting at the golf club, he made up his mind to tell Mr Robert the true reason for requesting yet more time off work. If they had a good time at the club Mr Robert would be in a good mood and might grant him a few days off.

Saleem watched as the main doors opened and was surprised to see the memsahib emerging from the club on her own and then walking briskly down the steps and into the car park. Her face wasn't very visible in that dim light, but by her brisk walk he could tell that she was either upset or angry. Then came his engineer sahib a few spaces behind. That was unusual, he thought, because they usually went everywhere hand in hand. Saleem, curious, watched as Mr Robert caught up with his wife and tried to put an arm around her shoulders. She pushed him away, saying something he could not hear, and walked quickly toward the car.

Pretending that he had not witnessed their discomfort, Saleem got out of the jeep and held the door open.

'Memsahib. Sir,' he saluted, as if everything was normal.

Mr Robert nodded but Miss Edwina climbed into her seat in silence and turned her face to the window. All the way home, not a word was exchanged.

As he drove, Saleem understood that this wasn't the right time to put his request to Mr Robert.

After safely depositing them at their home, Saleem turned the car round and headed for the house of Charan Das, a follower of Gandhi.

*

Saleem climbed the wooden steps to the attic room. It wasn't large but was big enough to seat ten people comfortably on straw mats. The metal-framed window was wide open to let in the night's breeze and to cool the room from the afternoon's heat.

As the meeting was already in progress, Saleem went in silently and sat next to Akbar, whom he knew as a freedom fighter.

Charan Das, who chaired the meeting, was speaking: '...for example, what happened in South Africa in 1906? The government wanted all Indians to be registered and be finger-printed like criminals. They called it the "Asiatic Registration Bill", but our Gandhi-ji called it the "Black Act".'

Everyone clapped. Charan Das took a sip of cool water that someone offered him from an earthenware pot in a corner of the room.

'And in 1913,' he continued, 'they said that only marriages performed under Christian rites were legal.'

'Does that mean all the other marriages were irrelevant?' Akber asked.

'Yes. Exactly.' Charan Das cleared his throat and looked at everyone. 'But again, thanks to Mahatma's fight for justice, now those marriages are fully legal too and the head tax has been abolished.'

Everyone clapped and cheered and called, '*Mahatma Gandhi ki Jai!*'

'Actually, Gandhi-ji had been extremely considerate to the government, even though they have arrested him several times and...' Charan Das continued.

'How? Why?' The speaker was interrupted by a chorus of voices asking the same questions.

'Well... he led a march supporting mine workers in South Africa. At that time European railway workers went on strike and the government was in real trouble so Gandhi called off the Indian action, not wanting to take advantage of the opponent's weak situation.'

'So why won't the governors listen to our pleas to reform the

system and make the rules and regulations less harsh for Indians?'
Akbar asked.

Charan Das looked at him. 'Because we Indians are less important
to them than the whites.'

'But it is our country!' shouted Akbar.

'Exactly! That's my point too!' Saleem stood up. 'They are ruling
our country and we are sitting like Buddhas, not uttering a word,
while they cut our throats and break our heads.'

'Yes, we shouldn't just sit with our heads bowed and bodies bent,'
Akbar said. ' I agree with you.'

'We should be the ones who decide what is good for the country,' a
man in the second row said.

'What makes you think that? Don't you know that they regard us
as uneducated idiots?'

Charan Das waved his hands to calm his audience and motioned to
Saleem to sit down. Only when the room was quiet did he continue.

'The only hope for us now is, as Gandhi-ji said, *satyagraha*.
Satyagraha means truth, love and non-violence and it is the policy of
our Congress party. Only through this weapon can we put into action
non-cooperation, and that's what we have to do if we want our
independence.' The speaker nodded to his audience as he finished,
and in response came angry shouts of protest from every corner of
the room.

'*Mahatma Gandhi ki Jai!*'

'Long live Mahatma!'

'British Raj, down! Down!'

The men applauded because they had been moved and stirred by
the speech and because they agreed with the speaker's words. Then
a man sitting near the window put up his hand and asked, 'What if
things go wrong? I mean, if independence comes too fast?'

'What do you mean?' Saleem frowned.

'I mean, what is the point of rushing headlong for independence?

Do we know what to do with it? Are we really prepared?'

The room went silent.

'Don't you think more harm than good will come to this country?' he added.

'In what way?' asked Charan Das.

'If it wasn't for the British, we wouldn't have any justice, education or civilisation…'

'Civilisation?' exclaimed Akbar. 'You mean to say that we are sitting here waiting for them to teach us how to be civilised?' He glared at the man. 'Do you mean we have to start eating with knives and forks, and speaking English, and that we have to wear a hat instead of a turban and play golf and polo? Is that what you mean by "civilised"?'

'What about our own ancient civilisation? Don't you know how rich our culture is?' Saleem said.

'Hear! Hear!' There was loud applause for Akbar and Saleem.

'What about our own civilisation which we have had since before the British emerged from their dark, cold and minute speck of a country?'

'It might be a minute speck,' the man in the turban replied, 'but look who is ruling the world! We just don't have the ability or the knowledge yet.'

'Stop it!' Akbar banged his fist on the floor. 'Don't forget that our Taksha-shila was the world's first university!'

*

It was almost the early hours by the time Saleem reached home.

'You went to that meeting again?' Prakash asked as he opened the door for him.

'Yes.'

'Do you know what time it is?'

'I know.'

'Why, Saleem? What is all this about? You are not going to gain anything from attending these meetings.'

Saleem shrugged and said, 'Do you know, apparently there are some Hindus attending weekly Bible-reading classes in the church.'

'So?'

'Why should they?'

'It's up to them, Saleem.'

'The English churches are bribing them.'

'Why does that worry you?'

'Do you know that the government is imposing heavy taxes on poor peasants?'

'Saleem…!'

'I am ashamed that I work for a man who belongs to the race I hate.'

'Saleem, I think you are going mad. Just forget about the British for a moment and read this.' Prakash pointed at a postcard on the windowsill. 'This came in the morning post.'

Even before Saleem looked at it, he knew it was from the money lender reminding him of the monthly interest that was already overdue.

'How could you afford to fend for your family if you didn't work for the engineer sahib? He pays you well…'

'Yes,' Saleem nodded, 'but I sacrifice my dignity for that.'

'Oh, stop feeling sorry for yourself, Saleem! You were the one who used to sing Mr Robert's praises.'

'I still agree that he is kind and exceptional.' Saleem paused. 'But his wife, Miss Edwina, takes pleasure in humiliating her servants, including me.'

'Don't take it personally. Some of them just don't understand us,' Prakash said thoughtfully.

'Exactly, for many of the British, Indians are weak, mindless and mannerless brutes.'

'It might get better in the future, Saleem. Now that they have introduced the Government of India Act, and about five million people have been given the right to vote.'

'Ha! Ha-ha! Very kind of them!' Saleem laughed sarcastically. 'Don't you know that the right to vote has been granted only to those who are already very wealthy and are in with the whites? How cunning of the government! What are five million compared with the total population, Prakash? It's a drop in the ocean.'

'Yes, but at least it's a start. There is discussion about giving India some sort of self-rule.'

'That's rubbish. They just talk. They know very well that it would lead to the break-up of the British Empire.'

'Yes, I suppose so,' Prakash yawned, leaning back on his pillows. 'Let's leave it for tonight. We both have to be up very early for work tomorrow morning…'

Taking the hint, Saleem got up and, opening the curtain, retreated to his section of the room.

Chapter 23

It was only the beginning of summer and Anjali was finding the scorching heat in the south much more unbearable than in her hometown Girigaov. The straw curtains at the wide-opened windows and doors were not moving at all. It was so sultry that the water which Anjali sprinkled on the curtains only served to make the air more humid and suffocating. Even a short walk to the bathroom outside blistered her feet. It was only when the evening finally drew in, and the fierce sun went down, that she could breath easily. Having a cold bath to wash away the sweat and heat was a delight, and afterwards Anjali sat on a stone bench under the almond tree to dry her hair in the breeze.

'Anjali, where are you?' Kalyani came out holding a bottle of hair oil and a comb.

'Oh, Anjali, I have too many tangles in my hair and my hands ache from combing them.' She sat next to Anjali.

'Let me help.' Anjali poured some perfumed oil into her hands and applied it along the length of Kalyani's hair. First untangling it with her fingers, section by section, she began combing it until it shone. It reminded her of Saleem's mother and how she used to massage her hair just like that with scented oils. A feeling of nostalgia tugged at her heart and Anjali worried yet again whether Saleem was safe.

'What's the matter, Anjali?' Kalyani asked when Anjali didn't respond to her chatter.

'Nothing… it just reminded me of…' Her voice broke.

'Are you worrying about your friend again? You desperately want to see the astrologer, don't you?'

'Yes.'

'I can take you there.'

'How?' Anjali stopped combing. Her hands dropped to her sides. Kalyani, who had been watching Anjali in her handheld mirror, saw the hope on her friend's face, and smiled.

'I can put in a request to Mohini to visit the temple and take you with me.'

'Do you think she would allow us?' Anjali said, twisting Kalyani's hair into a coil.

'Of course, if she is in a good mood.'

'And we could see the astrologer there?'

'Yes, because he is also a priest in the temple.'

'When do you think we could go?'

'Tomorrow evening perhaps. But I will have to wait and catch Mohini in the right mood for her to grant us permission.'

The next day, as promised, Kalyani managed to persuade Mohini, and the two young women set out in a palanquin to the outskirts of Roypuram, to the temple of Ganesh, the elephant god. The ancient temple was carved of one gigantic single stone, and was a miniature replica of the thousand-pillared temple in Harikonda. There were no doors as such but the archways and pillars divided it into three sections. Anjali marvelled at the flowers and birds, animals and people carved so elaborately on the outside walls and pillars.

'Look at that.' Kalyani was pointing at one particular carving. A dancing girl was bending sideways to put her anklets on. Her eyes were looking downwards, her long hair flowing down one of her shoulders, and the creases and folds in her transparent robes were highly realistic. Anjali stood transfixed, admiring the sculptor's skill in bringing stone to life.

Once through the porch, they stepped up on to the slightly raised, circular dance floor and then on into the main temple. In the altar was a carved statue of Ganesh, son of Lord Shiva, polished and gleaming from sacred water, ghee and milk that the priests and devotees brought every day in heavy jugs to pour over him. Both the girls stood in front of the altar and watched the astrologer performing the *pooja*, by chanting a series of *mantras* and *shotras*, praising the lord. Kalyani placed the coconuts, bananas and flowers on the offering plate on the threshold of the altar. Then they stood silently, their eyes closed and palms together, so as not to disturb the astrologer until the prayer ended. As the *pooja* came to a finish, his voice rose to a climax, and he ended the ritual by ringing a small silver bell which he held in his hand. At this signal the girls reached up to ring the large, heavy brass temple bells that hung from the ceiling.

Kalyani nudged Anjali and whispered, 'You know what to say, don't you?'

'No, tell me...'

'Just say, "Please answer my question."'

'That's all?'

'Yes.'

'But how does he know what's in my mind?'

'He will know and you will see.'

Anjali watched as the astrologer lit another silver lamp. He offered the *prasadam* of bananas and coconuts to the deity and sprinkled more flowers over him before turning and bringing out the holy flame, burning camphor on a silver plate, which he had lit as part of the prayer and blessing. Anjali and Kalyani lifted their hands above the flame to accept the blessings before bowing to Ganesh and then to the astrologer.

'May you live longer.' The astrologer gave them the traditional blessing and placed a spoonful of holy water and some banana and coconut pieces into their cupped hands. They went back out to the porch to eat the *prasadam* because they knew that this was not the end of the astrologer's duties and he had more tasks to complete before he could devote time to them.

By the time the astrologer finally came out, Anjali had worked herself up into a bundle of nerves. Much too quickly, she jumped up and asked, 'Please can you answer a question for me?'

He stood gazing at her for a moment. Then he closed his eyes. Anjali watched him anxiously while he whispered something in Sanskrit and counted the lines on his fingers. Time stopped. After what seemed an eternity, he opened his eyes and looked straight into hers.

'You can stop worrying,' he said. 'Your friend is alive. You will meet him before long.'

'Sir!' Anjali stared back, speechless.

He nodded. His silent presence was gentle and reassuring. Somehow, instinctively, it seemed that he knew how much this news meant to her and how troubled she had been. With his simple answer, he had given her back the hope she craved.

'Thank god,' she said. 'He is still alive!'

Chapter 24

As the summer progressed, even the nights became stuffy and unbearable. People moved their beds out into the open, on to the rooftops and balconies. Anjali and Kalyani slept in makeshift rope cots in the back garden under the almond tree.

It was past midnight, and the breeze was gradually getting cooler. Still Anjali found it impossible to settle down. She tossed and turned restlessly in her cot. Though she was delighted with the astrologer's pronouncement, it raised more questions in her mind. Where was Saleem now? What had prevented him from meeting her at the station all those months ago? And if the astrologer was right, when and where and how was she going to meet him again? Why hadn't Kalyani given her more time to talk to the astrologer when she had so many more questions she wanted to ask him? She fanned herself with her *sari pallu*; these tangled thoughts made her feel even hotter.

Perhaps she should visit Harikonda again. There was still a chance she might find Saleem there. As that thought took shape, she sat upright in her bed. How on earth was she was going to get permission from Mohini? How could she convince her? Would Mohini understand her worries?'

'Can't you sleep?'

Startled by her voice, Anjali turned to see Kalyani yawning in next bed.

'You are awake?'

'How can I sleep while my friend is restlessly yearning for someone?' Kalyani laughed teasingly.

'Actually,' Anjali paused for a moment before daring to say, 'I want to go to Harikonda.'

'Harikonda! Whatever for?

'I need to. To find out about Saleem.'

'But you don't even know whether he is alive.' Kalyani was leaning on her elbow. 'The astrologer could be wrong, you know.'

'He could be wrong, but my instincts tell me that he is right and that Saleem is alive.'

'And what makes you think that he is in Harikonda?'

'That's where he works. Please, Kalyani, do you think you could get permission from Mohini for me to go there? Please, just this once?'

'Are you mad?' Kalyani replied. 'Do you know how difficult it is to get permission to even step over the threshold? Of course I can't persuade Mohini…'

'But that's why I am asking you. It seems you are the only person who could possibly convince her. You managed it yesterday. She let us go to the temple.'

'Impossible. She won't let you go. Besides, the date for your dance *arangetrum* is already arranged.'

'I know,' sighed Anjali, 'but that's a whole month away.'

'You need to practice.'

'I will be back soon.'

'No, you won't! Not if you find him. He won't let you come back to dance.'

Anjali was silent for a while, then asked, 'Why don't you dance, Kalyani?'

Taken aback by Anjali's abrupt question, Kalyani frowned. It was something they had not discussed before.

'Mohini wouldn't teach me.'

'Why?'

'Because I am not pretty like you.' Kalyani made a face.

'Don't be silly, Kalyani. You know you are a very pretty girl.'

Seeing Kalyani's expression, Anjali regretted her question. Was there perhaps some other reason for Mohini not teaching Kalyani to dance?

'I am sorry, Kalyani, I shouldn't have asked. I didn't mean to pry.'

Kalyani stretched out her arm and patted Anjali on the shoulder. Then she took a deep breath.

'Listen, Anjali. I am going to have to be blunt with you. Sometimes you seem very naive about your situation here. Don't raise your hopes. In your position, it's going to be very difficult to persuade Mohini to let you go anywhere.'

'Why? She doesn't own me.'

There was a long silence before Kalyani replied, 'In fact she does. She does own you now.'

Knowing that Kalyani was right and it was impossible for her to get out, Anjali fell back on her pillows. How naive she had been. Had she thought Mohni had been giving her dancing lessons out of the goodness of her heart? Wake up, Anjali, she told herself. You are nothing but a puppet and the strings are in Mohini's hands. What to do? It would be impossible to run away from this place with so many watching eyes and guarded doors and gates. How could she possibly escape?

With all hope of sleep long gone, she watched the moon playing hide and seek through the branches and leaves, just as she had played with Saleem all those years ago. She longed for home with an almost unbearable despair and yearning. She finally understood that she was no more free than one of the exotic birds that fluttered helplessly in Mohini's silver cages. She was trapped and vulnerable.

Chapter 25

Anjali had discovered that she liked to dance.

As she learned the energetic yet graceful steps, the emotive facial expressions and meaningful eye movements, and as she came to appreciate the complexity and intricacy of this art, so it gave a purpose to her days. While dancing she could forget all her troubles and anxieties. However, the date for her debut performance was now fixed and with it came feelings of dread and anxiety. What if she did not dance well on the day? Her instinct told her that the zamindar would be there as an honoured guest, and that robbed her of the oblivion that dancing usually brought. One thing Anjali was glad of was that she was going to dance in the temple rather than in the Gadi palace, but the thought of dancing in front of the zamindar was still daunting.

Under Mohini's instructions, Malli the beautician had been giving her special treatments for weeks now, to enhance her beauty. Every morning she massaged her hair with sesame oil mixed with a powder of berries and hibiscus leaves to give it a shiny lustre like black liquid glass. Over her face and body she massaged in a paste made of fresh cream from buffalo milk, turmeric and sandalwood powder, letting it sink in then washing it off with lukewarm water, to give her skin a golden glow. After weeks of a diet of fruit, vegetables and milk mixed with almonds and saffron, her eyes sparkled and she glowed with vitality. The intense routine of dance made her body lean and agile.

The preliminaries for the debut dance had started months earlier. Mohini had ordered her own personal tailor to design a costume for Anjali, a made-to-measure magenta *sari* with a gold border. She brought in the goldsmith so that she could select matching jewellery in wonderful designs to emphasise Anjali's beauty.

As the day approached, she became increasingly nervous. Kalyani noticed how ill at ease her friend was becoming.

'Just don't worry. Imagine that you are dancing for the Lord Ganesh and keep your eyes on him and then you will be all right,' she advised.

'Thank you, Kalyani. When you are with me I don't worry.' Anjali tried to smile.

'I am sorry, Anjali, but I can't be with you on that day.'

'Why not? Aren't you going to sing for me?'

'I am afraid not. Mohini has said she won't allow me to.'

'Why?'

'I am not sure. You can ask her. I didn't dare.'

'Why is Kalyani not going to be singing at my *arangetrum*?' Anjali asked Mohini later, as she bent over to tie her ankle bells during her next rehearsal.

'Don't ask me questions. Just concentrate on your dancing.'

'Why can't I sing, Mohini-*amma*?' Kalyani, who was sitting to the side, also picked up the courage to ask, though she spoke in a low, deferential voice.

Mohini didn't answer except to glare at Kalyani.

But Anjali, seeing Kalyani's distress, persisted. 'But…who is going to sing?'

'I am.' Mohini's answer was curt.

'I am sorry Kalyani, I am so disappointed. How can I dance without you there singing? I don't think I can go through this.' In the quietness of their room, with Kalyani resting on her bed, Anjali paced up and down, upset at this latest news.

'It's all right, Anjali, I am used to being treated like this. But you must dance well, for your own sake. For your own satisfaction and confidence. You have worked hard and now is your chance to shine.'

'But why won't she let you sing?' Anjali would not let it go.

'I think she doesn't want the zamindar to see me.'

'Why not?'

'I don't know. I never understand her. She never lets me perform or even show myself in front of the zamindar. I don't think he even knows that I exist.'

'Really!'

'Yes. Rangi used to tell me that even as a baby she used to hide me from him.'

'She must be jealous of you because you are young and pretty.'

'I used to think that was the reason but now, since you came, I am beginning to suspect that it must be something else.'

'Why?'

'Because if she allows a girl like you to dance in front of the zamindar, she wouldn't have any problems with me... don't you see?'

'Yes. Rangi might know. Why don't you ask her?'

'Many times I have thought about asking her but I am scared.'

'What of?'

'I don't know. Perhaps the truth. It might be painful and I might get hurt.'

They talked quietly until very late into the night, until they heard the front door open and close.

'Ssh!' Kalyani placed a finger on her lips.

In the serene silence of the night they both heard the jingling sound of Mohini's bangles in the corridor outside their room. 'Who is coming in at this hour?' Anjali whispered.

'Come and see,' Kalyani gestured.

They both watched, keeping hidden to one side of their window, and saw Mohini, dressed elaborately in red silk and ruby jewellery, walk to the front room to welcome the zamindar, who then followed her to her bedroom.

Anjali couldn't believe what she was seeing. Speechless and with wide eyes she looked at Kalyani. 'What about his wife? Doesn't she mind?'

Kalyani sighed. 'You know what? I have only seen her a couple of times in the flower garden. She is good looking but not as attractive as Mohini.'

*

The morning after, when Anjali had finished her final rehearsal and was just emerging from the dance room, she heard a commotion. There was a loud swishing and thudding sound outside the garden wall, followed by a piercing scream. Then she heard a jumble of voices and running footsteps. She quickly ran up the stone steps to the rooftop. Leaning on the parapet wall, she looked down through the gaps between the branches of a tree. Her eyes widened with terror. Not far from where she was standing, Samba, the cowherd, was tied to a tree with a rope. The zamindar towered over the fifteen-year-old boy, his face red and fuming. The whip in his hand drummed on Samba's thin body, lashing it until it jerked. The screams got louder as the zamindar whipped more furiously. Those who had gathered around were rooted to the ground, staring in disbelief with their mouths open. Gradually the screams faded to faint groans until finally there was silence. Anjali watched in horror as the boy's head collapsed on to his chest. At last the zamindar seemed to tire of whipping, his anger spent, and he threw the weapon on the ground. His red eyes stared at the boy and then at the crowd of servants. His only gesture, proud and arrogant, was to stroke his upturned moustache. Then he turned and walked away. His deliberate, heavy steps reverberated like thunder in Anjali's chest as she watched him.

The crowed didn't dare move until the zamindar had gone. Then someone ran to untie the boy as Rangi, his grandmother, pushed through the onlookers, running and howling. She sat beside the unconscious boy and cradled his head in her lap. Someone sprinkled the water over Samba's face. Everyone looked on in shocked silence.

Anjali held her breath for what seemed like a very long time until he opened his eyes.

Chapter 26

The day Anjali was dreading had arrived.

Anjali barely recognised herself when she looked in the mirror. She saw a young woman wearing a figure-hugging magenta costume and gold jewellery.

'See, Mohini was right to choose this colour for you. It really emphasises your golden complexion. You look as beautiful as an *apsara*, the dancer in heaven.' Kalyani was watching her friend with a mixture of admiration and sadness.

'I am scared, Kalyani.'

'Of course. It's only natural, but don't be. Do as Mohini suggested and look far above the heads of those in the audience and just concentrate on your dance.' Kalyani lifted Anjali's face to apply the final touches of make-up.

'Kalyani, I can't go on my own. You must come with me.' Last-minute nerves made Anjali tremble and cling to her friend.

'I understand how you feel, but you know that Mohini won't allow me. You heard what she said. Go now, or you will be late.'

Kalyani put her arm round her friend's shoulder and pushed her gently towards the door.

'Good luck,' she called, as Anjali walked down the stairs.

Wearing her ankle bells and guided by Mohini, Anjali walked to the dance floor. At first there was a hushed silence, then a few seconds later loud applause. She looked out at the large crowd that had gathered in and around the temple to watch her; the whole village seemed to be there. The important men in the front rows stared in admiration at her beauty. They did not hide their desire.

'*Wah! Wah!*'

'*Bahut sundar, Bahut sundar.*'

When she bowed to the audience, Anjali caught sight of the zamindar, sitting in his privileged position right at the front and looking directly at her. She felt his eyes crawling all over her, examining every inch of her body. Her heart drummed in her chest. She remembered his cruelty to the servant boy and it repulsed her. Now, although there was no trace of his former fury, he looked hard and fierce. She quickly averted her gaze. Her knees trembled, her steps faltered, and drops of sweat appeared on her forehead. She felt breathless and dizzy.

'This is Anjali,' she heard Mohini announce to the audience. 'The new *nach-girl* – the dancer.'

'A dancing doll!' someone called.

'An *apsara!*

'*Wah! Wah!*' the rest agreed.

Someone whistled.

Almost frozen by fear, she forgot what she was to do next until Mohini nudged the drummer to start playing the drums, announcing the start of the dance.

While the musicians tuned their instruments, Mohini looked at Anjali and cleared her throat, ready to recite the opening *raga*.

Doing what Mohini had instructed her to do, Anjali bowed towards the altar before touching the dance floor with her hands in a gesture of respect. Mohini whispered to her to go and touch the zamindar's feet before she took the first steps of her dance. Anjali obeyed, keeping her head bowed. The zamindar smiled at her as he placed his hands on her head and blessed her.

'May you dance for my heart's desires,' he said.

His words didn't register. Anjali was too nervous to take in what he had said to her. Quickly she returned to the dais.

Despite her nerves, as soon as Mohini started singing, Anjali's body obeyed of its own accord, moving in harmony with her teacher's melodious voice. Soon she wasn't aware of anything or anyone except the music. At every new gesture – an artistic pose or a fast rhythmic step – she was vaguely aware of the audience clapping and shouting.

'*Wah! Wah!*' they called.

She danced as if she were in a daze, absorbed by the music and completely at ease with her body's movements. Nothing else existed. She was alone on the stage and alone in the temple, oblivious of her surroundings. Only when she had finished her performance, when she made the respectful gesture of the *namaskaram* to the audience, did she notice the zamindar smiling at her, his eyes full of lust. Anjali looked down. The joy that she had felt while dancing was extinguished like a candle flame caught in the rain. It flickered and went out.

She excused herself and walked quickly to the inner quarters of the temple. Sita, the astrologer's daughter, smiled at her from the floor where she was seated making garlands ready for the evening prayer. Anjali stared at the girl in the white coarse *sari*. Her *pallu* covered her shaved head and bare shoulders.

'You danced very well.'

'Did you see it?'

'Yes. I sat behind that door.' She pointed at the half-closed door. 'I could see you from there.'

'Thank you,' said Anjali, removing her ankle bells. Neither girl knew what to say to the other. Anjali tried to imagine what Sita would have been like before she was widowed, but it was hard.

'Do you make garlands every day?'

'Yes,' nodded Sita.

'Anjali! What are you doing here?' Mohini came rushing in and grabbed her hand. 'Come, come, the zamindar is calling for you.'

Anjali had no choice but to obey. Walking behind Mohini, she turned round to see Sita following her with her eyes. Those eyes were full of regret and sorrow.

Her hands shook as the zamindar presented her with a set of diamond earrings. For Mohini there was only a pearl necklace, thrown at her with barely a glance. The zamindar had eyes only for Anjali and his open stare made her very uncomfortable.

*

Despite the success of her performance and the appreciation of the audience, it was the look in the zamindar's eyes that remained with her later and disturbed her. Her nights became broken and she slept badly.

It was the Friday after the dance, the day of the zamindar's weekly visit to Mohini. It was mid-morning and Anjali hadn't done anything except to wash her hair but she felt tired because she was sleeping so badly. Giving in to her weariness, she leaned back against her pillows and closed her eyes, allowing herself to reminisce about the strange series of events that had happened in her life. She had coped with being separated from her father by avoiding thinking about him but she knew she was pushing away memories that she had to deal with. Lately, when she was feeling strange and alone, she allowed her thoughts to linger on him. Like a silent procession of the dead, then came her late husband. Today her mind was open to memories and she let herself dwell on him too, a fierce man who had frightened her at first, but whom later she had come to know as a gentle soul. He had treated her as his own child. Anjali sighed, rubbing her forehead, as her thoughts drifted next to Saleem. She never stopped thinking of him. Deep in her heart she knew he was alive. But where was he? She believed that he had been searching for her. She flinched. If any of the men in her life knew where she was now, with a woman like Mohini, and dancing as a *nach-girl* in the zamindar's court, they would be horrified and ashamed.

'Anjali!' Kalyani rushed into the room, interrupting her thoughts. 'Mohini is calling you. Come, come.' She pulled her by her hand.

'Why?'

'You'd better go and see for yourself.'

Kalyani followed her, but hid behind the door when Anjali entered the front room. She could see perfectly.

Mohini smiled at Anjali and gestured to her to sit next to her on the couch. A woman servant was there too, holding a large silver tray covered with pink silk. Anjali recognised her as one of the zamindar's own. When Anjali was seated, the woman servant came forward, and bowed before placing the tray at her feet. Puzzled, Anjali looked at Mohini.

'The zamindar has sent it for you.' Mohini again smiled at her encouragingly and said, 'See what it is.'

Anjali slid back the silky cloth and stared in astonishment at a gold-threaded purple silk *sari* and a set of heavy gold and sapphire jewellery.

'Oh, my lord!' Mohini gasped, unable to hide her own surprise. 'What expensive and exquisite gifts!' She ran her fingers over the soft shimmery material of the *sari* and lifted up the jewellery to look at it in the light that came from a window. 'You are lucky, Anjali! The zamindar certainly knows a rare beauty when he sees one.'

Anjali stared first at Mohini then at the servant woman. She was not gladdened by the presents and felt only suspicion and unease. Why had he sent them?

The woman then said that, according to the zamindar's instructions, from now on she was to be Anjali's personal maid.

*

As the sun disappeared into the horizon, in the orange glow of the oil lamps, the woman massaged perfumed oil into Anjali's hair, before she combed it smooth.

'You have such beautiful long hair. It is so soft like black velvet. The zamindar is lucky,' she said.

'Why? What is it to do with the zamindar if my hair is beautiful?'

'Oh, Anjali-*amma*, don't you know?'

'Tell me please, what is this all about?'

The woman stared at her in disbelief. She had not come across one like Anjali before. 'Don't you know? Really? Mohini sold you to the zamindar. At a good price, I hear. In a few hours he will be here to take you back to his palace.'

Anjali stared blankly at the woman while her stomach somersaulted and her mouth tasted metal. She should have recognised the signs. It was all so obvious.

'Why is Mohini doing this to me?' Anjali asked at last, the words faint and barely audible. As if she had suddenly woken from a bad dream, she gripped the servant's hands tightly and pleaded, 'Please help me… to get out of this place. I can't stay here.'

'Anjali-*amma*, I am sure you know that it's impossible for anyone in this village to go against the zamindar's wishes. All you can do now is think positively. You will live like a queen.'

'No!' Anjali's voice quivered with fear. 'I don't want to live like a queen. I just want my freedom back.' Anjali got up and ran towards Mohini's room.

'Why are you doing this?'

Mohini looked up, surprised.

'Why?' Anjali repeated.

Mohini stared at her hard. 'Don't forget who you were before I brought you here. You were a homeless widow, remember?' Mohini's voice rose. 'If anyone had reported you to your people, your in-laws might have taken you straight back to that funeral fire! If I hadn't taken pity on you, the street dogs in Harikonda would have made a meal of you by now! Just thank your lucky stars. Now go and get ready!' She pointed one finger at the door.

'Why me? Why don't you send Kalyani?'

'Don't talk nonsense. Just get out of here.'

So there was no point in talking to Mohini. The woman had made her deal with the zamindar and had now washed her hands of her. Anjali ran to her room sobbing, straight into the arms of Rangi, who was cleaning there.

'Sit down,' Rangi said. 'Calm down.'

'She's sending me to the zamindar.' Anjali's sobs quietened now that she had found someone she could talk to.

'I know,' Rangi said. What she didn't say was that everybody knew. It was no secret. They had watched Mohini preparing Anjali from the very start.

'Why doesn't she send Kalyani?' Anjali sighed.

'She can't.'

'Why?'

Taking pity on Anjali, Rangi decided to speak the truth. 'I shouldn't say this to you but... Kalyani is Mohini's daughter.'

The shock of this news stopped Anjali's weeping as no sympathy could have done.

'Do you mean...?' she wiped her tears.

'Yes. The zamindar is her father.' Rangi nodded.

'My god!' As Anjali's lips uttered those two words, everything fell into place and made sense.

'Does Kalyani know?'

'No.'

'What about the zamindar?'

'He has no idea. I don't think he is interested in these details.'

'Details?' cried Anjali. 'We are talking about a man's daughter!'

'It means nothing to him. It is routine for these rich and powerful men to buy their pleasure, and when they have taken it, the thought that they might have fathered a child would not cross their minds. Or if it did, it would be of no interest to them.'

Finally understanding her situation, Anjali realised that there was no choice but to obey Mohini's orders. While she sat and stood and turned, limp and unhelpful, she was dressed by others in finery as if she were to be a bride. She sat motionless, staring into space, as her new maid made her beautiful. Her mind was in such a state of shock that she could not even think about plans, about running away. Time was ticking by fast. When Mohini came in to inspect her, she stood up, as commanded, but she was shivering.

'Please, let me go to the bathroom first,' Anjali pleaded, and without waiting for a reply, she ran past everyone towards the back yard. Once inside, she bolted the door and leaned against it. She had to take gulps of air into her lungs to compose herself. She knew if she didn't think fast, very fast, she would be a prisoner in the zamindar's palace forever. Or until he tired of her and found someone younger. She looked at the tiny window with iron bars across it and knew it offered no means of escape. Then she caught her own reflection staring back at her in a small mirror that hung on the wall – a pale, ashen face with terror-stricken eyes – but also in that mirror were a couple of objects that Anjali had not noticed, and she thanked her fates for revealing them. She turned round and took the razor and scissors from the alcove behind her.

Chapter 27

Although it had been more than a year since he had lost Anjali, still Saleem was in anguish at not knowing what had happened to her. He still received letters regularly from Anjali's father, which recently had become frantic. In the end Saleem couldn't avoid replying. He wrote a brief letter saying that Anjali was fine and blamed the postal services for not delivering his previous replies.

Guilt-ridden, Saleem felt bad for lying to a respectable gentleman, but he knew he had no choice. He didn't want to cause more worry to a man who was already missing his daughter desperately.

Even though Saleem's hopes were fading, he never gave up on his search for Anjali. He enquired after her everywhere he went. Whenever he drove Mr Robert to different areas, he asked for some time off so that he could spend a few days searching for any trace of Anjali. For Mr Robert's kindness, Saleem was immensely grateful, yet his bitterness towards the British remained unchanged. Gradually he found himself softening towards Mr Robert, especially when he witnessed his constant fairness towards the natives, which, from what he had heard, was received with nothing but scorn and anger from his wife, Miss Edwina. Apparently it had become quite an issue between them. She called him weak for his tolerance.

It was while Saleem was driving Miss Edwina for her afternoon tea parties that he overheard her complaining about her husband to her friend Stella.

'Robert is too lenient. That's why the servants behave like they do,' she said.

'I know. Sometimes I am actually scared of my own servants,' Stella replied.

'Did you hear about the incident last month?'

'You mean the Kingsford incident?'

'Yes.'

'The natives swore that it was an accident but it was obvious that it was a murder. It seems that it was Mrs Kingsford's driver, Jayram, who was to blame. They dragged her cart into the ditch and left her and the horse there to die while he climbed to safety.'

'How awful!'

'Apparently the man said that his memsahib was driving the cart herself and had ordered him to stay behind and watch.'

'Well he would say that, wouldn't he?'

'You know what annoys me the most?' Edwina lowered her voice. 'Robert agreeing with the protesters that it was an accident.'

'I am glad that the driver was sentenced to death.'

'Yes, thank heavens. Justice was done,' Edwina said, self-righteously.

Saleem sighed silently and bit back bitter words. He remembered Mr Robert reading him an extract of the same news from the Manchester Guardian while he had driven him to the office the previous day.

'Amongst English judges and English juries in India, there are very few fair and right-minded officials left,' Mr Robert said, folding the paper.

Before Saleem could respond, they heard a young man on the street shouting, '*Vande Matharam*! Hail motherland!'

Within seconds an excited crowd gathered around him and soon they were all roaring anti-colonial slogans.

'*Jayram ki jai*! Victory to *Jayram*!'

'British Raj *murdabad*! Death to the British Raj!'

'Obviously they have heard the news of the death sentence too,' Mr Robert said quietly, as if to himself.

Every Indian newspaper published an article praising Jayaram's courage in not protesting when he was dragged to the execution platform, thus preserving his dignity. Saleem thought that his actions could mean either that Jayram was guilty, or that he knew it would be useless to put up a fight since he had no chance of winning against an all-powerful British opposition. On the other hand, all the English papers wrote articles which argued that the judge had sentenced Jayram not only because he had murdered his mistress but because he was involved in making explosives to be used against the government. Saleem didn't know which papers to believe.

*

A few days later, Saleem was driving Mr Robert and his superintendent Mr James home after a meeting, and overheard the discussion between them.

'These coolies do so much without any mechanical help. They carry tons of cement and concrete on their backs and pull enormously heavy stones with ropes using their bare hands. I think the government should provide them with the right machinery,' Mr Robert was saying.

'Heavens, Robert! Have you no idea how much it would cost us to import machinery from home?' James asked.

'But they should have the machinery they need. Lives are being lost and men injured. At the very least, the contractors should bring in bullocks to drag those heavy stones.'

'It's not necessary, my boy,' said the superintendent 'These natives are tough. How do you think we completed the Uganda railroad in 1901?'

'I know, James, they carried six hundred miles of iron tracks and laid them in appallingly dangerous conditions. The men were brave, but they had no choice. Now these coolies are working long hours doing back-breaking work, and we pay them so little for their hardship and suffering. Don't you think they deserve better?'

James laughed as if at a naive child. 'My dear young man, don't you know it wasn't cheap? It cost us six million pounds.'

'Yes, but I am not talking about Ugandan coolies, I am talking about our coolies here in India. Now.'

'Well, Robert, it's up to the contractors how much they pay the labourers. We are pouring thousands of rupees into their hands and the government certainly can't afford to increase the amount they pay the contractors, not until the bloody natives pay their taxes properly.'

'The taxes that the government is imposing are rather high, and the zamindars won't pay a *paisa* out of their own pockets. They enforce the taxes on the poor peasants and coolies who can't even afford one meal a day.'

James went silent for a while. 'You sound like my wife! She's soft on the natives. I have to let her have her way. Grace is a strong woman. Anyway, what do you want me to do?'

'Would you please send an order to the contractors to hire out bullocks? That will help, sir.' Robert had been quietly persuasive and in the end James had agreed.

'All right, young man, if you wish, certainly I will draft an order tomorrow morning.'

That night, when Saleem sat down to eat a meal with Prakash, he said, 'You know, I am beginning to feel some respect for my engineer sahib. I get to overhear quite a lot as I drive him and others around, and he is always on our side.'

Prakash looked up, surprised. 'I thought you always liked him?'

'Yes I did, but you know after that Jallianwala-Bagh shooting, when Anjali became separated from me, I disliked every single white person I saw. I couldn't even bear the sight of them.'

'But Saleem, that is not right. Every British person is not an assassin and the entire white population should not be treated with suspicion. You already knew your engineer sahib very well and knew how well he treated his natives. There was no reason to turn against him.'

'I know that rationally, but when you feel bitter, you feel bitter towards everything – even towards life itself. My anger and bitterness spilled on to him too. For a while, I hated him.'

Chapter 28

That Christmas, Saleem received a brand new uniform and ten rupees as a gift from Mr Robert and was deeply touched by his employer's generosity. Even though he didn't celebrate Christmas himself, being a Muslim, he quite enjoyed the festive atmosphere in the British cantonment area. Mr Robert and Miss Edwina spent their Christmas at the Wilsons' so Saleem had a day off, which he used to search for Anjali in the neighbouring villages, but without any success. He returned home saddened.

On New Year's Eve, Miss Edwina announced that she needed Saleem as a bearer for a party she and Mr Robert were giving. His duties would be to serve drinks and cocktails. He didn't mind helping at these parties, even though he was employed as a driver, not a house servant, because it was one way he could repay Mr Robert for his kindness.Miss Edwina always picked Saleem as a bearer; she once said, 'You are the only good-looking, good-mannered one amongst all our staff so I like you being amongst our guests, serving them and attending to their needs.'

'Saleem,' she called, as he was spreading a tablecloth over the dining table.

'Yes, memsahib.' Saleem abandoned the cloth and ran to her.

'Oh, there you are. Have you set everything?'

'Yes, memsahib. Everything is ready.' He gestured at the bottles of beer, gin and whisky, wine, mixers and glasses on the sideboard, from where he could serve the guests.

For once Miss Edwina looked impressed.

'Are we all ready then?' Mr Robert came into the dining room. He looked quite smart in his dinner jacket.

'Yes, sir,' nodded Saleem.

'Good, good. Well done.'

'Saleem returned the barest smile.

'You look lovely,' he said, walking over to his wife and putting his arm around her waist. He kissed her cheek. 'Here's to a successful evening.'

When Saleem had first worked for Mr Robert, any couple displaying affection for one another in public had looked odd, but as the years passed he got used to the English custom.

'Oh, Robert!' Miss Edwina wriggled out of her husband's embrace. Her mood changed. 'You and your guests had better be satisfied with my efforts. I have tried my best. Everything is so dreadfully difficult and complicated out here.' She gestured to Saleem to pour a gin and tonic for her.

Her words seemed to have no effect on Mr Robert. He remained calm and took deep breaths as he inhaled the strong scent of the *Rat-ki-rani* flowers that were blooming in abundance and peeping in through the open windows.

Miss Edwina kept looking at her watch. 'It's half past seven. The guests should be arriving any minute now. I went to a lot of trouble to decide on the menu and show the cook what to do. If they don't like it… well… tough luck.' With that she swallowed the last drop of her drink and, after handing her empty glass to Saleem, walked into the kitchen to inspect the food. As she opened the door, the most delicious aromas floated out. Mr Robert crouched down by the gramophone and placed the needle gently on a record, and the house was filled with syncopated jazz.

Some hours later, the party was in full swing. Saleem, with much misgiving, had just served Miss Edwina yet another whisky. She had been drinking steadily and he was concerned. She was already wobbly on her feet and her speech was slurred. Of course he did not dare refuse her, so she drank on.

'Saleem *bhayya*,' Vimala, the chief maid, who was standing next to him, whispered, 'look at Miss Edwina. She is drunk already...'

'I know.'

'Earlier, she made a big fuss in the kitchen.'

'What about?'

'About nothing, really! It was the colour of the jelly. She didn't like the orange, she wanted it red – you know, cherry or something – and the chef explained to her how he tried to find that colouring but couldn't get it anywhere in Harikonda.'

'And what did she say?'

'She just banged the table in anger and stormed off, saying, "Bloody place! I can't get anything I need here."'

Everyone was drinking, smoking and nibbling the snacks that the cooks and bearers brought out on huge trays. Some were chatting away as usual about politics, or the latest news from home, and even about Gandhi. Miss Edwina was sitting amongst a group of women, discussing husbands, babies, knitting, embroidery and servants. Saleem could see that Miss Edwina was not interested and barely joined in. He watched her leave the hall and walk unsteadily to the back veranda, where she leaned against a pillar. Her fingers, encased in white gloves, fumbled with a cigarette, trying to place it in her scarlet lips, but her hands were shaking uncontrollably. Quickly Saleem ran and pulled out a bench for her. 'Please, memsahib.' He made a polite gesture that she might like to sit down but she waved him away. As she looked past him, a slow smile came to her lips. She had spotted someone drawing away from the crowds.

'May I?' a male voice interrupted.

Completely ignoring Saleem, Mr Vincent pushed past him and leaned forward to light Miss Edwina's cigarette.

'Thank you, Vincent,' she half giggled and half hiccupped.

'My pleasure, my dear!' Vincent placed his hands on her shoulders and pushed her gently but firmly down on to the bench.

'Oh, Vincent…'

It was unsettling the way Miss Edwina could switch moods so quickly. Saleem had seen her do it before, many times. Now she was playing someone weepy. 'Oh, Vincent,' she repeated, 'I hate this place and I hate these parties. Robert doesn't care about me. And,' she continued, slurring her words, and trying for sympathy, 'do you know he puts the servant's needs before mine? I can't stand much more of this. I want to go home…'

'Never mind about him, my dear,' Vincent consoled her, swirling the whisky in his glass before lifting it to her lips. Clearly he did not care if she had drunk too much already.

'Oh, Vincent, you are so kind…' the words came out thick and unclear.

It seemed strange to Saleem to see a man putting his arms around another man's wife. Then he smiled to himself and thought everything that the British did looked odd to the Indians anyway. Who was he to judge? Not wanting to witness anything more, and thinking, not for the first time, that for some English the servants were invisible, he silently walked back into the hall, where the party was still in full swing.

Mr Robert, unaware of how much his wife had been drinking, or perhaps knowing full well but choosing to ignore it, was talking passionately about a major construction with one of his colleagues. Saleem felt a twinge of pity for his engineer sahib because he had heard what Miss Edwina had said and knew that her accusations against her husband were unfounded. It must take a lot of energy and patience for a man to manage a temperamental wife like Miss

Edwina, he decided. Compared to many English men, never mind Indians, Mr Robert was a saint. Saleem both admired him and felt sorry for him.

Later, when Saleem returned home, in the early hours of the morning, he couldn't help but say to Prakash, 'I don't think Mr Robert can be happy.'

'In what way?'

'I mean in his marriage. Of course he is loyal and doesn't say much but I have been watching him and Miss Edwina tonight – and on previous occasions – and things are not right. She behaves so badly…'

'Perhaps it's time he left her.'

'Prakash, Mr Robert is a gentleman. He would never do that. She is his wife and he brought her out here. I suppose he thought she would cope better…'

'Saleem,' Prakash interrupted with a wry smile, 'why are you worrying about your Mr Robert when you loathe the British? And when it's not Mr Robert, it's that girl you are always searching for. What's her name… Anjali? It's time to lighten up.'

'But Prakash…'

'No, that's quite enough for today! Go to bed and get some sleep. You have to get up again in a few hours. So do I!'

Prakash went back to his own area, shaking his head, and saying, 'What a soft heart you have, Saleem. Despite your anger and your restlessness and your extreme political views, you are a complex character – but then that's why I like you so much.'

Chapter 29

'Looks like you are off on your travels again. Where to this time?' Prakash asked, watching Saleem packing his bag.

'Yes. To Roypuram. The engineer sahib has been appointed to set up a new project there. He is going to organise the building of a new road from Roypuram to the city of Aryanagar,' Saleem replied, placing a neatly folded clean towel into the bag.

'Roypuram? Never heard of it.'

'I know, because it doesn't come under the Harikonda district. Apparently it is the biggest village in the Aryanagar district and home to a very wealthy zamindar.' Saleem looked up. 'But you know, I think this is all a big ploy of the government.'

'What do you mean?'

'By running a bus service from the city to the village, the government changes the status of the village to a municipality. Then they can raise taxes.'

'Yes, yes,' Prakash nodded. 'Look at my village since they changed it to a municipality – people are struggling to pay the higher taxes now.'

'I know, and only the poor like us are suffering. The rich don't care. They are happy as long as their status is raised and they gain influential British friends and colleagues.'

'Well, what does your engineer sahib say?'

'Nothing. I don't think he has any say in the matter. His job is just to organise the building of roads and bridges. He does as he is told by his superintendent, who gets his orders from the government.'

By the time Saleem walked across to the British cantonment, Mr Robert and Miss Edwina were sitting under the shade of an almond tree in the front garden, sipping tea. The cook was serving breakfast.

'Good morning, sir, memsahib.' Saleem raised his cap and saluted them before going to the portico to get the jeep ready. He wiped the already clean seats and dusted the dashboard. As he began polishing the outer surfaces of the jeep, he couldn't help but overhear Mr Robert and Miss Edwina talking.

'It will be a change for you, Edwina,' Mr Robert was saying. 'Even though it is a village, the guest house has modern European amenities. The team of servants will be at your beck and call. The jeep will be there if you want to explore the place.'

'For god's sake, Robert, can't you see, I'm already sick and tired of driving all over the place. I don't want to travel to some even more remote village. Just leave me alone here, please.'

'Darling,' Mr Robert tried to coax her, 'the zamindar himself has sent us an invitation. We are honoured. The contractor said the grand palace, the Gadi of Roypuram, is magnificent and well worth a visit. You might enjoy looking round it, Edwina.'

'How many more times, Robert? Have I not made myself clear? I don't want to see any more wretched villages, or temples, or palaces... nothing! I've seen all I want to see. Now leave me alone. I am not going with you, not on this trip, not on any other bloody awful trip. I've had enough.' She threw her napkin on the table, stood up abruptly, and pushed back her chair with such force that it fell backwards with a thud. Saleem heard her stomping off into the house. Mr Robert sat there silently staring at the fallen chair. Then he too got up, tossing his half-eaten toast on to a plate.

For most of the journey Mr Robert was immersed in his own

thoughts and Saleem drove the jeep in silence.

As he thought about Roypuram, Saleem's heart fluttered with a new hope. He never imagined that Anjali would have gone so far, crossing into another district, and yet anything was possible. Roypuram was only thirty miles from Kalipet station so Anjali just might have gone there. God willing, he might find her. Saleem's hope never faltered.

As the jeep rolled forward, jerking and dancing on the uneven dust road through the jungle, Mr Robert brightened up and said, 'Imagine this as a proper road and think how comfortably people could travel. Soon the buses will be running along this way and people will be able to reach the city in no time at all.'

'Yes, sir.' Saleem smiled at the engineer's enthusiasm. As was their custom, they fell back into their own pleasant thoughts. There was no need for further talk. They were comfortable and relaxed with one another.

Soon they saw a sign saying 'Roypuram', carved on a stone in local script as well as in English. Next to it was another carved stone representing a goddess with an outstretched tongue and four arms. Some offerings of fruit and flowers had been laid at her feet.

'Who is that?' asked Mr Robert, pointing.

'That is Kali, the goddess of the destruction of evil. I think the villagers placed her there, at the entrance, believing that she would protect the village.'

They passed through rice and maize fields, mango and orange groves, while the coolies stopped their work to stare at Mr Robert and the jeep. Some children were already running behind the unusual vehicle. Saleem explained to Mr Robert that the villagers might not have seen a jeep or an English person before in their lives. Mr Robert smiled. Of course, he knew all this, but he did not want to spoil Saleem's pleasure in explaining it. It was his country, after all.

The dock-bungalow, the guest house, was situated a mile away from the residences of Roypuram and was surrounded by woods. As they drove up to the gates they heard a band playing and saw a crowd already gathered there to welcome Mr Robert, the first white person to grace their village.

Saleem had to stop the jeep even before they reached the gates. The crowd cheered happily as a neatly dressed and well-educated looking person placed a garland over Mr Robert's head.

'My name is Venkat,' he said. 'I work for the zamindar – Jeevan Roy – as a secretary.' He spoke in English. 'On behalf of our zamindar, we welcome you to Roypuram,' he said, saluting Mr Robert.

'Thank you,' Mr Robert smiled.

'Please,' Venkat bowed, 'our zamindar says he will be happy if you would kindly accept his invitation and grace his palace at your convenience.'

'I will. Certainly. It will be my pleasure.'

Chapter 30

After a number of frantic bangings on the door, Anjali slowly emerged from the bathroom. She had been in there a very long time.

The expression on Mohini's face was a sight to behold. Her eyes boggled and she let out a scream as if she had seen a ghost. Kalyani put her hand over her mouth and moaned as if in pain. All the servants gathered around to see what was going on.

'*Bh-ag-van*! What – have – you – done!' At last Mohini managed to say something, one syllable at a time, while everyone else stared in utter disbelief.

Stripped of her fine clothing and jewellery and wearing a white cotton *sari*, Anjali stepped out. She looked directly at Mohini and smiled.

'I am a widow, remember?' she said in a small but firm voice, pulling her *sari pallu* over her shaven head. On the floor behind her, jet black clumps of long hair glistened.

'How dare you…' Mohini's voice shook with anger and her eyes glared at Anjali. The next thing Anjali felt was her cheeks on fire. Mohini slapped her hard on both sides of her face, then, as if her hands were tired, took a cane and danced it all over Anjali's body. She was rooted to the spot, doubled up in pain from these unexpected lashes, too shocked to move or run away. She tried to protect herself with her arms, but it was futile. She cried out loud. Finally a fierce blow knocked her off balance and she fell backwards, hitting her head on the wall, and everything went blank.

She didn't know how long she had been in that state but when she came to, a woman's voice was calling her name and sprinkling water on her face. Anjali opened her eyes but everything was a blur.

'OK. She's fine.' It was Mohini's voice this time, sounding relieved. She too was in the room, watching. 'Now get her out of here.'

'But Mohini-*dorsani*, she has only just woken up and is still in a lot of pain...'

'Don't argue with me, Rangi. Do as I say. She's alive and she can walk. Get her out of this house.'

Anjali heard Mohini shouting these orders in a voice that trembled with rage.

Given no time to gather herself, or to wait until the room had stopped spinning, Anjali felt Rangi grabbing her by the arms, and with another woman's help, she was hauled up and set on her feet. Her legs wobbled and her whole body quivered with pain.

When she woke again at the first call of a cockerel, it was still dark. Her head swam and her body ached. She tried to move her limbs but they felt as if they were pressed down by a ton weight. Her mouth felt dry and parched. She put her hands to her head and, with a shock, felt the smooth surface of her skull, instead of thick hair bound in a long glossy plait. Remembering what she had done, she moved her fingers tentatively from her temples to her neck. Her head was still sore from being shaved. Her fingers found a lump, which hurt, a reminder of Mohini's blows. For a moment she fought back tears.

The bed felt hard and cold. Just pulling her knees to her chest made her shiver but she had to get up and see where she was. Slowly her eyes grew accustomed to the darkness and she realised that she was lying on the floor on a straw mat in a strange room. Where was she? It was an effort, but with difficulty she managed to sit up and then get to her feet. She could only stand by leaning against a wall for support. In the faint light, she understood that she was in a mud hut with a thatched roof.

She saw a clay stove with used firewood in it and some pots and pans on a shelf above. In another corner was an earthenware pot with a lid, which she guessed was a water pot because a nickel glass was placed on top of it. It was too far to reach. She tried, but her body refused to move. She sat recalling the previous night's events. It was the first time in her life that she had suffered any kind of physical abuse at the hands of another human being. Her eyes filled with tears as she remembered her father, who had never lifted a finger to her. Even her step-mother, cruel as she was, had only abused her verbally. But now… what had happened was beyond her imagination.

Finally it dawned on her that she had been placed in the servants' quarters. She would not be re-entering the house. Good, she thought. I would rather live as a servant than in the zamindar's harem as his kept woman.

She was thinking about the change in her circumstances when the door creaked open and the morning light flooded in. Anjali tried to smile at Rangi but the muscles in her face would not move.

'You are awake!' Rangi said, coming towards her.

Anjali nodded.

'Look at you. Why did you do that?' the older woman looked at Anjali's shaved head while she untied a knot in the corner of her *sari pallu*, revealing a pot of ointment.

Anjali tried to speak but her swollen lips refused to part.

'I got this from the astrologer. He said the worst of the swellings will calm down within a couple of days.'

Anjali tried not to scream as Rangi applied the slimy green balm to her face and body, rubbing it on the bruises and cuts. Although its coolness relieved the burning sensation, even the gentlest touch from Rangi's fingers was agony.

After helping Anjali to walk to the bathroom in the back yard,

Rangi gave her a walking stick and said, 'Be careful where you step. It's very slippery. You have enough injuries without falling as well.'

When she returned from the bathroom, the clay stove was bright with burning logs and something was boiling in a clay pot.

'Here, drink this.' Rangi handed her a cup of hot broth made from sago and water. With a pinch of salt it tasted tolerable. 'We don't drink tea like you do,' Rangi said apologetically. 'I am sorry, but Mohini ordered you to live like a servant widow until you grow your hair back.' She looked at Anjali with sympathy.

Anjali looked up from her cup and tried to say, 'Why doesn't Mohini give up on me?' Her voice was weak and she could only speak a few syllables at a time but Rangi understood.

'Why would she give up on such a rare beauty as you?' Even with your shaven head, you still look lovely.'

'Please... please help me to get away from here,' Anjali pleaded, tears welling up in her eyes.

'Don't you dare say that again, girl!' Rangi scolded suddenly, wagging a finger. 'And don't you dare cut your hair again because if you do, it will be my head, along with your hair, that will be chopped off.'

Anjali stared at Rangi in disbelief, thinking perhaps that she was teasing to lighten the awful situation.

'Seriously, Anjali. I have been ordered to watch you closely and it is my responsibility to make sure that you grow your hair back, however long that takes. The zaminder has a weakness for thick, glossy hair.' She got up and took a bottle from the alcove. 'So you have to let me massage your head with this special oil.' She dragged a stool close to Anjali and sat down heavily on it. Anjali removed the *sari pallu* from her head. The pungent smell of herbs from the oil hit her nostrils. Then she had to close her eyes tightly at the pain of the oil being rubbed into her bruises and cuts.

It took several days for her body to start to recover from the shock.

Gradually the lump on her head shrunk and her pain and stiffness subsided. But still her mind was in turmoil. What could she do now? It seemed that it was impossible to get away from this place and she was certain that eventually she would be a prisoner in the zamindar's harem. What more do I have to do? she asked herself. Despite what Rangi says, I have made myself ugly and still they keep me here.

Anjali bent her smooth head and wept.

Chapter 31

In the beginning, Anjali found it difficult to adapt to living in the mud hut, which was half the size of her room in the mansion. Rangi kept it very clean. Every morning, she mixed red clay dust and cow dung with enough water to form a paste and, after dipping a piece of cloth into it, applied it to the floor with sweeping movements. The floor shimmered as smooth as velvet. Anjali was surprised to see that this one room could accommodate three people. A few pots and pans occupied a tiny space in a corner. Rangi and her fifteen-year-old grandson, Samba, had only two sets of clothing each, one for wearing and one in the wash, or hung on tree branches in the sun, ready for the next day. The only rope cot they owned was kept outside, in front of the hut for visitors to sit on. At night, they slept on a couple of straw mats, covering themselves with threadbare hand-loom bed sheets which had been discarded and handed down by Mohini. Every morning, all the bedding was rolled up and put away in a corner to make space for other things.

Even though she could be a bit dominating, Rangi treated Anjali with kindness. She insisted that Anjali sleep in the rope cot, which Samba brought inside, while she slept on the floor next to her grandson. Anjali was touched by her thoughtfulness, but lying in twisted, prickly ropes was far from comfortable and she was covered only by a thin bed sheet.

At first Samba was too shy to do anything but smile at her, but with Anjali's encouragement he began to respond and to speak to her. His polite smiles slowly developed into friendly chatter. Anjali of course remembered that he had been the victim of the zamindar's fury a few weeks earlier and she felt sorry for him. Slowly, they became relaxed in one another's company and took pleasure in their conversations.

One day Anjali asked, 'What did you do to make the zamindar so angry?'

'I didn't pay the tax.'

'Tax? On what?'

'The honey I collected from the forest and sold in the village.'

'Do you have to pay the tax even on honey?'

'Yes, nowadays we have to pay tax on everything.'

'Why didn't you pay?'

'I didn't know then that I had to pay for something I had collected myself.'

'How did you collect it?'

'I walked miles and miles into the forest to find the honeycomb on a tree. You know it is very dangerous to disturb the honeycomb? The bees don't like it and they can swarm around you and sting you to death.'

'How did you do it then?'

'I covered myself from head to toe with a thick blanket and made two holes for my eyes. I lit a fire near the tree with wood and leaves so that the smoke would disperse the bees.'

'You are very brave.'

'I watched the tribal people doing it.'

'So what did you do with that money?'

'It wasn't much. Only enough to buy a cup of tea in that roadside stall.' He looked at her. 'You know, I never tasted tea in my life, but I inhaled the aroma and wanted it so badly. So I took one of my friends with me and we had a cup each with that money... it was delicious.' Samba licked his lips.

'Oh, Samba! You endured such cruel punishment for such a small pleasure!'

In the mud hut, the time went slowly. Rangi and Samba woke up very early. They swallowed some broth that Rangi had cooked from sago or from the previous night's left-over rice mixed with water, and left for work by sunrise, as did all their neighbours. By eight in the morning, the whole area was deserted except for a stray dog or two, roaming around looking for food. The silence was only disturbed by the occasional bird cooing in the trees. At first, not knowing what to do with the endless empty days that stretched ahead of her, Anjali stayed in bed most of the day relaxing and restoring her health and energy. But soon her wounds began to heal with the regular application of the green, slimy balm, and her hair began to grow in short tufts with Rangi's daily oil massages; she knew that her peace would not last forever. Every time she looked at herself in the mirror, Anjali worried. She was well aware of Mohini's intentions and she had no doubts about what was to come when her hair had grown back to its former glory. She consoled herself that it would take a long time yet. Ultimately, though, there was no way out, either of her predicament, or from the zamindar's territory where she was held like a prisoner. The whole place was surrounded by a tall compound wall and inside it were hundreds of watching eyes. As each day passed, Anjali grew more troubled.

Anjali lived from day to day. Time passed. But finally the moment arrived. Rangi was at the door and, from the expression on her face, it was clear that she had brought the news that Anjali had been dreading.

'Every single day recently Mohini has asked me to take you over to the house, but I managed to put her off with all kinds of lies, like your wounds hadn't quite healed or you were still limping slightly… any excuse I would think of… but now she is threatening to come here herself to see you, so there is no avoiding it. You will have to come with me.'

'Why does Mohini want me to live there again?'

'She wants you to be my assistant. To help me. Every day from now on, you must accompany me to Mohini's house as a servant and a chamber maid. It could have been worse.'

'That's fine,' she said. 'I don't mind doing that sort of work.' Secretly Anjali was relieved, but Rangi looked at her sympathetically before explaining what she would have to do each morning at Mohini's house.

Even though it was difficult and she struggled with work that she had never done before, Anjali was happy thinking that she was out of danger, at least for the time being. That thought kept her going, but her mind never stopped searching for ways to get out of the place.

Although Mohini was still furious with Anjali and refused to look her in the face, she also insisted that she must keep up her dancing practice in the dance room. Now and then she would insist that Anjali remove her veil so that a servant could examine her head and measure the growth of her hair. Anjali was thankful that her hair was not in a hurry.

*

It was a morning like any other morning. Anjali swept the back yard and splashed buckets and buckets of water mixed with cow dung on the ground to prevent the weeds growing. The whole yard became a velvety khaki colour, in contrast to the white and pink *nagamalli* and *nandivardhana* flowers growing on the small bushes. Then she drew some more buckets from the well to water the *hibiscus* and *parijata* in the corner. The scent of the flowers brought back powerful memories of her father's house. She closed her eyes, remembering the past, her childhood. Every morning Tahera, Saleem's mother, would comb her hair smooth to plait it and then decorate it with the flowers she had picked in the garden. And her father would smile at her with moist eyes and whisper, 'I wish your mother could see you now.' Later, she and Saleem would collect up the long tubular stems of the *boddumalli* flowers that had fallen to the ground. When they blew into them, the sound was exactly like that of a flute. Anjali wiped a tear from the corner of her eye. Where was her childhood friend now? Once more she imagined him not surviving the station fire. She shook her head to dispel the thought and instead trusted her instinct that he was alive and well.

'Haven't you finished your work yet?' Kalyani came running. 'Let me help you.' With a kind look, she took the *chembu*, the water container, from her.

'No, don't!' Anjali said. 'Mohini will see you and I will get into trouble.' She tried to grab the *chembu* back.

'It's OK. Mohini is busy with the beautician. I think the zamindar is visiting her today,' Kalyani whispered. Then she looked at Anjali. 'Oh dear, I think you had better cover your hair properly. It's grown quite a bit. '

Anjali pulled her *sari pallu* over her head.

What Mohini had said to the zamindar, Anjali didn't know. Kalyani claimed that Mohini had kept her shaved head a secret and no one talked about it. But then she whispered, 'The zamindar visited Mohini the same night you shaved your head. The following morning she didn't come out of her room. In fact she stayed in there for two days. When she eventually emerged, she had dark circles around her eyes and she was limping.'

Anjali wasn't surprised. She guessed what kind of treatment Mohini had suffered at the hands of the zamindar. As she tried to imagine what life was like for Mohini, Anjali began to feel truly sorry for this middle-aged, unfortunate woman. Was her life any better than Anjali's own? Was she any more free?

'I miss your company very much,' Kalyani said.

'Me too,' Anjali replied, turning away so as not to show too much emotion.

She looked at her friend fondly. Even though Kalyani was ordered not to communicate with her, she visited her in secret, even if it was only for a few minutes and to exchange few words. Anjali was grateful for that and appreciated her friend's courage.

The sound of the drums outside interrupted their conversation. While Kalyani ran indoors, Anjali watched the servants abandoning their chores and heading out into the street. A short while later the drums stopped and Anjali heard a loud male voice calling out to the crowds.

'Attention! Attention! I have an announcement on behalf of the zamindar. From now on there will be an increased tax on firewood, fruit and honey. Without obtaining a licence from the government, no one is allowed to enter the forest to gather any of those things.'

Anjali heard the gasps of the shocked villagers.

'Silence! Silence!' came the voice again. 'This is nothing to do with the zamindar. This is due to orders he has received from the governor of the state, Sir Simon Hall.'

With that, the drums started up again, fading into the distance. Anjali guessed that the announcer was moving on to the next street. All the servants returned to the house and grounds with worry etched on their faces. No one spoke. They continued with their chores in shocked silence.

Chapter 32

That same evening, everyone gathered for a meeting in the communal yard in front of the servants' huts. Anjali sat behind Rangi at the entrance of their hut so that people couldn't see her but she could peep out through a gap between Rangi's shoulder and the doorway.

The leader of the group, Veeramallu, sat leaning on a *neem* tree, smoking a cheroot. Everyone squatted on the floor, the men smoking or rolling their tobacco leaves and the women either tending their babies or weaving intricate straw mats and baskets, even in the faint moonlight. Anjali marvelled at the patience and stamina of the hard-working women.

'This is very disappointing news,' Veeramallu explained to the crowd. 'Some of us work in the fields for the zamindar, but many of us depend upon the forest for firewood and honey and fruits. The taxes are already high, and people have had to starve to pay them, but now with this further increase, you can guess what will happen. We may not be able even to survive. How can we when the government denies us our traditional ways of making our living?'

'How can the zamindar do this to us!' shouted someone in the crowd.

'He says it's not him, it is the government,' Veeramallu answered. 'But can you trust him?'

'Shush!' A man put his fingers to his lips. 'Be quiet. Don't you know, even walls have ears nowadays.'

'But, can't the zamindar do anything? Can't he help us?'

'I don't think so. What can he do?' Veeramallu said in a low voice.
'You all know that he is one of them. He likes them – I mean the
English. He wants to be friends with them and he wants to live like
them. Last year he imported hunting rifles from London. They are
very expensive and do you know who paid for them?' He looked at
everyone and his eyes were red; Anjali couldn't decide whether it
was because of his anger or because of the cheroot smoke filling the
air. Pausing for breath, Veeramallu banged his chest with his fist and
said, 'We... we paid for them. They squeeze money out of us, the
poor, by raising the taxes on everything so that they can pay for their
own luxuries.'

For a few seconds silence hung in the air, as dense as the smoke.
The leader was breathing heavily and quickly.

'And,' he raised a finger in the air, 'as if that wasn't enough, the
zamindar has sent gifts of pearls and rubies to some governors.'

Again a gasp went round the room, then sighs.

'And this year, guess what he wants to buy?' Veeramallu asked the
audience, stretching out his arms to encourage them.

'A motorcar?' someone shouted.

'Yes! You are right! So how many of you agree with me that the
taxes on the firewood, fruits and honey go towards a new motorcar
for a man who is already very wealthy?'

'You think that was the reason that white man came to our village?'
an elderly man asked.

'Of course! Why else would he come to a village like ours in his
plush motorcar?'

'He must be the one who asked the zamindar to impose these
ridiculous taxes on us.'

'Definitely! No doubt about that.'

'Have you seen him?'

'No, but Samba went with Venkat to welcome him,' Veeramallu said, looking at Samba.

In response, Samba beamed, feeling important not only because he worked for a man like Venkat, but because he was the one who had brought the news to the village of the arrival of a first English official.

'Yes, I did,' he replied.

'And what does Venkat-saar say?'

'He says, this man is not a taxman but has come to build the roads from our village to the city.'

'They say that, don't they?' Veeramallu sighed.

A young man stood up and said, 'That's why there is a strike in Narsapore.' His voice rose in excitement. 'They not only refused to work for their zamindar but also attacked an Englishman who visited their village.'

For a few moments there was total silence, then everyone was talking at once, giving an opinion or asking for clarification.

'Perhaps we should do the same.' At first a single voice made this dramatic suggestion. Then a couple of others agreed. Then more and more people were nodding their heads and shouting for justice.

'Yes, beat the hell out of him until he agrees to abolish the taxes!' one man shouted.

Hearing that, an elderly man stood up and tried to restore some calm. 'I don't think that is wise. I don't think we should be talking about violence. We don't even know who this Englishman is.'

'You think he really came to build the roads? You are being naive!' a young man shouted.

'What are we supposed to believe? They won't tell us the truth,' someone else said.

'But no violence. Not yet. Definitely not yet. We must wait and see who this man is before we act,' the elderly man repeated.

'Don't you become another Gandhi and preach non-violence!'

The leader, Veeramallu, saw that he had to calm the crowd before things got out of hand.

'As the grandfather said, let's wait to identify this white man before we do something we might regret. We will find out who he is.'

He rose from his seat and placed his feet in his tattered *cheppals*. He took his shoulder cloth from the chair and wound it round his head. Then he set off for work as a night watchman in the zamindar's fields.

Taking this as a sign that the meeting was over, the other villagers departed one by one, into their huts. Soon the lamps were out and silence crept into every corner of the area, where it settled for the night.

Anjali, stretched out in her rope cot, watched the stars and the flickering fireflies through a hole in the wall. All this was new to her. Never had she been involved so closely with the poor and been able to observe their lives. As she began to understand the difficulties and sufferings of these innocent and simple people, she also understood how different their lives were from how she had lived with her father and her husband. The truth shocked her. What would they do next? What would be the consequences of any action they took, especially if they chose violence? What would happen to the younger ones like Samba? Lost in the troubles of others, she stopped thinking about herself. She turned over and looked with concern and tenderness at the boy lying fast asleep next to his grandmother.

Chapter 33

For the past week, ever since he had come to Roypuram, Saleem had redoubled his efforts to find Anjali, but no one could give him any information. He was puzzled because he wasn't met with people shaking their heads, but with a kind of blankness, as if everyone he asked was avoiding his questions. Then he met Samba, Venkat's servant boy. The boy was fascinated by the jeep and visited the dock-bungalow every morning just to admire the motorised vehicle. He had never seen one before. He offered to polish it, and while he did so he bombarded Saleem with technical questions about how the engine worked and the mechanics of the gears and the breaks. They got on well. Saleem was generous with his time and the boy was relaxed in his company. He thought about asking Samba about Anjali, and waited and chose his moment when the boy was occupied with greasing some part of the car's engine.

'Have you noticed a new girl in this village by any chance?' he asked casually.

'A new girl?' Samba scratched his head.

'I mean, has anyone come to this village recently and stayed?'

'Not recently, but a girl called Anjali came to live in Mohini's house about a year ago.'

Hearing her name, Saleem's heart skipped a beat and he found he was breathing hard. He gripped Samba's shoulders and said, 'Are you sure her name is Anjali?'

'Yes. Why? Do you know her?'

'Is she very pretty with big eyes and long hair?'

'Yes. That sounds like Anjali. Everyone around here says she is a beautiful girl.'

For a long moment Saleem was silent. He had to sit down to give himself time to gain some self-control so that Samba would not suspect anything. How long had he waited for someone to say these words to him?

'Yes,' he finally replied, trying to stop his voice trembling. 'She comes from my own village. She was my childhood friend.'

Much as he wanted to pursue this conversation, time was getting on and Saleem needed to attend to his other work for Mr Robert. He left Samba by the jeep and went on his way. He tried very hard to control his excitement while he carried out his morning tasks – preparing Mr Robert's breakfast, laying out his clothes so that they were ready when he came out of the bathroom, and spreading the newspapers on the table. All the while Saleem's thoughts were elsewhere and he found it difficult to concentrate. After Mr Robert had eaten, Saleem drove him almost in silence to the building site, and then went off on his own to collect letters from the post office and to post some important papers that Mr Robert had asked him to take care of. The day passed slowly. Much too slowly. When evening fell, Saleem drove Mr Robert back to the guest house, again saying very little.

The *punkha* coolie, who squatted outside Mr Robert's bedroom and whose task it was to pull the rope to set the heavy cloth fan swinging, was asleep at his post. So too was the gatekeeper in his chamber near the gate. The night was cool. Except for the noise of the crickets and the occasional distant dog barking, it was silent. Peace reigned, but in his cot on the front veranda, Saleem couldn't sleep for anticipation and excitement.

He got out of bed without making any noise and climbed a flight of stone steps leading to the flat rooftop. Leaning on the parapet wall, he looked out at the serene lake and the sleeping village under the starlit night. The thought of Anjali asleep in one of those houses, not far from where he now stood, was momentous. Was it really true?

'Anjali-ji, how are you?' he asked the stars.

'You can't imagine the relief I feel to know that perhaps soon I will see you again,' he said to the lake.

Then came the question, 'Who is this Mohini?'

He stayed under the canopy of stars for a very long time, thinking about the past and wondering about the present and dreaming about the future, until the fields on the other side of the lake grew hazy, and until the stars started to fade. Unable to find answers, and knowing that he could ask Samba in the morning, he finally left his lookout post and went to bed. Sleep came instantly and as a welcome friend.

'Saleem *bhayya…*'

He thought the wind was whispering his name.

'Saleem *bhayya…*'

He heard it again. When he opened his eyes, Samba was there outside the gate, peeping through the metal bars. Realising that he had overslept, Saleem leaped out of bed.

Soon Samba was polishing the jeep, which was already gleaming, and Saleem took an opportunity to drop his questions into the conversation.

'So, who is Mohini *dorsani?*'

Samba moved closer to Saleem and whispered, 'She is the zamindar's courtesan.'

'A courtesan!'

Unable to hide his embarrassment, Saleem bent to look under the jeep, as if searching for a problem, while he came to terms with what Samba had just told him. In the village where Saleem and Anjali had lived, courtesans had been talked about in whispered voices and with shame. They were called 'fallen women'. A courtesan was not respectable. But Anjali… Having made up his mind, he stood up. 'I would very much like to see Anjali. Would it be possible?'

Samba thought this through for a while before replying, 'It would have been very difficult when she was living in Mohini's house but now that she is staying with us, I think it would be possible for you to see her. I don't know. Perhaps you should arrange to meet her when everyone is at work.'

'Good idea,' Saleem said, relishing the thought of finding Anjali alone so that they could talk in confidence. He had to hear her side of the story before he made any rash judgements. 'When would be the best time?'

'Tomorrow afternoon? I will come here and take you to see her.'

'Thank you, Samba. I am grateful for your help.' Saleem shook the boy's hand with heartfelt gratitude.

When the boy had left, Saleem silently went over this new information. Anjali living with a courtesan? The thought was shocking. If a girl as beautiful as Anjali had been living under a courtesan's roof for more than a year then the zamindar's eyes must have already sought her out and… He shut his eyes, unable to dispel the unthinkable. Perhaps it wasn't Anjali but another young woman with the same name? That might be preferable. Or would it? Saleem didn't know what would be worse – to have found someone with the same name, or to have found his own Anjali living in disgraceful circumstances. Doubts and hopes followed one another in rapid succession until he leaned on the jeep, too dizzy to think any more.

Chapter 34

That night, when they all sat down for their evening meal, Samba announced that he had some good news for them.

'What is it?' Anjali and Rangi asked in chorus.

Adding a pinch of salt and some green chillies and onion to his cornmeal porridge to keep them in suspense, he said, 'Guess.' he was enjoying teasing them.

'I know. Has Venkat-saar decided to pay you an extra *paisa*?' Rangi's face lit up.

'No.' Samba shook his head.

Rangi's smile vanished and she sighed heavily. She didn't bother to ask him anything else. They got on with their meal in silence.

Anjali felt sorry for Rangi. She looked at her bowl of cornmeal porridge which was their evening meal almost every day. Sometimes they ate it with red chilli and garlic paste, other times with a green chilli and a piece of onion. The lumpy porridge and the heat of the chilli gave her heartburn and indigestion, but when she realised that this food was all they could afford, she ate it. During the day Mohini's cook served them leftover rice and lentils, for which she was grateful. Very rarely, if Samba received an extra *paisa* because Venkat-saar was pleased with his services, his grandmother would go to the market and buy them a treat – a finely made sweet *laddu* or fresh *jilebi*, spiral pastry soaked in sugar syrup.

'The good news is not for you, *avva*. it is for Anjali-*akka*,' the boy said at last.

'For me?' Anjali was surprised.

'Yes,' Samba smiled.

'What is it?'

'I'm not telling you. You have to guess.'

'Oh, come on Samba, don't drag it so much. Tell us what it is,' Rangi frowned.

He smiled at Anjali, his eyes twinkling. 'Someone is coming to see you tomorrow.'

There was a moment of surprised silence, followed by another chorus: 'Who?'

He opened his mouth to speak but at that precise moment, Lachi, Mohini's personal maid, came through the open doorway, calling for Anjali.

'What is it, Lachi?'

'Mohini has sent me to fetch Anjali. She wants her immediately.'

'Now? Why?' Rangi asked. 'We're in the middle of eating.'

'I don't know,' Lachi sighed, sitting on the floor next to Samba. 'Just a minute ago the zamindar sent a message to Mohini. I think he wants Anjali to dance tomorrow in his palace.'

Unable to speak, with her heart drumming against her chest, Anjali stared at the woman wide-eyed.

'What is the urgency?' Rangi asked, putting a protective arm around Anjali.

'I think the zamindar is going to invite that Englishman to his palace tomorrow and he wants Anjali to dance as part of the welcoming ceremony.'

'Oh no!' Anjali let out a scream. 'Please, please tell her my… my hair hasn't grown yet.'

Lachi looked at her with sympathy. 'I'm afraid you won't get out of it that way. Mohini knows how to attach a fake extension to your hair. It's long enough now. Her hairdresser is skilled at that. I've seen her do it before.'

'I don't want to dance,' Anjali said quietly.

'Well, perhaps we can think up an excuse on the way, but you had better come now before Mohini gets angry with both of us.'

With great reluctance and dread, Anjali followed Lachi out of the hut. At the door she turned back to Samba, giving him a questioning look, but he shook his head, telling her that this wasn't the news that he had been going to give her.

Chapter 35

Mr Robert was relaxing in his chair on the veranda, quietly engrossed in *Young India*. Sitting on the bottom step of the same veranda, Saleem watched with somewhat jaded curiosity as Venkat, at the head of a party of noisy villagers, approached the gates. Close behind Venkat came the important members of the village holding gold-capped walking sticks and looking fierce behind their long upturned moustaches and dressed in their white *dhotis* and silk *kurtas* with gold buttons. Their pointed shoes were richly embroidered. Behind them walked a group of female servants in colourful *saris* and veils, who held silver trays with brightly lit oil lamps and garlands of flowers, while the males in red and gold and turbans carried banners bearing Mr Robert's name and words of welcome. Though misspelt, the words were in English. A blue and gold uniformed band came next, playing the usual welcoming tunes. Bringing up the rear was a heavily decorated elephant draped in a velvet cover with tiny mirrors and beads that sparkled in the sun. This was the traditional escort that accompanied Mr Robert to the zamindar's palace. Saleem sighed. He had seen this kind of thing before and felt it rang a false note of luxury and arrogance on the part of the zamindar.

The commotion interrupted Mr Robert, who tossed aside his magazine and jumped to his feet. Saleem could tell that even though his master was expecting somebody to collect him, he had not imagined anything on this scale. The pomp and grandeur must have amazed him. Saleem wondered if Mr Robert would enjoy it, or whether he would put on a brave face and make himself be polite so as not to cause offence.

The procession came to a halt right outside Mr Robert's veranda. Venkat climbed the steps and placed a garland over Mr Robert's head. The band stopped to allow him to speak a few cordial words on behalf of the zamindar to this visiting Englishman

Some of the villagers had seen Mr Robert on his previous visit, but for many, this was their first sight of a white English man and they found it hard to contain their excitement. Many pairs of eyes stared at Mr Robert in wonderment. They stared at him as if they were seeing a strange specimen from another world. Samba peeled away from the others and proudly walked towards the jeep, showing it off to his friends. For his age group, the car was much more fascinating than any white man, wherever he came from.

Even while talking to the engineer sahib, Vekant's eyes too often turned towards the jeep. Noticing Venkat's curiosity, Mr Robert asked him to please dismiss the elephant, and suggested that Venkat and his assistant Samba accompany him in his jeep. His invitation was met with delighted acceptance.

Saleem drove Mr Robert, Venkat and Samba through the grand gates of the palace, but his thoughts were very much elsewhere. He should have been seeing this short ride through his employer's eyes and wondering how he felt, but for Saleem there was a much more dramatic moment ahead. His heart pounded. He couldn't help but smile to himself. In a few minutes he would be free to go with Samba to meet Anjali. Would she be happy to see him? Of course she would. He must make arrangements to remove her from this place soon. But would she leave all this luxury behind her to be with him? He thought of an urgent question for Samba, who was sitting next him, but was mystified when Samba turned his gaze away. He needed to be patient. He waited for an appropriate moment, when Mr Robert and Venkat were immersed in a conversation about politics, and said to the boy, 'Samba, remember you are taking me to meet Anjali today.'

Samba looked down guiltily as if he had committed a crime and said, 'Sorry, bhayya, she is not staying in our house anymore.'

'What do you mean?' Saleem's hands shook the steering wheel so hard that the car swerved slightly. Fortunately no one noticed. Nor did they notice that his mouth was open in shock and disappointment. His driving continued to be somewhat erratic.

'Sorry,' Samba repeated. 'She is with Mohini again now.'

'Why did she go back?' Saleem's foot pressed the accelerator too hard.

'What could she do? It was Mohini's order.' The boy sounded close to tears. 'But... you will see her tonight.' Now what was the boy saying?

'Where?' Saleem asked, not caring now whether the men in the back heard him or not.

'She will be dancing here on the podium of the palace.'

'She will be doing... what?'

Anjali was surely not a dancer? Not a dancer in a zamindar's palace? Saleem's long-cherished hope that he would find her as he had left her, a respectable woman, was cruelly crushed by this latest news. Surely it was not true. Samba must be wrong.

Saleem managed to slow the jeep to manoeuvre it through the palace gates and kept it gliding smoothly before coming to a halt in front of the main entrance. The zamindar himself came down with out-stretched arms, smiling broadly, to invite the first white man to grace his village into his palace. He garlanded the engineer sahib and shook hands with him in the English manner. The band played the welcoming tunes once again. The zamindar himself led Mr Robert to a throne in a vast room of immense grandeur whose walls were decorated with ancient, gold-framed paintings, life-sized portraits, and the prized heads of wild animals that the zamindar and his ancestors had shot while hunting.

After driving the jeep out of the main palace, and parking it in its designated place, Saleem looked at Samba. Any anger he had felt vanished as he saw the thin, vulnerable teenager and understood that he was expecting far too much from someone of his age. He needed to pose his questions more gently.

'Is there anyone who might help Anjali to leave this place?'

'You know how it is here, bhayya!'

'Of course.' Saleem understood perfectly well that all the servants would be frightened even to approach Anjali with any kind of assistance in case they were caught and punished by the zamindar. He knew there was no way he could even send a message to her through Samba – that would only get Samba into trouble. Saleem had already seen the marks of the thrashings on his body from his previous punishment, the criss-cross lines on his back still visible. Even though the wounds had healed, the skin on the injured parts was thick and pale.

Saleem knew that the zamindari system was established centuries ago as a kind of feudal order, introduced by the Mughals. The zamindars were employed to collect money from the peasants, but many of them abused their power by imposing unnecessary and very high taxes. When the peasants couldn't pay the revenue, the zamindars used violence to take their lands as punishment. That was the reason why people like Samba's grandmother became so poor and the zamindars became richer and richer, owning thousands of acres of land. Saleem wasn't surprised that the practice still continued, even under British rule. He had expected far too much of Samba and had not thought hard enough about the risks that he might have exposed him to in asking him to take him to Anjali.

He smiled at the boy and ruffled his hair. 'Go and meet up with your friends,' he said. 'I don't need any more help, thank you.' He hoped he was not disobeying Venkat in letting the boy go. Anyway, he could explain.

After Samba got out of the jeep and ran proudly towards the other boys his age, Saleem collapsed in his seat feeling utterly helpless. He couldn't do anything now except wait until evening, until Anjali had finished her dance. And there would be no immediate opportunity to rescue her then – after all, she did not even know that he was there. Unable to think of any solution, Saleem leaned back and rubbed his brow in frustration.

Chapter 36

Once again, and very reluctantly, Anjali sat motionless in front of a mirror while the beautician, with the help of Kalyani, took charge of making her ready for this most special of occasions. The room spun. Anjali was unable to focus on anything due to fear and anxiety. Her emotions mirrored the feelings she had on Ranjit's funeral day. Her dread now was almost as overwhelming as the knowledge that they were going to burn her alive, lying alongside her dead husband. She knew that in a few hours' time her life was going to be turned upside down. Again. As if she hadn't gone through enough already.

A rumour had been whispered in the huts and around the grounds that the zamindar was planning on selling her to the Englishman who had arrived in the village. Anjali had picked up the words on the breeze and had trembled. Was it true or not? If it was, the consequences that might follow from her dancing before Mr Robert that evening were unthinkable. She would be a prisoner, sold as a slave or a concubine. Her life would be unbearable, her existence no longer her own.

Mohini had woven a tight web around her, like a spider burying a fly deep in its thread. How could she escape from her predicament? There was no one to help her or to rescue her now. Not even Kalyani. It was a miracle that she had escaped the funeral pyre last year, but miracles only happen once, her father used to say.

'*Pita-ji…*' She closed her eyes as longing for her father engulfed her. It was painful to be so far from him, and even more so in the shameful situation that she found herself in now. Her father would feel such disgrace. He would be so disappointed in her.

Suddenly she saw him. He was there and his fingers reached out to wipe away her tears. He smiled at her reassuringly and showed no anger, and nodded as if to tell her that there was still hope. Her mother was there too, a shadowy figure behind him, smiling gently. Anjali sighed with relief and experienced feelings of calm and peace that had not been in her heart for many months. She breathed more slowly. Her heart quietened. She could face whatever lay before her.

'Anjali! Keep your head straight so that I can attach this hair piece.' The beautician interrupted the joy of Anjali's vision, and with her mundane words, her father and the shadow of her mother faded and were gone. She blinked, trying to bring them back, wanting to reach out and touch them. But she was back in the present, back in this difficult day when her fate might be sealed – and with those thoughts, her hopes dwindled once more, replaced with despair and anguish. She gave a distraught sob.

'Anjali… what is it?' Kalyani asked her softly.

'Oh, Kalyani,' she gripped her friend's hand tightly, 'what is going to happen to me? Please… please think of a way to help me get out of this place.'

Kalyani looked helplessly at Anjali, who understood that her friend was completely at a loss. What could Kalyani possibly do to help her, when she herself lived like a prisoner? They were equally helpless. Equally at the mercy of others. Anjali could see that Kalyani knew that this time there would be no escape for her friend but could not being herself to say so bluntly. She did not want to cause pain. Instead she wiped Anjali's tears and, ignoring the other woman in the room, whispered, 'Please don't be sad, Anjali. You are a good person and I believe nothing awful will happen to you.'

Anjali nodded, knowing that Kalyani was doing the only thing she could, which was to say something kind.

The beautician entwined garlands of jasmine all along the length of the hairpiece until Anjali looked almost as she had before she had shaved her head. Moon- and sun-shaped jewels, studded with white and orange stones, were pinned on either side of her parting. The precious stones lit up against the background of her velvety black hair. Just as the beautician was putting the final touches to her make-up, Mohini entered the room.

'Kalyani,' she ordered, without sparing a greeting for Anjali, 'make sure you bring her out in five minutes. Exactly.'

Mohini's eyes swept up and down, assessing Anjali like a piece of ripe fruit on a market stall, as if looking for flaws. Her expression said that she found none. Anjali could not look at Mohini and averted her eyes in disgust.

'How can a woman inflict on another woman the same misfortune and humiliation that she herself has suffered?' Anjali thought, while reluctantly slipping into an orange costume with a black and gold border.

And then it was time to go. Kalyani led a tearful, hesitant Anjali out of the room. Her steps faltered and she stumbled along like a terrified lamb being dragged off to the slaughterhouse. Completely lacking her usual grace, she walked on to the front veranda where Mohini was waiting for her. A look of anxiety crossed the older woman's face as she saw Anjali's obvious reluctance. At the bottom of the steps, in the courtyard, a palanquin with a plum-coloured velvet cover awaited her. Anjali barely saw the mass of decoration, the mirrors and beads. She took no notice of its splendour. It meant nothing to her.

As Mohini stepped towards her, Anjali opposed her with every ounce of her will. She listened to words from deep inside, perhaps from the lips of her parents, whom she had seen at her side such a short time ago. You have to do something now, and fast, otherwise she will trap you in the zamindar's harem or you will become a slave to that Englishman for the rest of your life. Isn't it better to die than to become a slave or a concubine to either of them? Remember, you come from a respectable family and you are about to lose all respect and self-esteem. You can't let this happen to you. So… go! Go! Get out of this place. If you don't go now, you never will. This is your last opportunity. Afterwards, you won't even get the chance to commit suicide.

Something flared up and pushed her into action. She turned abruptly and knocked Mohini roughly to one side. Not listening to the screaming and shouting, or Kalyani's frantic footsteps behind her, Anjali ran as fast as she could back to her room and opened her trunk. Grabbing her *burqa*, she ran to the back yard, bolting the back door behind her. That would slow Mohini down, as she would have to run all the way round to the side door. It took all her strength, but she managed to lift a heavy stone and threw it into the well. The loud crash as it hit the water camouflaged the noise of her opening the back gate. She jumped the high step and ran and ran through the empty streets until she reached a turning which took her down a track where no one could see her. Hiding behind a wall, she slipped the *burqa* over her head and carried on walking. She walked on, dazed, not knowing where to go or which direction to take. She just kept walking.

Chapter 37

The evening was pleasant, with a slight breeze that came from the lake. The stage in the courtyard of the Gadi palace was exquisitely decorated under a canopy of interlocked coconut leaves. With countless Petromax lamps focussed on it, it shimmered bright and clear. On one side sat the musicians, in a half circle, playing a soothing evening raga.

Mr Robert was seated in a cushioned armchair, in the centre of the front row, conversing with the zamindar and his family. In the second row, on wooden chairs, were the important people of the village. Standing behind them were the villagers, who were more interested in this new white man than the dance performance.

Sitting on the floor amongst the servants, at the side of the stage, Saleem braced himself for Anjali to enter and grace the dance floor. While he waited, he ran through various plans for rescuing her but none were clear and most were impossible. His mind drifted between the past and the present. He became restless, waiting for her entrance, because he was desperate to see her. Perhaps the sight of her would clear his muddled thinking and inspire him to come up with a plan to get her out of there. Time passed very slowly. Saleem was aware that the dance should have started, but Anjali had still not appeared on the stage. The audience, noticing the time, was becoming impatient.

Finally the blue curtain was raised and the audience applauded the dancer who entered the stage, her anklets jingling. Saleem sat upright and leaned forward for a clear view of the dancer's face. His jaw dropped. The woman on the dance floor was not Anjali but a much older woman with refined features. Had Samba made a mistake in referring to this woman, who perhaps had the same name as Anjali, as a girl? He didn't think so. This woman was old enough to be Samba's mother. Confusion and relief and disappointment followed one another in rapid succession. Was it possible that Anjali was in the village, but was not a dancer? He was making wild guesses, he told himself. It was pointless speculating. The fact was that he knew nothing.

What started as a low murmur amongst a few people in the audience spread and grew until almost everyone was whispering. Saleem heard the name 'Anjali' pass from one person's lips to another's. He became alert and focussed. He listened hard. He sensed a kind of excitement. Something was going on.

'What's her name?' he asked the person next to him, gesturing at the dancer.

'Mohini.'

'Mohini?'

He searched for Samba in the audience. He hadn't seen the boy since the afternoon. In fact Samba was not far away, standing at the side of the stage, amongst a group of helpers, not watching the dance at all but scanning the audience, and staring at the important guests. When finally their eyes met, Saleem beckoned him over. There was an urgency in Saleem's gesture that Samba did not dare disobey.

'Where is Anjali?' Saleem asked as soon as the boy was within earshot.

'She has escaped!'

'What do you mean, escaped?'

'Oh, there has been a lot of drama around here. At first everyone thought Anjali had jumped into the well because we all heard a loud splashing noise. And since there weren't any men servants in the house at the time, I had to climb down into the water! Imagine. But there was nobody there and by the time I had climbed out again, and everyone realised she had run away, it was too late to run after her.' Samba looked at Saleem's face, knowing that his story would have quite an impact. At first Saleem stared straight ahead as if he hadn't heard. Then, suddenly coming to life, he grabbed Samba's hand and said quietly, 'Come with me.'

In the audience, everyone had settled down and was immersed in the skill and grace of Mohini's dance. Without disturbing anyone, and without anyone noticing, Saleem crept out, dragging Samba with him.

They didn't speak until they reached the jeep. As he climbed into the passenger seat, Samba said, 'She must have thrown a heavy object into the well to make everyone believe that she had committed suicide. It was to distract people so that she would have enough time to escape.' He paused to take a breath. 'Mohini was seething with anger. I am sure she would have killed Anjali if she had found her. However, she didn't have a chance to send out a search party because she had to get herself ready to step in for the dance.'

'What about you? Why didn't you go after Anjali?'

'What would be the point? She didn't want to dance and she hated living under Mohini's roof. I thought, "It's good that's she's got away from this place." I was pleased that she had managed it.'

'So, where do you think she would have gone?' His voice quivered with relief and anxiety.

'I have no idea, but don't worry, she couldn't have gone far. She doesn't know the way out of the village. We might find her if we go after her in your jeep.'

'Let's go.'

Knowing that Mr Robert would not need him for a while, Saleem started up the jeep. When they reached the exit, the caretaker saluted him and opened the huge gates. The jeep shot out into the road and roared away. If Saleem had not been so focussed on his driving, and had not been so intent on scanning the streets for a face he longed to see, he would have noticed that Samba was smiling broadly, enjoying this fast, crazy, unexpected ride. Saleem listened carefully as the boy directed him through every street, every bazaar and every gully of the village. Most people were at the celebrations, but a few villagers stopped and stared at the frowning man, driving much too fast, and the boy beaming with excitement, racing along the narrow roads and swerving around the tight corners.

Chapter 38

The evening light was fading fast when Anjali saw a group of women ahead, drawing drinking water from a street well. Some had picked up their heavy burdens and were on their way home, the water pots balanced on their heads. Since a Muslim woman was a rare sight in that part of the village, they all turned to look at her. Her heart pounded and she felt hot but she was too scared even to lift her hand to wipe the beads of sweat that covered her forehead. Even though she was wearing a *burqa*, she was terrified that someone would recognise her. The faster she walked, the more her legs trembled.

She was forced to stop in a narrow lane by a herd of cattle. The bells around their necks tinkled as the cowherds made them run faster by twisting their tails. Pressing her back to the wall of a house, she waited for them to pass, but an old woman, who was gathering the cow dung left behind them, smiled at her and asked, 'What is the matter, *begum sahiba*? What are you doing here? If you are looking for the alchemist, he lives in that street.' She pointed in the direction of the astrologer's house.

Anjali nodded in response. She was relieved that the woman didn't ask any more questions. Knowing that it was impossible to walk unnoticed around the village, even hiding under her veil, she decided that she had to find a hiding place very soon and stay there, at least until the village was asleep. But on this day of celebrations, the village wasn't going to sleep until midnight. By now, the whole village must have gathered at the Gadi palace to see the rare sight of the Englishman and the entertainments that would follow. On she walked on to the Brahmin street, where the astrologer lived.

Checking over her shoulder once more in case she was being followed, she walked with frantic steps towards the astrologer's gate. In the faint light of the crescent moon, through the grille, she could see a woman placing a clay lamp in the alcove of the porch. She put her hand on the gate and gently pushed it. As it opened, it squeaked. The young woman turned round at the sound and pulled her *sari pallu* over her face.

'Who is it?'

Recognising the astrologer's daughter, Sita, Anjali spoke. 'Could I see the astrologer, please?'

'He is not at home now,' Sita answered, climbing down the steps towards Anjali.

'When will he be back?'

'Begum sahiba?' Sita was surprised to see a Muslim woman at that time of the day. 'He won't be back until tomorrow afternoon.'

'Oh, no.' Anjali couldn't help herself. It was too hard a blow.

'Why, is it urgent?' Sita asked, hearing the fear and panic in the other woman's voice.

'Yes. I desperately need his help.'

Sita opened the gate slightly. 'Are you not well? Come in and tell me what's wrong and I will see if I can give you something from my father's medicine box.'

'Thank you.' Anjali folded her hands together in gratitude.

Knowing that no one from the other castes was allowed to enter a Brahmin's house, Anjali normally would have waited at the bottom of the steps, but, terrified that someone from the street might recognise her in the light of the oil lamp, she climbed up to the veranda and crouched down in the shadow of a pillar inside the archway while

Sita went to fetch the medicine box.

Now what was she going to do? It was impossible to stay in the village until the next evening without someone finding her. Was it safe to reveal her identity to Sita? Would she, a woman as helpless as herself, be able to do anything for her? All kinds of dreadful possibilities crowded into her mind as she sat crouched on the floor of the veranda, making herself as small and as invisible as possible. Her head throbbed and she had a blinding headache. Leaning back against the pillar, she closed her eyes and waited.

*

'Anjali... Anjali...'

Someone was calling her with a voice that was soft and gentle. Who was it? At first, forgetting where she was, she thought it was Mohini. But no. Nor was it her step-mother. Perhaps it was her own mother? Why couldn't she see her? Her head swam.

'Anjali...'

The voice again, but this time with the sound came a cool splash of water on her face. She woke with a start. As her vision cleared, she saw an anxious Sita bending over her, concern etched on her face.

'Are you all right?' Sita put a glass of water to Anjali's parched lips.

She nodded, grateful for the cool liquid that slid down her throat. 'Sorry to trouble you...'

'No, no, not at all, but tell me,' she gestured at the *burqa*, 'why are you wearing this?'

Anjali's trembling hands went up to her head as she realised that her face was visible. She gathered up the veil that Sita had removed to splash water on her face, ready to put it on again.

'I thought that you were dancing in the palace this evening?' Sita said.

'Please...' Anjali let the silky material slide from her fingers, and, folding her palms together, pleaded, 'Please help me...' Tears welled up in her enormous eyes.

After only a moment of hesitation, Sita placed a hand on Anjali's shoulder and helped her to her feet. 'Come inside, and tell me what has happened.'

Chapter 39

It was already late into the night and Saleem had searched every street, pathway and gully, but Anjali was nowhere to be found. Desolated, disappointed and worried, Saleem dropped Samba home and returned to the palace to resume his duties. When he heard Mr Robert offering Venkat a lift, he cursed his employer under his breath because it meant yet more driving and more time-wasting.

As he drove through the empty streets of the village, his hope of finding Anjali fading, his rage and anger mounted. He hated himself, he hated Mr Robert, and he hated his lack of freedom. If only he didn't have to take Mr Robert home he could have searched the forest and neighbouring villages, and who knows, he might have found her. Saleem never lost hope, although at times it was almost impossible to remain positive. He looked in the rear-view mirror and saw Mr Robert fully immersed in a conversation with Venkat. Even though it was night, in the faint streak of moonlight, their faces, one white and one dark, were still visible – more so Mr Robert's. The old familiar bitter feelings of hatred for the man and his race, emotions that he thought he had suppressed, welled up inside him. He loathed himself for serving a man who belonged to a race that had come to rule his country and rob every ordinary man like himself of his freedom and independence. If he had not gone to that peaceful meeting to discuss the plight of Indian people, if he hadn't, like hundreds of others, been shot at while penned like an animal in a cage, if the soldiers had not been ordered to fire on civilians, if he had not been injured… remembering the brutality and atrocities were casually inflicted by the soldiers, he had no doubt that the colonial government was to blame for his separation from Anjali. And much, much more besides. That night, many lives were lost and ruined. For what? For a desire to discuss the situation in their own country.

With mounting anger he banged his foot on the accelerator, and the jeep leaped forward with such force that the men in the back seat were jolted hard and stopped talking.

'What's the matter, Saleem?' Mr Robert's voice, still calm and soothing, reached him and brought him to his senses. He eased his foot from the accelerator.

The jeep was bouncing along the ruts in the mud road from the outskirts of the village to the guest house. They passed the temple and heard a band playing. Saleem stopped to give way to a wedding procession. Mr Robert leaned from his window to look with curiosity at the bride and groom in the palanquin. In the bright light of Petromax lamps, the couple were clearly visible. The child bride, barely eight, looked exhausted. She was falling asleep, her head nodding forward on to her chest. The groom, perhaps in his late thirties, looked elated. Mr Robert stared in disbelief and dismay.

Once the procession had passed and Saleem had restarted the jeep, Mr Robert asked Venkat, 'Supposing you had a daughter, at what age would you arrange her marriage?'

'At five… at seven… and I must marry her before she reaches the age of nine,' Venkat answered without hesitation.

'And if you didn't, what would happen?'

'What would happen?' He repeated the question as if it puzzled him. The answer was obvious. 'My whole community would cast me out. None of them will dine with me or invite me to any ceremony. No one will consider my sons as possible bride grooms for their daughters. I will be isolated and spurned and looked down on to the end of my life. And when I die, no one from my caste will offer to carry my body on their shoulders to the burning-ghat.'

'And the girl herself, what would happen to her? If she were not married?'

'The girl? According to our customs, when she reaches maturity I must turn her out of my house and send her alone into the forest. There I must leave her for the wild beasts.' He paused a little before adding, 'You see, she is considered even lower than a widow.'

Mr Robert sounded shocked. 'But surely it is the parents' responsibility to look after their own children? How could anyone do that to their own daughter?'

Venkat sighed. 'The parents look after the sons and the Gods look after the daughters.'

'Is this the reason why the death rate for females is so much higher than the death rate for males?' asked Mr Robert.

'It's all in god's hands,' replied Venkat.

'But isn't the practice of burning a widow illegal today? *Suttee* was forbidden by the British government some twenty years ago.'

'But Mr Robert, sir, re-marrying a widow is impossible. Marriage is not a personal affair but a social and religious agreement. That is how we regard it.'

'I gather the zamindar's son is in Oxford now, studying law. Supposing he met a widow and fell in love with her, might he decide to marry such a woman, having seen the way we live in Britain?'

'No,' Venkat replied without hesitation. 'If he married even a virgin widow, it would make the headlines even in the reformed newspapers. It would be impossible.'

'Don't you think forcing widowhood upon little girls is a cruel thing to do?' Mr Robert asked. Listening in, Saleem picked up both his master's shock at hearing about such outdated customs and his reluctance to offend Venkat. 'Recently I looked at those doctrines of the *shastras* and *upanishads* and the *bhagavad-gita*, but none of them advocates this kind of widowhood. Personally, I think it was imposed by a man who misinterpreted the doctrines and customs long ago. Don't you think it degrades your religion?'

'No, no, sir, it doesn't, because these are the age-old traditions and wise rules set by our great ancestors, which we must respect and obey.'

'Do you know, a newspaper reported that even Mr Gandhi said that marriage is a tragedy for these young girls? He condemned it. He tirelessly questions old teachings that are kept alive simply by the sheer force of custom, unquestioned and accepted without thought for the victims. He observed that in India even the most ignorant and worthless men enjoy a superiority over women which they do not deserve and shouldn't have.'

'Please, sir, we want no more of Gandhi's doctrines. He is a deluded man.'

Hearing this conversation, and listening to the humanity expressed by his master, Saleem's heart again warmed towards Mr Robert, while his blood boiled at Venkat's answers. How dare the man insult Mahatma? What does he know about Gandhi's teachings to say that? He wanted to turn round and shout at him. If only, if only Anjali's father had waited, at least until she was a teenager, or if he had arranged a marriage to a younger man, things would have been so different for her now. Her life would not have been the endless trauma that it was.

Chapter 40

In a modest room, lying side by side on straw mats, Anjali and Sita talked for most of the night, Anjali unburdening her troubles, Sita revealing what it was like for her to live as a young widow. And what her life had been before.

'I was only five when I got married,' said Sita. 'I don't even remember the marriage ceremony. He was a widowed cousin, fifteen years older than me. His first wife had died in childbirth.'

'Was he kind to you?'

'I don't know. I don't even remember his face...' Sita turned to look at Anjali.

'So, how long were you married before you... you know?'

'Perhaps a year. He died of malaria. I still remember the afternoon it happened. I was playing in the back garden and my mother came out crying, followed by my father and grandparents. She took me into her arms, hugged me tight to her chest and howled like a wounded animal. I remember this, because I had never heard such heart-wrenching cries before or after in my life. She just clung to me, and wouldn't let anyone take me from her. She yelled at my grandparents and my father for rushing to get her only daughter married so young.

'After that... after that... when she saw me living like this, she was heartbroken and lost the will to live. She never recovered. I lost her six months later.' Sita's voice shook and, overwhelmed by emotion, she couldn't continue.

'I am sorry, Sita…' Anjali had tears on her own cheeks. She didn't have the heart to press Sita further about her personal circumstances, so she stared into the darkness for a long time, knowing Sita too was lying there lost in her own thoughts. They had so much in common. Each understood what the other had gone through and they felt sympathy for each other.

After a long silence, Sita whispered, 'At least my father hasn't got married again. It must be horrible to have a step-mother like yours.'

'Yes, it was difficult.'

And so they started talking again, not just about their own situations but about those of others like them, finding always that they thought the same way, until they felt that they had known each other all their lives. Two gentle women, two kindred spirits whose fates had dealt them a similarly cruel hand.

'I don't think it's safe for you to stay here tomorrow, because during the day the house swarms with students, patients and other people who come to see my father,' Sita said with concern.

'Yes, I know.'

'But don't worry, in the morning you could come with me to the temple and stay there until my father returns home.'

Anjali nodded. Then she said, 'But people will come there as well.'

'Not into the store room. Not without my permission. I think we should go there very early in the morning, I mean around 4 am, before the village wakes up, and we should walk there separately.'

Anjali nodded, grateful for her friend's kindness. 'Now try to get some sleep. At least an hour or two.' Sita yawned and stretched out.

Within minutes Anjali knew, by her regular breathing, that Sita had fallen asleep. But her troubled mind didn't grant her sleep that easily. Anjali watched Sita as her chest rose and fell under the threadbare cover. She observed how terribly slender she was – the result of a widow's diet of one bland meal a day. Her gaze lingered on her shaved head; she touched her own thick hair, remembering what a bare scalp had felt like. She saw the coarse white *sari* that was the only garment Sita was allowed to wear now, in the future, and until the day she died. Most of all she looked at her face. It was so young, so vulnerable, so innocent. What had this girl done to deserve such a hard life? Anjali felt the injustice more for Sita than for herself. Yet they shared the same fate. Widowhood had made them invisible. They had neither hope nor freedom, nor any kind of a future. They had both lost their mothers when babies. Now they were victims of religious rules written long ago by some bigoted man and not questioned or over-turned even today, in this modern age. Anger replaced pity as Anjali watched this sleeping child – because that was what she was – a young woman unfortunate enough to be widowed before she had started growing up. It was wrong, Anjali thought. Horribly wrong. Even though Sita's father was one of the more powerful men in the village, even he did not dare disobey the traditions and customs, even to help his own daughter. Again came the same question: Why should a widowed woman have to endure so much pain while a widower could pick up the pieces of his life and re-marry within three months of his wife's death? No one seemed to be able to provide a convincing answer. So far all she got was simple platitudes. 'This is her karma' or 'She must have sinned in her previous life'. How come being born female was a punishment for what one did in one's previous life? Was that true? Did that mean that no man had ever committed a sin in his previous life? Was that why men were so chauvinistic? It was convenient, wasn't it, for the men to forget that they wouldn't exist without a female, a mother? Each question produced another until Anjali's head was spinning. In the end, with none of them resolved, she closed her eyes and finally drifted into an uneasy asleep.

Sita woke her early next morning and as planned they walked separately to the temple. After letting Anjali into the store room,

Sita got on with her chores around the temple and in the room that adjoined the store room, where the altar was.

There was a wooden chest in that room that contained all the costumes and jewellery for the deities. Light from a tiny window was just sufficient to illuminate two medium-sized wooden chests and a couple of tin boxes which held everything that was needed for the *pooja*, the prayer. The alcoves were stuffed with camphor, incense sticks and cotton wicks. In a corner was a large basket, filled with flowers that Sita picked fresh each day from the temple garden. Their heavy scent filled the room. Anjali understood that Sita's duty was to get everything ready for the prayer, before her father entered the temple every morning.

Behind the closed doors Anjali could hear Sita cleaning the inner temple, the splashing sound suggesting that she was washing the deities before the temporary priest, a Brahmin boy, who was also a student of Sita's father, arrived. Soon he was there too; Anjali could hear him chanting the *mantras* of the morning prayer. The powerful words contained in the precise, rhythmic melody soothed her nerves. Then, the buzz of hushed voices and the soft tread of many footsteps told her that the temple was gradually filling with devotees. The morning was beginning.

It was several hours before Sita reappeared, bringing the offerings, and some bananas and coconut pieces for Anjali. 'Please have some,' she said, leaving the plate on the floor. 'I must go home now.'

Anjali nodded, but Sita saw the fear in her eyes. 'Don't worry, I will come again this evening with my father. I am sure he will help you.'

'Thank you, Sita-*amma*.' Anjali's eyes misted over with gratitude for her new friend.

And then the door closed and all was silent. She listened as one by one the devotees left until she imagined herself alone in the temple. She shivered with fear, very aware of her solitude in that place. There she was, shut in a store cupboard in a temple with only the faint hope

that the astrologer might be able to help her. There was absolutely
nothing to do but wait for evening to arrive.

Chapter 41

Saleem was watching the labourers, not really engaging with what they were doing. The workmen were completing the job of site clearance by removing the vegetation and excavating the earth down to more solid ground. Male workers had already started laying the foundations by placing large stones in the cavity they had dug. The women coolies were sitting next to a mountain of rocks, hammering them into small fragments. Saleem's eyes stared at all the activity but his mind registered none of it. What a bitter blow if he had completely lost Anjali again! He had already searched every corner of the place. Feeling trapped and frustrated, he stood waiting for an appropriate moment to ask Mr Robert for a few days' leave so he could go on yet another search mission.

Mr Robert was sitting on a chair under the shade of a huge *banyan* tree, reviewing the drawings before he surveyed the position of the road. The contractor stood waiting for him to approve the work.

The whole area was filled with the sound of metal hammers hitting the huge rocks the men had brought down from the side of the mountain. The air was thick with white dust. There was an urgency and excitement amongst the coolies. Many of them were the poorest of the poor, the untouchables, and work was a godsend for them. They didn't question the conditions or the pay.

One man was filling the gaps between the stones with rock chips mixed with a porridge of mud and water. A heavy bulldozer then rolled over the pebbles to press them down into the ground to seal them in and make a reasonably even surface. It was monotonous work. Saleem had been aware of the tedium of it ever since he had started working for Mr Robert.

A piercing scream disturbed the familiar, rhythmic sounds and at once Saleem was on his feet and running towards the already gathering crowd. A man was lying face down on the ground, his legs crushed under a huge rock. Blood ran in rivulets from his wounds into the dust. Mr Robert threw down his papers and ran. He ordered Saleem to bring the first aid kit from the jeep. Everyone stopped what they were doing to stare at the injured worker. His agonised screams reached a shrill and shocking pitch. Next to him, on her knees, his wife, another site worker, was wringing her hands and wailing. No one knew what to do. Soon the whole village was there to witness the freak accident. Saleem, with help from some of the stronger men, moved the heavy rock off the injured man's legs. Mr Robert bent down and started to clean the gashes but he saw the severity of the injuries where the stone had crushed both feet and knew that there was little he could do. The man needed medical attention. Mr Robert managed to staunch the flow of blood by tying bandages round the man's ankles and he covered his feet as best he could, but it was clearly a temporary measure. Shooing everyone away, Mr Robert ordered his men to carry the worker to the shade of a tree.

'Saleem!' Mr Robert called.

'Yes, sir.' Saleem understood, and took the keys from his pocket.

Mr Robert turned to the other men, and said in Hindi, 'Lift him gently on to the jeep. We will take him to the mission hospital in Harikonda city.'

'No!' screamed the man's wife. 'Not that far,' she pleaded, her hands folded together. 'Please, sir, take him to the alchemist first.'

Someone shouted from the crowd, 'No one who goes to the city hospital comes back alive.'

'No, that's not true,' Mr Robert said, but he glanced anxiously at Saleem.

'All right, all right, we will do whatever is best.' Saleem lifted his arms to calm the villagers.

Then someone else shouted, 'The alchemist is not in the village.'

That was the news they needed. Saleem and Mr Robert were able to move things on and get the other workers to accept their decision. There was no other choice.

As the men lifted the injured man on to the back seat of the jeep, his wife and a few other villagers climbed in too and crouched on the remaining seats and the floor. Mr Robert tried for a while longer to talk to the hysterical crowd but soon gave in. They would not listen. Anyway, it was more important to get the man to hospital. He climbed into the passenger seat and nodded to Saleem to get going. Saleem leaned on the horn to clear the way, because people were running all round the car and racing after it. Then he put his foot down hard on the accelerator.

Later, Saleem couldn't help but admire the way Mr Robert had dealt with the incident, both in his treatment of the injured man, and in his efforts to quell the distressed crowd. Not only did he accompany the untouchable to the hospital, he personally asked the doctor to take good care of the patient.

'Of course, sir.' The Indian doctor felt honoured that a white man was almost pleading with him instead of arrogantly giving him orders. This white man actually seemed to care about his injured worker.

After thanking the physician, Mr Robert turned to the injured labourer to try to reassure him. 'Don't worry, the doctor will take care of you and you will feel better soon.' He took the man's hand in his. 'We will come and see you again on Sunday.'

Despite his pain, and with tears of gratitude in his eyes, the man saluted the engineer sahib. Mr Robert handed a bundle of bank notes to the man's wife for food and other expenses. Visibly moved, the woman made the traditional gesture of respect and gratitude by touching the ground at Mr Robert's feet. Saleem knew she wouldn't actually touch the engineer sahib's feet because she was an untouchable. Not many upper-class people would have accompanied an ordinary worker like that. Saleem looked with renewed respect at this very special Englishman.

By the time they left the hospital it was late in the afternoon. As Saleem had expected, Mr Robert wanted to visit Miss Edwina since they had come so far into the city. As always when they entered the British locality, with tree-lined, wide roads and neat rows of huge colonial houses, Saleem felt that he was stepping into a completely different world. The contrast was enormous. Even the sun was not as fierce and the wind blew more gently.

When they reached the gates of Mr Robert's whitewashed villa, Saleem spotted Mr Vincent's car in the driveway. He drew to a halt beside the gleaming Hillman. Remembering what he had witnessed at the party when Miss Edwina was drunk and almost unconscious in Mr Vincent's arms, he felt very uneasy and anticipated trouble. This unexpected visitor must have surprised Mr Robert too because before Saleem managed to get out to open the engineer sahib's door, Mr Robert had already let himself out. It was at that precise moment that a smug-looking Vincent came out on to the veranda, followed by a giggling Miss Edwina. Her pale blue dress shimmered in the sun and her light brown fringe blew about her face in the breeze. Her eyes were shining, her skin silken, and she looked more attractive than ever. Saleem bitterly noted how happiness could change a woman's looks, because Miss Edwina positively glowed. There was no protecting his master, who saw everything just as he, Saleem, saw it.

'Hello there, Vincent.' Mr Robert strode towards them.

Colour drained from Mr Vincent's face as he extended his hand. 'How nice to see you.' Mr Robert shook hands with him.

Saleem watched Miss Edwina turn pale, as if she had seen a ghost. Her smile faded and she looked shocked at seeing her husband so unexpectedly.

Then he heard Mr Vincent say, 'I have just dropped Miss Edwina off from the gymkhana pavilion.' An uneasy grin hovered on his lips.

'Good. Good. It seems ages since I played tennis. In fact, I've been too busy for any sport.' Mr Robert looked at Miss Edwina. She opened her mouth to say something but Mr Robert stopped her. 'I am glad to see you are keeping busy, darling.'

Saleem breathed with relief and returned to the jeep. There had been no argument. No scene. Mr Vincent slowly walked to his car and drove away. Mr Robert led Miss Edwina into the house.

Chapter 42

Early the following morning the news was everywhere. Mr Robert read aloud from the paper while Saleem drove.

'A police station in Chintapalli was attacked in the night. They think it was carried out by the hill tribes from the forest. Apparently a large group of men marched in and attacked the police: "The three constables in the station could do nothing against two hundred men who snatched eleven handguns, hundreds of bullets, grenades, swords, handcuffs, and fourteen javelins. In total they stole one thousand, three hundred and ninety items. The rebels then moved in the direction of Devipeta, where they captured two police constables who were returning from foot patrol, and seized more riffles and five rounds of ammunition."'

'I hope it is safe for us to drive to Roypuram this morning, sir,' said Saleem, turning on to the main road.

Mr Robert looked up from the paper. 'I think so – the security will be tight after what has happened. And we are heading towards Roypuram, in the opposite direction from Devipeta, so I don't think we'll meet any trouble.'

'Sir,' Saleem asked hesitantly, 'did they give any reason for the attacks?

'It is obvious, Saleem. The hill tribes are angry for the same reason that every other person in the country is angry. The heavy taxes.

They can't pay. They are impoverished. Many destitute.'

'Sir... I heard that there may be rebels in Roypuram, too.'

'If there are, it will be for the same reason.'

'Yes, sir. I heard that because of a bad harvest this year, the farmers are even less able to pay the taxes, and yet the landlord, the zamindar, is taking possession of their lands under the pretext of non-repayment of the loans. He says that it is the order from the government. They were already in an impossible situation, and now he has added yet another tax on the sale of firewood and honey, but collecting honey and wood from the forest is their only form of livelihood, sir. They earn very little from it as it is. I heard that a couple of men have died after being beaten by the zamindar and his men. Why beat farmers and poor people when they simply do not have any money? They are doing nothing evil. They are being punished for being poor. It is cruel.'

'No wonder your people are angry. It does not surprise me at all, Saleem,' Mr Robert replied.

Once they were away from the British quarters, and on to the main road nearing the *chowrasta*, the city square, Saleem had to slow down. The traffic seemed to be blocked and it was impossible to move forward. Mr Robert put down the paper and leaned forward, staring out to see what was wrong. They inched their way through streets filled with people shouting slogans.

'*Jaihind!* Hail India!'

'*Chale jao British!* British go back!'

The rebels had probably been encouraged by the events of the previous evening, and neither the earliness of the hour nor the threat of rain would stop them from pouring into the streets. The mounted British police, and Indian police on foot, joined forces to try to regain control and restore peace. When the crowd refused to disperse, they began to beat people with batons, metal chains and rifle butts. Some of the protesters were trying to stone the police, while others continued marching, heads held high, ignoring the pain when they were caught in the fray or beaten. Some protesters fell, too badly injured to continue.

When a police officer saw the jeep, he saluted and fired several rounds of ammunition into the air. He kept firing until he managed to clear the road so that the English engineer sahib could continue on his way. They drove on in silence, until they reached the outskirts of the city. The road into Roypuram seemed deserted and calm. Both men began to breathe more easily, but they were shocked by what they had seen.

'I didn't expect that the incident in the village would have repercussions in the cities, sir,' Saleem finally said, turning a troubled face to Mr Robert.

'Of course it will, Saleem. And the reaction in the cities will be much swifter and probably more violent than in the villages. I am afraid the trouble will spread everywhere now. It's like a match put to dry wood. It will all go up in flames. The injustice of the treatment of the poor has been smouldering for a very long time. It took just one final event to rouse your people to action, and I can't say I blame them. They have taken enough.'

'That's very kind of you to think like that, sir.'

'I am not being kind to anyone, Saleem, I am just stating the facts. I do know what's going on in the country and what is making the natives angry.'

Moved by his master's insight and concern, but unable to express his gratitude in words, Saleem turned to Mr Robert and saluted him.

Chapter 43

The tiny store room became unbearably humid during that monsoon night and in the early hours of the morning Anjali couldn't bear it any longer. She climbed on to the trunk and undid the bolt of the shutters of the one small window. The rusty hinges squeaked loudly but it didn't matter because no one would be in the temple in the dead of night. She leaned forward, hoping to catch a breath of fresh air. It was still dark outside but the faint line of light on the far horizon showed that dawn would break soon. She was just enjoying the freshness of those cool early hours when she heard something and ducked down. She had caught sight of a sweeper woman with a clay lamp in her hand walking into the yard facing the window. Even in that very faint flickering lamplight she thought, just for a fraction of a second, that their eyes met. Her heart beating fast, Anjali stretched up and very quietly closed the window. Feeling pathetic, she sat back on the trunk and prayed that the woman had not seen or recognised her.

The astrologer hadn't come home as planned the previous evening, leaving Anjali bitterly disappointed. Sita reported that he had sent her a message saying he would not be back for another two days. Anjali sprawled across the straw mat on the floor and closed her eyes. Her thoughts went back to her childhood. Trying hard to remember her mother's face, she strived to imagine that she was a child again, in her mother's lap. She was not sure that she remembered, but her father often recounted scenes from her earliest years until it was hard to know what was memory and what she had just been told.

Eventually the image came, and with it a lullaby her mother used to sing until she fell asleep.

She didn't know how long she slept but she was woken by a noise outside.

Just for a moment she didn't know where it was coming from. Confused and sleepy, still held in the dream of her past, she looked around, forgetting where she was. Then the door opened, blinding daylight flooded the room, and Sita breezed in carrying a basket of fruit in one hand and some books in the other, and saying, 'Good morning Anjali. Guess what?'

'Good morning, Sita.' Anjali sat up. 'What's all that noise?' She was trying her best to wake up and give her full attention to her visitor, who obviously didn't realise she had been fast asleep.

Instead of answering her, Sita asked, 'Did you open the window this morning?'

'I did. It was stifling in here. Why? Oh, no, did she see me?'

Sita smiled, 'Don't panic. But there is a rumour going around the village this morning like wildfire.'

'No!' Anjali put her hand over her mouth. 'They know I'm here.'

'Wait… let me explain. Apparently, the sweeper woman is very impressionable, and when she caught a glimpse of your face at the window, she ran straight out into the village screaming that she had seen a real goddess looking at her in the inner courtyard of the temple. She said the goddess blessed her.'

'A goddess?' Anjali's mouth was open wide.

'Yes, that's what all the noise is about. There are hundreds out there waiting to catch a glimpse of you. The goddess.'

'Oh no! Sita-*amma*!' Anjali clung to Sita's hand with fear, 'What shall we do now?'

'Well, I had to think of something quickly so I asked one of my father's disciples – you know, the young priest – to tell them that it was no good waiting. The goddess will certainly not appear before such a big crowd: she will only appear when she wants and to whom she wants.' Sita laughed. 'One unexpected glimpse of you has changed the course of the sweeper woman's life.'

'How? What happened to her?'

'They sat her down on a shrine in the middle of the village, smeared her all over with turmeric and vermillion powders, and placed garlands of lemons around her neck. People were queuing to see her and to take offerings to her.' She laughed again.

'Really!'

'Yes. The unexpected sighting of you at that eery time of night seems to have fired up her already volatile mind, and now she is acting very strangely.'

'What is she doing?'

'Well, she is sitting there in the village square, shaking all over, and reciting *bhajans* in a really loud voice. And now she swears that the goddess has possessed her and is talking through her to the people. It's almost as if she thinks she is a goddess.'

'Really?' Anjali repeated, too shocked to say more.

'Yes, and now the whole village thinks she is telling the truth. Personally, I think she may have had a glass too many last night – you know that alcoholic *kallu* they drink in the evenings?'

'Yes, I know. But aren't they all going to get suspicious that I am hiding here?'

'Don't worry, my father will be arriving soon and will sort everything out,' Sita said, glancing at the window to check it was properly closed.

'Are they searching for me? I mean me Anjali, not some imaginary goddess?''

'Of course they are. After feeding you for so many months and teaching you everything she knew, do you think Mohini would let you go just like that?' Sita clicked her finger. 'I saw Samba this afternoon and he is worried about you.'

'I hope you didn't tell him that I am here?'

'No, of course not. He is worried that Mohini's men might find you. And he's worried that if you were hiding in the forest, you might be in danger from wild animals. He said there are also a lot of violent men hiding in the forest.'

'Dear Samba...'

'Listen, Anjali. There is more news. A lot is happening out there while you have been stuck in this room. Rebels from the villages have joined the tribal people from the mountains and are attacking the police stations everywhere. So far they have attacked at least four stations.' Sita was wide-eyed.

'Why? What for?'

'For weapons. You know, for guns and ammunition...'

'What do they want them for? What are they going to do with them?'

'They say they need weapons for self-defence. And to fight the British soldiers.'

'Is it getting worse?' Anjali asked.

'Yes. Very much so. Do you remember that engineer sahib for whom you were going to dance?'

'Yes.'

'Well, Samba says he fears for his safety.' Then Sita looked up, suddenly remembering something. 'By the way, do you know anyone by the name of Saleem?'

'Saleem? Did you say Saleem?' Anjali was visibly shaken. 'Where did you hear that name?'

'Samba said a man called Saleem came searching for you.'

'I don't believe it... after all this time...' Anjali stood up and held Sita's hands in hers. 'Please, tell me where he is now.'

'So you know him well?' Sita asked, wondering why Anjali was so moved.

'Since childhood,' Anjali replied.

'Apparently he works as a driver for that white engineer sahib.'

'No!'

'Yes.'

'Sita-*amma*, is it possible for you to let him know that I am here?'

'I'm not sure. It would be a risk. Listen, Anjali, why don't you wait for my father to come home, just one more day, and he will know what to do. Anyway, enough of that. Can you read? I've brought you some books to help pass the time.'

'Yes, I can read. My father taught me when I was small. In fact he insisted against my step-mother's wishes that I learn to read and write. He used to say that it was ignorance that made people believe that it was not important for girls to be literate.'

'Yes, your father is right. It is unusual, but my father thinks the same.' There was a pause. 'You know, ever since…' Sita was flipping the pages of one of the books she had brought. She could not continue.

Anjali understood and placed a comforting hand on Sita's shoulder.

Sita smiled. 'You know, reading is like a therapy for me. I can easily get lost in a book.'

Anjali nodded in agreement, trying not to show her dismay and sadness at the sight of that pale, thin girl with the shaved head.

'Anyway, these are for you.' Sita held out the books. Anjali read out the titles. '*Rukmini Parinayam – The Wedding of Rukmini. Sita Swayamvaram – Sita Chooses a Husband.*'

'Even though they are very old books, I like the girls in the stories, especially Princess Rukmini. She is so brave. She runs away from home to get married to her love, Lord Krishna. Perhaps you have already read them?' Sita asked.

'Yes, I did, but it was a very long time ago. I would like to read them again.'

'In the olden days, girls had more freedom than us. They didn't get married until they were sixteen, and were allowed to choose their own husbands.'

'I know. Isn't it strange that in previous times girls were independent and educated while today we are lucky to get any teaching at all, and we have almost no freedom. There doesn't seem to be much progress, does there, Sita?'

They both sighed and remained silent for a long time, each lost in her own thoughts, wondering when and why everything had changed so that the fate of women was now so intolerable.

Chapter 44

When he thought he had found her, he lost her again. When he thought he could make some progress, something prevented him. Saleem wondered what fate was playing such cruel games with him.

Anjali had been missing for two days now and god knew how far she had gone. No one had spotted her. Apart from a few small villages dotted here and there, Roypuram was surrounded by forest, and if she was hiding in there, it could be very dangerous for her. Now, more than ever before, there was an urgency to finding her.

Saleem toasted bread on a griddle above a wood fire and made tea. He placed the teapot, a cup and saucer, butter, and a jar of honey on a tray, and set off to take breakfast outside. Mr Robert was leaning back in his chair, his newspaper lying open on his face. To see Mr Robert not working or reading was so unusual that Saleem could not help but think that he was worrying about something, perhaps his situation with Miss Edwina. Ever since they had returned from the city, Mr Robert had not been himself. He had been preoccupied and sometimes Saleem caught him looking troubled.

Saleem remembered that Miss Edwina had not joined Mr Robert for breakfast on the morning that they left. Nor did she come out to kiss him goodbye. Saleem did not want to pry, nor to make wild guesses, but the scene they had both witnessed on their arrival at the house must have been worrying for his master.

As he placed the tray on the table, Saleem wondered if the newspaper that covered Mr Robert's face was protecting him from the sun. Or perhaps he was asleep. Not wanting to disturb him, Saleem said quietly, 'Sir, your breakfast..'

'Thank you, Saleem,' Mr Robert said, without removing the paper. 'Leave it there and have a nice day.' Strangely, he waved Saleem away, without another word.

After giving him a salute, Saleem walked to the village to find Samba. The boy must know something about Anjali. On the way, he heard about the sweeper woman seeing the goddess through the window of the temple and smiled at her naivety. He also saw Mohini's people, still searching for Anjali. That woman never gave up. What did it matter to her whether she found Anjali or not? Saleem did not understand why she persevered.

When he reached Samba's hut he didn't need to knock on the door because it was already open. To Saleem's surprise, he heard the old woman, Samba's grandmother, calling her grandson's name and sounding very upset. She was surrounded by a group of people, mostly women, who were trying to console her. His heart lurched.

'What has happened?' he asked someone who was standing nearby.

'Her grandson disappeared.'

'Disappeared?'

'Yes, yesterday he set off to work but did not arrive at Venkat sir's house and no one knows where he is.' She pointed to the wailing woman. 'His grandmother is distraught, worrying about what might have happened to him.'

Saleem felt a knot in his stomach as he set off yet again. What else could go wrong? He walked through the village and looked around the edges of the forest, this time searching not just for Anjali but for Samba too.

By midnight, heartbroken that he could find neither of them, Saleem returned to the dock-bungalow. Mentally and physically exhausted, he lay down in his rope cot on the front veranda and closed his eyes.

Half asleep, he heard his name being called. Very quietly. At first he thought his troubled mind was playing tricks. Who would call him at that hour? He knew Mr Robert would be fast asleep in his chamber and the gatekeeper, on the other side of the veranda, was snoring with roars as loud as thunder.

He opened his eyes and lifted his head to look. He was not mistaken. In the light of the moon, he could see someone hanging on to the gate, trying to get his attention. The moonlight was so bright that he recognised him instantly.

'Samba?' he whispered, and got up to open the gate. The sight of the boy raised his spirits. 'Where have you been?'

'Shh!' Samba placed a finger on his lips and beckoned to Saleem.

'Samba, where were you? Your grandmother was so worried, and so was I.'

'I know. It couldn't be helped. I'm sorry.' Samba led him towards the deep shadow under a tree and sat down on the root of it.

'So, what's all this?' Saleem asked, sitting down next to him.

'I came to tell you something.' Samba looked at him. 'I was worried about Anjali and went searching through the forest.'

'Did you find her?' Saleem asked, gripping the boy's hand.

'While I was there, I found out that one of my tribal friends had been captured by the soldiers,' Samba continued, lost in his memory, not hearing Saleem.

'Why? What for?' Saleem asked.

'For joining the rebels and helping them to ransack the police stations.' Samba paused for a moment. 'You know, they killed him. There and then.'

'Oh, no!'

'Yes. So after that, I went to see the gang leader. He was the one who was leading the mourning for my friend and he spoke about what was happening. That really opened my eyes. I thought it all through carefully and I couldn't help but make a pledge with him.'

'A pledge? What pledge?'

'To fight against the British. Now I am one of them. One of the freedom fighters.'

'Samba! You are too young. So very young to fight.'

'No, I don't think so. I will be sixteen next month. I hate the British. Only your engineer sahib is the exception. I know that from what you have told me and from my own observation. But, Saleem *bhayya*, the others don't know that, and I had to come and tell you that his life could be in danger. I've come to say goodbye and to ask you to take care of Mr Robert. To try to protect him if you can.'

Saleem looked concerned. This was serious. The unrest was escalating and involving people he knew. How would it all end?

'And Saleem, Anjali is hiding in the temple.'

Samba stood up to take his leave.

Saleem remained sitting. He was shocked and speechless, trying to digest all the information that the boy had given him. It was too much to take in. Finally he got up and stared after Samba, who was already walking away into the darkness of the night. A young man with a purpose. A much more mature and confident Samba, as if he had grown up overnight.

'How do you know Anjali is in the temple?' Saleem called after him, but it was too late. Samba did not hear.

Chapter 45

'Anjali is in the temple… Anjali is in the temple…' Samba's words echoed loudly in Saleem's mind, blocking out the sound of his own hurrying footsteps. Saleem knew that the temple would be locked at this time of night but still he couldn't help running the mile of streets and alleys just to catch sight of the single-storey structure, whose black stone gleamed in the moonlight. He slowed from a run to a walk as he reached the wide steps and his heart sang at the thought of Anjali being so near.

Being a Muslim, he had never entered a Hindu temple before. He bowed to the deities that were carved on either side of the doors and asked their forgiveness for not being a Hindu. After climbing the steps, he gently pressed his palms against the carved wooden doors. Even though he had fully expected them to be locked, still he was disappointed to see a large metal padlock holding them tightly shut. Not wanting to give up, he walked round the temple several times, calling Anjali's name, but soon realised that it would be impossible for Anjali to hear him through those heavy granite walls. Saleem looked up and saw the full moon high in the cloudless sky. 'It won't be long,' he consoled himself. 'It will soon be morning.'

Inhaling the fragrance of the *parijata* flowers that bloomed abundantly on a nearby tree, he sat on the steps and decided to stay there until the morning, until the priest opened the doors. He wondered at his chances of success. Would they allow him, a Muslim, into the temple? Not wanting to even contemplate the possibility of being rejected, he leaned back against the doors, and soon his eyelids drooped and he slept.

And so he remained until the first bird songs woke him at dawn. For a moment he could not work out where he was, and stared wildly around him, but remembering that Anjali was in the temple, his mood quickly changed to one of elation. He stood up calling her name. He stared at the still locked doors, which appeared so much larger now in the misty light. Then it all started. He heard the drums before he saw the mob of people arriving from the direction of the forest. They were holding placards and shouting patriotic slogans. His first thought was that they were Mohini's people and, worried that his presence there might give them a clue as to Anjali's whereabouts, he ducked down behind the *parijata* tree until the mob had passed.

Minutes later, the astrologer arrived. He was just starting to mount the steps of the temple when Saleem came out of the shadows and bowed to him. 'Sir, Anjali…' he began.

'She is safe,' the astrologer answered without even waiting for Saleem to finish his question. 'You will meet her soon.'

'Sir…' Excitement made him unable to say any more.

The man in the orange robes looked at him with kindness. 'You had better go and look after your master. That is where you are needed now. There is trouble brewing. Anjali will be safe here.'

'Sir…?' Saleem looked puzzled.

'Didn't you see the freedom fighters marching past a while ago? Did you not hear the anger in their voices? Perhaps you are not aware that Gandhi was arrested last night.'

'Gandhi… arrested?'

The astrologer nodded without saying any more and continued up the steps.

Saleem knew he had no choice but to leave.

*

Before placing the newspapers on the table for Mr Robert, Saleem glanced at the front pages, and found Gandhi's photo splashed across every one. Although the headlines were written in capitals big and bold enough to read, he couldn't manage the rest of the articles, which were of course in English. Only Gandhi's name over and over. He waited patiently until Mr Robert had finished reading them.

'What is the news, sir?'

'Gandhi was arrested in the early hours of this morning,' Mr Robert replied.

'What was the reason for it, sir?' Saleem couldn't believe that someone had actually arrested a peace-loving man like Gandhi.

'For no reason, I suppose. Apparently he was planning a peaceful meeting, but the authorities thought he might provoke trouble and arrested him.'

Saleem stared at his master in shocked silence.

'It is stupid of them to arrest him. I fear that their action might incite more unrest and violence.' Mr Robert stood up to transfer his feet from his slippers to his work shoes. 'They ought to know it will only aggravate people more.'

'Of course, sir,' Saleem nodded in agreement. He was grateful for his master's unbiased opinions.

After dropping the engineer sahib at the site, Saleem's loyalties were torn. In his heart, he wanted to get straight back to the temple, but after hearing Samba's and then the astrologer's warnings, he decided that he would be more useful here, with Mr Robert. Knowing that Anjali was safe with the astrologer, he decided to stay close to his master.

Night had fallen by the time they left the construction site. They travelled through the fields in silence, except for the barking of the occasional distant dog. The jeep lights showed the uneven mud road ahead but Saleem couldn't see to the left or right because the tangled upper branches of the forest blocked the moonlight. Only the middle of the road was visible. It looked eerie and for the first time Saleem felt uneasy about driving along that isolated route.

Then suddenly, just as they were about to turn in the direction of the dock-bungalow, a gang of people appeared ahead of them and moved towards the car. Saleem slowed down and stared in astonishment. In the jeep's headlamps, he could make out their faces and in their hands he could clearly see weapons, which flashed and glinted. Immediately Saleem sensed serious trouble. He recognised some of the men from the village and knew that they intended to harm their enemy, the white man. Any white man. There was a wild and crazy anger in the men's eyes and as they marched toward the jeep, which had slowed to a walking pace, Saleem saw their mixture of envy and disgust at the sight of the car. Soon there were dozens of men, running at the jeep, shouting abuse, accusing the white man inside of Gandhi's arrest. Saleem didn't know what to do. Not thinking clearly, he pressed his foot down hard on the brake.

'Sir...' Saleem began, not taking his eyes off the mob, which approached closer and closer.

'Don't worry. I will talk to them,' Mr Robert replied, beginning to open his door.

'No, no, sir!' Saleem stretched out his arm to stop Mr Robert from climbing out.

Stones began to hit the vehicle. Grateful for the blinding headlights, which shone directly into the eyes of the rebels, so that they were unable to see exactly who was inside, Saleem whispered, 'Quick, sir, get out and run and hide somewhere. Cover yourself up. It's not safe for you here.' He handed his master a black blanket from the back seat.

'But Saleem...'

'I will be all right, sir.' Then he surprised himself by saying, 'Please go to the temple, sir. You will be safe there.' He didn't know what made him say it, except that he knew that the temple was situated on the outskirts of the village, well away from the forest, so it was a good place to head for when mobs were out on the streets. It would be a perfect refuge for a man on the run.

He didn't need to turn his eyes. He felt Mr Robert crawling into the back and out from under the canvas. Saleem held his breath. He heard no triumphant roar from the crowd, so assumed that Mr Robert had managed to get away without being caught. The mile and a half trek back through the fields to the temple would not be a problem for a fit man like Mr Robert. But what if he was seen? What if he was recognised? What if someone saw that it was a white man hidden under the black blanket?

There was no more Saleem could do.

Chapter 46

Anjali waited all day, sometimes listening behind the door, while the astrologer performed his duties in the temple until, at last, she heard him chanting the evening prayers and her spirits lifted. Soon he would come to her. She knew that the wise Brahmin would find solutions to her problems and soon she would be free from her confinement, and safe from Mohini and the zamindar.

And just as she thought this, the temple bells rang out as if the gods were confirming the same message. With renewed optimism she mimed the *bhajans*, the devotional songs, which the devotees sang until the evening turned into night.

Eventually the doors of her room opened and the astrologer entered, followed by his daughter. Anjali stood up and took a few steps forward to touch his feet, and he smiled in return, placing his hand over her head to bless her. At that precise moment they all heard running footsteps resounding across the stone floor of the temple.

Pulling her *sari pallu* over her head, Anjali slipped behind the door. Sita stood in front of her as the astrologer turned to see what was happening.

'Who is it?' he asked, stepping across the threshold.

While his quick glances searched the main temple, his hands pulled shut the doors of the store room. Anjali gripped Sita's hand in fear but the younger girl reassured her by patting her on the shoulder.

'Please may I stay here for a little while? There are people out there who want to harm me.' Both girls heard a man's voice – speaking in an odd dialect that he had not quite mastered, and looked at each other in dismay.

Before the astrologer could answer, they heard an uproar outside the temple, not far away.

'*Jai Hind!* Hail India!'

'Long live Mahatma Gandhi!'

'British Raj – Down! Down!'

Anjali looked at Sita.

'They are freedom fighters. They have been roaming the streets, with more and more men joining them.' Sita opened the door just a crack. Through the tiny gap, they saw a shocked-looking man towering over the astrologer. From his clothes, Anjali recognised him as British. He sounded out of breath and was struggling to get his words out.

'What is a white man doing here?' Sita whispered, but her words were drowned by the roaring commotion and thudding footsteps that were soon all around the temple.

'We know you are hiding in there!'

They could hear them clearly now.

'Bring the white dog out and kill him!' someone shouted.

It seemed they might enter the temple at any minute.

The astrologer leaped into action. He dragged the white man into the room and pulled the door shut behind him. Seconds later, Anjali found herself with a veil over her head, the strange white man dressed in Indian clothing at her side, both facing the deities in the main temple. A *dhoti* was tucked at his waist, covering the length of his trousers. A shoulder cloth was draped around his shoulders to hide his jacket. A turban hid his light brown hair and half of his face. Anjali thought that with his deep tan, he looked exactly like a very handsome Indian, except for his eyes. They sparkled like sapphire stones.

By the time the angry mob had forced its way into the temple, the astrologer was chanting the Sanskrit hymns in a loud voice as if to bless a couple. Before she realised what was happening, he handed Anjali and the white man the garlands that had earlier adorned the gods. Then he turned and raised his hands to silence the crowd, which had come to a halt just beyond the threshold of the main altar. Many obeyed him, though not everyone. The astrologer continued with the ceremony and, at his instructions, Anjali exchanged garlands with the strange Englishman.

Only then did the astrologer step out of the main temple to address the crowd.

'This is a sacred place and the Almighty only blesses goodness and love. Please take your anger and desire for revenge elsewhere.'

'Sorry, sir,' the leader apologised. 'We thought the Englishman had escaped into the temple.'

'No one, not even an ant, would enter the temple without the Lord wishing it. But you are welcome to search the place.'

There was a moment of silence, then a few murmurs and whispers. Finally a couple of men rather sheepishly went around the temple looking in corners and dark hiding places, and even in the store room where Anjali had stayed for the last few days. Anjali held her breath until the temple was once again empty and the crowds had left, disappointed. Even though her head was down, Anjali sensed that until now, like her, the white man had not breathed properly, or raised his eyes, not even once.

Confused and dazed and dumbfounded, Anjali had no idea what would happen next. Here they were, a priest, a white man on the run, a child widow and herself, all hiding together in the store room.

There was a moment's shocked silence before the white man spoke.

'Thank you, sir. Never will I forget your help. I owe my life to you.'

'Who am I to save you? It's all in His hands.' The astrologer gestured at the black granite statue of Shiva.

'You are very kind, sir.' Mr Robert bowed to him again, unable to find words for his heartfelt gratitude. He might deny it, but this man had saved his life.

'The god's blessings are with you. It was meant to happen. Please wait here while I arrange some transport for your departure.'

'I don't want to trouble you any more, sir. I'm sure my driver must be returning soon for me.'

'Don't you think they will recognise your jeep?'

'Of course they will,' answered the Englishman.

'Then we must make alternative plans. It will take me a couple of hours,' the astrologer said.

They all waited, immersed in their own thoughts, until midnight, until they gradually stopped trembling, and until they were sure that every single member of the mob was far away from the temple.

At long last someone rang the temple bells and the astrologer rose, saying, 'Your transport is here.'

To her surprise, the astrologer then took Anjali's hand and placed it in the Englishman's.

'You must take her with you.'

'Sir…?' Mr Robert was mystified.

'Yes. Now she belongs to you. According to Hindu custom, she is your wife.'

'Sir?' Mr Robert looked horrified. 'I am a married man.'

'Your marriage to Edwina is a sham. You are two people who live together but are apart. Your hearts are not united.' The Englishman could not have looked more shocked. Not only did this astrologer know his wife's name, he knew the truth about his failed marriage.

'Yes, you and Anjali are meant to be together. It is His wish.' He gestured at Shiva again.

Too astounded by what had happened to think clearly or to

understand the full significance of the astrologer's actions, Anjali just stared blankly at the deity, who was clothed in leopard skins and wore around his neck a snake ornament as blue as the Englishman's eyes.

Sita and Anjali embraced each other tearfully. They had grown close and Anjali was only too aware of how much she owed the younger girl. When Anjali bent down to touch the astrologer's feet, once more she was astonished at his quiet, final blessing. She did not mistake those words.

'May you have a beautiful child.'

Chapter 47

The wind that had howled during the night had died down and the birds had started singing. The sun came up, its rays penetrating the thickly entwined foliage to land in bright circles on the dark ground like spotlights. After making sure the place was deserted, Saleem came out from behind the bush where he was hiding. Holding on to the prop roots of a huge *banyan* tree, he climbed slowly and noiselessly up from the bottom of a narrow gorge at least six feet deep.

After only half a mile, walking along a rutted track, he saw the mangled skeleton of his burned-out jeep. Although he had guessed what the mob would do to it, in the daylight the sight was unbearable. Angry, wretched tears welled up in his eyes. 'What's the difference between the brutal British and our freedom fighters when they both use this kind of violence? How can they say that they are the followers of Gandhi?' Exasperated, he looked all around him, but the thugs had not left a trace of their identity – no weapons, not even footprints. Only scattered pieces of charred metal covered in black soot remained as evidence of the previous night's violent drama.

He spread his shoulder-cloth on the ground beside the heap and, facing towards Mecca, prayed to Allah for peace and for Mr Robert's safety. When he opened his eyes he found himself looking straight into the gaze of two armed men, staring at him without the slightest sign of pity. Quickly he was on his feet but before he had a chance to run, the men leaped at him and caught hold of him, twisting his arms behind his back. He knew that there was no point in struggling against men as heavy and powerful as these. He opened his mouth to scream but they stuffed a rag into it to silence him.

They bound his arms and legs and blindfolded him. Like throwing a sack of potatoes, they chucked him on to one of their horse's backs and soon they were all moving off, his body shaken from side to side by the motion of the animals. Where they were taking him? What would they do to him? Only by the smells of damp plants and the sounds of woodland birds and animals did he guess that they were penetrating deep into the jungle. After the initial shock came sickening fear. He guessed that he had fallen into the hands of extremists, who had arrived the previous night disguised as more reasonable freedom fighters. This could be the end for him.

His thoughts turned to Anjali. These were terrible, turbulent times and he had no idea whether she was safe. All he could do was hope that the astrologer would protect her. Everyone in Roypuram said that he was a humane man, and as long as he remained in the village the violence would not get out of hand. In this moment of utter helplessness, he wanted so much to believe them. He wanted to believe that Anjali would come to no harm under the protection of the holy man.

An hour must have passed before he was dragged off the horse and flung to the ground. The surface he landed on was hard rock and stone, making him cry out with pain, but no sound escaped his mouth. He gagged as the rag suffocated him.

It was a long time before his legs were unbound and the blindfold was removed. Only then did he realise that he was imprisoned in a dark, narrow cave. He was dragged to his feet by a guard and pushed through the entrance of another, much wider cave that was lit by burning torches. The guard gave him another push and Saleem stumbled. A group of people dressed in black were sitting on the floor in front of him. A tall, stout man stood on a raised platform, waiting to speak. He held a thick whip in one hand. Saleem guessed that he was their leader.

'So here we have the disloyal Hindustani, the slave of the white dog!' the leader's voice thundered, his eyes full of hatred.

'Yes, sir,' the guard answered.

'Infidel! Why did you help your master, the white man, escape?'

What to say? How to answer so as not to provoke more anger? 'I didn't,' Saleem risked.

'Then who did, your grandfather?'

The leader cracked a clay water pot with his whip.

'I didn't help him, sir. He ran away from the jeep.'

'Don't try to fool me. Tell me where he is.'

'I don't know, sir.'

'You don't know…' The chief stepped down, twisting the rope of the whip around his hand. 'We will see if you don't know!'

The whip danced over Saleem's back. The pain was so excruciating that Saleem blacked out.

Chapter 48

Once again, unable to predict the future, Anjali was taking a journey to another unknown destination, but this time with a stranger at her side.

The moon, high above a thin layer of cirrus clouds, cast a silver light over the land, but inside the horse-drawn cart it was dark behind the curtains drawn on both sides. Sensing that they were exiting the village, Anjali's heart ached for Sita. Their acquaintance had been short but the bond they had formed was strong. She wished her friend was travelling with her.

The *tonga* driver avoided the forest and took them instead on a narrow track through paddy fields and castor bushes. Only then did he lift the front curtain as a sign that they were in safe territory. They passed through a number of sleeping villages, taking a circuitous but much safer route into the city. In that otherwise silent night, Anjali was very aware of the squealing cart wheels and the hard sounds of the horses' hooves on the stony ground. What if someone heard them? She looked up and saw the Englishman still wearing Indian clothes. He sat in silence, perhaps lost in thought. She could make out his blue eyes staring straight ahead, apparently at the hazy surroundings, but it was obvious that he was taking nothing in. Because there was limited headroom, he was somewhat bent over, and looked exhausted and uncomfortable. Every time the cart hit a bump in the track, he was bounced upwards and hit his head. Anjali felt sorry for him.

Could he be the man that Saleem worked for, she wondered. If so, where was Saleem? Was he still in the village? Why wasn't he there with his master? She cursed herself for not asking the astrologer about Saleem but took comfort in the thought that this man must know his driver's whereabouts. She opened her mouth to ask, but hesitated when she saw that the stranger had closed his eyes and was rubbing his brow. Her questions would have to wait. This man had been through a terrifying experience; she remembered only too well the angry mob that had broken into the temple brandishing glinting weapons. Being alone in that situation must have terrified him. It had certainly been frightening for her. She shivered, remembering again how easily they might have recognised her if not for the swift thinking of the astrologer. She would have been captured and imprisoned by Mohini and the white man would have been murdered.

But Anjali could also understand the anger of the freedom fighters. She had heard from Sita that Gandhi had been arrested without justification, and that riots and protests were breaking out everywhere. She remembered Sita's words: 'The entire country is turbulent with unrest and violence.'

Exhausted from the traumatic events that the day had thrown at her, she couldn't keep open her drooping eyes.

*

She woke from disturbed sleep and realised that her head was resting awkwardly against the wall of the carriage. Her eyes stung and her neck ached as she tried to sit up straight, and her heart skipped a beat at the sight of the stranger trying to smile at her out of politeness. Feeling terribly self-conscious, she pulled her shawl tightly around her shoulders and looked out to see where they had arrived. The sun was by now high in the sky and people were hurrying about their business. Trams, *tongas*, bicycle-rickshaws. The noise and hustle and bustle told her that they had reached a city.

'What is your name?' At last the Englishman spoke, breaking the claustrophobic silence and leaning forwards to talk to the driver.

'Samba,' the driver answered.

Anjali was stunned. 'Oh, Samba! Is that you, the same Samba?'

'Yes, Anjali-*amma*,' he laughed, turning back just for a moment to reveal his face.

'Oh, Samba!' Overwhelmed by her relief at seeing someone she knew travelling with her, she did not know what to say. She wanted to ask whether he knew where Saleem was but Mr Robert's voice interrupted.

'The city must be in turmoil after the news of Gandhi's arrest. Perhaps it would be better if we avoid the main roads and junctions, Samba.'

'Of course, sir. You are quite right.' Samba turned the cart into a narrow gully off the main road.

Peeling off his Indian robes and revealing the dark suit beneath, the white man asked, 'Do you know where Saleem is?'

Here was this stranger showing his concern and asking the very same question she herself had wanted to ask. Anjali listened carefully.

Samba nodded before saying, 'The last time I saw him, he was running away from the jeep, sir. But don't worry, sir, they are unlikely to harm him. He knows how to look after himself.'

'Running away from the jeep?' Anjali repeated quietly to herself. 'Why, Samba?' she asked.

'Don't worry, Anjali-*amma*. Saleem will be fine.'

Anjali understood Samba didn't want to pursue this conversation, but from what she had picked up so far, she could piece together what had happened on the previous night. Gripped with worry, she prayed for Saleem's safety.

Again silence held them until they entered the immaculate, tree-lined residential area of the British. At the entrance they were stopped by a couple of uniformed security guards, but recognising Mr Robert, the Ghurkas saluted and waved them on.

Anjali was awestruck at the grandeur of the place. Carved lamp posts topped with porcelain globes lined the roads. Every variety and style of motorcar sat parked in the vast grounds inside this protected compound. As they passed the houses, Anjali caught glimpses of well-dressed memsahibs on their shady balconies and verandas, sipping drinks which Anjali imagined were icy cool. Some of them read. Some knitted. Some sat and chatted with other women.

Anjali found herself in front of a two-storied white mansion. Flat-roofed with pillared verandas and an imposing portico, it was surrounded by green lawns and flowering plants, which blossomed richly against a dense background of palms and ancient trees.

Samba saluted Mr Robert and took his leave. Then he turned to Anjali and said, 'Please don't worry. You will be safe here and Saleem will come soon.'

Samba didn't wait any longer than necessary. Before she could even thank him, he sprang on to his seat and flicked his whip to move the horses forward. There they stood, two people who were complete strangers to one another, watching the speeding *tonga* until it disappeared around the corner.

Chapter 49

'Please come in.'

Anjali turned her gaze from the empty road at the sound of Mr Robert's voice. The gatekeeper saluted them as she nervously followed Mr Robert through the grounds towards the house.

As she climbed the wide steps, Samba's words, 'Saleem will come soon', echoed in her mind, giving her strength and hope as she stepped into a house so different from any she had seen before. A female servant put down her watering can among the plants on the veranda and came running towards Mr Robert. She bowed.

'Memsahib will stay in the guestroom and you will see to her needs,' Mr Robert told the servant. Then he turned to Anjali, 'Please feel free to ask Vimala for anything you need. She will be at your service.' Anjali thanked him and followed Vimala upstairs.

On the landing she stopped for a moment and looked down on Mr Robert, who was still standing in the hall as if in a trance. It was clear from his worried expression and the lines across his forehead that he was deeply affected and disturbed by the previous night's events. How could he not be?

As if tuned in to her thoughts, he wiped the sweat from his face with a handkerchief before turning to climb a different stairway that led from the hall in the opposite direction. Although she was separated from him by quite a distance, Anjali heard him sigh deeply as he started his ascent.

Anjali stepped into a room that took her breath away. As she crossed the threshold, her only thought was that she should not be there. She did not belong there. Without taking in the details, she was aware of luxury and comfort and expensive furniture. At the sight of the huge four-poster bed draped with a mosquito net in the centre of the room, she shook her head in amazement. This was not for her. She felt uncomfortable and lost, many miles away from the people she knew and with whom she belonged. She wished that she could be with her father once again. The initial shock slowly gave way to waves of exhaustion and sadness. There was no avoiding the huge bed as she was hardly able to hold herself upright. She collapsed on to it and sobbed into a white linen pillow.

*

After some time a gentle knock on the door awoke her.

'Yes?' she called, quickly sitting up and trying to look composed.

'Would you like to have a bath, *amma*?' Vimala asked. She came into the room carrying a bundle of new towels. 'Are you all right, *amma*?' She could see that Anjali had been weeping.

'Yes, I am fine. Just tired,' she managed to say.

'You look as if you haven't slept for a fortnight.'

'Yes, you are right… I have not managed to get much sleep lately.' Taking the towels from the maid's hands, she followed her through a door into another room, which Vimala explained was her own private bathroom. Anjali had never even seen a bathtub before.

While Vimala filled the tub with buckets and buckets of warm water, Anjali opened a small bag that Sita had packed for her and placed in her hands as she left the temple. She gasped to find a couple of small packets of turmeric, vermillion, dried fruit and nuts, and a gold-bordered red *sari* inside.

'Oh, Sita!' Anjali murmured. These were the few traditional things one would give to a new bride. She had been too embarrassed by the memory of sitting next to Mr Robert in the temple while the astrologer chanted the wedding *mantras* to think through its significance. At the time, her mind had been in turmoil and she had followed the astrologer's instructions because the noble man was doing something – the right thing – to rescue two people who had come to seek his protection. But now, as she remembered the astrologer's words for the first time, she understood the implications of what had happened to her. The thought of her being tied to a stranger, a white man, a man who just happened to be sheltering in the temple when she was, filled her with horror. She did not understand why the astrologer had performed a marriage ceremony instead of some other rite, and why neither she nor Mr Robert had protested. The only way she could come to terms with it at all was to imagine that it was some kind of fate, karma or destiny that had been written on her forehead even before birth. Perhaps she herself had little control over her future. She sat for a long time staring at the new red *sari*, trying to work out how she had arrived in this astonishing situation, until the maid interrupted her to tell her that her bath was ready.

In the bathroom mirror she saw a woman in a widow's white *sari*, the same *sari* she had been wearing ever since she had shaved her head at Mohini's, but on this widow's forehead was a dot of vermillion, placed there by Mr Robert at the astrologer's instructions during the ceremony. This was surreal. Was she a widow or not? The startled face stared back at her. 'I don't have any answers for you,' she wanted to say.

Should she wear vermillion or not? She didn't feel like a married woman, but she didn't feel like a widow either. For Ranjit, she had never been a wife, not in the fullest sense of the word. In her mind he was always a father figure, never a husband. Finally her instincts overcame her misgivings. She had worn vermillion all her life, so why not now? She placed a fresh red dot between her eyebrows.

Certainly it was refreshing and relaxing to immerse herself in the warm water. For a while, she leaned back in the bathtub and refused to listen to her confused thoughts. Enjoy these few simple moments of pleasure, she told herself. You are tired and dirty and exhausted.

She had no choice but to wear the red *sari* as she had no other clothes, except the *burqa* that Sita had packed. 'Thank you, Sita,' she whispered in appreciation of her friend's thoughtfulness. Who knew? It might yet be useful one day, especially now she was living on white man's territory. She put the black garment back into the bag.

She went and stood on the balcony, breathed the clean, scented air, and surveyed her new surroundings. The immaculate English neighbourhood. Here were luxurious properties that belonged exclusively to the whites. Dense bougainvillaea draped the residences and their compound walls. All the grounds were neatly manicured. But what struck Anjali the most was the silence. There was no noise and shouting and chaos. Just the gentle rhythm of white men and women going about their normal activities – a drive or a walk through the tree-lined streets and parks.

The second thing that struck Anjali was the complete absence of her own people, apart from those who were employed as servants and ayahs. She understood that it was a no-go area for natives. Although she had heard about the English living away from Indian life in their cantonments, she hadn't seen one before. It was another world, shielded from the real one. How strange. It felt as if she was not in India. What would she do here? What would happen to her? She did not belong.

And so her thoughts turned to Mr Robert and her heart sank. What if Mr Robert accepted and desired the marriage that the astrologer had performed? The very idea terrified her and she made up her mind that despite the astrologer's wishes, she would tell the engineer sahib she would not agree to be his wife. The marriage was a sham. For her, it meant nothing.

A knock on the door startled her, but hearing Vimala's voice outside, she composed herself and let her in.

'Mr Robert is asking for you, *amma*.'

Her heartbeat quickened. Anjali stared at the woman. 'Why is he asking for me now?' she stuttered.

Vimala smiled. 'For breakfast, *amma*.'

'Oh!' She let out a sigh of relief. Calm down, she told herself.

Embarrassed about what had been going through her mind, and feeling overdressed in her new red *sari*, Anjali pulled her *pallu* over her head and timidly walked out on to the veranda. It was a peaceful space, shaded with pink and white jasmine creepers. The breakfast table was already set.

'Please, come and join us,' Mr Robert said, standing up and offering her a seat. 'This is my wife, Edwina.'

Feelings of surprise were followed by enormous relief. Mr Robert was already married.

'*Namaste*.' Anjali offered the traditional Indian greeting to the elegantly dressed woman sitting in the chair opposite Mr Robert.

'This is Anjali. She almost saved my life last night,' Mr Robert said. He was calm but serious and gave little away, but when he looked up and smiled at Anjali, she felt that somehow he could read her troubled mind.

It was awkward for Anjali to sit with a couple of Europeans eating a breakfast of toast with butter and jam and cups of tea.

Sensitive as always, Mr Robert noticed her discomfort. 'Please, if you don't like this breakfast, ask for something else. The cook will make you something Indian,' he said in her native tongue.

'No, no, sir, this is fine.'

All through breakfast Anjali saw that Miss Edwina's eyes never left her face. She stared openly but said not a word to her, almost as if she were not there. In fact they all finished breakfast without speaking much at all, except for a necessary word or two with the servant. Anjali was desperate to ask Mr Robert about Saleem, but of course she could not possibly begin on this topic with Miss Edwina present. It would not be appropriate.

Eventually, when Miss Edwina excused herself and left the table, Anjali mustered up the courage to ask, 'Sir, do you know where Saleem is?'

'Do you know him?' Mr Robert's voice sounded surprised as he looked at her questioningly.

'Yes, sir,' she said in a low voice. 'He is my childhood friend and I heard that he works for you.'

Mr Robert nodded, wiping his mouth with a napkin, and asked, 'Are you the girl he was searching for?'

'Yes, sir,' she said with renewed hope. 'Samba said he was searching for me. For a long time I didn't even know whether he was still alive because, you know, after that Jallianwala-Bagh shooting...'

'Yes, yes, I know...' he said with quiet compassion. 'He was badly injured.'

'Sir, is he coming here today?'

'I was hoping he would but I'm really not sure...' There was concern in his voice and he paused for a moment. 'But don't be concerned, the police are aware of the situation and I am going to their offices now to enquire about him.'

'Enquire about him?'

Mr Robert looked away. 'He is still in Roypuram...'

'In Roypuram?' Her eyes opened wide with fear. 'He will be in trouble, sir. If the rebels know that he is your driver...' She couldn't finish the sentence. Her voice broke and tears filled her eyes.

'Please don't worry. He will be back here soon,' Mr Robert said softly. 'Now, if you will excuse me, I must go to my office. Please take some rest and feel free to ask Vimala if you need anything.' He stood up.

'Thank you, sir.' Anjali watched him stride away.

Drained physically and mentally but comforted by Mr Robert's words, Anjali went back to her room and lay on her bed.

Not once had either of them mentioned the marriage ceremony.

Chapter 50

When Saleem regained consciousness, his body felt like burning pulp and the open wounds on his face made him flinch whenever he moved his eyes or mouth. 'Where am I?' he groaned as he tried to prise open his eyes.

He couldn't see anything; it was pitch dark. He shivered uncontrollably.

'Saleem,' someone whispered. He felt a hand on his shoulder. 'Here, take a sip.' The speaker lifted Saleem's head and placed a glass of water to his parched lips.

After taking a couple of welcome gulps and gathering his wits, Saleem opened his eyes fully, but still he couldn't make out who had spoken to him.

'Saleem, it's me, Samba.'

'S-am-ba...' He tried to repeat the name but his lips and mouth were too parched.

'Shush, don't talk,' Samba hushed him. 'Just listen. Anjali and Mr Robert are safe.'

Saleem sighed with relief.

'I am your guard for tonight but you must act as if we don't know each other, and don't you dare open your eyes. You must pretend to be unconscious if anyone comes in.'

Saleem nodded, understanding the situation.

Then there was silence. Saleem waited for a long time for Samba to speak again, but he didn't even know whether Samba was still there. Not wanting to take any risks, he closed his eyes and once more exhaustion took him.

*

For the next two days he didn't see Samba or anyone else except two armed guards who took turns to parade in front of the narrow opening of the cave. He made a guess that the gang must have gone off to hunt down another victim, and he was worried about Samba's whereabouts. When it was time for the guards to throw in a dry chapatti for his lunch, Saleem plucked up the courage to speak a few words with them, but they offered no reply, only a cold, disdainful glance.

Saleem was chained to a heavy stone. He did not know whether he would escape death. His situation was physically and emotionally unbearable and only the hope of Samba returning with more news of Mr Robert and Anjali kept him from giving up. He passed every hour listening for Samba's return.

After what seemed an eternity, he thought he heard a voice he recognised amongst others that had arrived outside the cave. There was a lot of shouting and laughing. He could smell wood burning and guessed that the rebels had made a fire outside. More arrived and the noise began to sound like a party. Then, finally, a figure slipped into his cave and crouched at his side.

'Saleem, I'm here. I'm back. It's been difficult to get away.'

'Thank god. You have no idea how good it is to hear your voice.'

'It must have been very difficult.'

Saleem's silence told Samba everything.

'They are celebrating out there,' Samba whispered.

'What for?'

'For killing a white man this morning.'

Again Saleem was silent. What was there to say?

'They found him riding a long way in front of his servants. When they finally caught up with the rebels who held their master, and saw that there were at least twenty of them, they fled, leaving their master to his fate.'

'Terrible.'

'I know.'

'Were you with them?' Saleem asked, after a few moments of silence.

'Don't ask too many questions now. I will tell you later.'

'They are not real freedom fighters, are they?'

'No. They are a violent bunch.'

'But… You…?'

Samba went silent for a moment. 'You know, Saleem, I didn't know that when I first heard their leader talking. I was impressed and he made us believe that he was the follower of Gandhi.'

'Follower of Gandhi!' Saleem spat. 'You must be joking. He is using violence against everything Mahatma has preached about non-violence.'

'I know,' Samba sighed.

'Can't you get away from these people?'

Samba squirmed and said nothing.

'Oh, Samba! It's impossible for you, isn't it? I was being naive.'

'One day I might manage to get away,' Samba said with a wry smile as he pulled a blanket over Saleem's shivering body. 'Ah, one more thing…'

But Samba had to jump up and stop in mid-sentence as other men entered the cave. First just a few, then many more came in and sat down on the floor, ignoring Saleem as if he did not exist.

The chief climbed on to the raised platform, not far from him.

'Comrades,' he began, once everyone was settled. 'We are celebrating tonight. Not only have we succeeded in catching and killing one of our enemies, we gained seven horses and a pouch of money as well.' He paused for a moment. 'And also, I have found out about another one. Not white, but an enemy, and he sits right here with us.' Saleem's pulse raced as all eyes fell on him.

'No, not him. He is nothing. I am talking about the man who helped the Englishman escape from the temple.'

'From the temple…'

'But we searched the temple, sir.'

'The white man was not there…'

Astonished voices rang out from the assembled men.

'Yes, you did, but they fooled us. And do you know how? With the help of one of my most trusted men.' His crude laugh echoed around the cave.

Everyone looked at each other in dismay. The guilty one was amongst them.

The leader played with his men, staring around the room, his glance falling on one, then another. Finally he stared at Samba and there his eyes rested.

'You think you can betray me, fool?' the chief's voice roared. 'Don't think that I don't know what you did, and how you helped the white dog escape!'

Panic-stricken, Saleem watched Samba staring at the leader wide-eyed and open-mouthed. Wanting to protect and help the vulnerable boy, he struggled helplessly against his heavy chains. It was extremely difficult to keep control of his emotions, but anything he did now would probably make things worse for his friend.

The next moment the stone walls of the cave resounded with gunshot. Everyone sat motionless. No one dared to blink. Not even a murmur was whispered between the men for a long time.

Samba's lifeless body lay in a pool of blood.

'Take the bloody thing out and throw it in the river.' The chief's command broke the tension.

'No!' A few men glanced at the bound man in the corner of

the cave, but he was of no significance. 'He is only a boy!' Saleem shouted.

'Shut up or you will follow him,' a man said in warning. Saleem looked at him helplessly.

'You. Remove it,' the chief barked, pointed at one of the guards.

As Samba's limp and bleeding body was dragged out of the cave, Saleem could not even wipe away his tears because his hands were bound with rough rope.

Then the men went outside, and the noise of celebration started up again. The pungent smell of crude palm wine mixed with the aroma of barbecued food. The men drank and laughed and clapped one another on the back. How could they, Saleem wondered? Was there not a single person out there who felt sorry for the dead boy and shame at his killing? 'Oh, Samba, I am sorry, I am so sorry.' He banged his head against the wall of the cave. 'I have watched you being killed and I have done nothing. Perhaps I could have dragged myself between you and the gun. You were only a boy, yet you showed more courage than most. What will happen to your grandmother? How will she cope with the news that she has lost you?'

Saleem stared into the darkness for a long, long time. He was drained by his sorrow, exhausted by replaying the brutal scene, tormented by guilt at his inability to help his friend, lost to the real world.

*

A blast brought him to his senses. Then shouts and screams. The fire of rifles and guns. He strained forward to see through the narrow opening of the cave. The fire that had been burning was gone and in the faint light of early morning, he could make out only dust and smoke blowing in the air, carried this way and that by the wind. But as his eyes grew used to the haziness, he saw with horror that the dark-clothed rebels were fighting with men on horseback. From where he was tied, Saleem could see the fast rise and fall of horses' hooves and the tangle of men caught between them. Bullets flew into the cave, making holes and dents in the walls and stones around him. Saleem lay down behind a rock and waited as the fighting continued.

Finally, at day break, the firing ceased. Saleem could hear the moaning and groaning of the injured. 'Oh, Allah…' he closed his eyes, knowing that there had been yet more bloodshed outside.

Then came the blinding light of a torch shone in his eyes. More torches lit patches of wall, parts of the cave floor. Saleem heard men shouting as they found the store of stolen rifles and other weapons.

'Look! There is a man hiding here. Who are you?' The man who had spoken lifted his gun, but as he shone his torch and saw that Saleem was bound hand and foot, he put it back in its holster.

'He's a prisoner… What's your name?

'My name is Saleem Khan.'

'The engineer sahib's driver?'

'Yes, sir… They killed Samba.' It was his first thought. His only thought.

'You mean the young boy from the village?'

Saleem nodded.

'Yes, we know,' the uniformed man sighed. 'We were investigating the murder of Mr Carpenter, the Englishman, and we came across the boy's body in the shallows of the river. That's how we discovered this place. We followed the bloody footprints.'

Saleem tried to stand up but faltered. His back was stiff from being bent for days, and he flinched from the pain of his wounds. His hands and feet were numb and the rope burns on his wrists and ankles had drawn blood. Two men held him and helped him stand.

'Look at this!' one said, clearly shocked at the severity of Saleem's injuries.

'Brutes,' the other said. 'They've left him here bound with untreated wounds. We need to get him to a hospital.'

'You poor man. We'll get you treated now,' the first man said, touching Saleem's arm. 'When you feel ready, we'll get you out of here and get you some help.'

Three men walked slowly out of the cave. The one in the middle was supported on either side and walked with his head bowed. His legs gave way every few steps, but he pulled himself up and insisted on carrying on. He gave no thought to his own injuries. He was remembering his young friend.

Chapter 51

'It's four o'clock. Tea time, *amma*.' Vimala's voice woke Anjali.

She had fallen asleep again. Ashamed, she got up.

'Memsahib thought you would like your tea here.' Vimala put a tray on a bedside table.

What a relief that the memsahib didn't wish Anjali to join her.

'Is the engineer sahib back?'

'No, *amma*.'

Three days had gone by without any news from Mr Robert about Saleem and Anjali was becoming ever more concerned. Her own situation was equally upsetting. Nothing had been resolved. Nothing had even been said. Although she didn't feel the same tension and fear that had always been with her when she was with Mohini, nevertheless she felt as if she had been transferred from one jail to another. Was that unfair of her, she wondered. Mr Robert was treating her with kindness and consideration, but she remained very much alone.

Miss Edwina didn't bother to communicate with her and occasional visits from Vimala were her only connection with the outside world. In a way she was glad to be left alone with her thoughts and she felt little desire to leave her room. But remaining alone for hours on end made her claustrophobic. Not knowing what was going on and what her future might be was the worst. She could never relax. She worried continually and fretted about what would happen next. For some reason, she felt she was being kept in the dark. She could only hang on to the hope that Saleem was safe and alive and she would see him soon.

She lost her appetite and could only pick at the meals that Vimala brought her. Each time she pushed away her plate, she would look at Vimala with a questioning glance, but the answer was always the same.

'We have heard nothing yet, *amma*. No need to worry. The engineer sahib wouldn't let any harm come to Saleem.'

'Could you ask your memsahib? Perhaps Mr Robert has told her something?'

'As you very well know, *amma*, this memsahib won't discuss things like that with the servants.'

Anjali sighed helplessly.

As the days passed, Miss Edwina's silence bothered Anjali more and more. Thoughts of Mohini came to her. At least she would have spoken to her by now. Unable to cope with the total lack of communication, in desperation Anjali opened the door of her room and set off towards Miss Edwina's private quarters. It was a stupid thing to do but by now Anjali's nerves were frayed. She had to do something.

Halfway down the hallway, Vimala came running towards her, carrying a white envelope and a brown parcel in her hands.

'These came for you, *amma*.'

'What are they?' The envelope had her name on it. Recognising the writing, her heartbeat quickened. Unable to wait, she tore it open. Her eyes followed the uneven rows of words on the sheet of white paper. She whispered the contents aloud to herself and a wide smile came to her lips. She repeated the letter, this time a little louder, just to make sure that she wasn't dreaming.

'Anjali-ji, I am glad to hear that you are safe and with the grace of Allah and the kindness of the Engineer Sahib I am safe as well. It might take a few more days before I see you. Please take care, Saleem.

Vimala heard the words spoken and saw Anjali's happy face. 'Good news, *amma*! Thank god he is safe.'

Unable to speak as emotion overwhelmed her, Anjali smiled back with tears in her eyes. She took a deep breath before turning back towards her own room. Vimala followed her with the parcel still in her hands.

For a while Anjali sat quietly on her bed, allowing herself to rejoice in the news that Saleem was safe. Finally, she turned her attention to the parcel and was surprised to find her name written in English, in a different hand. Without opening it she placed it on the table.

'Do you know who it is from?'

'Saar sent you this with Mr James's driver.'

'You mean the engineer sahib?'

Vimala nodded.

'Who is Mr James?'

'He is another big engineer sahib.' Vimala raised a hand high above her head. 'You know, bigger than our saar.'

Wondering what it was, Anjali toyed with the string that tied the parcel for a while before removing it hesitantly. Both women gasped as the paper fell open. At least half a dozen very expensive silk *saris* in many colours slipped from the brown paper. They reminded Anjali of the *saris* she wore so long ago when she was living at her late husband's grand house.

Already embarrassed that she was living in his house, to accept this expensive gift from a white stranger seemed too much for Anjali. The possibility that he might be thinking that she had accepted the marriage took away all pleasure in the beauty of the *saris*.

Even Vimala looked stunned to see them.

'Vimala, please tell him I can't accept his gift.'

'But he is not here, *amma*…'

'Then you keep them with you until your master returns.'

She re-tied the parcel with string and placed it on the table.

'Vimala!' It was Miss Edwina shouting outside the door. Startled, they looked at each other. Miss Edwina didn't come in but shouted again, 'How long are you going to stay in that room? Have you forgotten whose maid you are?'

'Sorry, memsahib. I'm coming,' Vimala said apologetically as she opened the door.

'Tell that darkie that I need her room tonight because a guest of mine is coming to stay.'

'But, memsahib, where will *amma* go?'

'Send her to the servants' quarters and start cleaning the room at once.'

'But, saar said…,'

'Oh, what is it with you all servants? Always "sir said this" and "sir said that"! What about me? Listen, Vimala, just do what I say!'

'Yes, mem…'

Vimala came back in, but couldn't look at Anjali.

Anjali smiled at her. 'Don't worry, Vimala. Honestly, I will feel more comfortable in your quarters than here.'

'I am sorry, *amma*,' Vimala apologised.

'It's not your fault. Come and show me my new room.' Anjali put her hand on Vimala's shoulder.

The servants' mud houses were situated at the back of the building where Miss Edwina could see them from her balcony. In all, there were twelve houses, which, grouped together, looked like a little village. Vimala allocated Anjali a small but clean hut, saying, 'Only this one is available, *amma*.'

'That's fine, Vimala, I like it.' Anjali stood looking around the single-roomed hut, which reminded her of her time with Samba and his grandmother. Her heart ached at the memory of the old lady. How well she had looked after her. As if she were her own granddaughter.

'Who lives in the other houses?'

'The sweepers, water carriers, laundrymen, gardeners and *punkha-wallahs* – the fan people – and several other servants.' Vimala paused for a moment. 'Whenever Saleem needs to stay, he stays in this same hut.'

'Doesn't he live here permanently?'

'No. He prefers to live away from here. He says he can't breathe freely in this area.'

Anjali nodded, understanding. 'Do you live outside the compound as well?'

'No, I don't have any choice because Memsahib wants the maids to live here so that she can send for us at any time, even in the middle of the night, you know.' Vimala lowered her voice. 'She is not like Engineer Sahib. Very different.'

'I've noticed how considerate he is. And the way he treats his servants…'

'Yes, *amma*, he is not like others. He seems to like us and our customs and the way we live. I always think he looks content and at home here in this foreign country.'

'But…' Anjali looked at Vimala.

'Memsahib doesn't even like this country. She hates being here. She always fights with Mr Robert because she wants to go back to England. But the engineer sahib is not only committed to his job, he likes living in India.'

*

The following evening, Anjali saw a man standing on the balcony of her old room and guessed that he was the guest that Miss Edwina had invited to stay. Later, when the cook was serving dinner on the same veranda where she had breakfasted two days ago, she saw him again. This time Miss Edwina was with him. She could see them through the open window of her hut.

'See what I mean?' Vimala entered the hut with a plate of rice and curry for Anjali.

'What do you mean?'

'She is not happy with our engineer sahib but she is happy with this man.'

'Who is he?'

'Mr Vincent is an officer who recently came from London. Because he didn't know anyone, Mr Robert saar invited him into his friends' circle, and now look how he has repaid his kindness.'

'Are you sure, Vimala? They could just be friends.'

As she finished the sentence, they heard loud laughter.

'See for yourself.' Vimala gestured towards the window. Anjali stood up to see Miss Edwina laughing uncontrollably and draping herself over Mr Vincent, while he put his arms around her.

'She is drunk,' Vimala whispered. 'She is always drinking, drinking too much, you know, and he…' Realising that she was revealing far too much information to a stranger, Vimala stopped talking and Anjali felt a pang of guilt for spying on Mr Robert's wife. It was none of her business. She closed the window.

'At least for the engineer sahib's sake, we shouldn't jump to wrong conclusions,' Anjali said as Vimala took her leave.

But later, when the laughter from the balcony grew louder, Anjali began to feel sorry for this good gentleman whom, she had been told, liked her country and its people and who did not deserve to be treated in such a way by his wife. Her heart melted for the man who indirectly had helped her escape Roypuram and Mohini.

Chapter 52

The next afternoon, on Miss Edwina's orders, Anjali went with Vimala into the kitchen. It didn't resemble any kitchen she had seen before. This one had dozens of cupboards and gadgets; she didn't even know what they were called. Though they were Indian, the cook and his assistant, busy preparing countless dishes, looked strange in their white uniforms. And to her astonishment, the chef stood at a waist-high cement worktop with a clay oven beneath it and several coal and gasoline burners on top. Anjali had never seen anyone doing this before. In India, women sat down to prepare and cook food.

The memsahib was already there, studying the menu for the evening's dinner party. She glared at Anjali and brusquely said to Vimala, 'Tell the darkie that she must help you serve the guests this evening.'

Anjali smiled when Vimala replied in protest, 'But she is a guest!' But it was to no avail; the memsahib just repeated her order and told her to do as she said.

Later, wearing a maid's uniform – a white *sari* with red border – Anjali followed Vimala and helped her to set the table in the dining room. It was as exquisitely decorated as the living room, with a huge table in the centre. She helped Vimala to polish the crystal glasses, the crockery and the silver cutlery.

'It has to be spotless,' Vimala said, 'or Memsahib will be furious. Not a smudge. OK?'

Anjali polished and polished until everything shone. Then Vimala showed her how to lay the table, with several kinds of knives and forks lined up for each person in the right order and in the right place.

'How do they eat with all those knives and forks?' Anjali asked, mystified.

'You will see,' answered Vimala.

'What are you doing here?' Mr Robert's voice, so unexpected, startled Anjali, who almost dropped a plate. 'Anjali, whatever are you wearing?' He stared at her, then looked questioningly at Vimala.

'Saar... Sir...' Vimala stuttered. Anjali remained silent, not knowing what to say.

'What's going on here? Anjali is our guest. Why is she working like a servant?'

'I wanted to keep myself busy, sir,' Anjali interrupted.

'No. You are kind to help, but this is all wrong.' Mr Robert gestured to Vimala to carry on with the preparations, then turned to Anjali. 'Please go and get ready for the dinner party. I want you there. I want to introduce you to our guests, especially to Mr and Mrs Wilson. They have been so kind, you know, helping us to find Saleem.'

Anjali was torn between simply obeying Mr Robert and saying nothing, and explaining that his wife had ordered her to help Vimala and to behave like a servant in the house. There would be consequences if she now turned up at the dinner party instead of waiting on the guests.

She asked, 'Have you seen Saleem, sir?'

'Yes, I have. Did you not get his letter?'

'Yes, sir.'

'He is fine. You can see him tomorrow.'

'I can see him tomorrow?' she repeated. 'Thank you, sir!'

Looking at his wrist watch, Mr Robert called to Vimala, 'Please stop what you are doing and help Anjali memsahib to get ready. We don't have much time before the guests arrive.'

Not having any choice but to obey Mr Robert, and with renewed hope in her heart that Saleem was safe, she followed the maid, who instead of taking her back to her hut, led her upstairs, saying, 'Mr Vincent left this morning. The room is all yours again.'

Anjali nodded, but her mind was on other things. 'Vimala, I really don't want to attend this dinner party. Whatever will your memsahib say?'

'Don't worry about Memsahib; it is not up to her now that the engineer sahib is home and he has invited you.'

Anjali looked aghast. 'Don't you understand? There may be a row. The last thing I want to do is to cause trouble.'

'I do understand, *amma*, but how can you refuse the engineer sahib's request?' Vimala turned to walk away, calling over her shoulder, 'While you wash, I will go and bring your things from the servants' quarters.'

Anjali took off the maid's uniform and looked at the red cotton *sari* that Sita had given her. It was crumpled, and hardly suitable for a dinner party. Nor did she want to embarrass Mr Robert by wearing her coarse, starchy white one. Since there was no other option, she picked out a new, blue *sari* from the package that Mr Robert had given her. It was not too ornate or showy, and the colour was soft and subtle.

Feeling extremely shy, Anjali walked slowly downstairs and into the living room, and was surprised to see that Mr Vincent was there again. He and Mr Robert were immersed in deep conversation side by side on one of the grand sofas. Miss Edwina, at the far end of the room, was staring out of the window and sipping golden liquid from a goblet. Anjali sensed that she was not looking at anything but had withdrawn from the others to be alone. The room was so huge that none of them noticed her enter and she had time to take in her surroundings and to note the tense expression on Miss Edwina's face. She felt an overwhelming urge to turn back, to leave them to it. She did not belong here. But Mr Vincent's question, addressed to Mr Robert, stopped her in her tracks.

'So, you approve of what Gandhi is doing?'

Anjali wanted to hear his answer.

'Yes, why ever not when our government is imposing such unfair taxes and rules on the people?'

'So you think our government is at fault?'

'Of course. There was no reason for General Dyer to order that massacre at Jallianwala-Bagh and there was no reason to arrest Gandhi when he was holding a peaceful meeting.'

'You call that "peaceful"? Look, Robert, that man is provoking the natives and even suggesting that we quit this country.'

'What else can he do when the government refuses to listen to their reasonable requests to reform the tax system?' Mr Robert replied. 'We are being appallingly harsh and barbaric towards the natives. Don't you agree?'

'How can you say that?' Mr Vincent raised his voice and was becoming red in the face. 'Look at what happened to you – you build roads for them and they thank you by attacking you!'

'Don't be absurd, Vincent. Everyone knows that the men who attacked me were not real freedom fighters. They were a bunch of thugs who took advantage of the situation. It is happening everywhere, I'm afraid, and it has nothing to do with Gandhi's beliefs…'

'Whatever you say, Robert, I don't believe that the darkies are capable of ruling their own country. They are uneducated and uncivilised and will float aimlessly in the sea of turbulent independence.'

'What kind of civilisation are you talking about?' exclaimed Mr Robert. 'If you think wearing hats and helmets and lying in the sun for hours and playing tennis and polo is civilisation, then you are completely wrong. I don't think we offer them much of a role model. Our behaviour out here is hardly exemplary.'

For a moment Mr Vincent was silent. Then he said, 'But we mustn't succumb to their radical demands for immediate independence. Don't you think they are intimidating us with their threats?'

'You are being very unfair, Vincent. In the past they have offered us a lot and they have our interests at heart, and what have we done? We have mistreated them very badly. I don't see that it would hurt us to try to understand their way of thinking, and even to adopt some of their requests…'

'Absolute rubbish! Liberal bloody rubbish!' Mr Vincent was shouting, out of control, but he stopped mid-sentence when Miss Edwina's voice interrupted him from across the room.

'And,' she added, as if she had been listening to and following all of their argument, 'my dear husband actually said that a couple of darkies had saved his life. Not only that, he has thought fit to bring one of them here, into our house. She…'

Miss Edwina's savage speech was cut short as she spotted Anjali standing at the door. Whatever she had been about to say was left unheard.

Following his wife's gaze, Mr Robert immediately stood up and made his way towards Anjali, his arms outstretched. His blue eyes lingered for a moment on her. And she could not fail to see his gentle admiration and even… No. She gazed down at the floor. Don't be ridiculous, she told herself. Stop imagining things. He is just being polite.

'Yes, Anjali is one of the people who saved my life,' Mr Robert announced as he reached her. 'Please come and join us,' he added in Hindustani, inviting her to take a seat close to him.

'How do you do?' Mr Vincent stood up and stretched out his hand.

Having never interacted socially with Englishmen before, Anjali put her hands together and greeted Mr Robert and Mr Vincent with a '*Namaste.*'

Miss Edwina drained her glass, stared at Anjali as if she could not believe her eyes, then seemed to make a decision to completely ignore her. She shouted for the boy to fill her glass again.

Anjali meanwhile sat on the very edge of her chair, an observer and a stranger. Mr Robert asked if she liked lemonade and ordered some for her. Then, while she sat glass in hand, he went to the gramophone, placed a record on the turntable, and lowered the stylus. The room was flooded with the quiet sound of Western music.

Mr Vincent got up again and, also ignoring Anjali, walked across to Miss Edwina. Wrapping one arm around her back, and taking her hand in his, he began to dance slowly with her around the vast space of the room. How easily they conversed and moved together, Anjali thought, watching them. They danced with grace, moving in practised harmony, and leaned in towards each other to whisper and smile at shared snippets of conversation that no one else could hear. How intimate they appeared, and oblivious of the rest of the world, even with Mr Robert right there in the room. Anjali glanced at him, expecting to see embarrassment and concern on his face, but it was as if he had not even noticed. Or did not care. He tapped his fingers on the arm of his chair and occasionally looked up at Anjali.

Anjali felt sure that Mr Robert knew exactly how uncomfortable she felt to be observing the scene in the room. Even she, a foreigner in this house, sensed that something was wrong here, like a bad taste. The vibes translated easily from Western to Eastern sensibilities and she was disturbed by Mr Vincent's behaviour and its possible effect on Mr Robert.

Chapter 53

At half past seven, Anjali stood at the window and watched the guests arriving, struck by the fashionable elegance of the English women's frocks, hats and handbags. Their Western hair styles and mannerisms fascinated her. However, compared with Indian women, their jewellery seemed very minimal. Perhaps each piece was very valuable.

When a couple in their fifties arrived, Mr Robert introduced them to Anjali as Mr and Mrs James Wilson. While the gentleman barely acknowledged her, Mrs Wilson took her hands in hers and exclaimed warmly, 'My dear, you're absolutely beautiful!'

Noticing that Mr Robert smiled in agreement, Anjali looked down, embarrassed.

'Come and sit next to me,' Mrs Wilson continued, leading Anjali to one of the sofas.

Warming to her openness, Anjali began to relax and feel at ease with this new English woman. No longer so self-conscious, she joined her in polite conversation about everyday happenings. Neither of them broached anything more serious. This, after all, was a party and their first meeting.

While trying not to appear rude, Anjali's eyes roamed the room, opening in wide surprise at the sophistication of the behaviour of the women. Fingers with long, crimson nails held long, thin cigars in elegant gold holders. With an air of complete confidence and ease, the women blew smoke rings from blood-red mouths while sipping wine or vodka or gin and tonic from thin-stemmed glasses. Anjali noticed that they left behind a smear of lipstick after each sip. The atmosphere was jovial and good-natured. Even Miss Edwina seemed more relaxed as she enthusiastically did the rounds among her guests, stopping to laugh and chat with each group. Her face became alive and animated each time she started up a new conversation and she looked prettier than ever in her knee-length lavender floral dress. No wonder Mr Vincent was stealing glances at her.

When the last couple had arrived, a tall, turbaned butler, in white and red, entered and saluted with a flourish.

Miss Edwina threw back the remains of her gin and clapped her hands together to get her guests' attention. 'Let's go in to dinner,' she announced in a loud, clear voice, completely at ease.

Mr Robert and Miss Edwina escorted their guests to their respective places at the enormous table, where crystal glasses and silver dishes glinted in the last, orange rays of the sun sneaking in between the half-drawn shutters. Down the middle of the table were extravagant decorations of flowers and fruit. Beside the place settings, the name of each guest was written on card in an elaborate script. In the background stood a row of well-trained attendants.

Mr Robert and Miss Edwina took their places at each end of the table. Anjali had been seated next to Mrs Wilson. It was a nerve-racking experience for her to be in the presence of so many British people and she felt awkward and tongue-tied as the conversations flowed in all directions. Some of the men and women gave her friendly smiles, while others ignored her, but Mrs Wilson soon immersed her in conversation, telling her all about the English way of life in India and explaining how the wives filled their days.

'We have coffee mornings and needle-craft afternoons,' said Mrs Wilson, 'and in the evenings, well, there is the club house. We play bridge, bingo, and tennis when it is cool enough; there is even a tennis league, in which I'm very near the bottom. Of course, we have a swimming pool and swimming galas, and film evenings. We're shown the latest British films, you know, and the news reels. Very entertaining.' Mrs Wilson paused for breath. 'And I have my own project which I shall tell you about later. Mr Wilson doesn't approve but I take no notice. We have been out here a long time and he is resigned to me doing what I want."

Even though she could only speak a little English, Anjali understood most of the conversation. Secretly she thanked her father for hiring Miss Garland to help her learn the language. Until her step-mother took charge and stopped the lessons. Anjali also thought of her late husband, who encouraged her to sit in with his small children when they were learning to read and write with an Anglo-Indian lady who came to teach them at home.

As Anjali conversed very softly with Mrs Wilson in her limited English, she was aware of an expression of pleasant surprise across Mr Robert's face. He seemed to be watching and listening to her with an increasing fascination, which he did not try to hide.

'My dear Edwina,' a woman in red with lips to match called across the table. Then she whispered loudly, 'Tell me, is she the one who rescued Robert in that village?' She stared straight at Anjali.

Miss Edwina nodded.

'So, what exactly did she do to save him, my dear?'

'I would rather not talk about it now, Tessa.'

'Oh, please do tell,' insisted her friend.

'I don't know exactly what she did.' Miss Edwina shrugged her shoulders. 'But you know how some women are? They don't hesitate to use their feminine charms to manipulate men like Robert. To gain favours,' Miss Edwina shot a look of cold dislike in Anjali's direction.

'Oh, I know… I have seen the sort,' Miss Tessa made a face. 'Edwina, I will tell you about an incident I encountered. At my first dinner party in this country, I met a young man fairer than you and me. I thought he was new to the country and, thinking I would put him at ease, asked politely if he was with anyone. He said, "Yes, with my sisters." Of course, I immediately asked who his sisters were, and he pointed to two very dark women opposite. Well, I shrieked with laughter, thinking that he was joking, but later in the evening, I saw him climbing into a car with the very same women and I nearly fainted. So,' she gestured alternately at Anjali and Mr Robert, 'these days you have to be careful. We don't know who is related to whom or what connections they have.'

Until Mr Robert looked meaningfully across at her, Anjali did not realise that he too had been listening to Miss Tessa's conversation with Miss Edwina.

'Don't worry about her,' he said. 'Her speciality is fiction.'

'Oh, is she a writer?'

Mr Robert laughed heartily. 'She might be, if she stopped blabbing and put her pen to paper, but I fear she does not have that talent, nor any other.'

Anjali heard what Mr Robert did not say out loud. She heard his unspoken criticism of the ignorant woman and his apology for her hurtful words, and once more she was grateful.

Chapter 54

Mr Robert's friendliness at the previous night's party, and Miss Edwina's absence at the breakfast table, gave Anjali the courage to talk openly for once and to ask the questions that needed answers.

'Where is Saleem now, sir? And, as you said last night, am I going to see him today?'

'Yes, you will see him soon. But tell me first, did you say that Saleem is your childhood friend?'

'Yes, sir.'

'He worried so much about you when you went missing.'

'I knew he would, sir. He is the brother I never had.'

'A brother?' A curious smile played on Mr Robert's lips.

'Yes, sir, we grew up together and he always looked after me like a younger sister.'

'I see.' Mr Robert looked at her. His smile disappeared and his tone became serious. 'Saleem is fine now but he is in the hospital.'

'Oh, no! Why? Is he ill, or…?'

'He was captured by some thugs,' Mr Robert answered.

Anjali stared at him for a few seconds before saying, 'Captured? What… what did they do to him?'

'Believe me, there is nothing to worry about. He is recovering quickly. You can see him yourself soon. I didn't want to say anything to you before until I knew that he was going to be all right.'

'One awful thing after another has happened to him. That time at the Jallianwala-Bagh and now this…' Anjali's eyes filled with tears.

'I am sorry that he was caught up in those terrible events.'

Wondering why he sounded so terribly serious, and not knowing what to say, Anjali nodded.

Later, in the car on their way to the hospital, Mr Robert gently broke the news about Samba's murder. Distraught, Anjali covered her face with both hands and wept.

'I am really sorry,' Mr Robert said softly. 'I was going to tell you last night but Edwina had already organised that dinner party. Partly that, partly I just didn't have the heart to upset you all over again, when you had gone through so much yourself. So I waited until now.'

Anjali nodded helplessly and turned away from him as hot tears soaked her cheeks. She did not bother to wipe them away.

They travelled in silence until they reached the hospital.

Seeing Saleem in the hospital bed so soon after hearing about Samba's death pained Anjali immensely. The two friends, distressed beyond words, stared at each other. And as if Mr Robert understood that his presence was a barrier between them, he found an excuse to take his leave. 'I will go and talk to the doctor,' he said, leaving them to comfort each other.

'Anjali-ji!' The minute they were alone, Saleem tried to sit up in bed and held out his hand to his long-lost friend. One emotion after another travelled across his face like clouds across the sun. He looked much thinner than she remembered and there were bandages around his forehead, arms and legs.

'Saleem… are you all right?' she asked, dragging a stool to the side of his bed and sitting down.

'I have been searching for you so long…'

'I know…' More tears welled up as she took his hands in hers. 'I am sorry that I gave you so much worry.'

'No. Please don't apologise. It wasn't your fault. I made a big mistake in letting you travel on your own.'

'I should have waited for you in Harikonda.'

'You don't know how happy I was when I found out that you were in Roypuram.'

'I know… Samba told me…' Her voice shook.

'Samba… Poor boy!' Saleem looked down and sighed heavily. 'He didn't deserve that.'

And then once more they were silent, unable to express their grief. They wept together for the loss of their friend. They wept for the past. And in the end they wept with happiness at seeing each other.

'Anjali-ji…' Saleem was smiling as he leaned forward to wipe away her tears.

He hadn't seen her properly since the day she was married. Not even when he brought her to Adhira – she was always covered in a *burqa*. He remembered her as a pretty child but now she had grown into a young woman more beautiful than he could ever have imagined.

*

However much he disliked the idea of Anjali living in the British area, he knew that his own shared room in the slums clearly wasn't suitable for her. He was torn when Mr Robert suggested he move into the servants' quarters at the back of the engineer sahib's house until he was well again. On the one hand he would be going against his own principles of never staying in a white compound but on the other he would be very near Anjali. Perhaps his sigh was for his own weakness.

The day Mr Robert brought Saleem home, Anjali was waiting to welcome and care for him. She had asked permission to take a few cushions to his room to make the place as comfortable as possible. That first day, he was too weak to say much, but she stayed with him until he slept, stroking his hand and smiling encouragement if he opened his eyes. The following day she was there again, bringing

drinks and food that he would find palatable. And so the days
continued. During the daylight hours, Anjali stayed with him; only
late at night when the stars came out did she go back to the guest
room to sleep.

As his strength returned, they talked endlessly about everything
– their childhood, Anjali's marriage, Saleem's experience at
Jallianwala-Bagh and his life after the massacre, his strong beliefs and
political views. Anjali told him how she had ended up with Mohini in
Roypuram and about Kalyani not knowing the dreadful secret that
Mohini hid from her. She told him about Sita, suffering in silence as
a child widow. They also talked often about Mr Robert and were in
total agreement that he was different to the other English masters. He
had a heart. He was intelligent. He understood India and its people.
Regarding Miss Edwina, they kept their opinions to themselves.

Between them, though, lay one unrelated episode which Anjali
stepped over each time she entered Saleem's hut and left at the door.
She could not bring herself to tell Saleem what had happened in the
temple when the astrologer saved her and Mr Robert by performing
a marriage ceremony for them. That whole episode, over so quickly,
still felt like a dream and had no reality for her. Still, she could
not bring herself to talk about it, even with her childhood friend.
Especially with her childhood friend. Especially with Saleem, who
waited each day for her with such eagerness.

Chapter 55

Having Anjali always near him gave Saleem the strength he needed to recover quickly, but his mind was never quiet. Even though he said nothing, he was constantly thinking about how he could take Anjali away from Mr Robert's house. He knew that his small rented room, shared with Prakash, wasn't suitable and that it would not be safe for Anjali to live by herself in the slum area when he went away on tours with the engineer sahib, but he was sure that if he paid a little more rent, he could find better, two-roomed accommodation for both of them in a reasonably decent area. However, that plan meant he would have to move out of the place that he shared with his friend, leaving Prakash to pay twice as much in rent, unless he could find someone else to share the room. He decided to return to his own accommodation so that he could talk things through with Prakash. He was sure that his friend would understand his circumstances.

So immersed was he in his own thoughts that he had covered the two miles to the Gudem area before he even realised it. As he strode through the familiar narrow gullies, the children playing on the streets with sticks and broken tiles gave him friendly smiles. Women, sitting on their doorsteps weaving their palm-leaf baskets, asked him how he had been. And the men in their front yards, making shoes or producing long ropes out of coconut fibre, greeted the driver of a white man with respect. Despite the untidiness of the place and the stench of the gutters, he realised just how much he had missed his home. He had visited Gudem only a month ago, on a Sunday, when he had come to see Prakash. But because of everything that had happened since then, it seemed like much longer ago.

The doors were locked. Guessing where his friend might be at that time on a Sunday, he turned around and set off again. Lately, Prakash also seemed to be bitten by the freedom-yearning bug.

As he expected, Prakash was in the meeting room at Charan Das's house, eagerly waiting for the follower of Gandhi to start his speech.

'Saleem…!' Prakash stood up as soon as he saw his friend. 'Thank god you are safe! I've been worried about you.' He gave him a big hug. 'We heard the news about the thugs kidnapping you and…' Prakash's words were drowned as the assembled men raised a cheer for Saleem, acknowledging his bravery. Recent events flashed through Saleem's mind and he couldn't speak as he thought of Samba. He felt hollow inside. Anjali's presence had been like a balm for his grief, perhaps washing away some of the sharpness of recent memories, but now it all came back. Of course he still mourned the brave boy and felt wretched about losing him in such a terrible way.

'I am sorry to hear what happened in Roypuram. We all prayed for you every day but with the grace of Lord Rama, you are alive!' Charan Das said, greeting Saleem. 'It is bad enough for us to use violence against the British, but Indians harming Indians? I can't believe it!'

'No wonder the freedom fighters got angry with him. He works for an Englishman,' someone at the back said.

'Hear, hear!' others cheered, raising their hands.

Saleem looked down, embarrassed.

'It is ridiculous to think,' Charan Das said, 'that just because he works for an Englishman, he is against us. You all know very well that some of us have no option but to work for the British for a living, not only to support ourselves but our families and extended families too.'

He paused and looked at those who had thought to stir up trouble. 'Here we are, professing to be followers of Gandhi, but by supporting people who use violence under the pretext of fighting for freedom, are we not going against the Mahatma's principles?'

'What else can we do?' someone said. 'Haven't you heard how an officer made some Indians crawl on the ground when they passed along the road where an English woman had been attacked?'

'English woman or not, attacking an innocent person is a crime and a sin. Isn't it?'

'Yes, but they should punish only the offenders. Why punish every Indian?'

The atmosphere in the room had changed. Saleem was hearing more angry voices and more insults aimed at the British. Saleem felt suppressed resentment surfacing as he listened to anger and hostility that he felt was not justified. He did not want to hear any more. He stood up and walked out of the room.

The cooler air outside did not quench the fire of his fury but increased his agitation, not just for his own hopeless situation, but also for the circumstances that had brought Anjali to Mr Robert's house.

'Saleem…' Prakash was running after him. 'Come on. Let's go home. We can talk more easily there.'

Chapter 56

The following morning, before he left for work, Prakash woke Saleem with a cup of steaming tea. It was rare that they made tea; only on special occasions or when one of them had a headache or fever. Saleem was touched by his friend's kindness. He smiled gratefully.

As he sipped his tea, relishing every mouthful, the unpleasantness of the previous evening gradually faded. He rejoiced in the freshness of the morning. When he looked out of the window, the dew drops on the red hibiscus flowers in the back yard reminded him of Anjali. Whistling the theme song from a recent play, he got ready to leave.

It was then that the postman arrived with a letter. Recognising the handwriting on the envelope, he stopped whistling, but his face did not crease with worry. Instead a smile spread on his lips. It was from Narayan. Finally he would not have to pretend or lie; he could write honestly that his daughter was safe with him. Going to his tin trunk, he collected all the previous letters he had carefully kept for Anjali. He placed the new one on top, tied them all with string, and set off.

When he walked through the gardens of Mr Robert's mansion, there was Anjali, at the breakfast table, in the shade of veranda. Opposite her was Mr Robert, talking to her with ease. Empty plates and cups suggested that they had finished their breakfast some time ago. Beside Mr Robert was an empty chair, pushed back where no doubt Miss Edwina had been sitting.

Mr Robert must have made a joke because Anjali laughed a little. Seeing the dimple on her left cheek, Saleem's heart fluttered. He hadn't seen her laugh like that since she was living as a married woman. He remained at the bottom of the steps, staring up at her as if he had never seen her before. Her hair looked freshly washed. She wore it lose and it fell down to her hips like a waterfall. Her skin shimmered like gold in the crimson silk of her *sari*. Tender feelings stirred in him and his heart ached for her.

'Ah, Saleem, good morning! You are here early.'

Saleem averted his gaze and, feeling perhaps that he had interrupted something, stepped forward and saluted Mr Robert. He greeted Anjali with a nod before quickly walking away towards the servants' quarters.

Anjali did not follow him as he had expected. Saleem sat on his bed, disappointed, staring at the wall in front of him. There he brooded on what he had just seen. Along with Anjali's loveliness, had he not caught a look of admiration in Mr Robert's eyes? Could it be true, or was he mistaken? He shook his head in frustration. It was suffocating and too hot in his room, so he went out and sat under a *neem* tree, where the breeze soothed his hurt feelings and cleared his head a little. Was he mistaking Mr Robert's friendliness towards Anjali for something else? It was so confusing. What is it with these English people? They touch one another by shaking hands and with pecks on the cheeks. How is anyone supposed to interpret an innocent-looking touch, especially where a beautiful girl like Anjali is concerned? Why can't they keep their distance with the opposite sex, like Indians do? It is forbidden for a woman to talk to a man and women must remain in *purdah*, hidden behind a veil to protect themselves from the lustful eyes of a man. This was right, he thought. And his respect for his own culture returned with renewed conviction.

Because he was grappling with his thoughts about different cultures, he was oblivious of Anjali's approach.

'Saleem!' she called.

He looked up, still confused.

'What's the matter? You look worried.' She gave him a quizzical look.

'No, no, I am all right. I'm fine.' Saleem cleared his throat. 'A letter came for you this morning,' he said, wiping the cement bench under the tree with his shoulder-cloth. 'Please sit down and I will get all your letters from my bag.'

The sight of her father's handwriting made Anjali very emotional. She looked at them for a long time before saying, 'Thank you for keeping them for me, Saleem.'

'I am ashamed to say that I haven't replied to most of them. But later, when I sensed that his anxiety for you was increasing, I wrote one or two. I am afraid I lied to him. I wrote that you were safe here with me.'

'Please don't worry. You needed to do that. That was thoughtful of you,' she replied.

'Yes, but he must have been wondering why you were not writing to him.'

'No, Saleem, I think he will understand that it isn't safe for me to write in case my letters get into the wrong hands and...'

'Yes, your father and I discussed that possibility. That's why we have a code name for you. Ananth.'

'Ananth!' Anjali laughed with tears in her eyes. 'That's a boy's name.'

Saleem also laughed, 'Can't you guess why we decided on a boy's name?'

'Yes, I can,' she smiled.

'He also sent this for you.' Saleem handed her a thick envelope.

'What is it?' She pulled out a bundle of notes and stared at him mystified.

'It's the money he sent you some months ago.'

'Oh, *pita-ji*…' she sobbed, putting her *sari pallu* to her face.

'Please…' Saleem tried to console her but he could see that she needed to be left alone in the company of her father's letters and to immerse herself in her own thoughts and memories and emotions. 'Please read them in the privacy of your room. I will be back this evening,' he said quietly, and left her.

*

After spending the whole day in her room, reading and re-reading her beloved father's letters, addressed to Saleem but intended for her, Anjali acknowledged once again how much Saleem had done for her. With feelings of overwhelming gratitude, and wanting to thank Saleem fully, she walked towards the servants' quarters.

Saleem sat under a *tamarind* tree at the back of his hut, obviously lost in thought. Anjali had been rushing to thank him, but observing him like this, she slowed down and approached him with quiet footsteps. She was almost beside him when he finally heard her. He turned and gave her a warm smile but Anjali sensed the anxiety behind his greeting.

'Saleem,' she asked gently, 'is there something wrong? You looked so worried just now.'

Saleem was silent for a while. Then, summoning up the courage to be honest with her, he admitted, 'I feel bad that you are living here in a white man's house.'

Anjali nodded, understanding his concern.

'Where should I go instead? Do you want me to move in with you in your rented place?'

'I would love that,' he replied, 'but it's not safe for a girl like you to live in that area. I thought I might look for somewhere more suitable… some accommodation with two rooms… perhaps I could live in the second room and take care of you. Would that be acceptable to you?'

She nodded. 'But Saleem… until then I am afraid I have to live here.'

'It looks like there is no other option for you.'

'Is this what's worrying you? I can see something is.'

'I also feel bad about working for an Englishman.'

'But why, Saleem? You know he is not like the others.'

'I know, but other people don't know that.'

'Why bother about that? Do other people's opinions matter to you so much?''

'I went to a meeting last night… and… you know…'

'Again, Saleem…?' Anjali looked at him disapprovingly. 'You know how dangerous these so-called meetings are.'

Saleem smiled. 'This was not like Jallianwala-Bagh, Anjali ji. This was held in someone's family home.'

'But still, Saleem! If you are not working for Mr Robert, who will you work for?'

'Who do you think? I would work for an Indian, of course.'

'So what is the difference? At least Mr Robert treats you well. You can't guarantee an Indian employer would be as considerate.'

'I know, but at least all this wouldn't have happened, and you wouldn't have endured all that you did at Mohini's.'

'Saleem, if you hadn't been working here, it would have been impossible for you to rescue me, and I wouldn't be alive now.'

'Anjali-ji…!'

'Saleem… I think there must be more to this.'

'It is just…' After some hesitation, he told Anjali what had happened at the previous night's meeting.

Anjali said, 'Saleem, you are never going to get the freedom you want. If the British left, you would be working for a rich Indian and there is no guarantee that he will treat you like Mr Robert. In fact, it might be much worse for you.'

'I know, but for some reason my heart won't accept that argument. A person like Mr Robert is very rare, but I still feel guilty working for a British man.'

'I understand how you feel because that's exactly how we women feel. Not with the British but with the men of our own culture.'

Surprised, Saleem looked at her.

'Yes. You say that you have no freedom but where is the freedom for the women of this country? Are we not deprived of it by our own people, our own families?' Anjali smiled wryly. 'I want to work because I don't want to be a burden to anyone, but you said once that a woman shouldn't work.'

'Yes, that's right. Our society doesn't respect a working woman.'

'But why, Saleem? What is the problem with a woman working and finding satisfaction the way men do? And you've just said that you can't let me stay in your home because it's not safe for me to live in that area. So tell me, where is the freedom for a woman? Why does she have to suppress her feelings, wants and desires?'

Saleem looked aghast. But Anjali continued.

'Look at Sita and Kalyani... even Mohini... What sort of lives are they leading? Why does our society punish such women with cruel labels and a complete lack of respect when they haven't committed any crime?'

'It is the way of our culture. It is not thought of in terms of a punishment. We are just following the customs and traditions,' Saleem replied.

'In that case, we need to question our customs and traditions, because they are unjust and unfair.'

'I don't think other people feel things as deeply as you. They are content to follow the rules of our ancestors. In fact, no European culture respects and protects women like we do.'

'Oh, come on, Saleem! Are you so brainwashed that you boast about our culture and look down on others?'

'Anjli-ji!'

'You criticise Western women, but at least they have the freedom to express their thoughts and men seem to value their opinions. For me, that is a kind of respect I would greatly value.'

'I agree with you, Anjali.'

They both jumped and stood up. Mr Robert was standing close behind them. Neither had noticed him approaching.

'Please sit down. I just came out because it was hot inside. I am sorry but I couldn't help hearing what you were saying.'

'Sorry, sir!' they both said at once.

'Sorry for what? What you say is absolutely right, Anjali. Yes, I too am appalled at the way some women are treated here in India. And I know many of them suffer in silence. If even one suffers, that is one too many.'

He sat down on the bench, joining them as if it were the most natural thing in the world.

'I will bring a chair for you, sir,' Saleem offered.

'No, I don't need one. Please relax, Saleem… Anjali.'

Mr Robert waited until Anjali was seated at the other end of the bench and Saleem on the root of the tree, before picking up the thread of the conversation again. 'I thought they had passed legislation to ban *suttee*. I am really appalled that it is still going on.'

'It is, sir,' said Saleem. 'People ignore the rules, sir.'

'Shameful!' He paused for a moment before addressing Anjali. 'What sort of work would you like to do Anjali? I heard you say how much you would value your independence.'

'I would. I am prepared to do anything useful, sir.'

Mr Robert looked thoughtful. 'I have one idea. Perhaps you would consider…'

'Anything…' she repeated.

'No, not anything. We need to find you work that will use your skills and experience… and give you some satisfaction. I have given it some thought already because I am aware that you don't want to do nothing here. What would you think about working with deprived women and children?'

Anjali looked up, amazed at such a proposal. 'I would love to, sir.'

'If you like, I can arrange an interview for you with Mrs Wilson. She is involved in running a home for deprived women and child widows.'

'But, Sir, I don't have any qualifications…' Anjali protested.

'How many Indian girls can read and write and speak a foreign language like you?' He smiled. 'Exactly. Only those from wealthy families?'

Anjali could hardly believe how events were unfolding. A few moments ago she was arguing with Saleem about the fate of Indian women and now here was Mr Robert offering her a chance to be independent. It was unreal. A dream.

'Thank you, sir. I very much like the idea. I hope I will please Mrs Wilson. Work of that sort would give me a real purpose.'

As she finished, a servant came running, saluting Mr Robert. 'Sir, Mr James's driver is here with a message for you.'

'Excuse me,' Mr Robert said, standing up. Then to Anjali, 'I will keep all this in mind and talk to Mrs Wilson soon.'

*

Anjali had been so engrossed in Mr Robert's suggestion that she had almost forgotten about Saleem. She certainly hadn't noticed his reaction or seen his mounting anger and indignation.

'How dare he interrupt our conversation! It is not his business to decide whether you work or not!' he said with contempt, the minute Mr Robert was out of earshot.

'Saleem!' an astonished Anjali replied. 'It was only a suggestion and he was trying to help me.'

'Who is he to suggest anything to you? What does he know about you?'

'He knows that I want to work.'

'Why does he have to sneak out and eavesdrop on our conversation?'

'Saleem, he is a gentleman. He wouldn't do that. He just happened to come out and he overheard us. We were having quite a heated discussion!'

'He has shown himself to lack the manners of a gentleman,' Saleem muttered.

'Saleem, whatever's wrong with you? Mr Robert is trying to help me. I think there is much more to this than you are letting on.'

'Why do you have to agree to work for an English woman? Am I not here for you?'

'Of course. I know you are here for me. The only thing that kept me sane while I was at Mohini's was the thought of you searching for me. I knew you would remain loyal, and Saleem, I know how much I owe you.' Anjali looked at him. 'That was the reason I came looking for you earlier. To thank you for what you have done for me. It is because of you that I am alive today.' She looked at him with tears in her eyes. 'But, you know, the point is not whether I work for an English woman or not. You know that. The point is whether the work is useful. You heard what Mr Robert said: it involves the needs and interests of our Indian women and children. I have already met Mrs Wilson and like her. She is a humane woman.'

'Anjali-ji, it is not that straightforward. Their morals are wrong and different to ours. Most white people can't be trusted.. '

'Perhaps some, Saleem, but I believe Mrs Wilson's intentions are honourable.'

Looking down, Saleem remained stubbornly silent.

They sat immersed in their own thoughts and remained silent for a long time. Finally Anjali got up. She looked at the twinkling stars. 'It's too late to talk any more tonight. There is a lot for us both to think about. Good night, Saleem.'

Saleem nodded without a word. He watched her as she walked away and went into the house. He could see her through the large glass windows, climbing the stairs and disappearing into her room.

He couldn't bear to stay there, in the servants' quarters. He walked out of the gates and set off towards Gudem and his rented room.

Chapter 57

That night, feeling shaken by the latest turn of events, Saleem disclosed everything to Prakash.

'Mr Robert is luring Anjali with the promise of finding her a job in an institution where a Mrs Wilson oversees or helps with things. I have to get her out of there fast otherwise she will be living in Mr Robert's house forever.'

Prakash nodded. 'I understand.'

'I am sorry,' Saleem said, 'to be burdening you with all this but it concerns you too. I know if I move out you will have to pay double the rent, but I don't know what else to do.'

'Saleem, please don't worry about me. I can probably find someone else to share the room. But are you sure you can afford a two-roomed house in the city? The rent will be ridiculously high.'

'Somehow I have to manage it,' Saleem replied. 'I have already decided to give up smoking, tea, *paan* and that crude *kallu* that we drink in the evenings so that I can save some money towards the rent. I am also thinking of cutting down on the amount I send home every month.'

'Do you think your family can manage with less money?'

'They will have to.'

'One more thing, Saleem. Have you thought about the reaction of other people? What will they think if you and Anjali live in the same house?'

'People can think whatever they like, Prakash. I don't care.'

'You don't care, but what about Anjali? And how are you going to introduce her to your future landlord?'

Saleem's silence showed he knew that his friend had a valid point.

'They will definitely ask you, Saleem. Most of them will want to know what your relationship is with her before they offer you somewhere to rent. I doubt if you will find a landlord who will allow a man and woman like you and Anjali to live together. They will all jump to the same conclusion.'

'Yes. You are right. You know, in my anxiety and haste, I hadn't thought that through, Prakash. I realise now that there might be problems.' Saleem's face creased with worry.

'Are you in love with her?' Prakash asked.

To Saleem, the question might have appeared abrupt and even out of place, but he supposed it must have been obvious to Prakash for a long time that his feelings were no longer that of a childhood friend. Perhaps it was a relief to finally have it out in the open.

'You are, aren't you?' Prakash persisted.

'Perhaps I am…' he admitted.

'You are telling me that you are not sure?'

'Is it that obvious?'

'Of course. Even at the very the beginning I could see how forlorn you were – not eating… pining for her… You were like the real Saleem in the story *Anarkhali*.'

Saleem looked down, deeply embarrassed.

'I am sorry, Saleem, I don't want to dampen your dreams but have you thought about the consequences? Her religion is not your religion. Do you think your family would agree to you marrying her?'

'Prakash…!' Saleem looked at him flabbergasted.

He had never thought of marrying her. She was from a high caste, a Brahmin. His family had been working for them since his grandfather's time. He knew his limits and where he stood. He was nowhere near a match for her. But… yes… he knew he was in love. Hopelessly so. He had not revealed it to anyone until now because it was such an ill-fated match. But he had not thought it through either. For a whole year, thinking about her and trying so hard to find her had completely occupied his energies, and now seeing her every day was an incredible joy. Too lost in his own emotions for rational thought, Saleem was barely listening to what Prakash was saying.

'Saleem!' Prakash said again.

'Sorry, did you say something?'

'I asked if you knew how Anjali feels about you?'

'I know she is fond of me. We are friends.'

'Is that all?'

'I think so. Let me find some accommodation first.'

'I think you are doing things in the wrong order, Saleem. Are you genuinely going to remain just friends? You are not going to be able to hide your feelings for her for long. And is this what Anjali wants? I think you should go and discuss it with her openly and honestly first. It is complicated, Saleem.'

Go and tell Anjali that he loved her? To confess his true feelings was out of the question. Better to concentrate on practical matters first, he decided. His personal life was just too confusing.

*

More determined than ever, Saleem went in search of a suitable place for himself and Anjali, accompanied by his troubled friend. As Prakash had predicted, wherever they went the owners wanted to know how many people were going to live in the rooms and asked what the relationship was between Saleem and Anjali. Unable to give a convincing answer, they were turned away again and again until they had searched the whole city, for hours on end, and the light was fading. Saleem was beginning to lose hope.

'I don't know about you, but I am starving,' Prakash said. 'The machine of my body is refusing to work without fuel.' He dragged Saleem to a roadside tea stall.

As they sipped the sweet milky chai, Prakash suggested, 'The only solution I can think of is that you will have to tell them that she is your sister.'

'But that's not true.'

'Can't you lie?'

Saleem looked into his cup for a long time before saying, 'Yes, I can. But there is another problem. I am a Muslim and she is a Hindu.'

'Well, my friend, you will have to lie about your faith too. Or she will have to. You could change the way you dress to a *dhoti* and *angi*, and pretend you are a Hindu…'

Prakash was only half serious, but Saleem seized on the idea. While he knew perfectly well that it would not be easy to lie about his religion, and that even if he dressed as a Hindu he might be asked some difficult questions, he chose to ignore his doubts. Don't think about any of that now, he told himself. It will work out somehow. He told Prakash that his idea was brilliant.

'Thank you,' Saleem said. 'You have solved all my problems.'

'I am not so sure,' his friend replied.

So this was how, the next morning, Saleem, dressed as a Hindu, set off once more in search of somewhere to live. This time he was successful. He managed to convince the owner of a large bungalow that he and his sister, both Hindu, needed accommodation because their parents were in financial difficulties. The small, two-roomed outhouse behind the man's own bungalow was perfect. It was clean and tidy and had its own separate bathroom. It was even close to the city's amenities.

'This is it. I shall take it,' he told the landlord quickly, before they both changed their minds.

Chapter 58

The previous night's conversation with Saleem had disturbed Anjali. She couldn't understand Saleem's objections to her working. Why couldn't he see her point of view? Working in a women's home was an excellent opportunity for her, and Mrs Wilson was a kind if somewhat unusual woman, but Saleem didn't seem to believe that. Was he being paranoid? Ever since he had been involved in that shooting, he seemed to suspect every single white person.

A gentle knock on the door disturbed her thoughts. Vimala was softly calling her name.

'Come in, please,' Anjali answered lethargically.

Opening the door and stepping in, Vimala announced, 'Mr Robert went to play tennis and Miss Edwina has just left for the club house. But Mrs Grace is here requesting your company.'

'Mrs Grace, requesting my company…?' Repeating Vimala's words, Anjali immediately got up.

Mrs Grace was sitting on a sofa in the drawing room, waiting for her.

'Good afternoon, Mrs Grace,' Anjali said.

'Afternoon, my dear. Come and sit here.' She gestured at a chair beside her. 'And please call me Mrs Wilson. You are not my servant.'

'Thank you, Mrs Wilson.' Anjali sat on the edge of the seat while Vimala brought a tray of tea and biscuits. The aroma of fresh Assam tea wafted into the room.

Even though she had not experienced any kind of socialising with the British before staying at Mr Robert's house, Anjali was beginning to learn some of their wonderful ways and habits, like sipping tea at every opportunity from delicate china cups. She smiled, remembering how most Indians slurped tea boiling hot from bronze tumblers, passing the hot metal vessel from one hand to the other, and blowing in between gulps to cool the liquid down.

Mrs Wilson waited until Vimala had placed the tray on the table in front of them and said, 'Thank you, Vimala. We will help ourselves.'

Vimala bowed and left the room.

After pouring the tea, Mrs Wilson said, 'Mr Harrison has told me everything.'

'Everything?' repeated Anjali, holding her breath.

'He said you are interested in working for our women's institute.'

Anjali exhaled with relief. Of course he wouldn't have revealed what had happened in the temple of Roypuram. She was being ridiculous.

'I think working there is a splendid idea, if you are willing.'

'Thank you. I would really appreciate the opportunity, if you would accept me.'

'Why ever not? We need young, enthusiastic women like you.'

Anjali looked at her gratefully.

'Why don't you come with me now and we'll visit the institute. You can see things for yourself and it will give you some idea of what to expect.'

'Thank you, Mrs Wilson. I would like to.'

It all happened so quickly. Minutes later, she found herself sitting next to Mrs Wilson in her car, travelling to St Agnes's Women's Institute. They passed imperial government buildings flanked by splendid lawns, a race course, a magnificent cathedral and an ostentatious memorial to Maharani Victoria. It was all so foreign to her. Even the street names – Victoria Road, Kensington Street, Reginald Crescent – belonged to another country. Another world.

While Anjali marvelled at the surroundings, Mrs Wilson explained about the work of the institution.

'Apparently the mother superior of a convent started it early in the nineteenth century and it was run by the sisters of the community of St Mary The Virgin. Their initial aim was to rescue the young British girls and women who had come out here naively in search of a husband, but were either deceived or rejected by the men they had hoped would marry them. As a result, they were left penniless and with nowhere to go. Some were literally out on the streets.'

Anjali was shocked. 'Really? Does that happen in English society?'

'Of course. That kind of thing can happen in any society,' Mrs Wilson said. 'The institute housed the rejected girls in the hostel until it collected enough money to send them home. It doesn't happen so much now, not to British girls, because they are not so naive anymore. But I can't say it is not still happening. Even now, there are some parents in Britain who send their young daughters out here on a husband-hunting mission. The plan is that they will stay for two or three months with relatives or friends until they find a match. They used to call the girls the Fishing Fleet. Very unkind. Yet for these girls, perhaps from families that were not rich or fashionable, this was one of the few ways they might meet an eligible rich young man. The ones who were not successful returned to England, ruthlessly labelled Returned Empties.'

Anjali listened attentively and with sympathy for the girls who came all the way to India in search of a husband. So necessary was it to be married that they were willing to travel halfway round the world to find a man.

'I have been involved with the work ever since I came to India, some thirty years ago. I was one of those naive girls. I was only twenty-three when I travelled out on a ship named the *Viceroy of India*.

It took us a month to travel from Liverpool to Madras. In that four-week voyage, everybody got to know each other. I remember I went to a fancy-dress party with another girl wearing enormous great hats we had decorated with fruit and flowers. We both wore purple and pink dresses with slips deliberately showing underneath. I remember it so well. It was in the bar of the *Viceroy of India* that the young officers and girls met. Some were paired up by the time they reached Madras. That's how I met my husband. Far too hasty. I hardly knew him. Shocking, don't you think?' Mrs Wilson laughed. 'When we arrived in Madras, his colleagues were waiting on the quay to meet him and they looked taken aback to see us walk down the gangplank together.'

'Did Miss Edwina come out here as one of the Fishing Fleet?' Anjali asked suddenly, but seeing Mrs Wilson's smile disappear, she regretted it and bit her tongue.

'Good heavens, no. She was already engaged to Robert before she came over. She was considered quite a catch.' Then quickly changing the subject, she said, 'But then the British girls became fewer and Indian girls started to arrive, seeking help. They heard about us. You would be surprised to know how many native girls and young women have come to us in need of shelter and a place of safety over the years.'

'Did you accept them?'

'Yes, of course! We didn't have the heart to send them away. At least our English girls eventually went home, but the Indian girls had nowhere to go because they were abandoned by their families and society, or had run away from them in difficult circumstances. The only future ahead of them was either prostitution or suicide.'

Anjali listened, thinking to herself how much this account mirrored her own situation.

'Well, as the numbers grew, we couldn't accommodate everyone. We ran out of room. So ten years ago we set up a separate refuge for native girls. The priests and governers of St Agnes's Church, on the outskirts of the city, came forward and offered some buildings adjoining the church for the purpose.'

'That was extremely kind of them.'

'We split the accommodation into two units – one for the children, and the other a training home for older girls and women.'

'It must be very expensive to run. Where do you find the funds? I hope you don't mind me asking,' Anjali said.

'Of course not, my dear. I'm glad you are already thinking so clearly. It is maintained by charity subscriptions and staffed by voluntary workers who are paid only for their subsistence.'

By the time the car stopped in front of the church building, Anjali was speechless with admiration and gratitude towards this kind and compassionate woman who spoke so selflessly about the work she did and the organisation she helped to run. She got out of the car and saw a board with big bold letters on one of the buildings. It read, 'St Agnes's Home and School for Girls'.

Chapter 59

The whitewashed, flat-roofed, single-storied, rectangular building stood surrounded by small patches of green. Anjali could see coconut trees, tall and full of fruit, behind it, and marigolds, in shades of red, orange and yellow, blooming abundantly before its walls. She could tell it was of strong, ancient construction, with its stone walls and arched iron porches and gates.

As they entered the building, Mrs Wilson was still talking about the history of the institute. 'In the beginning, many girls who were suffering and fearful refused to come to this home.'

'Why?'

'Because they were brainwashed. People filled their minds with a dread of Christians. They were told by the orthodox conservatives that the Christians, after feeding them and fattening them up, would hang them upside down, build a huge fire underneath them and then extract human oil that would be sold for an enormous price for medical purposes in England. Some were even told that they would be put into mills, where their bones would be ground up...' Mrs Wilson looked at Anjali. 'You know what I mean. They were told shocking horror stories to scare them away. Besides, these ill-treated women couldn't understand how anyone would be kind to them unless behind their actions was a selfish motive.'

Anjali was shocked to hear this and shook her head. 'How sad!'

'I know. But slowly things changed. We are fortunate in having an extraordinary woman called Chandrabai, a social reformer, who put an end to the false rumours. Encouraged by her, we started this home with just four young women and a couple of child widows. Chandrabai convinced them that what they had heard was untrue, and slowly they started to trust us. After Chandrabai joined forces with us, she travelled all over the state, several hundred miles, by foot, on buses and trains, campaigning. Now our numbers have increased to nearly a hundred. The women have come from all backgrounds and faiths – not just widows, but child brides whom Chandrabai has rescued. They had been so horribly abused that they were terrified of the touch of another human being. Even older women who had been treated like animals and had suffered years of cruelty came seeking our protection.'

'Is Chandrabai a Christian?'

'Not by birth. She was born a Hindu and suffered as a child widow herself, but recently she converted to Christianity. Even though she reads pages from the Bible every day, she has promised not to put pressure on the girls whose religions are different from ours to convert to Christianity. She offers lessons on the Bible but only if they want to learn about it. Having said that, many of the women, through reading the Bible and observing Chandrabai's principles and behaviour, have converted to Christianity.'

St Agnes's Home contained two huge halls and a kitchen. One hall was divided into four sections by bamboo screens and was equipped with blackboards, chalk, slates and books. Anjali guessed this must be the school room. The other hall was used for many purposes: it was a living room, a work room and a craft room. There were several palm-leaf mats on the floor, with evidence that women had been working there. A box of multi-coloured embroidery threads, needles, finely sliced palm leaves, jute soaked in water to make baskets, a pile of discarded material and cotton wool to make toys. Metal containers of beads and coloured stones for making jewellery were arranged to one side.

'At night, it becomes a bedroom for the women,' Mrs Wilson said. 'We can only afford those,' she pointed to a pile of thin mattresses in a corner. 'The women lie down on them side by side, and the children sleep in the adjoining school rooms, ten or twelve in each, with one adult supervising them. Come, let's go to the church hall and meet Chandrabai.'

Chandrabai was sitting reading in a chair in one of the church halls and seemed very pleased to see Mrs Wilson and Anjali because she immediately jumped up and welcomed them with open arms. She was a dignified figure wearing a black and white *sari* with her hair in a chignon.

'You have arrived at a good moment. Would you like to join us for the prayer? It will be starting soon,' she smiled.

As she spoke, the doors opened and the church hall began to fill with women, girls and children, some as young as five. They all came to attend the prayer meeting and sat silently in rows on the wooden benches facing Chandrabai's chair, so that they could see and follow her. When Chandrabai started her prayer, Anjali realised that she made no mention of any particular faith but quoted, 'A life totally committed to God has nothing to fear, nothing to lose and nothing to regret.' With that, each and every one of the women and children present closed their eyes and prayed silently to their own god. Then the meeting ended and they all dispersed in separate groups, returning to the school rooms to attend their evening Bible or Bhagavad-Gita or Quran readings.

Anjali followed Mrs Wilson and Chandrabai as they went from room to room and quietly observed the girls and women. They were all shapes and sizes and of different nationalities, some wearing *saris*, some half *saris*, some the *shalwar-kameez*, some knee-length dresses and skirts. Many had covered their heads with scarves. Each was reading from her chosen book. Anjali could see that there were Hindus, Muslims, Jews and Christians. Some looked content – happy even – but a few looked subdued and disturbed. Anjali knew that they still had not got over the ordeal they had gone through. After the readings, the children were led away to do their homework, while the women gathered again in the hall with Chandrabai. They all remained standing as a mark of respect for the two women, Chandrabai and Mrs Wilson, who had given them this second chance of a life worth living.

'Thank you,' Chandrabai said, nodding to acknowledge their appreciation. 'Now, please sit down. You all know that many of you came here without skills and unable to recognise the letters of the alphabet, let alone read. Thanks to the kindness of the volunteer teachers, now, at least, you are getting some training in crafts that may help you earn a living.'

The audience nodded and some put their hands together in a gesture of gratitude.

'Now I want to introduce you to someone who has kindly come forward to take you all a stage further. She has offered to teach you to read and write.' She gestured to Anjali. 'This is your new teacher, Anjali.'

Everyone clapped and greeted Anjali with a chorus of, '*Namaste*, Anjali-teacher!'

Embarrassed but elated to hear a new title attached to her name, Anjali gave them a friendly smile and couldn't help but say, 'Thank you. It will be a pleasure for me and I hope you will accept me as one of you. I am really grateful to Mrs Wilson for giving me this opportunity. It is because of her kindness that I am here today, and my thanks to Chandrabai for agreeing with Mrs Wilson. This opportunity means so much to me.'

Chapter 60

By the time Mrs Wilson dropped Anjali at home it was late. For the first time in a long time, Anjali felt content. At last her life was beginning to take shape. Thanks to Mr Robert's understanding and quick thinking, she now had a purpose and could look forward to the future. Her heart filled with gratitude for the man who had showed her the right path and she felt a strong wish to thank him.

She knew the household routine by now. After dinner, Mr Robert and Miss Edwina usually took their drinks into the lounge, where they sat for a while. Eagerly, Anjali set off to tell Mr Robert the good news, but the lounge was empty. Disappointed, she sat down on a chair and recalled the day's events. She didn't notice the clock on the wall ticking away until it chimed ten and Vimala came in to switch off the lights.

'Anjali-*amma*, are you still here?'

'Yes. I was expecting Mr Robert... I mean... They didn't bring their drinks in here today?'

'No.' Vimala came nearer and whispered. 'They had a big argument at the dinner table and Miss Edwina stormed off to her room with a bottle of gin in her hands. I don't know where Mr Robert went but he drove off in his car.'

'Did Saleem take him?'

'No. He went alone.'

Oh, no, not again, thought Anjali, concerned about Mr Robert. The servants kept telling her things after listening at doors – things she mostly ignored because she was not interested in their gossip. But she had seen for herself the mounting tension between husband and wife.

'Mr Robert is a decent man and he has no bad habits and has so much patience and I don't understand why Miss Edwina is always angry,' Vimala said.

'We don't know what goes on in a marriage, Vimala. It's not our business to judge them.' Anjali stood up to go to her room.

'Goodnight, Anjali-*amma*. Is there anything you need?'

'No thanks, Vimala. I'll just get myself a glass of water.'

It had been an eventful day and although she was tired, her mind was much too active to let her sleep. After everything had gone so well, she had to admit that she was a little disappointed that she had not been able to tell Mr Robert and thank him. Her heart went out to the man. Even though she had been gently dismissive of Vimala's comments because she did not want to talk openly with the servants about their employers, she was in fact in agreement with her judgement. Nor could she understand why Miss Edwina was unhappy. Anjali wondered if it was simply living in India but then she recalled the scenes when Mr Vincent was with her, when she looked as if she hadn't a care in the world. After lying awake for hours, going over and over the occasions on which she had seen Miss Edwina with her husband and with Mr Vincent, she finally had to admit the truth: Miss Edwina was not in love with her husband. She didn't know whether he loved her still, despite her behaviour, but she could see he was a very patient man.

As her thoughts focussed on the man who had rescued her from the temple, she found herself reliving that scene too, and she remembered something she had not thought about at all since then. When he had looked at her for the first time, she had been struck by the amazing blue of his eyes. Now, instead of pushing the image away, she allowed herself to dwell on it, without feeling embarrassed, without even feeling uncomfortable. She wanted to remember it all in detail. She closed her eyes. Once again she was back in the temple, sitting on the floor at the end of the ceremony, when the astrologer had pressed her hands into those of Mr Robert, and she felt again his soft but firm touch. His palms, warm and slightly damp, had hesitantly closed around her fingers.

Aware that her cheeks were flushed, she opened her eyes. What was happening to her? Her heart was drumming against her chest. It was in this strange, emotional state that she heard the sound of a car entering the portico, its headlamps illuminating her window. Then the engine was switched off and her window became dark again. In the silence of the night she heard the front door open and the voice of the butler greeting Mr Robert. Footsteps – she knew they were his – came up the stairs and she swore that they momentarily stopped outside the door of her room, just for a second, before moving on. Not towards the marital bedroom, but to the spare room.

In the morning, hoping to find him at the dining table, Anjali went downstairs. Mr Robert was sitting alone, a cup in his hand. He looked at her with an expression that suggested that he had been waiting for her.

'Good morning, sir.'

'Morning, Anjali.' He gestured to a chair, inviting her to sit down.

Looking at him and remembering all the events and thoughts of the previous evening, she had no idea what to say. Things were no longer simple and straightforward.

His question saved her. 'So, I gather you went to see St Agnes's Home yesterday?'

'Yes, sir. Thank you, sir. Mrs Wilson took me there.'

'Did you like it?'

'Very much, sir.'

'Good, good. I am glad.'

'I am so grateful to you, sir…'

How stilted this conversation was, Anjali thought. How unlike their usual easy exchange of news. She felt tense. He looked tense.

'Anjali…' Mr Robert put down his cup and looked at her.

Hearing the seriousness in his voice, she looked up and saw how tired he looked. There were streaks of red in his eyes which told her that he hadn't slept last night. She wondered if perhaps the argument that Vimala had described was more serious than the many others she had heard.

'We… Edwina and I… are going to Ooty for a few days. All the servants will be here and if you need anything, please don't hesitate to call Mrs Wilson. She knows our plans. And of course Saleem will look after you.'

'Is Saleem not driving your car, sir?'

'No, he is taking us to the station. We are going by train.'

As he finished speaking, Miss Edwina emerged from upstairs and Mr Robert stood to leave.

Anjali watched the couple, who were clearly avoiding one another. Not even a glance was exchanged. As she too stood up, and followed them out of the room, she wondered why they had decided to go to a romantic hill station like Ooty straight after a dreadful argument. Then the answer came to her. Of course. They were probably going away from everyone to sort things out between them and to try to find a resolution. Perhaps, in that beautiful place, they would be reconciled.

All the servants lined up at the front of the house to bid them goodbye. Mr Robert nodded to them but the memsahib didn't look at anyone. With her pink dress fluttering in the breeze, her auburn hair tightly set in ringlets and her eyes hidden behind dark glasses, she could have been a film star. The lady of the house climbed into the car while her husband held the door open for her. Then he took his place beside her.

Anjali stood on the steps of the front veranda and waved goodbye to them. Mr Robert turned his head once, looked back, and waved at her as Saleem drove the car out of the gates.

Chapter 61

After seeing his engineer sahib and memsahib off at the station, Saleem came home happy. Anjali noticed that yesterday's misery had disappeared from his eyes and he seemed excited.

'Anjali-ji, good news!' he exclaimed as soon as he saw her.

'I have news as well,' she laughed. 'But tell me yours first!' She was sitting on a small stool in the corner of his room.

'I have found accommodation with two rooms in Krishnapura, in a pleasant locality very near to the *chowrasta*. The house is small but clean. The owners seem to be a nice family.'

'If it is near to the *chowrasta*, the rent must be high. I hope you didn't pay the deposit?'

'You don't need to worry, Anjali-ji, it's only a little more than I pay now for the room I share with Prakash. I have definitely decided to move out. It won't be a problem.'

'But Saleem... I want to tell you something as well.' Anjali hesitated, not knowing how he was going to take the news.

As he looked at Anjali, a fleeting shadow of doubt darkened Saleem's mind, and his face clouded. He recalled their previous conversation regarding her wish to work. But then he quickly composed himself and sat upright, ready to hear what she had to say.

'I have decided to work in the institute that Mrs Wilson runs.'

He had been half prepared for this, but even so, the expression on his face told Anjali that he was taken aback. He said nothing.

'Saleem, please don't look at me like that. You have no idea what it was like for me being in Roypuram. I was almost crippled by the fear of not knowing what was going to happen to me. But staying with Mohini and meeting Kalyani and Sita made me realise how undermined our Indian women are by the society in which they live. When I was hiding in the temple, I had time to think and to analyse the situation. It was then that I knew I had to do something, to try to make a difference. Many ideas swirled around my mind, but I didn't know how to put them into practice. Now that the opportunity has occurred, I don't want to lose it.'

Speechless, Saleem continued staring at Anjali.

'I can see you don't like the idea, but...' she said gently.

Saleem quickly wiped his face with a handkerchief. 'But you will have to travel quite far every day from Krishnapura.'

'No, Saleem, I don't have to because Mrs Wilson has offered me her outhouse.'

'Anjali-ji!' Saleem looked truly shocked. And angry. How could Anjali do this, knowing how he felt about inequality and unfairness under colonial rule? Not only was she putting her trust in a white woman, but she had agreed to live in her house? Didn't she care about his own feelings?'

Understanding what he was thinking, Anjali said, 'I won't be living in her house. The outhouse is situated far out at the back.'

'A *bibi-khana*?' Saleem asked bitterly. 'How can you possibly agree to live in one of those?'

'*Bibi-khana*?'

'Yes, you know. A long time ago, when the domination of the East India Company was young, there were no memsahibs in India. The English sahibs chose native women and no one objected. But when the company expanded and grew strong, memsahibs came out in shiploads. They openly despised men who associated with Indian women. These outhouses, which used to house the Indian women whom the sahibs fancied, were called "*bibi-khanas*". You can see how unfair it all was, even in those days. The English sahibs didn't let their mistresses live in their homes; they had to live separately in purpose-built, greatly inferior accommodation. Like servants.'

Anjali sighed. 'I think it is the same story everywhere. Regardless of their race, men have always treated women as inferior. What does it matter what they used to call the houses?'

She waited for him to speak but he had no more words. Deciding that he needed time to come to terms with her decision, she walked out.

Saleem sat motionless, immersed in his own thoughts. He realised that Anjali was no longer the little girl who had played with him, nor had she grown up into a traditional Hindu woman. Once she had spoken to him timidly, hiding behind a door. Now her thinking had developed and matured. She made her own decisions with care and confidence. When this change had taken place he did not know, but he realised that once she had made up her mind, she would see through whatever decision she had made. She was quite clear that she wanted to work for the institution and he knew, with a sinking heart, that he would not be able to persuade her otherwise. However hard he thought about it, he couldn't find a valid reason for making her change her mind. Whatever he thought up seemed like a ridiculous excuse, even to his own ears, and revealed him as selfish and narrow-minded.

He rubbed his forehead, restlessly pacing up and down until darkness swamped the room. With no desire to light a lamp, he collapsed on to the bed.

Chapter 62

Anjali went up to her room after telling Vimala that she did not feel hungry and needed nothing. Not wanting to put the lights on, she sat on her bed, but after her conversation with Saleem she was still restless and knew she was not ready to settle down for the night. She got up and went to the window. In the slanting light of a street lamp, the servants' quarters were visible. In most of the tiny frameless window holes oil lamps flickered, but she noticed that Saleem's room was pitch black. Like her, perhaps he too was sitting thinking, preferring the cover of darkness?

Her heart went out to him. She knew he was hurt, but what could she do? To some extent she could understand why Saleem did not want her to work. In her society and within her caste, women did not work; those who did were regarded as the equivalent of a fallen woman. But her father used to say that in Bombay, Delhi and the other big cities, girls from high-caste families were beginning to be educated. He said that he wouldn't be surprised if these girls become professionals one day soon, such as doctors, lawyers and politicians. From the way he spoke about it, she knew her father liked the idea, and probably that was the reason why he had hired Miss Garland to teach her. If her step-mother had not interfered and arranged her marriage when she was still so young, her father might have encouraged her to continue with her studies. She liked to think that he would have been proud of a daughter who was educated and independent.

Now, when she had found an opportunity to put her limited knowledge and experience to good use, it had made Saleem, her loyal childhood friend, sad and angry. She sighed as she reflected on how much he had done for her. She felt sad and guilty and uncomfortable with a situation in which her own fulfilment brought pain to someone who cared for her. There was no solution. How could she make Saleem happy but at the same time live on other people's charity? She understood Saleem's hostility towards the British and appreciated that he wanted to keep her well away from them. He would be more than happy to provide her with a home and look after her. But how could she accept that kind of sacrifice when she knew that she would only be an additional burden on top of his family commitments and responsibilities? How long did he think he was going to look after her?

'Saleem,' she said, as if he were there beside her, 'if you know me at all, you must know how desperately I crave the independence and freedom that I have never had. Besides, I want to do something that might help someone less fortunate than myself. Saleem, can't you see that for me to work amongst those unfortunate women is like a gift from the gods. I need a purpose in my life. I need work that is absorbing and stimulating. Let me choose a way of living that leaves me dependent on no one. A life which I will lead alone.'

Alone! Alone! Alone! The word that she had suppressed for so long echoed in the dark, and reverberated in her chest. She could hear it in her every heartbeat. Despite all the arguments that she had just rehearsed so clearly, she now envisaged a future that stretched before her like an endless dark tunnel. Realising that she was losing her courage over the huge changes ahead, she tried to calm herself and to think rationally. She returned to bed and pulled the bedcovers over herself. She closed her eyes, wishing her father was there to support and advise her. She blinked back the tears that welled in her eyes, refusing to give way to self-pity, and turned her mind to her new role at St Agnes's Home. For a while, imagining the scenes she had witnessed there, she managed to see herself in her new role. But soon, back came thoughts of Saleem, slipping into her plans. By the time sleep blessed her, she had come to a decision that she knew would please her childhood friend.

Chapter 63

Saleem woke early to the crowing of a cockerel and the beams from the morning sun, which played across his eyelids through the window hole. Yawning, he sat up in his bed and opened eyes that were gritty and sore from lack of sleep. Was he dreaming? He blinked twice. Anjali was there in his room, sitting on a stool in one corner, just as if she were waiting for him to wake up. In her soft blue *sari*, with her long hair tied back with a matching ribbon, she looked like a freshly bloomed golden chamanthi in a blue morning mist. He stared at her.

'Saleem…' she said softly.

He got out of the bed and stood up in a gesture of respect.

'I have come to say I am sorry, Saleem. After all that you have done for me, I have behaved ungratefully, and last night I know I hurt you. Please accept my apologies.'

'No… no… please…'

'I understand what you are trying to do for me. I know that you want to make me comfortable and happy and secure. Maybe I can explain again, more clearly. You see, just sitting at home and being waited on hand and foot by you will never make me happy. I need to use my energy to some purpose.'

Saleem began to interrupt but Anjali put up a hand to stop him. 'Let me finish. For a long time, through times of unhappiness and fear, I have been thinking about how I could do something useful. I didn't make the decision lightly. I have thought about it very hard. I am desperate to work but...' she looked up and smiled at him. 'Saleem, I have decided that I don't need to live in the *bibi-khana*. I would like to live in the house you have found for the two of us after so much searching. Can we go and see it?'

'Anjali-ji!' His frown vanished and in its place came a smile, which Anjali returned.

'Yes,' she nodded. 'I mean it.'

'But it will be so far for you to travel every day to the home.'

'Don't worry. I will be able to afford a *tonga*, with my remuneration.'

'Are you sure?' He was beaming now, unable to hide his delight.

'Yes.'

'Give me a few minutes and I will be ready.' Off he went to the bathroom, already whistling a cheerful tune, a spring in his step. Anjali watched him and was glad that she could repay him a little for everything that he had done for her. She was only too aware how much she was in his debt.

To Anjali's astonishment, Saleem emerged wearing a *dhoti* and kurta. She stared, open-mouthed, then laughed. 'You really look like a Hindu. You look like my real brother.'

The word '*brother*' startled Saleem. It was as if Anjali had slapped him 'Brother, brother...' he repeated silently to himself. It was a word he did not want to hear.

'Yes, Saleem, you are the brother I never had,' Anjali continued, cheerfully oblivious of Saleem's pain.

When, in the *tonga*, his face grew clouded and he kept glancing at her in a strange way, she decided that he must just be feeling emotional about her sudden decision. She hadn't prepared him, had just turned up and blurted it out. Of course he was feeling a bit unsettled about the future and how it would work out.

At the end of the journey, they alighted in a wide street lined with tall ashoka trees. It seemed much quieter than the other parts of town they had travelled through. Here there were no vendors with baskets on their heads, shouting about what they had to sell. At the far end of the street were a row of purpose-built shops selling household goods and a few fruit and vegetable stalls under canvas or fabric shelters. This was enough to tell Anjali that the people who lived in Krishnapura were middle-class professionals and merchants.

Slipping off the latch, Saleem opened the iron gate of the merchant's big house and held it for Anjali to enter, but she was absorbed in looking up in admiration at the fine windows and balconies. He smiled at her interest and pleasure. Then together they walked into the paved front yard, where flowers bloomed abundantly in clay pots, in the fashionable style of a city dwelling. Like everyone else's in India, the front door was wide open. They climbed the steps and, standing side by side, peered through it.

A woman was sitting on a wooden couch, combing a child's hair. They were chatting quietly. When she saw Saleem, she got up and greeted him.

'This is our landlady, Mrs Dhanamma,' Saleem said to Anjali, completely forgetting to introduce her in turn.

The woman asked them to wait while she found keys to show them their accommodation. 'So you have brought your sister this time?'

'Yes. I'm sorry. I should have introduced her. This is Anjali.' Saleem was hesitant about saying the word 'sister'. He seemed to have lost all his usual confidence.

'My brother wants to show me the place,' Anjali said, placing extra stress on the word 'brother'.

Saleem seemed to scowl. Where had his good humour gone, she wondered.

As they entered the two-roomed outhouse, which stood separately at the far back of the big house, Anjali whispered, 'This must also have been a *bibi-khana* at one time?'

'Perhaps, but at least it would have been an Indian *bibi-khana*.'

Chapter 64

Without Mr Robert and Miss Edwina, the house felt empty and subdued. The servants, more relaxed, did everything at a leisurely pace, chatting idly, and spent time hanging around in groups and smoking under the shade of the huge ancient trees at the back. There was no hurry to complete any of the tidying and dusting and polishing. Normally Vimala would check that Anjali was awake, but now she just left her to sleep on.

Three lazy days slipped by very easily. Anjali didn't feel the need to get up early or to dress formally to go downstairs. Her work at the St Agnes's Home didn't start until the following week. At the breakfast table each morning, she asked Vimala for a cup of tea and sat for ages taking small sips and thinking about the past. She wanted almost nothing to eat because her appetite had vanished. In this dreamlike state, she recalled brief conversations she had had with Mr Robert and remembered the bursts of playful laughter that had echoed along the veranda. And when she thought about his blue gaze, sometimes lingering on her, she smiled to herself and sighed.

Until Saleem asked her why she was so absentminded, she had not known that she appeared preoccupied and distracted by her own thoughts, or that others had noticed. Only then did the truth dawn on her and with horror she realised that she was missing this strange, handsome white man. She was ashamed that her heart relished the moments she had spent with him and at the same time was embarrassed that she had allowed her thoughts to run so freely. As her restlessness grew, she spent more and more time in Saleem's hut talking to him as a way of distracting herself.

'Mr Robert and Miss Edwina arrived back early this morning.'

Vimala's words made her jump.

'Why? It's only Thursday today. They are not due back this soon,' Anjali said.

'I have no idea, *amma*. They didn't even call Saleem to bring the car to the station. The gatekeeper saw them arrive in a hired horse-drawn buggy. Apparently they just asked him to attend to the luggage and entered the house very quietly.'

'Oh. That's strange.'

'I know. The butler who carried their luggage to their rooms said they looked tired and seemed strained. So none of us have dared approach them yet. We are just waiting to be called.'

'I wonder what happened in Ooty.' The thought remained silent. Anjali kept it to herself.

At lunchtime, Vimala told her that Miss Edwina had ordered a light lunch and that Mr Robert had gone out on his own without eating anything. By night, Anjali was disappointed that she hadn't seen him at all that day, and looked forward to the next morning. Mr Robert never failed to turn up for breakfast on the veranda; ever since she had been there, it had been their routine to meet and talk to one another there every morning.

As she had hoped, Mr Robert was sitting at the table in the shade of the slanted roof. The wide open arches were swamped with white jasmine flowers and an abundance of red bougainvillea that spilled out in untidy clusters, spreading their sweet fragrance everywhere. Seeing him looking tired and preoccupied, just as he had been the morning they had left for Ooty, she felt desperately sorry for him. But before she could decide whether to leave him alone or to greet him, he looked up

'Good morning,' he said abruptly.

So that was decided. Anjali went and sat at the table in front of him as usual, deliberating over whether or not to ask him about his Ooty trip.

'How have you been doing?' Mr Robert broke the awkward silence that hung for several minutes between them.

'Very well, sir.'

'I gather you have started working at St. Agnes's Home?' His smile seemed forced.

'Yes, sir. Mrs Wilson has asked me to teach the women to read and write, sir.'

'Very good! I am very pleased. I presume you are starting soon?' At last there was a glint of brightness in his eyes.

'Yes, Sir, Mrs Wilson said I can start next week.'

'Good, good.' he said, managing a smile.

Sensing that he understood her excitement, she said boldly, 'It's all happened because of you, sir. You have been so kind to me. Thank you for helping me… I am so grateful…'

'Hold on… hold on,' he put out a hand and Anjali was delighted to see that he was up to teasing her again. 'Why don't you write a book of praise for me?'

Feeling embarrassed at expressing her gratitude so openly, Anjali smiled sheepishly.

Then neither of them seemed to know what to say and the minutes ticked away silently again as Anjali became tongue-tied and Mr Robert slipped back into his own thoughts.

Wanting to break the awkwardness, Anjali decided that she should tell him the rest of her news. 'Sir… also…' But the butler came and interrupted her with a message for Mr Robert.

'Sir, there is a trunk-call for you, from your head office.'

'Excuse me, please.' Mr Robert rose, pushing back his chair. Anjali watched him stride away hurriedly.

Thinking that it would be a courtesy to inform Miss Edwina that she was moving out, and wanting to thank her for her hospitality, Anjali went in search of Vimala and asked her to get permission for her to see the memsahib. Minutes later Vimala returned to inform her that the lady of the house had decided to stay in her own quarters and would see nobody.

*

Much later, Saleem arrived dragging his feet and looking wretched.

'Saleem..?' Anjali asked, reading her friend's mood immediately.

'I've bad news,' he replied. 'This morning the engineer sahib had a call to inform him that everything is clear at Roypuram. Apparently the police have captured every single one of the troublemakers and Mr Robert was reassured that Roypuram is now a trouble-free area.'

'And...' Anjali prompted as Saleem became silent.

'It means we can continue our work in the village from next week onwards.'

Misinterpreting Anjali's shocked face, Saleem ploughed on.

'In fact, a brand new jeep has been delivered to the headquarters and I have to go and collect it.'

Looking at Saleem's serious face, Anjali asked, 'You are unhappy about this?'

He was lost in thought for a moment and then sighed, 'To tell you the truth, the news has come much earlier than I expected. I am not ready.'

'Oh, Saleem, of course!' She could imagine how nerve-racking it would be for him to go back to Roypuram after what he had experienced there. 'I understand how hard this is for you,' she said.

But Saleem's anxiety about returning to Roypuram was nothing – absolutely nothing – compared to his dismay and disappointment at having to leave her yet again.

On the way to Mr Robert's headquarters, Saleem deliberated

about whether it was sensible now to move Anjali to their new accommodation. Was it wise to leave her alone in a strange place while he was away? Since he didn't know the property owners – the merchant family – very well, it might be fairer to Anjali to suggest that she stayed where she was for the time being, in familiar surroundings, and with Vimala to look after her. It would mean postponing their move until he finally returned for good from Roypuram, and he had no idea when that would be.

'So we are returning to Roypuram, sir?' Saleem said, knowing full well that this was indeed the plan.

'Yes, but not for long.'

'Sir?' Saleem looked up. A tiny flicker of hope leaped in his heart.

'It is only for two weeks initially and after that we only have to be there for one or two days a week.'

Saleem tried to hide the relief that flooded through him.

'The construction work was already in progress before we left, and once we get it properly moving, I won't be needed there all the time. My junior and the supervisor can manage fine on their own.'

'Thank you, sir,' Saleem saluted cheerfully. 'I will go at once to collect the new jeep.'

Chapter 65

The news that Saleem would soon be going with Mr Robert to Roypuram put Anjali in a terrible dilemma. She became uneasy and worried at the chance that Saleem would find out about the secret ceremony between her and Mr Robert. In fact, to her worried mind it seemed inevitable. Sita or the astrologer might tell Saleem what had happened on that incredible night. Perhaps on the way to Roypuram, Mr Robert would casually talk about it. If he did, Anjali knew exactly how Saleem would take the unexpected news. His first reaction would be shock. He would be stunned. Then, he would probably feel betrayed by her. Wouldn't it be better for him to hear it from her rather than from others? But how could she knowingly hurt him by telling him such a painful truth? Of course he will be shocked, she reasoned with herself, but why do I jump to the conclusion that he will be hurt? Her thoughts were utterly confusing, but only because, as she now admitted, she had been deceiving herself. For a long time. She too had refused to admit the truth. Sometimes it was only a fleeting look, or a strange expression in his eyes, but Anjali knew in her heart perfectly well how Saleem felt about her. She recalled now the many times he had stared at her dreamily, as if searching her face for the answers to his unspoken questions. Of course she had noticed that gradually her friend had changed. He wasn't the same Saleem she knew when she was a child. Nor was it to do with the harshness of his recent experiences. No, this was different. She had to admit that there was longing in the way he looked at her. Although she was frightened to admit it, his attitude towards her was no longer one of brotherly affection.

Anjali took a long walk in the garden. Paced up and down the length of her room. Tossed and turned in her bed. Unable to make up her mind, she became furious and frustrated with herself. But all the thinking in the world did not produce any solutions. And deep down, she knew she was deluding herself in believing that there was an easy solution, a solution that would cause pain to no one. 'It is you who is being dishonest,' she heard her inner voice say. 'You hide the truth from everyone, including yourself. You are the one who has been playing games.'

And so, finally, she concluded that there was no option but to tell her story to her childhood friend. She prayed and hoped that it wouldn't increase his anger and hatred towards the British, and that his fury would not escalate into loathing for Mr Robert.

*

Anjali approached Saleem, who was waiting under a flame-coloured gulmohar tree that was in full bloom behind his hut. As she sat down, some distance from him, her body trembled. Knowing that if she waited any longer, she would never open her mouth, slowly at first but then with increasing speed, she narrated the episode of her hiding in the temple and the ceremony which had set her and Mr Robert free.

After hearing her out, Saleem was at first speechless. His mouth fell open and he looked right through her, as if she were not there. Then his skin turned pale. His face, with its rigid set jaw and clenched muscles, looked paralysed. Then that too changed and he looked at Anjali with such distress that she feared for his sanity. His eyes never left her face. He folded his arms around his body, as if to protect it, and rocked and swayed on his feet. Anjali thought he might faint.

Once more she was shocked at her own lack of foresight. She had not anticipated such a strong reaction, nor had she understood the depth of Saleem's feelings. For her, it had been a great relief to talk. The heaviness in her heart had dissolved as the words flooded out. Not once had she glanced up to see how Saleem was reacting. Not once did she stop to see if perhaps she was doing the wrong thing. Anjali had been lost in her own confession, making sure she missed nothing out and explaining the circumstances as clearly and exactly as she could. But as she looked at Saleem now, she understood that she had hurt her friend more than she had ever imagined. Ashamed, she lowered her gaze to the floor.

The long, long silence as the sky darkened told Anjali that her description of the scene in the temple – yes, that alone – had created between them a void so great that neither would ever be able to cross it. They sat motionless, immersed in their own thoughts for a long time, until they could no longer make out each other's features nor the vivid scarlet of the gulmohar tree.

The temple scene had came back to her vividly too. Before, it had been like a dream. Now, when she listened to her own voice talking about the event, it seemed as if it were yesterday, and it became very real. She shivered as a cool breeze blew red petals from the tree across the two of them, recalling the petals in the ceremony with Mr Robert. They were like blazing embers, ashes blown from a red hot fire. They burned all the easy friendship and all the fine, honest emotions that had once flowed between Anjali and Saleem. Afterwards, for each of them, there were only smouldering, silent emotions.

'Saleem…' she tried one last time, repeating what she had already said. 'It happened without either of us giving our consent. Neither I nor Mr Robert have ever taken the marriage ceremony seriously. We have never even mentioned it again. It was the only choice the astrologer had… The only way he could think of to save our lives.

Between the two of us, it meant nothing. Nothing.'

Saleem responded with silence. Then he rose and walked away through the back gates and disappeared into the night.

Chapter 66

Saleem didn't come back to his hut in the compound for the next two days. Anjali knew that he needed time to get over the shock of what she had told him, but it worried her that she did not know where he had gone. On the third day, there was a knock at her door.

'Who is it?' Anjali asked.

'May I come in, *amma*?' It was Vimala.

'Yes.' Anjali got up to open the door. 'What is it, Vimala?'

'I just came to tell you that Saleem is back.'

'Oh, good. Please tell him I will be down in ten minutes.'

The door of his hut was open but Anjali didn't just walk in as she would have done before. She stopped at the entrance and looked in. Saleem was packing his clothes into a trunk that he had placed on his bed. She gently tapped on the door. He turned. She had last seen him only two days previously, but the change was dramatic. He had lost weight, his face was pale and he was unshaven. His dull eyes were sunk deep in their sockets. Anjali was shocked. He turned away from her and went back to his packing. He said nothing.

'Saleem,' she called softly, hiding her disappointment that he hadn't invited her in.

He continued folding his clothes into his trunk.

'Saleem.' Anjali walked in, but he behaved as if she was not there. He took a towel and went into the bathroom, closing the door.

She waited patiently. When he came back into the room, he was buttoning his shirt.

'Saleem, everything happened so fast before we knew what was going on,' Anjali blurted out, so desperate was she to explain once again. 'We had no choice. Otherwise the thugs would have killed us. You of all people know what they are like.'

Finally Saleem looked at her.

She went nearer and said, 'Surely you understand, don't you?'

'You mean to say that the marriage the astrologer performed in front of the gods has no meaning? That you can ignore the *Veda mantras* the astrologer chanted to unite two people? You can just refuse to accept a Hindu marriage?'

'Yes, I can.'

'What if the engineer sahib claims you as his wife?' Saleem asked.

'Saleem!' Surprised that he could even put such an idea into words, she looked up and said, 'Of course he won't.'

'I asked you, "What if?"'

'He is a married man…'

'Anjali-ji, whatever you say, according to your Hindu religion you are now his wife, and that is a fact.'

With that Saleem closed the lid of the trunk and locked it.

It was a clear signal that their conversation had ended. Anjali left Saleem and turned to walk along the garden path, picking berries and flowers absentmindedly. She presumed that their plans to share a house were in ruins. She would have to move into Mrs Wilson's outhouse after all.

Apart from the servants' polite voices and soft footsteps, the atmosphere in the house was one of unbroken, uncomfortable silence. On the surface things ran smoothly and routines went unchanged, but four people were suffering, each caught up in a situation that was unresolved, each unable to move forward.

Anjali didn't find an opportunity to speak to Saleem again

until Monday morning, when he was about to drive Mr Robert to Roypuram. Looking very smart in his navy and white driver's uniform, he was in the portico, polishing the already gleaming dark green jeep.

Hiding her own hurt, Anjali greeted him with a smile.

'All ready to go?'

'Yes, we are leaving very soon,' he replied politely, as if to a stranger. The anger in his voice had disappeared but he didn't look at her. Instead he bowed slightly as he used to do in the old days when he came to her parents' house as a servant's son and messenger.

'Please look after yourself,' she said.

He looked up and she saw the pain in his eyes.

'He will.'

Mr Robert was standing behind them, tall and dignified, dressed in a charcoal suit with a white shirt and blue tie. He looked fresh, handsome and unexpectedly relaxed, ready to set off again to the fateful Roypuram. There was no trace of the wretchedness that had been a part of him for so long. Perhaps, with Miss Edwina being difficult, going to work was more appealing than staying at home. It was an escape from all the recent tension and unpleasantness. It was surely nothing to do with her. And Saleem? Perhaps he felt he had become just a bit too familiar with her and was simply stepping back a little. All this rushed through Anjali's mind as she tried to understand what was going on beneath the surface of their polite exchanges.

'I will make sure that he takes care of himself,' Mr Robert assured her.

Anjali avoided returning his smile because she knew Saleem was watching her closely, almost jealously. Mr Robert's blue gaze had set her cheeks ablaze and she turned away so Saleem wouldn't see. Ever since she had told Saleem about the ceremony, she felt uneasy in the presence of Mr Robert. But never had she felt as uncomfortable as she did now, standing in front of two very different men who were watching her with very different motives. It was like standing under a spotlight, Anjali thought, with an audience of two observing her every move, her every emotion. She could take no more. She turned to go.

'I understand this is your first day at work too,' Mr Robert said.

His words stopped her in her tracks. He had remembered. She turned back and nodded.

He gave her a brilliant smile. 'Good luck.'

'Thank you, sir.'

In all that emotional confusion, here was the ray of light that kept her sane.

As if saying a silent goodbye, Saleem gave Anjali a brief glance before starting the jeep.

Anjali remained where she was while all the servants lined up in front of the house, as they always did when their master went away for any length of time. It was very noticeable that Miss Edwina was missing from the scene. She hadn't bothered to come out to say goodbye to her husband.

Standing on the wide steps of the front veranda, Anjali waved after the departing jeep. Only Mr Robert waved back at her.

Chapter 67

After the two men had left, Anjali remained on the veranda for a long time, pacing from one end to the other, until the grandfather clock in the hall struck eight, reminding her that Mrs Wilson's driver would soon be there to pick her up. That at least was something to look forward to. Why was she not thinking about her day ahead and getting excited about it, instead of worrying about Mr Robert and Saleem? With a spring in her step, she went inside to get ready for her first day at work.

Wearing a simple pale yellow *sari* with a narrow border of deep green leaves, she climbed into Mrs Wilson's car with a smile on her lips. This felt right. It felt good.

The car dropped her off at the gates of St Agnes's. She stepped across the courtyard with enthusiasm and was met by Mrs Wilson and Chandrabai. They greeted her warmly and wished her well. Mrs Wilson then showed her the timetable, written on a square board, in columns, on the office wall, and explained that they had divided the girls into two groups, beginners and advanced. Anjali was to teach the beginners in the morning and the advanced in the afternoon.

'So that the two groups will have a chance to do their handicrafts as well,' said Chandrabai.

Anjali understood that producing their crafts, to sell in the market, was the only way for them to earn some meagre pocket money.

Chandrabai guided her towards her classroom. It was a rectangular mud-walled building with a thatched roof, set towards the back and separate from the main school building.

'It used to be a cow shed once,' said Chandrabai.

'Really?' Anjali replied, gazing at the newly laid cement floor and whitewashed walls. It looked fine for its current use.

And then she was alone in the classroom. Having never worked before. Having never taught anyone anything in her life. Lifting her head, she did her best to appear confident and comfortable so that her pupils would not pick up her anxiety. As she surveyed the room of benches, arranged in rows, a sea of women of all ages turned their faces towards her, stopped chatting, and stood up. At least twenty pairs of eyes were focussed on her as she bid them a nervous 'Good morning'.

'Good morning, Anjali-teacher,' they chorused back.

She asked them to sit down, conscious and proud of hearing her title on their lips.

'Let's start by introducing ourselves,' she said, clearing her throat. 'You know my name but I don't know any of yours and would like to learn them.' She turned to the girl on the end of the first bench. 'What is your name?' she asked.

'Lakshmi'

'And yours?'

'Kamala.'

Of course she would soon learn all their names but for now she could only remember the unusual ones, like Pushpavalli and Amritamba. But it broke the ice. She knew it was a game played more for her sake than for that of her pupils. She was giving herself time to adapt to her new circumstances. To this room. To her role as a teacher. All her pupils were friendly and polite, and soon Anjali was seated on a chair behind her table, taking the register and placing a tick on the tiny grid, next to the name of each girl and woman present. That done, she got up and wrote the auspicious word '*Om*' on the blackboard with a piece of chalk and, remembering how Miss Garland had taught her with quiet concentration and patience, began her first lesson.

Her hands shook as she wrote the letter 'A' on the board, saying, 'A for *Amma*.'

As everyone copied the letter, a girl asked, 'How do you say *amma* in English?'

Anjali smiled and said, 'Mother.'

'Mother... Mother...' everyone repeated.

After teaching the alphabet and the meanings of some simple English words for an hour, Anjali switched to teaching numbers.

It had been only two hours but it was tiring for Anjali because everything was new. Despite her efforts to relax, she was tense and worried, eager to do well. She was glad when it was time for the hour's break. In the staff room where she sat to eat her lunch of vegetables, rice and yogurt, she met two other voluntary teachers who had been with the younger class. She felt shy but they immediately made her feel at home.

'I am Jayanthi,' said one. Probably in her thirties, guessed Anjali. 'I teach the five- to ten-year-old girls.' Then she gestured at the young man, in his late twenties. 'This is Ravindra and he teaches the eleven- to fifteen-year-olds.'

'*Namaste*,' Ravindra greeted her politely. 'We both teach maths and English.'

'I am Anjali...'

'We know,' said Jayanthi. 'Mrs Wilson told us that you came to teach the women.'

'Yes.'

'It's quite difficult because there are only four teachers trying to teach every subject to nearly fifty children so we don't have time to teach the women as well. We're very pleased that you have come.'

'We need more good people like you to come forward,' said Ravindra. 'Everyone here deserves to be educated. Like Chandrabai, we all have to raise awareness and campaign as much as we can.'

'Of course,' Anjali nodded, recognising the zeal and energy of social reform in his voice. 'Another follower not only of Chandrabai, but perhaps also of Kandukuri and Gandhi,' Anjali thought.

An office boy brought them all glasses of tea and then it was time to teach the advanced groups. Anjali felt encouraged and happy. She had met her colleagues and started to feel that she belonged in this community.

*

Sometimes in her lunch hours, instead of going to have a chat with Jayanthi and Ravindra, she would stay behind in her classroom to sketch designs of flowers, birds and butterflies on pieces of paper for the women to trace using carbon paper on to the garments they were making in the craft sessions. They could add the designs in embroidery or beadwork. Soon the women were using Anjali's designs not just on silk and cotton *saris*, but on sheets and pillow cases. Each day when her formal duties as a teacher were over, she loved to go into the craft room to help out or to learn cross-stitch or chain-stitch from the skilful girls. Teacher and pupils learned from one another in a satisfyingly reciprocal way, strengthening the bonds between them.

In the evenings, she went home in a *tonga* that waited outside St Agnes's until she was ready to leave. To her surprise, she later learned from Mrs Wilson that Mr Robert had arranged this transport for her before he had left for Roypuram. Once again his thoughtfulness and kindness moved her and she felt indebted to him.

By the time she reached home it was always late, long past Miss Edwina's dinner time. Anjali liked it that way – not having to interact with the memsahib. Because she was at St Agnes's all day, she rarely saw her or had anything to do with her. With Mr Robert away from home, the pace of life was slower in the big house. No one rushed to do anything and the routine was relaxed. Vimala was always waiting for Anjali when she arrived back and insisted on serving her personally. 'Mr Robert's orders,' she would smile. During the day, while she concentrated on her lessons and the needs of her pupils, time passed quickly and she didn't have the space to think about her personal life, but at night, after she had corrected the homework and had prepared the next day's lesson, her thoughts always turned to Saleem and Mr Robert. She missed Saleem and in a strange way she missed Mr Robert too. The past still haunted her.

Mr Vincent's visits became more frequent, and on the days when he was there Anjali noticed that Miss Edwina grew lively again. Late into the night, Miss Edwina's bright and brittle chatter and laughter was carried by the wind, making Anjali sigh. How could she behave like that with another man?

But during the evenings when Mr Vincent was not there, Anjali often saw her shadowy figure walking around the grounds, head bowed. She walked like someone trying to solve a problem whose solution escaped her. There was something about her pacing that made Anjali think that she was troubled. Anjali too liked to walk in the grounds at night, when the scent from the plants was heady and the wind had dropped to a gentle breeze. It soothed her to walk and think as the light faded. Whether Miss Edwina was aware of her presence, she did not know, but their paths never crossed. And so in the evenings, when the sun had gone down, two women, together but separate, walked in the cool shade of the trees as the sky turned crimson and gradually darkness fell.

Chapter 68

Saleem found it almost unbearable to have Mr Robert sitting next to him in the jeep. He wished the engineer sahib would ride in the back like all the other English bosses. For some reason this white man had always insisted on sitting in the front next to him. Saleem could not look at Mr Robert because he feared that his own eyes might reveal his innermost feelings. He glanced sideways and saw that his master was as immersed in his own thoughts as Saleem was in his. He might have been staring at the official papers in his hands but it was obvious to anyone that he was not reading them. His mind was elsewhere. Was he too thinking about the past? About Anjali? Saleem wondered how he really felt about her. He had noticed that the engineer sahib was becoming increasingly fond of her. Would he claim her as his wife one day? Saleem flinched at the thought. A taste of bile rose to his mouth. Angry with himself at his own reaction, he gripped the steering wheel hard, as if her were competing in a rally, not driving along easy country roads.

His thoughts moved on to Miss Edwina. Had Mr Robert told her what had happened in the temple? If she found out, how would she react? For the first time since he had come to work for the couple, Saleem, to his own surprise, felt sympathy towards this woman who already hated the country she lived in and the limited options open to her. Perhaps she too wished for more freedom. The English memsahibs might have everything they wanted but did they find their lives fulfilling out here?

Despite having so much on his mind, the drive through the woods on country roads, away from the British-infested city of Harikonda, calmed him. His heart beat more slowly. The adrenalin did not flow so quickly through his veins. In this mood, eventually, he began to feel ashamed at his own unreasonable behaviour towards Mr Robert and even more so towards Anjali.

So lost was Saleem in this trail of perplexing thoughts that he did not even notice when they had reached Roypuram. The noise and commotion shook him into the present. The whole village had turned out to welcome Mr Robert with as much enthusiasm as the last time. Some villagers were running behind the car. Saleem wasn't surprised to see the zamindar himself on his elephant, waiting to welcome the Englishman at the gates of the guest house. He knew the zamindar's love of a European lifestyle. He also knew that the rich Indian man needed the engineer sahib's help to order and import a motorcar from London.

During the first few days, in order to avoid being with Mr Robert, in his free time Saleem roamed aimlessly around Roypuram. The loss of Samba felt like a heavy weight he carried around with him, making his experience of the place completely different. Wherever he went, he was conscious of Samba's absence. He walked with his head bowed, staying well clear of the temple, worried that he might bump into the astrologer or his daughter. He knew that he couldn't bear to hear the story of what happened all over again. He also avoided the villagers, not wanting to talk to them either. But some wouldn't leave him in peace. They wanted to talk about Samba. They wanted to talk about Anjali. A group of women in the street, carrying water pots, stopped him and asked if he had heard about the sudden disappearance of the new dancing girl. Not knowing what to say, he shook his head and tried to walk on.

'There is a rumour, you know,' said one of the women, 'that she ran away with a white man.'

Another woman came close enough to whisper, 'Some people even think it was your engineer sahib. Is that true?'

Saleem shook his head and pushed past them.

While the women whispered about Anjali, the men kept asking Saleem about his capture and his injuries and who the men were who had treated him so badly. He answered their questions with a nod or one or two dry words. He wanted to talk about none of this.

One afternoon, after hesitating for days, he plucked up the courage to visit Samba's grandmother, Rangi. That was the least he could do. On the way, remembering that she had a favourite sweet, he bought some *jilebi*, pastry spirals soaked in sugar syrup. As he got nearer, he worried about what he was going say. How could he possibly console her when he himself was the cause of Samba's death? He would have to find the words to explain to her that while trying to save Anjali and the engineer sahib, her grandson had sacrificed his own life.

The door of the hut was ajar but he knocked before he went in. There was no reply. Aware that Rangi would not have gone anywhere at that hour, gently he pushed the door open and saw the old woman lying on her bed, facing the wall.

'Rangamma,' he called softly.

She stirred in her bed and asked, 'Who is it?' It was barely a whisper.

'It's me, *dadima*, Saleem. Do you remember me? I came here with Samba... you cooked us a wonderful meal.'

'Saleem! Of course I remember.' She slowly turned her head to look at him. He saw with a shock how frail she had become. She was no longer the woman he remembered but a skeleton covered in skin, her eyes deeply sunken in their sockets.

A lump came to his throat. '*Dadima*...' He sat holding her until her trembling body settled a little. He sensed that she had no more tears to weep. No more energy to feed her shrunken frame. Perhaps no will to live. Saleem placed a pillow against a wall and propped her against it. Then he fetched a glass of cool water from the earthenware pot in the corner. When he put the tumbler to her dry lips, she didn't refuse, but sipped it slowly. Only then did her watery eyes focus on him.

'I am sorry… I am sorry, *dadima*…,'

She nodded. Without speaking, she showed him that she understood and that she felt no resentment or anger towards him. They sat in silence, holding hands, probably thinking the same thoughts, recalling the same memories. The time ticked away painfully slowly.

'Your engineer sahib is kind,' she said at last in a hoarse voice.

Saleem looked at her. 'Engineer sahib? Why do you say he is kind, *dadima*?

'He organised a grand… funeral… for my Samba.'

'He did?'

'Yes. And he sent me bundles of money so that I don't need to work for a living and I can employ a girl to look after me.'

'It was the least he could do for you and your brave grandson, *dadima*,' he said with a smile.

'My Samba managed to melt a white man's heart and made him feel sorry for me.' She smiled wryly.

Chapter 69

A week went by, just like that, bringing the unwanted Sunday. Anjali would miss going to school, miss her students and the conversations she had with her colleagues and Mrs Wilson. As usual she woke early, but feeling the October chill in the air she stayed in bed under the covers enjoying the luxury of not having to hurry. But she soon grew restless, pulled a shawl round her shoulders, and went to open the window.

The sun was struggling to come up, its weak rays barely warming the waking world. It was like a painting outside, everything softly blurred in the hazy light. On half-open, light green sampangi and yellow hibiscus flowers below her window, dew drops shimmered. The trees behind the servants' quarters were barely visible, as if brushed with a water-wash from a palette of pale colours. The servants and their families, already awake, were sitting together round a fire on their common ground, their faces glowing in the red of the rising flames. They sipped hot broth from brass bowls, their first meal of the day before they left for work. The crackle of snapping wood mixed with their low voices and the early bird song in the trees. Anjali looked at Saleem's empty dark hut and wished he was there to see and hear such gentle beauty.

Anjali remained at the window as the watery sun rose and burned higher in the sky and the fire died down until only embers remained.

Everyone had left to carry out their duties. She watched the sweeper woman working in the yard around the house and heard another servant sprinkling water on the ground to lay the dust. Anjali was still at her window when Vimala brought her a steaming cup of tea.

There was no hurry for her to get ready. She had no plans, so while she sipped her tea, she tried to structure the empty hours that lay ahead. First she decided to draw more designs for the girls at St Agnes's. Then she looked at the pile of books that Mr Robert had sent her before he had left for Roypuram, and began to wonder whether she would be able to understand the language. These books were difficult and more challenging than any she had read before. With her fingers, she traced their names, and picked up one called *Jane Eyre* by Charlotte Brontë. She made up her mind to try and read a few pages.

But before any of that she would take a long, leisurely walk through the grounds. She set off towards the gardens and was wandering dreamily along the paths, admiring the full blooms and savouring their scent, when she came face to face with the lady of the house. Both women were caught off guard. Both women stopped in their tracks and stared at each other without a word. It was Anjali who broke the silence, with a polite greeting. A deep red flush crept over Miss Edwina's cheeks. Turning to the gardener, who was tending the plants, she fumed, 'How dare *she* walk in to this side of my garden! Has no one told her that she is not allowed here?'

'Sorry... memsahib...' Anjali looked down.

Take her into the kitchen!' She shouted towards a female servant who came running. 'Tell Vimala to give her some work to do. I have friends coming for tea this afternoon and the cook needs help.'

Though hurt, Anjali wondered why the memsahib never spoke to her directly rather than through the servants.

Later, Vimala was curtly dismissed and once again Anjali found that she had stepped into the role of servant. After laying the table and arranging the flowers in the vases, she was ordered to serve the refreshments to memsahib's women friends. While pouring wine and gin and tonic into fine-stemmed glasses and handing round bowls of peanuts, Anjali couldn't help but overhear their conversation.

'I have spent eighteen months in India but soon I shall be thinking of going home. Sweet home,' Miss Edwina said languorously, after pouring a large glass of whisky down her throat.

'What do you mean, Edwina?' asked one of her friends.

'My parents said the thing about India was that in the end everybody loved it. Even if you hated it for the first few months, it would grow on you. But the thing is… I still hate it.'

'Why, Edwina, it is a wonderful experience! What are you lacking here, my dear?' asked another friend.

'It may be heavenly for you, and you might think me uncharitable and useless out here, but the truth is, I have failed to fit in and I can't find any satisfaction or fulfilment living in India. I can't bear the way everything is disorganised and dirty. And I feel homesick. I miss… oh… little things like curling up with a good book in front of a roaring fire in the evenings, and having a hearty roast dinner served on Sundays. No Indian knows how to cook a joint of meat so that it bleeds when you stick in the carving knife but is still crispy on the outside. I even miss bacon sandwiches! And yet… you all seem to be fine out here.'

'Edwina darling,' Miss Tessa had been staring hard at her friend while she had been speaking, 'forgive me for being blunt, but these sound to me like excuses. As if you are pining for something much more important than roast lamb. You wouldn't miss bacon sandwiches if everything else was going well, I promise you. Is there something else? Something more significant that lies behind all this complaining and unhappiness?'

'Well…I can't even use the bathroom or lavatory without fear…' Miss Edwina's voice grumbled, but with less vindictiveness. 'You see,

I encountered a snake once. It came through the hole in the wall where the bath water runs out. I am terrified of snakes, especially in the monsoon season, when it gets warm and wet…'

'Don't your servants check the room before you go in, my dear?'

'They do, but even then you never know. A snake could come in through the ventilator, which is too high to reach. I daren't close my eyes while having a bath. I have to look around all the time, just in case…'

'My servants put a cork in the hole and remove it afterwards.'

*

While clearing away the empty glasses and replacing them with tea cups, Anjali felt some vague sympathy for this English housewife who was homesick in a place she hated. No wonder she was dying to get back and kept asking Mr Robert when they would be returning. Perhaps Miss Edwina felt some of the same feelings she herself had felt when she was at Mohini's. But then Miss Edwina's situation was very different. Remembering that Miss Edwina was not alone, and recalling the courtesy and kindness of the engineer sahib, Anjali changed her mind and decided that there was little justification for so much unhappiness.

'Is it anything to do with Robert, my dear?' At last someone voiced the one question that up to now had remained unspoken. It was the question that always lingered in Anjali's mind.

'Even Robert…' Edwina stopped mid-sentence and glared at Anjali, making her self-conscious. The other women's eyes followed hers.

'Get out of my sight, you…' The delicate cup in Miss Edwina's hand rattled in its saucer. Her words were uttered with such spleen and vindictiveness that Anjali ran to a corner of the room, away from so much anger. But still she listened.

Taking the wobbling cup from Miss Edwina's hand, Miss Tessa asked, 'Are you all right, my dear?'

Miss Edwina nodded.

Miss Tessa picked up a spiced cashew and addressed the others as if Miss Edwina was not there. 'You see, she didn't want to come to India in the first place.'

'Why on earth did you come out then, my dear?' asked one of the others.

Miss Edwina was in no state to answer. She had been drinking steadily all afternoon and looked like she might pass out at any moment.

'You!' Miss Tessa shouted at Anjali. 'Come and help her.'

It was with some trepidation that Anjali walked towards the lady of the house, but Miss Edwina was in no condition to care who was taking care of her. With the help of a second female servant, they got her to a standing position, where she drooped and leaned her head on Anjali's shoulders. They walked the unsteady woman to her bedroom and lifted her on to her bed. As soon as Miss Edwina's head touched the pillow, she was gone. Anjali switched on the ceiling fan and returned to serve more tea.

The guests were whispering loudly, leaning forward in their chairs so as not to miss any of the gossip.

'You see,' Miss Tessa was saying, 'she had a pretty dull life in England and I believe that she just snatched at the opportunity. Oh, you know. It was one of those things that meant nothing to her except a chance to escape. And enough money. She set out to impress Robert and, naturally, a young man like him fell for her good looks.'

'Then why is she so miserable?'

'She says that Robert doesn't understand her feelings.'

'But he is…'

'I know, their characters are poles apart.'

'The main problem is that he likes India and its people and she doesn't.'

'I heard that she is convinced that he has an Indian mistress somewhere.'

And all eyes in the room turned to Anjali.

*

That night, in bed, for the first time since she had come to live in that house, Anjali felt a certain sympathy towards Miss Edwina. Perhaps her own presence in the house had added to the woman's misery and caused her further unhappiness. As she closed her eyes, she saw again the way the women had all stared at her and she remembered the hatred in Miss Edwina's eyes. How much did the memsahib know about what had happened in the temple? Had the engineer sahib told her everything? Was Miss Edwina worried that she might claim to be married to her husband? How ridiculous.

Feeling responsible for causing trouble between a husband and wife, Anjali got up and paced the room.

Chapter 70

Anjali shut her eyes tight but her troubled mind chased away all possibility of sleep.

Miss Edwina's behaviour haunted her and left no room for further doubt or self-deception. The woman hated her. Yet here she remained in her house as her guest. The thought of Miss Edwina's unvoiced accusations linking her with Mr Robert made her break out in a cold sweat. Her head pounded. The situation was intolerable. Anjali's only wish now was to get away from the place. To go.

Her thoughts turned naturally to Saleem. Perhaps he could still take her to the accommodation he had rented for the two of them. He was her friend and the only person who truly kept her interests at heart. She could rely on him for anything. If she were to ask him he would certainly help her.

But wait, she thought, catching herself going down the same old tracks. You are deluding yourself. You can't just turn to Saleem every time you are in trouble. Have you forgotten about his own feelings? For the first time, reaching out for Saleem did not feel right. It felt like imposing on him. Anjali had taken advantage of his kindness too many times already and should now make her own way, without asking for his help.

Anjali opened the window and stared out into the night. The half moon was playing hide and seek between midnight clouds, casting its silver light then hiding it again. She sat on the windowsill thinking until she heard the first birdsong of the morning. Seeing that day was breaking, she quickly closed the shutters and went to bed, hoping to snatch an hour's sleep before Mrs Wilson's car arrived to take her to St Agnes's.

In the car, she asked Mrs Wilson if she could possibly stay in the Home with all the other girls.

'But you don't need to do that, my dear. You are welcome to stay with me, as I told you. Or, if you prefer it, the outhouse is available,' said Mrs Wilson.

Anjali remained silent, not knowing how to tell this kind woman the truth.

'What is wrong, my dear?' Mrs Wilson picked up Anjali's mood.

'I just want to live on my own.'

'But the Home is already full. Why would you want to live in those cramped conditions when you can live in Robert's house or mine?'

'I just want to live independently, that's all.'

'I see.' A slight pause. Clearly Mrs Wilson did not understand. 'Not to worry. We'll think of something.' It was an attempt to change the subject.

'If it's no trouble to you, would it be possible to move into that empty building just outside our school?'

'You mean the store room?'

'Yes. But it isn't used now, is it?'

'Do you know what that was before we bought the place? I think I told you. It was used to store cow dung and clay and hay.'

'I don't mind, Mrs Wilson. Once it is cleaned, it will be fine.'

'But, Anjali, there are no facilities. You would have to share the bathrooms with the girls.'

'I don't mind that..'

'And the roof needs some repairs. In the last rainy season it leaked very badly.'

'For me these are all minor problems. At least it is not the rainy season now. I really like the thatched roof; it will be cool in summer.'

'If you say so, my dear. It sounds to me as if you have made up your mind already. I will see what improvements we could make to the room.'

'Thank you, Mrs Wilson. I am very grateful.' Anjali smiled with relief.

Mrs Wilson's driver found a couple of labourers from a local building site who were willing to work on the thatched room and to take on the other repairs. They piled fresh layers of hay on the roof and secured it with coconut-fibre ropes so that it would be warm and watertight through the coming winter months. Then they applied red clay to the outside walls, levelled the uneven floor inside and laid a surface of clay. When the floor was dry and smooth with a velvety sheen, the girls came and drew pretty patterns with lime paste in its centre. The newly whitewashed walls reflected the light and made the room fresh and almost new.

It had only been a few days since the tea party had opened Anjali's eyes to her impossible situation. Her new accommodation was ready.

Not wanting to wait until Sunday, until Saleem and Mr Robert came back, she decided to act at once. Once they were back, one or other of them might try to convince her not to move out, and it would be difficult for her to refuse or to disobey. Especially if Mr Robert voiced objections to her living in a store room. He would try to smooth over her concerns and would dismiss her worries as nonsense. No. She had better go while she could.

On Thursday morning, she packed her belongings in the small satchel that Sita had given her. She left most of the *saris* that Mr Robert had given her. Vimala made a fuss, and told Anjali how much she was going to miss her. Anjali gave her a big hug and thanked her immensely. Then she went and briefly informed Miss Edwina that she was moving out. The memsahib's response was to look away and pretend she had not even heard.

And so at last Anjali took her final steps out of Mr Robert's mansion, which had sheltered her for the past months. As she climbed into the car, she was surprised to see all the servants lined up at the gates. Moved by their loyalty and kindness, she waved to them with tears in her eyes. They had all been kind to her and she was going to miss them.

The one-roomed hut was surrounded by a two-foot-high unevenly built mud wall with a latticed cane gate. The small back yard was smothered in yellow pumpkin flowers, all blooming profusely. In front of the hut, outside of the gate, was a well that provided water for the Home, the school and the nearby houses. Inside, the space was adequate and the room clean. It was comfortably cool, with light entering through the door and a small window, both of which faced east.

At Mrs Wilson's insistence, Anjali accepted a small coal stove, a couple of saucepans and enough cutlery and crockery for one person and a guest. There was also a folding cot. Anjali thanked her profusely, touched by the English woman's kindness. At last she had a place she could call her own.

That evening, when Anjali lit the lamp in her own place for the first time, without anyone to look after or to shout for her or to follow her around, she sat quietly for a long time in the flickering yellow light and reflected on all that had happened. She relished her new solitude. She was content to be independent. Here she could truly be herself. Of course, eventually her thoughts turned to two very different men, both of whom had helped her over the past year. What would they think of her decision, she wondered, as her eyelids grew heavy and she leaned her head against the whitewashed wall and watched the sky turn black in the small square of window.

Chapter 71

Saleem was there, serving him breakfast, when Mr Robert received a phone call from his superintendent. At first, Saleem didn't pay much attention because the two men were discussing work, but as he was about to take the tray away, he heard a surprised pause at Mr Robert's end, and then, in a whisper, 'Anjali? Are you sure?'

Alarmed at hearing Anjali's name, Saleem stayed very still and listened.

'Away?'

Pause.

'Where?' Mr Robert was only managing to utter one word at a time.

Pause.

'Where is she staying?' The engineer sahib's voice shook a little.

Pause

'I wonder why she couldn't wait until...'

Pause

And then no more. The engineer sahib hadn't revealed the location. Where had she gone? Saleem's heart raced as he worried over the reason for her sudden departure from the house. Perhaps he had misheard. Or misunderstood. When Mr Robert finally put the phone down, he asked, 'Sir, I couldn't help but hear your conversation. I gather that Anjali-ji has moved...'

Mr Robert stared blankly at Saleem as if he was not taking in anything he was saying. As if he was not there.

'Yes,' he replied at last. 'Yes. Mr Wilson was telling me that Anjali has decided to move to a small building near to St Agnes's.'

'Did he say why she had moved, sir?'

'Only what I've just said. Anjali wants to live closer to St Agnes's.'

For one moment his hopes rose and he wondered if she had perhaps moved to the accommodation that he had found for the two of them – and on which he had already paid the deposit.

'Near to St Agnes's?' he asked again.

'Yes, that's what I heard,' Mr Robert replied, equally dazed.

But the Krishnapura house was nowhere near St Agnes's. It was further away. There had been one small ray of hope. Then nothing. The flame went out.

*

Why had Anjali moved out? However much he deliberated, Saleem could not understand this abrupt decision. He couldn't believe that a girl like her would suddenly take a big decision like that on her own, and go and live by herself. But who knew? Didn't she tell him that she was apprehensive about continuing to stay in the engineer sahib's mansion? She had told him often enough that she wanted her independence. What a fool he had been to believe that if Mr Robert offered formal marital status to Anjali, she would of course refuse and then, eventually, move into the accommodation that he had found for them. He felt his energy drain from his body. Still she had the power to pull on his emotions. He dragged himself out of the room to carry on with his other chores, wondering over and over why Anjali had not waited until he had come home to talk this through and to consult him. It seemed out of character, and he was worried.

It felt like an eternity waiting for Sunday. Saleem went through the motions of working and carried out his duties as he always did, but he felt no enthusiasm for the job. He felt dispirited and disengaged.

But watching Mr Robert, Saleem decided that he did not seem to be doing any better. Since coming to Roypuram, he too seemed less involved with his work, often distracted and distant. Saleem thought that his master, too, had his mind elsewhere. And so the two of them got through the days as if they were physically present but emotionally absent. Anyone watching them would have thought how similarly disconnected they both looked.

Eventually Sunday morning came. Saleem was up before dawn, pacing up and down by the jeep. He drove Mr Robert to Harikonda and as soon as he had parked, rushed inside to find Vimala. The maid confirmed everything that Mr Robert had already told him, but she also told Saleem about the tea party and her mistress's behaviour, and how difficult things had been for Anjali. It upset him that Anjali had not confided in him and told him about her difficulties coping with the memsahib. She had stayed there and tolerated it for long enough; surely she could have waited just a few more days, until he had come home and she could confide in him as a friend.

Saleem felt bitter. He returned with a heavy heart to his shared room and waited for Prakash to come home.

'What's wrong?' his friend asked as soon as he saw him.

After telling Prakash everything, Saleem held his head in his hands. 'What should I do now?'

'You must go and visit her and hear her explanation,' Prakash suggested.

'I don't know, Praksh. I feel betrayed, and can't help wondering…'

'Wondering what?'

'I don't know…' Saleem shook his head. 'My mind is turning into a devil's workshop.'

'What are you thinking exactly?'

'It is very wrong of me to think like this… but I can't help it… it seems to me that the reason she ran away from everyone, especially from me, was because… she might have feelings for Mr Robert. Do you think that's possible?'

'The only way you will find out is by asking her, Saleem.'

'Prakash…!'

'Yes, ask her directly. Otherwise this will go on forever, with you wondering what could be the reason…'

Saleem remained silent. He rubbed his head. 'And how do I find the words to ask her that question?'

'Well, you certainly shouldn't go now. Not when you are in this frame of mind. It is late, you are upset, and you are very tired. Let's have something to eat and try to get a good night's sleep. You will feel better tomorrow and when you visit her you will be able to think clearly and find the words you need.'

'Prakash, you are right. You are nearly always right.' Saleem smiled. 'But I still need to think of a reason to visit her. She has put all this distance between us…'

'Friends don't need a reason to visit each other,' Prakash interrupted. 'I sincerely believe she still regards you as a very good friend and will be pleased to see you. Now go to bed.'

Saleem heard Prakash sighing as he went into his own area of the room and drew the curtain. Perhaps, thought Saleem, he too was wondering why Anjali had made this sudden, dramatic move. Taking a deep breath, he leaned back on his pillow.

Chapter 72

Working in St Agnes's was a joy, and living independently in her own house was a comfort. For the first time in her life, Anjali felt she was her own person.

The week went faster than she had expected and as the weekend approached, her thoughts turned to Saleem and Mr Robert. Expecting them both back on the Sunday, she couldn't help wondering how both men would react to her moving into her own accommodation, especially Saleem, since she had turned down his offer of a shared home. And Mr Robert? Would he think her ungrateful, moving away just like that, without even waiting for him to come home, and without even saying a proper goodbye? Thinking it over, she worried that her behaviour had been impulsive and would be thought rude. Would they understand that she had acted out of desperation? Surely once she had explained why she needed her independence, Mr Robert would understand and forgive her. She would then go and thank him properly and fully for his kindness and generosity. It would be better if Saleem accompanied her so that there could be no misunderstanding with the memsahib.

On Sunday, her emotions swayed like a pendulum, back and forth. Yes, she looked forward to seeing Saleem and hearing about her old friends, Sita and Kalyani, but she also dreaded him turning up furious on her door step. She vowed to be honest with him and to tell him everything. But would it be wise to tell him about the memsahib's accusations? Wouldn't that upset him and provoke further anger towards the British? She would chose her words carefully so as not to trigger his volatile emotions. Still thinking this through, she started to prepare lunch, because she was sure he would arrive in time to eat with her. She made Saleem's favourite dishes – spiced lentils with tomatoes, rice, and small aubergines stuffed with fresh coconut, green chilli and coriander, which would make a spicy filling for parathas. For the sweet course, she fried thin vermicelli in ghee, adding just the right amount of milk and sugar and a few strands of saffron. Once the mixture was boiled and the vermicelli was cooked, she added fried cashews and pistachios. The final touch was a sprinkle of fresh cardamom powder. Then she took up her position, like a guard, at the window, waiting and watching the little girls playing in the school grounds. It reminded her of when she was little, playing with Saleem.

But the sun moved across the sky and Saleem did not come. The food went cold and unappetising. Anjali spent the whole day running to the front door each time she heard the slightest sound outside. The sweltering afternoon dragged on slowly and eventually gave way to a cool and pleasant evening. Anjali grew restless and even considered going to Mr Robert's to find Saleem, but the memory of the way Miss Edwina had looked at her stopped her. Hugely disappointed, and not knowing what to do next, she walked into her front yard and sat down under a huge *banyan* tree. A bougainvillea that had climbed into the branches of the tree and smothered it in deep pink flowers dropped petals like confetti as the light faded.

The hurricane lamps in St Agnes's were lit up. The children went inside. Except for the slight rustling of the wind through the leaves of the tree, the night was silent. The moon came up, a small crescent, illuminating the grounds and trees and buildings with a cool light, and still Anjali stayed under the *banyan* tree, deep in thought, perhaps unaware of time passing. The pink bougainvillea flowers changed colour in the moonlight. She remained there for a long time, until she heard footsteps and the gate opened.

'Salee…' she looked up. It wasn't Saleem. It was Mr Robert. She tried to hide her surprise.

'Sir…'

'Hello, Anjali. How are you?'

How good to hear that deep voice. How reassuring to see him after the disappointment of her long, lonely day.

'I'm fine, sir,' she replied.

'Please…' he gestured to the bench. 'I am sorry if I startled you.' He sat on one end of the uneven plank of wood that was nailed down on four crooked legs. Anjali sat on the other. In the darkness, he would not notice her flushed cheeks, nor could he hear how her heartbeat quickened. After rehearsing her explanation so many times, over and over, she plunged straight into her prepared apology.

'I am sorry, sir, that I left like I did without giving you any warning. It was rude of me. I was going to come to see you and explain why I did it…' Anjali felt shy and self-conscious. Her words tumbled out in a rapid stream, making Mr Robert smile.

'It's all right, Anjali. You don't need to apologise. I think I understand. I just came to see if everything is OK with you. Remember the priest did ask me to look after you.'

Anjali was speechless. Her heart thumped harder at the mention of the astrologer and the reminder of what had happened in the temple.

For several moments, an awkward silence hung in the air. Anjali twisted and untwisted the corners of her *sari pallu* around her fingers. Mr Robert stared at a bougainvillea flower that he had picked.

'Would you like some tea, sir?' This time Anjali broke the silence.

'Thank you, but no. I just came to talk to you. I wanted to tell you that I know why you left the house so suddenly.'

Anjali looked up. 'I am sorry, sir…'

'Please… don't be…' He looked at her.

'I should have waited until you came home.'

'That doesn't matter.'

Did he know what Miss Edwina had said to her? That she had more or less accused Anjali of being Mr Robert's mistress?

'Saleem and I are going back to Roypuram on Tuesday. Not tomorrow,' Mr Robert said at last.

Why had he told her that? Anjali looked up. The blue of his eyes shone like tiny mirrors where the silver light touched them.

'Sir, how is Saleem?'

'He is fine. Going back to Roypuram was a challenge for both of us.'

'Of course, sir. I understand. After what he went through. And you.'

'It hadn't really changed but it felt strange to be back there.'

Anjali nodded, glad that he was confiding in her. She wanted to hear more about Roypuram but Mr Robert stared at the moon as if not knowing what to say next.

'Sir, Saleem…'

'I think he went to see his friend, Prakash, today. He said he would definitely come and see you tomorrow and tell you all about Roypuram.'

'Sir.'

Another silence heavy with words not spoken.

'Anjali…'

She looked at him.

'You left because of something Edwina did, didn't you? It's all to do with her.'

'No, sir.' She said it quickly, looking away because he would see that she was not telling the truth, but she did not want to accuse his wife of anything and cause more trouble.

'I came to tell you something…' Mr Robert hesitated.

Anjali's heart was beating so hard against her ribs that she imagined it must be visible beneath her *sari*. Calm down, she told herself. You are being ridiculous.

'Anjali…'

This time there was no mistaking the emotion in his voice. He did not just speak her name but breathed it like a sigh. She held her breath.

'I came to tell you that Edwina and I have decided to split up.' His voice shook.

'Sir…' Again Anjali waited.

'She is going home soon.'

'To England, sir?'

'Yes.'

'But why, sir?' It sounded so false, even to her own ears, but she could not bring herself to tell him that she was not surprised nor to ask the question she wanted to ask: *What about you, sir?*

'Anjali, I suspect you know by now that Edwina is unhappy with me and that we don't get on well. I have tried but…it has become impossible to carry on.'

Anjali looked down, not knowing what to say. How could she possibly tell him that she knew that their marriage was unhappy? It was too delicate and sensitive.

'As the priest in the temple somehow knew, Edwina and I are not well matched. We are too different. We are not close.'

There – he was referring to the astrologer again, reminding her of what had happened in the temple. It seemed to be often on his mind. What significance did it have for him, she wondered. What would he say next? As if reading her thoughts, he clumsily changed the subject.

'I met Edwina at a dinner party in London only two months before I was due to leave England,' he continued. 'I have to admit that at the time I was attracted to her looks. Everything happened very quickly. Her family approved and encouraged us to go out together. Edwina seemed pleased. Certainly she encouraged me. But there was pressure on me to make a quick decision because I was very soon to sail to India to take up my new post. We saw each other a few more times, in social situations – parties and dinners – and then we became engaged. Looking back, we gave it very little thought. It happened in a whirlwind. I wonder now what would have happened if we had had more time... if we had got to know each other better. To be honest, I don't think we would have stayed together. We were too different.'

He sighed again, and Anjali wondered if he was blaming himself.

'As it was, we decided to get married as quickly as possible. Soon after I had arrived here, I wrote to her and asked her if she would be willing to sail out to India. We would be married here. She agreed immediately and in her reply wrote that her parents couldn't be happier. Edwina had never even set foot outside London, let alone England. I arranged that she would be accompanied by Mrs Wilson. Only days after she walked down the gang plank, we were married. I've had plenty of time since then to reflect on the way we rushed into marriage and I have had plenty of time to regret my thoughtlessness and impulsiveness. I was young and foolish. I was infatuated with a pretty girl I hardly knew. She thought India would be glamorous. She thought it was going to be such fun... an endless round of parties like she was used to in England. I should have made the time to disillusion her. To tell her what conditions were really like.'

'Sir...' Anjali could not help smiling at the notion of India being glamorous.

'Her happiness was short-lived. It was perhaps only a matter of weeks before I saw the real Edwina and understood how spoilt she had been as the only daughter in a very rich English family. She expected so much and was forever dissatisfied. Of course she grew increasingly bored and restless and hard to please. She made not the slightest effort to adapt. Nothing in India pleased her and nothing I did was right.' Mr Robert rubbed his forehead. 'We both knew what every single servant in the house knew. There was trouble, serious trouble, brewing between us. Things went from bad to worse over the following eighteen months. There were a number of incidents. I won't bore you with them…' Robert stopped talking and stared again at the moon, composing himself.

Oh but I witnessed a few of them myself, Anjali thought. Like the servants, I observed a lot and said little. I heard the shrill laughter on the balcony when Mr Vincent came to visit. I felt the leaden atmosphere when she was at home with you. I saw how much she drank, perhaps to drown her unhappiness. I saw her pacing the grounds at night, obviously unhappy.

'Anjali…' Mr Robert continued, 'do you know that lately she has even accused me of having an Indian mistress hidden somewhere? It became something she said every time we were in company.'

Anjali looked at him sympathetically. She knew this too. She had heard it herself.

'You must have guessed why we went to Ooty. To talk about our marriage and to see if we could sort things out. I wasn't hopeful because by then I felt little for her. It was there that she admitted to having an affair with Vincent.'

Anjali looked at him, shocked. Certainly she had heard the drunken laughter and seen the physical closeness between Miss Edwina and Mr Vincent, but that might have meant nothing. She had not wanted to judge other people, and anyway it was none of her business.

'The thing that really shocked me was that the two of them had already met,' Mr Robert said. 'It was on the ship when they were sailing out here from London. She said the attraction had been immediate and mutual. Despite Mrs Wilson's chaperoning of Edwina, she met Vincent often and of course in secret.'

'I am so sorry to hear this, sir.'

'She should have told me as soon as she arrived. It would have saved us a lot of heartache. I would have given her her freedom. In a way, I am relieved that it is finally all out in the open. I have asked Vincent to accompany her back to London and to take good care of her.'

'You asked him to go with her?'

'Yes. It's better this way.'

Anjali was truly astonished at the generosity of this man in putting his wife's wishes and feelings before his own, and in going to so much trouble to see the painful business through to its conclusion.

'I am sorry, Anjali, to be bothering you with all this.'

'I am honoured, sir, that you feel able to tell me.'

'I don't know why, but I wanted to tell you everything. I knew that you would listen quietly, as you have done, and understand.'

'I appreciate you confiding in me, sir. But I am also very sorry that you have had to go through so much anguish.'

'No… really. I am fine.' He tried to smile but it was not convincing. 'Tomorrow I have to go to Madras to arrange everything for Edwina's departure.'

'Sir…'

'If you need anything, please don't hesitate to call me or to ask Mrs Wilson. She knows everything.'

'Thank you, sir.'

He got up and said, 'I hope I'll see you again before too long.'

Anjali watched him turn and walk away. At the gate he gave her one last lingering look.

No, he is not fine, she thought.

Chapter 73

The first thing Saleem thought about when he woke on Monday morning was his conversation the previous night with Prakash. As he remembered his friend's wise but blunt words, he thought seriously about not going to see Anjali at all. Stop deluding yourself, Prakash had told him, although not in those words. It would be pointless and inconsiderate to argue with her about where she wanted to live or to try to persuade her to move into a house with him. He must come to terms with being no more than a friend to her. She had told him that she regarded him as a brother. He couldn't go on fighting like this, both with his own feelings and with Anjali. It was time to accept the truth.

He could see, even from a distance, that Anjali was there at the gate, waiting to welcome him. And to his surprise, it felt natural being with her, as if the barriers between them had suddenly come down. Perhaps it was because they were away from prying eyes, on their own at last. Here it felt as if nothing much had really changed. She was once again his childhood friend.

'How nice to see you! It's been two weeks, but it's felt like ages.'

'Yes. It has felt a long time for me too.' He smiled. 'I went to see my friend Prakash yesterday.'

'I waited for you but…' Anjali stopped abruptly. She certainly did not want to tell him about Mr Robert's visit before she had even asked how he was. For no good reason, she felt guilty. Almost as if she had committed a crime. She turned pale and looked at him with huge eyes. Saleem's heart melted.

'Are you all right, Anjali-ji?' he asked.

'Yes, thank you. Please do come in. Let me show you my house.'

Inside everything was as he had expected. The room was not spacious but it was neat and tidy.

'I thought you might come today so I made some puris and pitla with onions and tomatoes. Is it still one of your favourites? But would you like some tea first?'

'How kind of you, Anjali. Yes please.'

Offering him a low stool to sit on, Anjali lit the stove, filled a small pan, and waited for the water to boil. She busied herself pouring the scalding liquid into two glass tumblers, wanting to get her apology over with. 'Saleem, I am sorry I moved out of the house when you were away. I should have waited and told you my plans.'

'Why did you go so suddenly? I admit I am surprised.'

'I felt uncomfortable in Miss Edwina's house.'

'Why? I thought you were happy there.'

'Oh, Saleem, how can you say that? You know how things were between me and Miss Edwina. Don't pretend otherwise. She hates me. She wouldn't speak to me.'

'She hates every Indian.'

'Yes, I know.'

'Anjali-ji, are you happy here?'

'More than ever, Saleem.'

'This room is fine for the time being but you wouldn't want to live here permanently, would you?'

Anjali opened her mouth to reply but Saleem continued. 'I have a suggestion. Let me just put this to you. The Krishnapura accommodation is still available, and I would be very pleased if you would move into it. I will arrange for transport and help you…'

'Saleem, thank you for your concern and for this kind offer but as I said before, I am happy here where I am close to my work and where I can chat with the girls and women.'

Even though Saleem had expected this answer, the disappointment was still bitter. There had been just the smallest chance she might have said yes. But with her rejection of his offer, he knew that this was the last time they would talk about living together. He had to remind himself that it wasn't his position to tell Anjali where to live nor to persuade her what to do.

'I am sorry, Saleem,' she said again, knowing that she had hurt him.

Saleem nodded. 'As you wish.'

'Thank you for understanding. I really appreciate that. And I am more than willing to pay the deposit.'

'No. There's no need for that.'

For a while, they talked on about ordinary things. Anjali explained her work at St Agnes's. Saleem talked about Prakash and his ideals, and how he was now attending the freedom fighters' meetings.

As she placed the puris and pitla on his plate, Anjali finally asked, 'How is Roypuram?'

'The same as before. No change.'

'Did you meet anyone? I mean Samba's grandmother or Sita or Kalyani?'

'I saw Samba's grandmother.'

'I am glad. How is the poor woman coping?'

'Not very well. She is still mourning her grandson. But just thinking of Samba and remembering him seems to keep her spirits up.'

Anjali nodded silently as a lump formed in her throat. She could imagine how unbearable this elderly woman's suffering must be. First her son, then her grandson, so young, murdered pointlessly. Anjali took comfort in knowing that Rangi had always faced life, however cruel, with fortitude and courage. She could understand why she

BLUE EYES

had chosen to spend her last days with the memories of her brave
grandson.

Seeing the tears in her eyes, Saleem offered his handkerchief.

'No, I am fine,' Anjali smiled. 'And how is Kalyani?'

'I don't know. Rangi is not working for them anymore. I'm sure she
is fine. Why wouldn't she be?'

'You don't know, Saleem. That place is like a prison.'

'For you it was, but it's her home.'

'And Sita…?'

'No, I didn't see her, but I did see the astrologer briefly. I drove Mr
Robert to his house. He wanted to thank the astrologer in person for
his help.'

'And…' Anjali couldn't hide her curiosity.

'He asked Mr Robert about you…' Saleem gave her a meaningful
look then abruptly changed the subject. 'Do you know that Miss
Edwina is going back to England?'

Not knowing how to respond, Anjali just looked at him.

'Mr Robert took the train to Madras this morning to make all the
arrangements.'

'Did he?' she asked, wondering if her deceit showed in her burning
cheeks and trembling hands. She had no intention of telling Saleem
about Mr Robert's visit. There was no point in risking more upset.

'That was delicious,' Saleem said finishing the last piece of puri.
'Just as my mother used to make it.'

'Remember I learned it from her, when she used to cook for us?'

'Of course!' smiled Saleem.

'Have you heard from home? How is she?'

'Yes, I had a letter only yesterday from my brother. He says she's
fine but is missing me.'

'Of course she misses you, Saleem! She is a loving mother. When I
was young, I learned from her what a mother's love could be like. You
know how my step-mother treated me!' Tears welled up in Anjali's

376

eyes, but she blinked them away. 'I am so fortunate to have had your mother to care for me, Saleem…' For a few moments Anjali could not continue. There was too much to be put into words. Too much that was still unspoken between them. 'As I have always said, you are like a brother to me. You are the brother I always wanted.'

That word again. Saleem repeated it silently to himself, his emotions in turmoil. He looked at her for a long time. And instead of the grown woman, he saw the little girl, Anjali. He saw her as clearly as if she were there in front of him. He remembered how she used to follow him everywhere, pestering him to play with her. The image faded. Anjali was beside him, still pestering him to be a brother for her. A corner of his mouth lifted in the barest hint of a smile.

'Anjali-ji, you haven't changed a bit,' he said.

Chapter 74

Duty bound, Saleem returned again to Roypuram with his engineer sahib.

Under normal circumstances, he would not have worried too much about Miss Edwina's sudden announcement that she was leaving the country. After all, he had known that she would leave sooner or later because he had witnessed her unhappiness. But as he drove, he thought about the possibility of her leaving being linked to Anjali. He had always imagined that Miss Edwina had been joking when she announced drunkenly to all her friends that her husband was hiding an Indian mistress somewhere, but beneath the banter she may have half-believed her own accusation. And now... the truth went far beyond anything she had feared. Her husband did not have an Indian mistress but had been married to a beautiful Indian girl.

What would happen after Miss Edwina had departed? Would Mr Robert claim Anjali as his wife? Would Anjali accept marriage? He did not think that it was his imagination but in the last couple of months they seemed to have grown closer to each other. His thoughts haunted him day and night. To stop himself from thinking, he worked hard, volunteering to help the labourers at the construction site in his spare time. But the nights were more difficult; then his imagination roamed outrageously over images of Anjali with the engineer sahib.

One particularly bad night, he couldn't sleep, so he got up and went for a walk, hoping to refresh himself in the cool air. Not planning his route, he nevertheless found himself heading for the temple and walking towards the lake. Apart from the occasional barking of a village dog, the night was very quiet. Fireflies sparkled like tiny fireworks all around him as if competing with the stars. He could see the embankment clearly and noticed a figure moving along one side. Who else was out walking at this time of the night? He quickened his pace until he could make out a female dressed in white, standing on the embankment, looking down into the dark water. Her long hair was blowing in the gentle breeze, as was her *sari pallu*. She looked like a figure from a dream. Who was she? She couldn't be anyone from the village because no woman in her right mind would come out at this time.

He froze. His heart missed a beat. He had heard people say that female ghosts roamed around in white *saris* in the dead of night. A shiver ran down his spine. Saleem would have sworn that he did not believe in any of that nonsense, but now, given his agitated state of mind and the setting of the lake in the darkness, he wondered if it were true after all. The pale shape was climbing on to the embankment. And then Saleem snapped back to the present and knew that of course she was not a ghost but a person. As her intentions became obvious, he raced towards her. He acted instinctively, without hesitation and without thought. He grabbed her waist, dragged her down from the embankment and held on while she fought in his arms, trying to escape.

'Let me go! Leave me alone!' she screamed.

For a while she struggled, but he was much the stronger of the two and eventually she had to give in. She crumpled like a rag doll in his arms and wept bitterly. Saleem sat on the ground beside her, still holding her.

'What were you going to do?'

'Please…' she pleaded. 'Let me go. I want to die.'

He released her hands. 'Why?'

She didn't answer but continued to sob, hiding her face in her hands.

'Why do you want to die?' he repeated, looking closely at her for the first time. She was about Anjali's age. 'What will you gain by dying?'

She didn't answer.

'Don't you know that committing suicide is a crime and a sin?'

At last she looked up and blinked at him through her tears.

'As if I care,' she replied.

'Tell me the reason you are doing this?' Saleem asked more gently. 'Why do you want to die a horrible death like this? What has brought you to this?'

Still she said nothing but stared straight ahead, as if he were not there.

'Please, perhaps I could help?'

'Help… huh?' Finally she gave a wry smile and her sobs quietened. 'No one, not even a god, can help me now.'

'Please…' he said, looking at her swollen face and eyes. 'Don't lose hope.'

'Hope…?' she repeated as her eyes again filled with tears. 'When life is a sentence and my existence is a prison, tell me where is hope?'

'Why do you think death will solve anything?'

'For me, it will solve everything.' She laughed a painful laugh. 'It will allow me to escape a life that is far worse than death.'

'That's no way to think…'

But she interrupted him, her voice suddenly strong and bitter. 'What would you know about the life of a girl whose mother is a concubine? How would you feel if your mother expected you to follow her into the same way of life? And would you not feel repulsion to learn that the man who demands physical pleasures with you is the man who fathered you?' She was shivering uncontrollably while she blurted out her story to this stranger.

Removing his shoulder cloth, Saleem placed it around her trembling arms. He understood. This girl's desire to end her own life and her courage to do so had given her the strength to reveal secrets probably long held. Shocked, Saleem stared at her. The expression on her pale face told him that her dread of living had made irrelevant any fear of dying, leaving her no choice but to cross the fragile line from one side to the other. She would embrace death if it ended her misery.

At last he whispered, 'Kalyani? It is Kalyani, isn't it?'

'How do you know my name?' She was visibly shaken.

'Anjali told me about you,' he said.

'Anjali!' An expression of surprise followed by a small smile broke through her distress. 'You know her?'

'Yes.' He looked away. 'I am Saleem.'

'Saleem!' Her mouth opened wide. 'So, she found you?'

'Yes,' he nodded.

'I have heard so much about you from Anjali.'

'So have I… about you.'

'Have you?' She looked down as if suddenly remembering her situation.

'Please, go home. I will come with you.'

'So you want me to continue leading the life of a living corpse?' she asked.

'No, of course not.'

"I… have lost… everything,' she choked. 'Don't you understand? No. How could you? You are a man.'

'Kalyani, I do understand. Not all men are the same.'

'No,' she replied. 'Perhaps not.'

'Perhaps you could run away, like Anjali, and do something else… or marry someone…'

'Do what! Marry!' she said with scorn. 'And who will marry me? A concubine's daughter and a fallen woman?'

'I understand what society might call you, but you are also a young woman who is not to blame for her past and who has the right to live happily.'

She sighed. 'You are very kind, Saleem, but not many people would agree with you. I am worse than an outcast.'

'Please come with me. I would very much like to help. I know of somewhere I can take you… where you will be safe.'

'Where?'

'I will take you to Anjali.'

Kalyani looked up in surprise. 'I know she is my friend, but how can she help me? I don't want to be a burden to her. Or anyone.'

'I'll tell you more as we make our way there. Anjali works with women just like you, women who have been rejected by society. She will be very pleased to see you.'

Chapter 75

A knock on the door woke Anjali. It was still dark. Who on earth would be visiting her at this early hour of the morning? She got up, turned up the wick of a lantern, and with some trepidation went to the door.

'Who is it?' she asked, without opening it.

'It's me, Saleem.'

'Saleem! At this time! Are you not in Roypuram?' Anjali opened the door. 'Please... Come in.'

'I am sorry if we woke you or gave you a shock,' Saleem said, still standing there.

'Don't worry.' Anjali knew that it must be something serious for Saleem to disturb her like this.

'I have someone with me.'

'Who is it?' Anjali stepped forward, lifting up the lamp so that she could see the two faces. A young woman stood beside Saleem. She looked up from under her veil, her eyes brimming with tears. Anjali recognised her friend from Mohini's house.

'Kalyani! Both of you... come in.'

But Saleem remained where he was and the girl stayed beside him as if frozen to the spot. Why were her two old friends standing on her doorstep at this time of night? Why didn't they come in?

'Are you real, Kalyani, or am I imagining things?' Anjali began to smile, wanting to welcome someone who had been a very good friend and ally, but when she looked properly at Kalyani's face, she saw how pale and tense she was, as if she had been through some ordeal. Her eyes were expressionless. Anjali understood that the girl was in extreme distress, perhaps traumatised. What could have happened to her? She opened her arms. Kalyani ran into them, burying her head on her friend's shoulders. Anjali felt the tremor of her body.

'Kalyani…' She must wait to ask her what had happened. The girl seemed to be in shock. 'You are safe here with me. Take your time.' She tried to console her friend and assure that she was at least out of danger.

Finally the floodgates broke and Kalyani began to sob on Anjali's shoulders. Anjali waited patiently and in silence until Kalyani was calmer.

'Come inside… You can tell me what has happened.'

Saleem remained at the door. 'Anjali-ji,' he said, 'I'm so sorry but I have to go. I borrowed Mr Robert's jeep to bring Kalyani here and the engineer sahib will be waiting for me.'

'But Saleem… How on earth…'

'Kalyani will tell you everything.'

Anjali nodded.

'Kalyani, please don't lose hope. Anjali-ji will look after you,' Saleem said, looking at the distraught girl.

As Saleem took his leave, he gestured to Anjali to follow him. She settled Kalyani on the bed and walked with him to the jeep.

'Anjali-ji, please keep a close eye on her and don't ever leave her on her own.'

Understanding, Anjali nodded.

Saleem looked back one more time before he climbed into the driver's seat. He could see Kalyani through the open door, motionless. He felt desperately sorry for her.

'Please don't worry. You did the right thing bringing her here. I will look after her.'

'Thank you, Anjali-ji. I know you will. I will be back on Sunday again.'

*

Choosing her words carefully, Anjali gently persuaded Kalyani to talk. When she did finally respond, it was to pour her heart out, leaving nothing unsaid. Anjali listened in astonishment and horror. She kept an arm round Kalyani and wiped away her tears as she listened. The two young women spent hours talking and sipping hot tea until the first pale rays of the early morning sun touched their dark heads through the grills of the window.

'How did you find out that the zamindar is your father?' she finally asked.

'There was one night when I overheard Mohini shouting at him. Much louder and more persistent than usual, and I could hear every word. She shouted, "*You have fathered her. She is your daughter and how could you even think of such a thing?*" I knew it was me she was referring to. Mohini never told me, but I suspected from quite an early age. I look in the mirror and I see her. Only when I was older did I understood that she was protecting me from the eyes of the zamindar.'

'You knew. But you never said anything…'

'It was easier just to play along. It was a cynical game between us. Maybe she knew I knew. She did it to protect me, Anjali. I think she had my interests at heart. But on *Diwali* day, when the zamindar arrived at the house unexpectedly, I was there in the front room, all dressed up for the festival.' She flinched at the memory. 'You know, he had never seen me before. At first he stared at me in surprise and then his expression changed. His eyes narrowed and became… full of… lust. The way he leered at me terrified me. I felt sick. I just ran…'

'Oh, Kalyani…'

'Later that night, he came back and asked for me. Mohini was horrified. She pleaded with him. She told him I was his daughter – over and over and again and again. That was when I learned that he was my father. Mohini even placed her head on his feet, begging him to leave me alone. But there was no stopping him. He said he didn't want to hear any more lies and told Mohini that she was just making stupid excuses. He told her she was jealous.' Kalyani stopped, too upset to continue.

'How shocking for you, Kalyani.' What more could she say? It was unthinkable.

'Mohini fought as much as she could but in the end she had to give up…'

'No…!' Anjali gave a sharp scream.

'She had no choice… she was like a deer in front of a hungry lion,' Kalyani whispered. 'I… I… died that night.'

'Oh, Kalyani…' If she hadn't run away from Roypuram, she would have become the zamindar's new concubine, existing only to satisfy his lust. Anjali trembled at the thought. She wished she could have suffered that fate instead of Kalyani. She felt that it her fault that Kalyani had fallen into the zamindar's greedy hands. Kalyani had paid the price of her own escape.

They both sat for a very long time immersed in their own thoughts, until the first morning bell rang out across the courtyard, making both of them jump. It was six o'clock. Time for everyone at St Agnes's to stir and start a new day.

Kalyani broke the heavy silence. 'Tell me, Anjali, when everything in you is dead, except for your body – and that is no longer your own – what point is there in living?'

'I do understand your pain, Kalyani. As you know, I too have felt despair. But death is not the solution. Please believe me when I say that there is life even after the kind of death you describe. You may not believe me now, but you will when you have had enough time to start to heal. You look exhausted. Why don't you sleep for a while I get ready and cook us some breakfast? Then have a bath. Come with me and I will take you to St Agnes's.'

'Sorry, Anjali, I don't feel like going anywhere. I can't face anyone.'

'Of course you don't, but it is important, Kalyani. You need to take this first difficult step, and I will be at your side. I will show you many women and girls who have suffered as you have suffered, and who have come through. For now, you just need to trust me. Later, you will believe it for yourself.'

'What is this place?' Kalyani asked.

'It is a house of safety for women who been mistreated. For women who had lost hope.'

'And why are you here, Anjali?'

'It's a long story. I will tell you some time later when you have rested. I teach here. I am very fortunate.'

'I don't know. I don't understand what fortunate means anymore.'

'Oh, Kalyani…' Anjali sat down beside her friend again. 'Of course you don't. No wonder after what you have been through.'

'I trust you, Anjali. You too have suffered,' Kalyani said at last. 'I know you understand how I feel after…'

'When you are ready, we will go. Let me show you this place where I work. I think you will find you can start to recover here.'

'I am ashamed to go anywhere.'

'Why? You haven't committed any crime. You mustn't punish yourself and let that… animal ruin your life. You are going to have to be very strong, Kalyani, but I know you can do it. If you can try not to look back… and try to have some hope for the future.'

'Do the others have to know what has happened to me?'

'No. They need know nothing. Only that you need help and support.'

Kalyani nodded.

They made their way slowly across the courtyard to the main building, Anjali's arm linked through Kalyani's. Anjali forced her features to look hopeful, but she was shocked to the core. Thank god it was Saleem who had found Kalyani and knew to bring her here, she thought. Saleem again. How can I ever thank him for this, and for everything else that he has done?

Chapter 76

The night before Miss Edwina set sail for England, Mr Robert drove off in his jeep. The next day he was still nowhere to be seen. It didn't take long for Saleem to understand that he was not going to say goodbye to his wife.

Mr Vincent sent his car and driver for Miss Edwina. It upset Saleem to help the driver load the memsahib's luggage into Mr Vincent's car. Anjali was there too, feeling awkward and embarrassed. On the one hand, it seemed right to say a last goodbye to the woman in whose house she had stayed for so long, but on the other she worried that her presence might provoke further distress in the memsahib. The previous night, when Saleem had visited her and Kalyani, she had broached the subject and asked his opinion.

'You haven't committed any crime, Anjali-ji. It isn't your fault that Miss Edwina is leaving. Since she is on her way back to England, it might not provoke her to see you one last time,' Saleem had suggested.

When Miss Edwina came down, wearing a smart travelling suit and dark sunglasses, Anjali timidly went up to her and wished her a safe journey. Since the memsahib didn't take her goggles off, Saleem couldn't tell whether the woman acknowledged Anjali's gesture, but he thought he saw a slight nod of her head. Perhaps embarrassment prevented her from doing more. He guessed that she wanted to be gone as soon as she possibly could.

As usual all the servants lined up in the courtyard and saluted Miss Edwina. Then, one by one, they went up to her to say goodbye and she gave each a gift of money. Most of her employees looked upset. Saleem wondered why. It was not as if she had treated them well or they would miss her. He did not hear the whispered conversation that flew along the solemn row of uniformed natives. 'Even though the memsahib was unhappy and difficult a lot of the time, she did not treat us very badly,' they said to one another very quietly as she climbed into Mr Vincent's car.

'Every Christmas and *Diwali* we received generous gifts from her,' Vimala explained to Anjali, who, like Saleem, was watching with surprise.

'Hmmm,' Saleem said. 'At least they got something out of her.'

Standing next to each other on the steps of the veranda, Anjali and Saleem felt the same mixed emotions as they watched Miss Edwina leave her Indian home for the last time. They knew it was the only possible course of action but they were sad that her stay in their country had caused her so much grief. Saleem imagined that once she was in the car, she would breathe a sigh of relief to be on her way to meet Mr Vincent, who would accompany her to Madras. There they would board the *Viceroy of India* and set sail for England. Saleem imagined them standing at the railings high above the sea as the engines started up and the ship pulled away from the dock.

Anjali and Saleem wondered how Mr Robert would react to his wife's departure. It was one thing making the decision but another living with the consequences. Probably all the servants were thinking the same because no one moved. They all stared at the open gates for a long time, perhaps each thinking about the future. Even the gatekeeper remained where he was, as if he couldn't bring himself to close the gate on his memsahib.

Two weeks went by. The household muddled along with neither

master nor mistress present. Saleem didn't feel like staying so he asked Vimala to take care of everything while he visited Prakash. He returned occasionally but there was never any sign of Mr Robert.

'I know he has taken time off work but I have no idea where he is,' he told Anjali. 'I hope he is all right.'

'Mrs Wilson was saying that he is a strong man and that he will get over it. He will return when he is ready. That's all,' replied Anjali.

*

Things at St Agnes's went on as normal. For Anjali, having Kalyani in her house was an additional pleasure. She observed, while appearing not to, the efforts Kalyani made to put behind her the shocking ordeal she had been through. What helped her most was that Mrs Wilson and Chandrabai asked her if she too would like to help the girls and women at St Agnes's by teaching music. By day, Kalyani had a busy schedule and didn't have time to think about herself, but at night she was still troubled by nightmares, though they gradually became less vivid and stopped waking her. The change was slow but Anjali noticed how much Kalyani's mood improved. Day by day her friend was getting better.

With Mr Robert on leave, Saleem of course had no work to do, so he stayed with Prakash and frequently visited Anjali and Kalyani. Anjali noticed how his presence made Kalyani happy. She would always volunteer to make tea or cook food for him. Saleem was unfailingly kind and pleasant with Kalyani, and spent long hours talking quietly with her. It was as if he was doing what he could to give her back her will to live. Sometimes when her eyes filled with tears and she apologised for being emotional, he comforted her by quoting beautiful lines by Urdu poets like Ghalib, who wrote about love and life.

Heart it is, not a brick or stone.
Why shouldn't it feel the pain?
Let not tyrannise this heart
Or I shall cry again

'More please…' Kalyani would beg, clasping her hands together.

And Saleem would continue, hoping that wise words might help restore Kalyani's hope in the future.

What then is the need to cry?

The drop dies in the river of its joy.

The pain goes so far, it cures itself.

At last it is here I receive recompense for the anguish I endured so long.

'Oh, Saleem, I love to hear you recite verse. You speak the lines so well,' she said.

He could even make Kalyani laugh by telling her funny stories about his childhood with Anjali. He teased Anjali and was relaxed with her now. Anjali was delighted to see a steady change in him too. He was becoming more and more like her childhood friend.

And so the days passed peacefully for the three friends. At last, each day had its own purpose and pattern and they fell into a routine that offered a quiet pleasure. This was the first time they felt safe and settled.

Mrs Wilson had said all along that Mr Robert would return after two weeks, and so it was. He went home briefly, then set off to Roypuram, taking Saleem with him. Anjali guessed that he would fill his days with work and immerse himself in the completion of the road. Work would give him a purpose and a routine, and would fill the hours.

But what about the nights? Anjali knew what it was like to lie awake with thoughts that would not be silenced. Each evening when the moon rose, her thoughts turned to Mr Robert, and she worried.

Chapter 77

Meanwhile a remarkable event was unfolding at St Agnes's. One morning, in the prayer meeting, Mrs Wilson said that she had a special announcement. She told everyone that the maths teacher, Ravindra, had asked for permission to marry one of the girls who was resident at St Agnes's. She was a child widow whose name was Kamala.

'It is my pleasure to tell you that Kamala has agreed wholeheartedly to this marriage proposal,' Mrs Wilson said.

This extraordinary news sent a wave of excitement round the room, which erupted in joyful clapping and cheering. Surprised and elated, Anjali looked at Kamala and imagined from the expression on her face the happiness that was bubbling in her heart. The twenty-year-old girl was looking down shyly, trying to hide a smile that could not be disguised. Chandrabai then invited the couple on to the stage and all the girls gathered round and congratulated them. They admired Ravindra's courage and Kamala's good fortune.

Anjali knew that her colleague was an idealist but she hadn't thought him audacious enough to challenge his parents, go against the customs and traditions of society, and stand so firmly by his principles. Marrying a widow was forbidden for Hindus because they considered it would bring bad luck on the boy and his family. They believed that the girl must have sinned in her previous life to be left a widow in this one. Hindus were certain that such a woman, once widowed, would become a widow a second time. Parents were terrified of accepting a widow as a wife for their sons.

'We would like to thank Mr Ravindra and offer our appreciation of his ideals, his principles and his modern way of thinking. He believes that women are not inferior to men and that child widows are not cursed,' said Chandrabai. 'The marriage ceremony will take place next Sunday morning here in this room. It is the first marriage of its kind to be celebrated since St Agnes's was founded ten years ago. It will also be the first time, in this district, that a man has chosen a widow for his bride. Once again we congratulate Ravindra and Kamala.'

The day before the wedding, all the young girls gathered in the prayer room to decorate it with fresh flower garlands, mango leaves and coloured paper chains. The women prepared a simple but delicious wedding breakfast of *tamarind* rice, puris, potato kurma and sweet halwa.

Chandrabai had bought a new *sari* for the bride and on the day Anjali helped Kamala to dress and braided her hair with garlands of fresh jasmine while Kalyani made up her face. Wearing bright yellow instead of white, and with clusters of flowers in her hair, Kamala was transformed. Her eyes sparkled. Between her eyebrows was the vermillion dot that she had never before worn. Her happiness was obvious in her smile and the look in her eyes.

Several guests were already seated in the front row, and Anjali listened attentively as one of them, Mr Koneti Devraj, gave an inspiring speech about the importance of a woman's role in society and how a mother was a teacher as well as a carer.

Just as the ceremony was about to begin, there was a commotion at the main entrance and someone ran in to announce that the final guest had arrived. Chandrabai got up and went quickly to greet him and to bring him into the room. Moments later, Anjali's eyes became

wide with dismay and her heart skipped several beats. She gasped as
Mr Robert entered the wedding hall. It was three weeks since she had
seen him, and she was relieved. But although he looked as dignified
as ever in his dark suit, he had lost weight and his face was serious.
Why had they invited Mr Robert to be their main guest? She was
still wondering when everyone, including the other guests and Mrs
Wilson, stood up to welcome him. They showed him to his chair.

'We are honoured that you could be with us to grace this occasion.'
Chandrabai said. Then she turned towards the audience. 'I would
like to introduce you all to our special guest, Mr Robert Harrison. It is
very kind of him to accept our invitation to this auspicious ceremony
and on behalf of you all I would like to thank him with all my heart.
I want to tell you something that perhaps many of you don't know.
Mr Harrison has contributed very generously to our Home. Without
him, we wouldn't be here today.'

Astonished, Anjali looked at her colleague, Jyothi, who sat beside
her. Jyothi smiled, her nod indicating that she knew this already.

'I know nothing about it. No one has told me,' Anjali said.

The ceremony was very simple. The bride and groom exchanged
flower garlands and Ravindra tied the three knots of the wedding
necklace around Kamala's neck. Then they signed the marriage
certificate and the registrar announced them man and wife.

Anjali had been so lost in thought that she was unaware that the
ceremony had ended. The noise of cheering and clapping brought
her back to the present. Ravindra and Kamala were standing
together joyfully as a married couple, and Mrs Wilson was asking Mr
Robert to say a few words. He stood up.

'First, my sincerest congratulations to Ravindra and Kamala. I wish
you every happiness. It is my pleasure to attend the first ceremony
in which a man has taken as his bride a woman who, through no
fault of her own, happens to be a widow. I hope you won't mind if
I quote two great social reformers from the last century whom you

may already know and who campaigned for the rights for women, including the rights for widows to re-marry and to own property. First, Sir Raja Ram Mohan Roy, who actively opposed the *sathi* system and the practice of polygamy. What he said was, '*Hindu women are uneducated, illiterate, deprived of property rights, married before puberty, imprisoned in purdah and murdered at widowhood by a barbaric custom. By treating women as equals, Indian society could free itself from social stagnation.*' Secondly, and more recently, Sir Kandukuri Veereshlingam, a local hero whom we sadly lost quite recently. His words '*the denigration of women has ruined society*' still echo in my mind. As many of you know, as long ago as 1881, he organised the first marriage in this state between a widow and her husband to be.' He turned to Ravindra. 'Today this remarkable young man follows in the footsteps of our great reformists. He has shown us that by positive and forward thinking it is possible to lift the barbaric rules that have been ruining the lives of women for centuries. Mr Ravindra and Kamala have set an example by daring to break a taboo that is utterly meaningless. I am sure that many more young men will follow in his footsteps.'

Everyone stood up and clapped, drowning out Mr Robert's final congratulations and good wishes.

Anjali felt dizzy as she listened to his speech. Her heart swelled with pride and gratitude towards this very unusual man who was willing to talk with fairness, eloquence and humanity about the oppression of women in India.

Suddenly the blue eyes searched for hers and he smiled at her. Her heart missed a beat. His gaze lingered for several moments longer than politeness warranted. What did Anjali read in that look that darted across a room full of people, searching her out? She would have said she saw vulnerability and longing. Yes, a yearning for something he desperately wanted.

As she had done many times before in the company of this charismatic man, she chided herself for her overactive imagination.

'You don't know,' she told herself firmly. 'You have no idea what he is thinking. You don't know what he wants.'

Chapter 78

The following week almost every local newspaper printed photographs of the newlyweds.

The headlines read: 'Idealist Marries Child Widow', 'Widow Re-marries: Kandukuri's Dreams A Reality'.

There were several other pictures, including ones of Mrs Wilson, Chandrabai, Mr Robert and Devraj. Mr Robert was looking at the photographs with Saleem one morning and telling him all about the event when Saleem spotted a group photograph clearly showing Anjali and Kalyani in the background.

Alarmed, Saleem asked, 'Sir… have you seen this?'

'Yes.' He looked at Saleem. 'I know what you're thinking. The zamindar might see it too and then he will know the whereabouts of two girls who have escaped him.'

'And knowing what he is like, he will go to any lengths to get them back, sir.'

'Yes, I thought about that too, so I phoned Mrs Wilson this morning and asked her to alert the police and to be very careful about security. If the zamindar tries to enter St Agnes's, he will find it under heavy protection.'

'I'm glad you have done that, sir, but…'

'Saleem, he may be brave enough to hunt a tiger but he doesn't wish to make the white man his enemy.'

Saleem looked unconvinced.

*

The next morning Saleem was surprised to receive a letter from Anjali. He was even more surprised and shocked to read what she wrote. Whatever was she saying? He stared at every word as if he couldn't make sense of them. He turned over the sheet of paper and looked at the blank side, as if searching for answers there, until it was time to drive Mr Robert to work. He folded the paper and put it in his shirt pocket, where it felt like a ton weight against his chest.

After that, he spent his nights lying awake thinking about Anjali's astonishing request. He knew she meant well and did not mean to cause him any distress, but the letter wrought havoc with his emotions. Saleem spent the entire week totally confused and undecided. If the suggestion had come from anyone else, he would simply have ignored it. But it came from Anjali, who did not ask such things lightly nor without careful thought and consideration. And so he remained in a state of restlessness, not knowing what to do or how to answer the letter.

The next Sunday, Mr Robert decided that he wanted to go home. It had been a long time. Perhaps he felt that he was finally ready to face his new domestic circumstances and settle down to living by himself. That gave Saleem an excuse to delay replying to Anjali, as well as an opportunity to discuss the matter with Prakash. He knew his friend always saw things very clearly and would offer sensible advice.

'How could she write this?' Saleem asked, handing the letter to Prakash.

For a while there was silence.

'I don't see why not,' Prakash said, looking up after reading it.

'Prakash!'

'Try to understand, Saleem. I know you still find this difficult to accept, but Anjali thinks of you only as a brother. We've discussed this and there is no more to say. I think it's time you became realistic. Try to think of this request as fair and sensible. At a practical level. It solves problems.' Saleem looked down, lost in thought. 'She is asking you to consider marrying Kalyani. What is so terrible about that?'

'But Prakash...' Saleem interrupted.

'No, wait. Let me finish. Anjali has also written that this poor girl loves and admires you,' Prakash said thoughtfully. 'I'm sure that's the truth. Think about it, Saleem. I will tell you what I would do if I were in your place. First, I wouldn't have wasted half my life longing in vain for a woman who clearly has never loved me in that way, and has been open and honest in saying so. Second, if I considered Anjali my close, trusted friend, I would accept her suggestion that I now marry another young woman who is deeply in love with me.'

'But Prakash... I...'

'Do you have any reservations about Kalyani? I mean in terms of her past?'

'No. Nothing like that. Her past is of no interest to me, except that I know she has suffered.'

'Saleem, you have seen how unfair life is in this country for girls like Anjali, Kalyani and Sita. And you told me how much you approved of Mr Robert's speech and how much you admire people like Rajaram Mohan Roy, Kandukuri and now Mahatma Gandhi. Are they not all saying the same thing? By marrying Kalyani, not only will you give this girl an opportunity to start a new life, but you will be a pioneer for other young men in this country. You will set a fine example and others may decide to follow in your footsteps.'

Saleem remained silent for a long time.

'Take your time and think it over before you make any decisions,' Prakash advised.

*

Anjali did not let Kalyani know that she had written to Saleem, knowing she would be mortified, but she did tell her that she had sent a letter about Sita to her father, the astrologer. Two weeks went by and Anjali became anxious that she hadn't received any response from either of them. She knew Saleem needed time to work through his emotions and to digest her request before making any decision either way. But the astrologer... She hoped that he had not misunderstood her.

'Since he is a Brahmin and strictly orthodox, do you think he would consider your suggestion?' asked Kalyani.

'I hope so,' answered Anjali. Her hopes had not yet faded.

'You know, he does obey all the traditional religious rules.'

'I know, but from what I have seen of him, he is also very practical and is forward- thinking.'

'If you say so. But is he modern enough to let his daughter live in a home run by Christians? As you know, he is a very influential person in Roypuram so he will have to think hard about his own reputation.'

'Sita is his daughter and he loves her very much.'

'Would he want the daughter he loves to leave home and live somewhere where she receives charity?'

As Anjali listened to Kalyani, her hopes dwindled, but her instincts told her that the astrologer might yet consider her suggestion.

That very night, as the world slept soundly, there was the unmistakable sound of a *tonga* drawing up in front of Anjali's house. What else would make that crunching noise on the gravel? Anjali knew in her heart that Sita had arrived.

'Kalyani...' she woke her friend.

'What is it, Anjali?'

'Listen, I think it's Sita.'

'Don't be silly...' But then Kalyani too heard the gate open.

As the two friends got to their feet, there was a knock on the door. And there was Sita, standing in front of them. Her father had accompanied her.

'*Namaskaram*, sir,' Anjali and Kalyani greeted him and bowed in respect.

'Welcome, Sita.' Anjali gave the girl a warm hug before inviting them both in. 'Thank you for bringing Sita here, sir,' she said with heartfelt gratitude.

'You are very kind…' smiled the astrologer. 'I do hope my daughter will be happy here.'

'I hope so too, sir.'

Taking Sita's hand, he placed it in Anjali's. 'Anjali, you have persuaded me with your eloquence to break all the rules and to ignore religious barriers that have ruled my actions throughout my life. Bound by them, I was unable to help Sita. I obeyed the rules for widows and watched helplessly as she suffered, and would have continued to suffer. She was a little girl when she became a widow. Only five years old. No girl deserves a fate like that. She had no childhood. She became a widow long before she grew into a young woman. It killed my wife…' he broke off to cope with the emotion that overwhelmed him. Then he wiped his tears and said, 'At last Lord Shiva has given her this opportunity to make a new life with you. Who am I to say no to that?'

Sita too was in tears as she leaned her head against her father's shoulders.

'Please look after her,' he said, his arm lingering around Sita's shoulders. 'She is my only child.'

'Of course we will. Thank you. From the bottom of my heart.'

Anjali and Kalyani watched as father and daughter took leave of each other, both in tears and both finding it painful to part. Then the three young women stood at the window and watched the *tonga* pull away. They watched until it faded to a small, blurred shape moving through the darkness.

Chapter 79

It took three months for Saleem to come to a decision.

He still visited Harikonda with Mr Robert, but not as frequently as before, because he felt uncomfortable seeing the three young women. What made it particularly awkward was that he could never catch Anjali on her own. Inevitably with Kalyani and Sita sharing her tiny house, one of them was always there or might arrive at any moment so that it was impossible to speak to Anjali properly. Even his conversations with Kalyani, which used to be so easy and spontaneous, were now strained. Poor Kalyani, she must have noticed the puzzling change in Saleem's behaviour. But because she remained oblivious of the situation, she could not understand what was wrong. Now neither of them managed to finish their sentences. Their meetings felt stilted and even claustrophobic because of what was not said and resolved.

Although Anjali had told Saleem to think over what she had proposed, he was aware that he was taking a ridiculously long time. He chided himself for the irrational thoughts that still blocked his ability to make a decision. In his heart, he knew what held him back. He still could not quite shed his love for Anjali. He was like a snake struggling out of an old useless skin whose last shreds still clung to him. But finally, after more long talks with the ever-patient Prakash, he wriggled free and felt almost ready to move on. Only a slight uncertainty still lingered. Prakash suggested that he try to get to know Kalyani a bit better before he gave Anjali a definite answer, and that seemed a reasonable idea. With this plan in mind, and feeling calmer, he set off one Sunday to make the journey to St Agnes's. He would discuss everything with Kalyani.

Anjali was the first to hear the rickshaw pull up outside. As always, she was very happy to see him. And maybe he brought news for her at last.

'It's Saleem! Saleem!' she called to the others. Sita and Kalyani ran outside to join Anjali, who was already in the courtyard, and the three together welcomed him and invited him in.

'It's been so long, Saleem,' Kalyani said.

'Are you well?' Sita asked.

Seeing the three women together, and knowing that they were leading independent, purposeful lives, Saleem's heart swelled with pride, especially for what Anjali had achieved. What an incredible difference she had made to the other two young women. He never imagined that he would see Kalyani so full of energy and enthusiasm as she was now. And Sita. Her hollow cheeks were rounded and her eyes sparkled with new hope. Her hair had started to grow and as Anjali had predicted, she looked a fine young woman. Saleem wondered what the astrologer had told the villagers about her disappearance, because her name was never mentioned, not even by those who loved to gossip. He smiled at the thought of them seeing her as she looked now. They would not recognise her.

'I just made some *aloo vada*. Would you like some?' Kalyani's question made him jump. He had been lost in his own thoughts.

'Yes, please,' he said, taking the plate. It was one of his favourite snacks: boiled potato mixed with onions, green chillies and spices, shaped into balls and dipped into a rice and lentil batter, then fried in sesame oil until golden brown. Crunchy outside and soft inside, it was delicious.

'Um… very tasty.' He looked at Kalyani appreciatively.

'Saleem, because today is Sunday, Kalyani insisted on making them, just in case you came,' Anjali teased.

'Thank you, Kalyani.'

She smiled at him shyly. It was obvious that she liked him.

When Kalyani busied herself making tea, with Sita helping her, Saleem took the opportunity to say quietly to Anjali, 'Actually, if you would permit me, I would like to talk to Kalyani on her own.'

'Of course, Saleem! Do please talk to her. She will be very pleased.'

Later, Anjali excused herself, saying that she had to see her colleague, Jyothi, about something, and took Sita with her, leaving Kalyani alone with Saleem. Not knowing how to start the conversation, Saleem asked her to tell him her recipe for *aloo vada*.

Kalyani looked at him in amazement. 'I didn't know you were interested in cooking,' she laughed, but she gave him a list of ingredients and told him how she made them.

At last, after many false starts that were nothing to do with what he had come to talk about, he managed to ask her opinion about inter-caste marriages. And that opened up a real conversation.

'You know that Ravindra and Kamala are not from same caste?'

'Yes.'

'What do you think about inter-caste marriages like theirs?'

'In my opinion, it's the wrong word to describe a marriage. When two hearts are united, don't the two castes become one?'

'Of course,' agreed Saleem. 'So would you say the same thing about a marriage between a couple whose religions are different?'

'Yes, I would. I don't think religion is a barrier to a happy married life. Again the two will become one.'

'But what name would you give such a couplet? Say, for example, a Hindu married a Christian, would you call the couple Hindu or Christian?'

'I am afraid I would call them neither.'

'Neither? Then...'

Kalyani laughed. 'Their religion will become Love.'

'No, seriously.'

'Why do they have to follow the rules of any particular religion or be labelled in some particular way? Can't they live freely, as they wish?'

'Yes, I think so. I believe that married individuals just have to accept the religion of a husband or a wife if it is different from their own and from the way they choose to behave. Each should be free. What do you think?'

'I agree. You know, Rangi used to tell me a story...' Kalyani's face clouded over as the name brought back memories of Samba.

Sensing her sadness, Saleem had to persuade her to continue. 'What story did she tell you? I'd like to hear it.'

'Oh, a long time ago, when she was a girl, a Hindu girl and a Muslim boy ran away and got married, but they kept their own faiths. Apparently, she wore her traditional *bindi* and *sari* and did the *pooja* everyday. And he did the *namaz* three times a day, facing Mecca. They celebrated all Hindu and Muslim festivals equally. The marriage was a happy one.'

'That's interesting to hear. I'm glad it worked out.'

Kalyani smiled. Saleem looked at the ground. Then up again.

'Kalyani... As you know, by birth I am a Muslim, but I am not interested in following the rules of my religion because I believe they are man made and arbitrary. In my opinion, I see no reason to divide mankind, created by the supreme being, into different and conflicting groups and segments. By giving each group a different religious name, I think we are causing segregation and misunderstanding and hostility.'

'Of course. I agree with you.'

Saleem looked at Kalyani, somewhat surprised that she had obviously thought all this through, just as he had done, and was offering her considered opinion. His respect for her deepened.

'So, it seems that you don't have a strong belief in our caste system and you look on religion with some healthy scepticism?'

'Yes. I think that sums up my thinking. I've seen too many women and even men damaged by the rules of religion… But why are you asking me all this?'

'I'm asking you… I'm trying to find out what you think because… I'm interested in your views…'

Kalyani looked at him in amusement while he struggled to find the right words.

'Because… Would you mind marrying me, Kalyani?'

'Saleem! What did you just say?' Kalyani's amusement changed to disbelief.

'Yes. Will you marry me? Like the woman in your story, you can keep your own religion.'

'Saleem… I never thought you would ask me… I mean… Oh, I don't mean that… I mean that I don't deserve you.' Tears slid down her cheeks.

'Kalyani…'

'Yes… But how can you… I am a fallen woman.' She sobbed as if her heart would break.

'No, Kalyani. Please don't ever say that word again. Society has failed you. That is all.'

'Oh, Saleem…' She looked up with gratitude. 'What a generous way of describing my situation.'

He wiped her tears. 'It's not generous. It's the truth. You have committed no crime, so why should you be labelled so cruelly and shunned by society? You had no choice. It was an accident of your birth.'

'Thank you, Saleem. I will try to honour the trust you have placed in me,' Kalyani said, taking both his hands in hers, and bowing her head low over them, she covered them with kisses.

The snake was finally free and slithered on its way, so much lighter in its new skin.

Chapter 80

Anjali was the first to hear what Saleem had decided, and was overjoyed for her two dear friends. Sita became excited as she planned and discussed the details of the wedding. And as for Kalyani... She walked around in a daze, unable to believe what was happening to her. If anyone so much as mentioned Saleem, her eyes filled with tears. A smile hovered permanently on her lips.

The women set the wedding date for March, when both Mr Robert and Saleem would be back for good because the construction work in Roypuram would be finished. Mr Robert offered to pay for the wedding, partly in appreciation of all the work Saleem had done so willingly for him, and partly as an expression of his fondness for him. He said it was a gesture he was happy to make.

Since Saleem and Kalyani wanted a very simple civil ceremony, there was not a great deal of organising to do. Even so, Anjali and Sita would sit together for hours on end discussing the colour of the wedding *sari* they would choose for Kalyani and the flowers she would wear in her hair. They planned the menu and talked in endless detail about the different dishes they would prepare for the wedding breakfast. Kalyani never joined in these earnest debates. She would pop her head round the door and listen for a while but she found it hard to concentrate on anything practical for more than a few minutes. Then she would drift away. Her friends teased her about being absentminded and thinking about Saleem all the time. She just smiled shyly.

'No I'm not,' she would tell them. But they knew that she meant 'Yes I am'. And it was true that she was missing him.

March approached. Sometimes, amid the preparations, Anjali would stop in the middle of what she was doing and look at Sita. She wished that someone suitable would come along for this innocent, wise, delicate-looking young woman, just as Saleem had done for Kalyani. As her thoughts passed from one possible husband to the next, one image kept returning. Saleem's friend Prakash. She hadn't met him but based on what she had heard from Saleem, Prakash seemed a level-headed, open-minded, kind man and she felt sure that he would appreciate the gentle Sita, with her sensitive personality. Once or twice, she secretly mentioned her idea to Kalyani. Kalyani's suggestion was not to wait until Saleem came home, but to go and see him soon and ask him directly. Nothing wrong in doing so, she said. You have nothing to lose. Surely a man like Prakash wouldn't have any reservations about talking it through. In the end, they persuaded one another that it was a very good idea.

*

Late one afternoon, after finishing her lessons at St Agnes's, Anjali set out in a *tonga* to travel to Gudem. By the time she reached the bazaar in the village, it was late. On the uneven pavements, the snack carts selling food were already lit by lanterns made of old tins and jars. Thick cotton wicks protruded from them, sucking up the kerosene and producing flickering flames and pungent black smoke. The heady smell from the burning lanterns mingled in the air with the aromas of cooked rice, pulses, vegetables and spices. The sweet stalls were more exotic and expensive, displaying trays of square, round and diamond-shaped confectionary. Anjali breathed in the wonderful aroma of melted ghee, sugar and boiled milk, mixed with saffron and cardamom. She bought a small pack of mixed *mitthai* for

Prakash. After all, it would be auspicious to offer him sweets at the same time as she offered him Sita.

Even though Gudem was in the poor, neglected outskirts of Harikonda, it was as busy as the town centre itself. It was noisy as well. The vendors shouting *pakoras, chilli-bajji, chudva* at the tops of their voices competed with the non-stop buzz of people talking and calling to one another and arguing loudly. Most of them stood around in groups, chatting idly to pass the time; others made their way on foot or by bicycle in and out of the narrow gullies, off to whatever destination. Small children were out playing and harassing their mothers to buy the sweets and fruits that were temptingly displayed in cane baskets all along the narrow streets. And in the midst of it all, a few cows and buffaloes stood still at the roadside or sat on the ground as if meditating while fanning themselves with their tails. Goats searched for banana skins. Ravenous stray dogs fought one another for discarded scraps at the rubbish heaps or circled the stalls and their vendors, sniffing and barking.

There were no names for the streets here and no numbers on the doors. The *tonga-wallah* who was driving Anjali was obliged to stop and ask people, 'Do you know where two friends called Prakash and Saleem live?' Finally he was given directions and stopped the *tonga* at the beginning of a very narrow lane. Anjali was surprised to see that it would be impossible for the *tonga* to drive down it. Asking the *tonga-wallah* to wait for her, she got down and walked along the lane to the house beside the coconut tree.

The door was open and through it came the cheerful whistling of a tune from a popular *bhajan*. She knocked on the door. A man in loose pyjamas came out. His whistling stopped at once and he stared at her in astonishment.

Even though she guessed who he was, she said, 'I am sorry to disturb you but are you Prakash?'

'Yes, but… You are…?'

'I am Anjali.'

'Anjali… ji… Saleem's friend…'

'Yes, I am his friend, Anjali.'

'Oh, please come in. But Saleem is not here,' he said, quickly wiping the dust off a chair with his shoulder cloth so that she could sit down.

'I know. Saleem is in Roypuram.' She looked discretely at the small room with the partition down the middle. She guessed that the other half was Saleem's.

'Of course you know. He will have told you.' A look of puzzlement crossed his face. Anjali gave him no help because she was wondering how to begin. Perhaps this whole idea had been a stupid mistake. They sat in silence for a few minutes.

'It's been very hot today. May I offer you a glass of water?' He was completely at a loss as to why she was there.

'Oh, yes please. That would be nice.'

He went to fetch a glass of cool water. Handing it to her he said, 'A woman like you shouldn't have taken the trouble of coming all the way out to this poor area. You could have sent a message and I would have come to you straight away if you needed me.' He was clearly embarrassed – about both his modest home and her unexpected arrival in it.

'Don't worry. I wanted to come.'

'Is there anything I can do for you?'

'Yes, a big favour…' Anjali looked at him. He was just as good-looking as Saleem, though his skin was a shade darker. She couldn't help but imagine Sita sitting next to him and a smile came to her lips. She had already learned from Saleem that Prakash was earning a reasonably good salary as a clerk in a railway office. But he was living in this shabby house in this poor area because the rent was cheap and he was saving up for his younger sister's wedding and his brother's education. Like Saleem, he was shouldering a heavy responsibility for his family and Anjali admired the generosity of these two friends.

'A favour…' Prakash repeated, waiting for Anjali to continue.

'Yes. Do you have a few minutes to spare? I would like to talk to you.'

'Yes, of course.' Prakash sat down. 'Is it about Saleem?'

'No…' Anjali shook her head.

Prakash's friendly face looked mystified but something about his expression encouraged Anjali to continue.

'Prakash, I have heard so much about you from Saleem. First, let me thank you.'

'What for?'

'I know that it was you who helped to persuade Saleem to be realistic and to consider marrying Kalyani.'

'Anjali-ji, it's kind of you to say, but I didn't do anything. Saleem is a very open-minded person. You know he was suffering… he just needed some reassurance, that's all.'

'I know that you two are real idealists,' she smiled. 'I am very proud of you both.'

She stopped there, not knowing how to move on to the subject that had brought her there.

'Anjali-ji, surely you didn't come all the way out here just to thank me?'

That was just the cue Anjali needed.

'Prakash, Saleem has probably told you about Sita, whose father brought her to St Agnes's.'

'Yes, he did tell me about her. Poor girl. But it's the same kind of story for half of all Indian women,' he sighed.

'Well… Sita is the reason I have come to talk to you.'

'But how lucky she is to be with you and Kalyani now.'

'Yes. But I think she would be happier still if a nice man came along with an offer of marriage,' Anjali replied, after a deep breath. 'Like Saleem did, bringing such joy to Kalyani.'

He looked at her thoughtfully.

'Yes, Prakash. I know already that you are progressive in your thinking. Now that I have met you, I know too how kind-hearted you are.'

'Anjali-ji!'

'Yes, Prakash. I am asking you to consider marrying Sita. Please would you at least think about it?'

It was not such an unreasonable suggestion, yet she could see that Prakash felt very uncomfortable.

'I will completely understand if you object to what I ask.'

'No. It's not that.'

'Prakash, please take your time. I understand that this is a life-changing decision for you and Sita. You certainly don't have to give me an answer now.'

Another silence made Anjali doubt her whole mission. She was putting this kind, thoughtful young man under too much pressure.

'It's just that I have my mother to think about. As you can imagine, she is old-fashioned and very traditional, and she loves me very much.'

Anjali nodded, her hopes sinking.

'Have you talked to Sita about it?' he asked.

'No, not yet. She doesn't know that I am here.'

Prakash nodded. 'Anjali-ji, I have no real objections to what you propose, except that… she is a Brahmin girl and I am from a Reddy caste.'

Anjali sighed with relief. 'I know,' she replied. 'For Sita this is not an issue but perhaps it is for you…'

'She might not mind but what about her father? After all, he is a priest. Of course he adheres strictly to many orthodox religious rules.'

'Yes, he does, but that's a personal thing. He would not force his views on other people. We know that because he allowed Sita to come and live at St Agnes's. Prakash, he once said, "A person shouldn't automatically become a Brahmin by birth, but by deeds. Anyone, educated not by schooling but by observing life, who believes in goodness and truth, should be able to be a Brahmin." My feeling is that he will be pleased that a man like you might consider marrying his daughter.'

'Anjali-ji, before I say any more, I would like to talk to Sita. As my father is no more, and as I am the eldest son, I have many family responsibilities and commitments. I might not be able to offer her the kind of life she is used to.'

'Prakash, what kind of life do you imagine it was?' Anjali tried not to sound indignant. 'You know perfectly well how a widow has to live in this country. Sita is a sensible, sweet-natured girl. She is not remotely interested in living in luxury. She will be grateful if you treat her with kindness and affection, that's all.' She added silently, And even more grateful if you grow to love her, which I'm sure you will.

Prakash did not reply. Anjali held her breath.

'I will come and see her on Sunday,' he said at last.

'Thank you, Prakash. Sita will be very happy to see you.' She stood up and looked at him with heartfelt gratitude.

There was more heavy silence, both Anjali and Prakash lost in thought about what had just passed between them.

'Please accept these sweets. I bought them on the way here for you,' Anjali said at last, awkwardly handing him the paper parcel.

'Is this some kind of bribe?'

Anjali looked up, worried, but Prakash was smiling.

'If you want to call it that,' she laughed.

'Thank you,' he said, untying the cotton thread around the parcel. 'They look and smell delicious.'

Anjali breathed out, a long low sigh, as she looked up at this fine young man. And dared to hope.

Chapter 81

The clouds gathered in the evening sky. A cool breeze rustled through the leaves of the *tamarind* trees. Anjali heard a *koel* bird singing sweetly in its branches. It was so tempting. She put down the lesson she was preparing and went outside to wander alone in the grounds of St Agnes's.

It surprised her that two months had already passed since the gift of sweets that had sealed the fate of Sita and Prakash. What excitement had ensued at St Agnes's when a double wedding was announced and then celebrated. Anjali recalled how pleased Prakash had been that he had managed to persuade his mother to accept Sita as her daughter-in-law.

For the first two weeks after the wedding, the days passed very slowly. On one hand, Anjali missed her friends terribly. On the other, she didn't mind because she loved her newfound space and solitude. The three of them had been a bit cramped in that small room. The important thing was that her friends were happy. She smiled to herself, remembering one vivid memory after another. She saw the joyful smile Saleem gave Kalyani when the marriage ceremony came to a close. She remembered vivdly the primrose yellow of Sita's wedding *sari*. She saw again the astrologer, who risked so much to come to see his daughter married. For Sita, her father's blessings meant that the occasion was more than a dream come true.

As the two couples were exchanging flower garlands, Anjali looked at Mr Robert. In his casual Indian clothes, he looked exactly like the man who had knelt next to her in the temple all that time ago. His gaze met hers and held it. He gave her a steady knowing smile. She blushed and quickly looked away as the heat rose to her cheeks. She sighed as her heart beat too hard against her ribcage. There was no denying the intensity of her feelings every time she saw him, every time he visited her. She shook her head as if to deny it all once more. It was because her friends had just been married and all the romance was rubbing off on her. Oh, Anjali, she asked herself crossly, why do you continue to delude yourself?

*

Bathed in the warmth of her memories, Anjali was startled to come across Mrs Wilson standing in the doorway of the main building, looking worried and carrying a newspaper.

'I was just coming over to see you,' she said.

'What's wrong?' Anjali asked, reluctant to be dragged from her gentle thoughts.

'They've shot Malladi, my dear. There will be more trouble.' Mrs Wilson handed the paper to Anjali, where the headlines shrieked:

'Fearless freedom fighter Malladi Nagabhushan Rao shot dead without a trial'

During her time with Mohini in Roypuram, Anjali had heard much about this patriotic and brave young man. His kindness towards the poor and his courage in challenging the government had been welcomed and praised by the locals. Now he was dead at the age of twenty-eight, killed in a shocking and terrible way. Already people were taking advantage of the political situation as an excuse to carry out personal revenge. This incident would breed more violence. She was concerned at the loss of life that would inevitably follow. She sighed heavily.

'I fear it is going to be bad,' she said. 'Although perhaps the police will be prepared this time, and will contain any further violence. Here. You can read about it for yourself.'

'Malladi Nagabhushan Rao was popular and loved by the poor,' the paper read. 'He was a brave heart who was ready to fight the British without a single weapon. He was the first to adopt Mahatma's Non-violence in the district. With his powerful weapon of oration he even turned some of the British army against the Government and against each other. As the soldiers fought amongst themselves, Malladi became a nightmare for the British authorities. Since they couldn't find a fault with his non-violent strikes, it was only with connivance and foul play that the British accused him falsely and charged him for a murder of an English officer in the forest and were finally able to gun him down.'

'Oh, no!' How cruel it is to kill an innocent person in that way! Anjali whispered to herself. There was no doubt that the murder of this young man would provoke further riots and bloodshed. There would be anarchy and uproar again. Her thoughts turned immediately to Mr Robert, who had set out for Roypuram a couple of days earlier, invited by the villagers for the inauguration of the new road. After the opening ceremony, Mr Robert had stayed on to sort out a few last administrative details which would conclude the project, but he had sent Saleem home so that he was not away from his new wife for too long.

On his return, Saleem had brought Kalyani to visit Anjali. He had described the first bus that had set off from Roypuram on the new road.

'They decorated it with flowers and tinsel, and stuck posters of gods and goddesses all over it,' he laughed. 'They even placed a small brass statue of Ganesh on one of the front seats for good luck. After praying together, everyone climbed into the bus until you couldn't have fitted a needle inside. More people climbed on to the rooftop. They all wanted to experience a ride on a bus! They didn't care where it went. The driver complained but he had no choice but to start the engine. The bus moved in a heavy, slow and stately way, rather like a pregnant woman almost at full term.'

'It must have been very exciting for the people in Roypuram,' Anjali smiled.

Noticing her lack of interest and the expression on her face, which suggested that her thoughts were elsewhere, Saleem looked at her knowingly and said, 'Mr Robert will be coming home very soon.'

Saleem's words, which were then so reassuring, terrified her now. She knew that Mr Robert would be travelling in his jeep alone through the same forest roads where he had been attacked and Saleem had been seized. The roads were out of the way, with trees towering over them, making them hidden and dangerous.

'Mrs Wilson, Mr Robert is still in Roypuram...'

'I know. I was concerned about him too but my husband has already responded by placing a trunk-call to Robert. He wasn't in the office, so he left a message with the clerk, insisting that Robert come home immediately. I am sure the message will have reached him by now. If he sets off straight away, he should be home this afternoon.'

'Thank you, Mrs Wilson.' Anjali left it at that. There was no point telling Mrs Wilson her fear that the message might not reach Mr Robert because there was nothing either of them could do. She would just have to wait and pray for Mr Robert's safe return.

Now, with the summer temperatures soaring, the children, young women and teachers worked only until lunchtime. Then they would rest in the enervating heat until it relented in the evening. Restless and not knowing what to do, Anjali spent the long afternoon at home, waiting patiently and hoping to hear from either Mrs Wilson or Mr Robert himself. Her fingers were black from turning the pages of the newspapers and re-reading the same articles about the fear of escalating violence. Finally she could take in no more information. She sat motionless in her chair until darkness clothed her room in shadows, but still no message came for her.

As Anjali had predicted, the riots started up again, and much sooner than even she had expected. Even though St Agnes's was situated on the edge of the city, in the distance she could hear the sounds of people shouting. Soon after that, she heard what could only be the reaction of the mounted police as the thud of batons and screaming of shrill whistles were added to the noise. She imagined the horses being turned towards the crowds. It was not long before Harikonda sounded like a war zone, with gunshot fire echoing across the streets and the scraping and jangling of metal chains. Anjali heard people crying in pain, shouting in anger and howling like animals.

Anjali raced outside, wanting to find Mrs Wilson, but a security guard stepped up to her and blocked her way.

'I'm sorry,' he said, 'the situation is very volatile out there. I have orders from the authorities to ask people not to leave their rooms, nor to walk in the grounds. It is not safe. Please go back inside.'

And so Anjali had no choice but to return to her own house and wait. The noise of the demonstrators clashing with the police continued. Anjali could only imagine the carnage.

Chapter 82

Anjali heard loud voices and then a sudden crash a little way off and rushed to the window. She saw a crowd of miltants, some holding weapons, milling around the gate of St Agnes's. They had got there despite the increased security organised by the police. She watched in horror as they hurled stones, the repeated clank clank of rock on metal jarring her nerves. With her window wide open, the chanting was perfectly clear:

'Beef-eating Christians won't interfere with our faith!'

'Who are you to question our culture!'

'How dare you organise widow marriages?'

'You bring shame and misfortune on the country! You will rot in hell…'

Anjali could imagine how difficult it was for the guards and the police to control the angry crowd and to stop them breaking through the gates. They clashed for a long time, until with a shout from one of the men, the protesters at last turned around and slunk away. Or so it seemed. But the peace did not last: soon they were back, this time with burning torches.

There was a sudden, blinding flash of red and orange. Anjali saw flames leaping up just outside her door and heard the unmistakable crackling of fire. Terrified, she closed the window and rushed back into her room. She didn't know exactly what happened next, but she was aware of a sizzling heat and of smoke pouring in. The flames engulfed the only door. Red-hot tongues poked around the wood, licking the hinges and trying to get through the gaps. Shocked to the core, Anjali looked around the room for a means of escape. The two small windows had strong iron grilles fastened over them. She wasted precious minutes rushing about in a state of panic before seizing the water pot and throwing the water at the door. It did nothing to quench the thirst of the flames. And there was no way she could get out.

'Help!' she screamed, but the noise outside drowned her cries. She remembered with a sinking feeling that in any case Mrs Wilson would have gone home. And her house was invisible from the women's hostel, unless somebody came outside. Not only was it late at night, but because of the rioting, the windows and doors of the hostel had been shut tight. Having heard rumours of further violence spreading through the city, Chandrabai, before she left, had suggested that Anjali sleep in the hostel with the girls for her own safety. But Mr Robert might send a message, Anjali had thought, so she stayed in her house. What a fool she had been!

She didn't know if anyone could hear her cries, or see her burning door. The guards at the gate and the police were too busy dealing with the protesters to look inside the grounds. Even if they noticed the fire, by the time they reached her, it would be too late. What a macabre coincidence that she should find herself in this situation. She had escaped the funeral pyre but now she faced more flames. She stood no chance. Her fate must have followed her, cunningly hiding until it had the opportunity to spring out again in the same form as before. After all, if the Almighty had written that her life was supposed to end in flames that swallowed her alive then no one could prevent it.

The heat in the room was intolerable. The fire swept through the wooden door. It would not take long before it leaped across the floor.

Sweat soaked her *sari*, her stomach churned and she coughed as smoke filled the room. Darkness folded over her.

*

Later, Anjali could not say how long she was unconscious. Maybe only minutes. When she came round, she was gasping for air. Her throat was raw. Thick smoke made it impossible to see even as far as the window. She was starting to choke on the poisonous fumes.

'Anjali…'

She heard an urgent voice. Someone was trying to reach her. She wanted to call out in reply but couldn't. Her throat was too parched. Her lips dry as dust.

'Are you in there, Anjali?' The voice came to her again through the wall of black smoke. Then there was silence. She opened her mouth to answer but no sound came. Only a choking noise. Nausea. The burning heat.

She felt a pair of arms around her, lifting her from the floor. She felt herself held very tight to protect her from the flames. She was aware that she was being carried out of the burning house and placed in a vehicle. As she lay on the back seat, someone leaped into the driver's side and drove like a madman through the dark, empty streets. Both windows were wide open so that the cool air from outside blew in. She gulped it down, down into lungs that felt burned and bruised with smoke. But she was able to breath again. At first her skin glowed with heat, as if on fire itself, but soon she found herself shivering. Hot and cold. Burning and freezing. She closed her eyes, putting her trust in whoever had rescued her.

Anjali drifted in and out of a half-sleep, while the vehicle carried her along. She was aware of it slowing down and passing through some tall gates. She heard the familiar noise of tires crunching across gravel and felt it stop. Now she was being lifted carefully and gently, being taken out of the car.

She was being carried upstairs to a room. She was being placed gently on a bed.

Someone came in and washed her face and hands with a rag dipped in warm water. Anjali heard the clinking sound of bangles... Was it Vimala?... Was she dreaming? Then there were voices, some of which she recognised. One sounded agitated. Another calm.

'She is fortunate... I don't think she inhaled too much smoke.'

'By the time I reached her... She was unconscious...'

'I think it was fear, more than the smoke or the heat that made her faint...'

'The fire was only inches away from her. Had I got there even a minute later...'

'Don't think about it...'

'Will she be all right?'

'She is in mild shock at the moment. She should be much better in the morning. She needs some rest now.'

'Thank you, doctor.'

*

As the first rays of light fell in bright stripes across her pillow, Anjali opened her eyes and lay very still for a long time. Her mind was clear, her body relaxed. Was she really here? She thought she had been dreaming last night, but she was wrong. She looked around, comforted by the familiarity of her surroundings. Then the memories flooded back. She went back to the previous evening and relived it until she had recalled every detail, making a jigsaw out of the pieces. With a sharp intake of breath, she realised how close she had been to death. Then her heart jumped with joy at the thought of who had saved her.

'Anjali...'

She heard her name. Her heart raced. When she lifted her head to look at him, there was no mistaking the concern and tenderness etched on his face. She gazed back as if she had found someone long lost.

'How do you feel?'

'Oh, Mr Robert! Thank god you are safe. I was so worried about you driving back through that forest…'

He smiled and came nearer to her bed.

'When someone special is thinking about you, then you are protected from harm,' he teased.

She looked down shyly. 'I waited all day for you. I was worried you had been hurt…'

'Never mind about me,' he interrupted. 'Tell me, are you really feeling better?'

'Much better.'

'I'm so glad.' His voice became serious. He spoke with pain. 'When I saw the flames I was terrified that I might have lost you.'

'You saved my life,' Anjali said. Tears welled up and for once she did not try to stop them. She sobbed as she listened to his account.

'I don't know why, but as I drove towards Harikonda, I felt a strong urge to turn off towards St Agnes's. I abandoned my original plans and followed the road to your house instead… I could see the fire from the road… I didn't know if you were inside…'

'You put your own life at risk for me…'

'Anyone would have done the same.'

For a moment neither spoke as each acknowledged what might have been.

'Try not to think about it now.' He placed a finger under her chin and lifted her face. With his other hand he wiped her tears. She shivered, recognising the look in his eyes.

'Anjali…' he said softly, once she had composed herself. 'Do you remember the marriage ceremony that the astrologer performed for us?'

'Yes… How could I forget?'

'Does it mean anything to you?'

'Yes,' she said, 'if it means something to you.' She held her breath as she waited for his reply.

'It means everything to me,' he said.

If the *koel* bird had looked in the window, it would have seen a blue-eyed man and a black-eyed woman entwined as one. As it was, it continued to sing, oblivious, on the gulmohar tree. A gust of wind touched the branches and shook them. Blossoms, as red as passion, blew into the air and floated to the ground like confetti.

GLOSSARY

Akka	*big sister*
Aloo vada	*snack made from potatoes*
Amma	*Mother. Also a respectable woman of equal status.*
Angi	*shirt*
Arangetrum	*debut dance performance*
Attar	*perfume*
Avva	*grandmother*
Baishakhi	*harvest festival*
Banyan	*a tree*
Batthanis	*snack of dry chickpeas*
Bazar	*street/market*
Beti	*daughter*
Bhai	*brother*
Bhajan	*devotional song*
Bhangra	*a dance*
Bindi	*vermillion dot that married Hindu women wear between their eyebrows*
Bishaki	*festival*
Boddumalli	*flower*
Burqa	*a long garment muslim women wear from head to toe*
Chamanti	*name of a flower*
Chapathi	*flat bread*
Chowrasta	*town centre*
Dadima	*grandmother*
Dhoti	*a traditional clothing worn by men*
Divali	*festival*
Diwali	*festival of lights*
Dorsani	*a title for a respectable lady*
Gidda	*a dance*
Gopuram	*domed roof of the temple*
Hartal	*a protest or demonstration*
Jaihind	*hail India*

Jai-hind	*victory to India*
Jeedi	*a seed*
Kallu	*crude alcoholic palm drink*
Koel	*a small black bird*
Kurtas	*shirts*
Mahout	*elephant keeper and driver*
Mantapam	*dias or stage*
Mantra(s)	*chanting verses or hymns*
Mitthai	*sweets*
Muhurtam	*auspicious time*
Murdabad	*down down*
Nach-girl	*dancing girl*
Nan	*Indian bread*
Nandi	*name of the bull that carries Shiva*
Neem	*a tree*
Paisa	*Indian money, equal to an English penny*
Pakoras	*Indian snack*
Pallu	*the shoulder piece of a sari*
Pooja	*prayer*
Prasadam	*offering*
Prem-devi	*goddess of love*
Puja	*prayer*
Pundit-ji	*addressing a learned man with respect*
Punkha	*fan*
Purdah	*curtain/veil*
Raga	*tune*
Rat-ki-rani	*flower creeper*
Roties	*flat roasted breads*
Sari	*female dress*
Sari-pallu	*top end of sari*
Satyagraha	*fighting for truth*
Shastras	*sacred verses*
Shotras	*verses of hailing gods*
Tamarind	*a tree*
Tonga	*horse drawn buggy*
Upanishads	*sacred/wise verses and hymns*
Vande Matharam	*hail motherland*